INEVITABLE SEDUCTION

"I shall tell you one thing, *Mr.* Cutter," Velvet said with grim determination, "you shall never have what you want—never. I shall burn in the blistering flames of hell before I give you that."

"I can always . . . take it," he said evenly.

Velvet's eyes blazed. "Yes," she challenged. "I concede that you are stronger than I."

"But that isn't the way I want you. You know that, too, don't you?"

Velvet could only nod. Some barely reasoned instinct told her that Cutter was offering unimagined mutual pleasure. She could not move, could not think. She only felt.

"I don't want it to be any way at all," she whispered. "Not with you."

Cutter took her shoulders and, for all his roughness, turned her tenderly to face him. "But it *will* happen," he said softly. "*And* with me . . ."

HEARTFIRE ROMANCES

SWEET TEXAS NIGHTS   (2610, $3.75)
by Vivian Vaughan

Meg Britton grew up on the railroads, working proudly at her father's side. Nothing was going to stop them from setting the rails clear to Silver Creek, Texas — certainly not some crazy prospector. As Meg set out to confront the old coot, she planned her strategy with cool precision. But soon she was speechless with shock. For instead of a harmless geezer, she found a boldly handsome stranger whose determination matched her own.

CAPTIVE DESIRE   (2612, $3.75)
by Jane Archer

Victoria Malone fancied herself a great adventuress, but being kidnapped was too much excitement for even Victoria! Especially when her arrogant kidnapper thought she was part of Red Duke's outlaw gang. Trying to convince the overbearing, handsome stranger that she had been an innocent bystander when the stagecoach was robbed, proved futile. But when he thought he could maker her confess by crushing her to his warm, broad chest, by caressing her with his strong, capable hands, Victoria was willing to admit to anything. . . .

LAWLESS ECSTASY   (2613, $3.75)
by Susan Sackett

Abra Beaumont could spot a thief a mile away. After all, her father was once one of the best. But he'd been on the right side of the law for years now, and she wasn't about to let a man like Dash Thorne lead him astray with some wild plan for stealing the Tear of Allah, the world's most fabulous ruby. Dash was just the sort of man she most distrusted — sophisticated, handsome, and altogether too sure of his considerable charm. Abra shivered at the devilish gleam in his blue eyes and swore he would need more than smooth kisses and skilled caresses to rob her of her virtue . . . and much more than sweet promises to steal her heart!

Available wherever paperbacks are sold, or order direct from the Publisher. Send cover price plus 50¢ per copy for mailing and handling to Zebra Books, Dept. 3058, 475 Park Avenue South, New York, N.Y. 10016. Residents of New York, New Jersey and Pennsylvania must include sales tax. DO NOT SEND CASH.

SWEET VELVET PASSION

CAROL KING

ZEBRA BOOKS
KENSINGTON PUBLISHING CORP.

To Thomas IV, Amy Marie, and Juliet Ruth—
Each with their own treasures
Each treasured unconditionally.

This book is dedicated to Miscellaneous, Inc.
With love and thanks
"Make it Last Forever"
and

To the Gerling Reference Library
With gratitude

ZEBRA BOOKS

are published by

Kensington Publishing Corp.
475 Park Avenue South
New York, NY 10016

First printing: June, 1990

Printed in the United States of America

Chapter One

Screams, keen and panicked, pierced the serenity of the languid afternoon. The arrow-straight white pines, shooting hundreds of feet into the pinkened sky, seemed to shudder at the sudden, sonant eruption. The man's head swung up. Unsure of what he had heard, he listened. His eyes narrowed behind thick wire-rimmed spectacles. The small rock he examined slipped from his big hand to the forest floor. Again the screams sounded, silver-sharp on the quiet air. Without further hesitation, the man bounded to his horse and mounted with one powerful swing of a long thigh. He jerked the reins. The animal reared mightily and wheeled, then, spurred to a pounding gallop, headed in the direction of the disturbance.

Man and horse crashed through trees and came to a halt in a shrub-brushed clearing. Several blue-coated men struggled with something at its center, their broad backs obscuring their prey. The rider dismounted and made for the group in a forward dash. Noting his challenge, the assaulters abandoned their victim and turned almost casually. They faced the bespectacled avenger with cocked smiles.

"What are you doing here, Cutter?" asked one of them lazily.

"Got a problem, old man?" another queried.

Cutter stopped suddenly, his stance wide-legged, guarded, his big fists clenched. "I heard a woman scream," he answered tersely.

"Did you now?" a self-assured fellow said as he stepped forward. The others advanced as well, their lips twitching with ill-concealed humor.

"And what did you intend to do about it?" a fourth man inquired loftily.

The sun glinted on Cutter's round-rimmed lenses, and he removed them, swathing each dusty surface with a wrinkled kerchief as he attempted to see beyond the wide shoulders of the uniformed men. At last, his eyes locking with their collective, amused perusal, he said, "Just what are you un-civilized louts up to?"

The young men's mirth, jogged by the question, sent them into spasms of laughter. "Uncivilized louts!" one of them repeated in Cutter's haughty tone. "Oh, Cutter," another ejaculated, slapping his thigh, "you really are a piece of work!" At that moment, as the group's high spirits sent them scattering in all directions, there appeared, in the center of the clearing, a small jewel-kissed creature, the shimmer of her jacinth-yellow, hoop-skirted gown, the con-fection of her gold-rilled onyx curls—and her smile—per-fectly unperturbed. She twirled a lacy parasol tranquilly.

"Is there a problem, sir?" Her voice was sun-sparkled honey.

Cutter's gaze took in the remarkable vision. Slowly, he placed the spectacles into the pocket of his vest and pulled his soft hat from a tousle of dark curls. He held the hat, relentlessly mashed in a large fist against his chest, as he studied her. "Are you all right, miss?" he asked at last.

An impish glitter kissed the bright aqua of the young woman's heavily lashed eyes. She pouted prettily. "These nasty boys were about to toss me into the water."

Cutter looked past her at a small lake sparkling in repose beyond the group of young people. His eyes, the cool quartz gray of that clear water, drifted back to the woman. "You are not, then, in any real danger," he said quietly.

She shrugged delicately, the action causing her light froth of a shawl to slip, baring, with practiced significance, an elegant shoulder. "Well, I suppose that would depend en-tirely on what you call 'real danger,'" she murmured with a flutter of tangled lashes. Cutter noted the enticing drawl that sweetened her tones.

One young man, his lean body doubled over in laughter at the exchange, guffawed, "Did you really think to save a damsel in distress, Cutter?"

The bigger man's jaw tightened as the uniformed lads jostled him in good-natured—and not so good-natured—derision.

"Now that'll be the day—that'll just be the coldest goddamned day in hell—" the lad laughed—"when J. Eliot Cutter decides to put himself in harm's way!"

"I think you boys are being just a tad unfair," murmured the lady, the music of her voice slicing sweetly through the laughter. She moved toward Cutter, making a path for herself through her companions with light, pointed flicks of her closed parasol. At last she stood before him. She paused, shading her gaze with delicate fingers against the milky glaze of the mountain sun, and studied the man frankly for the breath of a second. "Won't you forgive them, sir?" she said finally. Her words rippled like a warm Southern breeze over the ragged terrain. The ivory smoothness of her brow wrinkled tantalizingly as she frowned. "You've no reason to forgive them, I'll admit, but"—here she offered a dazzling smile—"you're such a gentleman, I just know you will." She glared over her slim shoulder at the sniggers she heard behind her. "Well, he *is* a gentleman," she said, smoothly arching a raven brow, "unlike some others I could name." She returned her wide blue-green gaze to Cutter. Her smile restored, she continued. "It isn't many men these days who would ride so gallantly to save a lady. Where I come from, we reward gallantry. For all these boys are my very dear and loved friends, their behavior is so typically *Yankee*. It just curdles my blood to see them acting so disdainful of your chivalry." She glanced once again at her chastened suitors, and then graced Cutter with a flutter of her silken lashes. "At last I've found a gentleman in this dismal Northern wilderness," she breathed. She extended her small white hand and as Cutter took it, bowed over it, she curtsied prettily. "My name, kind sir, is Velvet McBride, only recently of these infelicitous environs." She watched his tall form as he straightened. His tanned and weathered countenance had an unmistakable air of command. "And you are J. Eliot Cutter?" she inquired. He nodded. "So very, very nice to meet you, J. Eliot," she said. "I'm presuming I may call you J. Eliot," she added, tipping her gaze piquantly. Again Cutter responded with only the suggestion of a nod. His glance shot up as he heard evidence of the young men's unsuccessfully reined mirth.

Velvet offered them an oblique warning. "Where I come from," she said, lifting her chin, "J. Eliot would be the rule and *not* the exception. And he would certainly — most certainly — *not* be made an object of ridicule. You boys ought to be ashamed of yourselves," she went on. "You could learn a great deal from this fine specimen of manly courtesy."

Cutter cleared his throat quietly. "I thank you for your . . . protection, Miss . . ."

"McBride," Velvet offered. "But please call me Velvet."

"Miss . . . McBride," Cutter repeated. "I assure you, however, it's hardly necessary." His gaze narrowed as he targeted the young men. "The taunts I regularly receive from these buffoons have ceased to disconcert me." He bowed curtly. "Meeting you has been a pleasure, Miss . . ."

"McBride," Velvet said again, impatiently, bemused by the man's seeming indifference to her most practiced flirtations. "But please *do* call me Velvet." Cutter merely nodded once again and pushed his wide-brimmed hat back onto his head. He turned abruptly and strode toward his horse. Velvet's eyes widened in astonishment at the sudden rebuff.

"Just . . . just a moment, sir," she said hastily, hiking up her billowing skirts and following him. "For heaven's sake, won't you allow me to thank you properly?" Cutter noted the flash of a trim ankle.

"That is hardly necessary," he intoned as he swung easily into his saddle. He glanced down at Velvet. "After all," he said, "I did nothing."

"On the contrary!" Velvet protested. "Suppose I really had been in danger. Suppose these boys really had been threatening my life, or *worse!*" She lowered her lashes as she unfurled her parasol and lifted it up and over one shoulder. "Why," she said, the nectar of her tone dripping helplessness, "you might have saved my *virtue!*"

Cutter's mount danced impatiently. He held the horse in check with one big hand. "Your . . . virtue?" he asked.

8

There was only a hint of mockery in the crystalline chill of his eyes, and Velvet missed the hint entirely.

"Well, of course," she answered breathlessly, looking up. "Now, you must not leave before your gallantry has been properly rewarded." Cutter once again reined his prancing mount. He eyed Velvet's small upturned face. "I insist," she continued, tilting him a quick, sweet, sideways smile. "I quite simply *require* . . . that you accept an invitation to call on my uncle tomorrow and allow him to thank you." She lowered her lashes, flicking them delicately over the soft curve of her pinkened cheeks. "We're having a small gathering anyway in honor of those silly boys going off to that war everybody's talking about," she said gravely, her little chin trembling. "I suppose you'll be going, too?" she murmured. She lifted her robin's-egg gaze.

Cutter studied her from the height of his mount. "No," he said quietly. "I will not be going." His response was rewarded with Velvet's sudden, sunlit smile. She shrugged off the grumblings of the young men who stood nearby, though she noted that Cutter's jaw tightened and his gaze hooded as he eyed them.

"Pay them no mind," Velvet said lightly. "They're just jealous."

Cutter's firm lips became etched in a slow smile. "They're not jealous," he stated, his gaze never leaving theirs. "Are you, lads?" The boys nodded and groused a collective affirmation.

Velvet's brows winged in a delicate frown and dismay pouted her lips. These men, she grumbled silently, they are always drawing each other into some sort of private bond. Whether it was affection they shared, or animosity, they seemed bent on excluding females from their world. Well, Velvet determined defiantly, she would not allow it. She had already shared too much of their attention with this ridiculous war.

She flicked her lashes pointedly, and Cutter's regard returned to her. "My uncle Duff would be just heartbroken if he wasn't given the opportunity to thank you himself," she said. "I'm staying at the Duffy spread till this silly war is

9

over," Velvet explained, her tones bubbly and carmelized, "and I would so enjoy making a new friend hereabouts." She paused. "Won't you come?" Her request was made simply — and with no allowance for refusal. At last Cutter nodded.

"I know your uncle well," he answered evenly. "I shall be riding up tomorrow anyway."

"Really?" Velvet responded in surprise. It seemed everyone here in this Northern wilderness knew everyone else. She nevertheless checked her dismay and dimpled shyly as though Cutter's acceptance of her invitation had been gained by her charms alone. "You won't be sorry," she said. "I promise to show you a glorious time."

"How long has it been," one of the young men interjected snidely, "since you've felt the restraint of a stock around your neck, Cutter?" The others laughed unrestrainedly. Velvet shot them a dangerous glare.

"Don't you go chiding this man," she admonished prettily. She turned her gaze back to Cutter. Perusing his loosely collared, rough cotton shirt and his lean-fitting trousers, she offered a dazzling smile. "Pay no attention to them, J. Eliot," she said. "You look just fine." Then, after pausing delicately, she added, "Though, it might be . . . for your own comfort . . ." She regarded him through a veil of lowered lashes. "It might be best if you wore your party clothes," she murmured.

Cutter hid a grin. This little minx was certainly formidable enough, though whatever brawn she possessed was well hidden beneath a finely laced and perfumed exterior. "I shall try not to embarrass you," he said with deliberate solemnity.

Her wide gaze shot up. "Why . . . why, that never occurred to me. It quite simply never entered my mind," she protested. Her little parasol whirled energetically. Reining her discomposure immediately, she added with a bright smile, "We'll expect you about three." Touching the brim of his hat, studying her with one last raking perusal, Cutter rode off.

Once horse and rider had disappeared into the woodland surrounding the clearing, Velvet slowly turned to her companions. They noted that her gaze had darkened perceptibly. Her cutting scrutiny stifled any humorous remarks they might have been tempted to make. Wordlessly, she glided past them in a rustle of lace and satin. One of the young men dared an observation.

"I hope you don't really expect that priggish rustic to appear at the party," he called hesitantly.

Velvet swung to face him, her skirts swirling turbulently. The blue-green storm of her gaze riveted the young men to their places. She paused significantly before speaking. When at last she did, her words were like delicate, dangerous gunshots.

"*I* hope," she began, "for your sakes, that priggish rustic *does* appear at the party. If he does not, I will hold each one of you responsible." She aimed her parasol like a frothy épée. "So far, I have been very patient with you oafs because you're the only men, besides ill-smelling loggers and the occasional peddler, who inhabit this godforsaken wilderness. But my patience is at an end. If J. Eliot Cutter does not appear at the party, I am personally going to tear the hide off each one of you and nail it to the nearest hemlock tree." She lifted her chin and unfurled her parasol with a snap. The young men glanced cautiously at each other. There was little doubt in their minds that Velvet McBride would carry out her promise as succinctly as she'd made it. "It's just about time I met a gentleman," she asserted.

"Cutter, a gentleman?" blurted one of the men. For his insolence, he was impaled with a truculent glower. He flinched and backed into the protective company of his friends. Those brave and true comrades merely peeled off in several directions, leaving the young man to stand alone. Velvet approached the offending gallant menacingly.

"Don't you dare impugn that man's conduct," she hissed. "What would you know about being a gentleman?" Her lip curled derisively and her narrowed gaze took in all the young men. "All you talk about is your silly war, and you expect me to tell you how brave you are, and to simper and flirt and bat my lashes for you. And for all my trouble, I get to be pawed and slobbered over. I get to listen to endless accountings of your anticipated triumphs on the field of manly honor. What do any of you care about me? You haven't the manners of a gaggle of sloven boars." She lifted her chin and a winged brow snapped up. "If you would talk about something that interests *me* once in a while," she pouted tartly, "I might just forgive your lapses. But none of you seems to have the slightest concept of how to treat a lady properly. All any of you seem to care about and talk about and think about is yourselves and the subject of your ridiculous soldiering."

"Somebody's got to fight the war, sweetheart," ventured one lad soothingly. He recoiled immediately as fury stiffened Velvet's supple form. "What . . . what would you have us do?" he stammered.

"I don't care what you do," she railed, her eyes blazing blue-green fire. "Just don't spoil my chances for some respectable male companionship while you do it!" She flipped her skirts contemptuously, and turned in a perfumed huff. "J. Eliot Cutter is the first man I've seen in weeks who doesn't sport a uniform as some sort of badge of masculine honor," she threw over her shoulder as she marched off, "and I intend to see that he becomes otherwise diverted before he decides to do so." She made a sweeping exit from the clearing, as the lads watched disconsolately.

They were left to eye each other sheepishly, to make attempts at consoling each other, to justify their current employment as United States soldiers — and to wonder how a man like J. Eliot Cutter had so easily ruined their lives.

Chapter Two

Clouds of vapor were only now rising from the jagged, mountainous peaks as Velvet opened her sleep-misted eyes. Once fully awake, she gathered her resources rapidly, breathing deeply of the cold morning air. Huddling into a thick wrapper, she ran to the window and shooed the light draperies aside. She gazed out onto the uncultivated landscape that had become her home. For all her complaining, for all her discontent at being trundled from her dear Sweet Briar Hill with its rolling lawns and manicured shrubs, she was captivated by this rare and almost primordial wilderness, especially in the mornings.

She looked out over the pine-crested horizon, far into the misty Adirondack distance where a purple postdawn mantle shrouded the lofty summits and the deep, mysterious hollows. This land, this limitless land, was far beyond the boundaries of man's firm control. It was tempestuous, unyielding, savage in its honesty. Its stony peaks towered, forthrightly unreachable. Its cavernous depths, fern-shadowed, moist, tree-twisted, candidly bespoke danger. There was no comfort here, yet Velvet felt a hint—the promise perhaps—of deep serenity when she perused this quiet, enigmatic, uncompromising wilderness. The contradiction frustrated her, made her uneasy, for in all her life she had never experienced such a disarrangement of her emotions.

Since birth, Velvet had known only deference, affection, gentleness in the refinement of her docile surroundings. Her land, familiar in its textures, its colors, its constancy, had promised much and had delivered all. Velvet had been nurtured in a land where man had gallantly battled with nature, and had won—or had seemed to. Her father and her greatgrandfather before them had tamed a portion of the southeastern seaboard of the United States, had offered it

13

green, cultured, and pungently ripe to their children. She saw her land now, pictured it superimposed on the ragged terrain outside her window. Verdant lawns rolled down from the white stone of the Big House steps to the neat fence rows below, mockingbirds twittered among the stately oaks, light breezes rippled the pink and white magnolia blossoms. She could hear the murmur of song from the workers in the fields. They would be setting out the young tobacco plants or hilling up the soil around the corn or straightening the rows of yellow wheat. There was no question, no uncertainty as to her land's intent—as long as man followed the rules.

Here, in this unbridled expanse of cliffs and caverns, it seemed there were no rules. There was no measured formula on which man could depend in order to bend nature to his needs. There could be, Velvet supposed as her pretty pictures evaporated in the strengthening sunlight, deriving a certain comfort from knowing that. One might take solace in absolute, final surrender to a superior essentiality. Velvet, however, was not yet ready to surrender.

Her eyes focused reluctantly on the rock-powdered panorama, on the jagged, shorn, and awesome tract before her. War or no war, she reflected fervently, she did not belong here. She slowly turned from the window. For all its enchanting magnificence, this land was not her home.

Intellectually, Velvet knew why she was here. She understood that her parents, concerned for her gently bred sensibilities, had felt it necessary to send her away when this terrible War Between the States, as it was being called, had intruded upon their neatly patterned lives. She sat heavily on a rocker made of twined and twisted grape vines and surveyed her rustic surroundings. There certainly were no patterns here that Velvet could see—not of nature and not of matter.

The floor of her room was constructed of rough pine logs that often infected her bared feet with splinters. Her wood-framed bed was covered with a blanket made of small squares of colored cloth. She examined its rumpled surface from where she sat, and decided that no real pattern—no

14

rhyme or reason that she could detect—existed in its bright, patched conformation. She eyed the ragged log walls. Except for the fact that they were placed in a horizontal configuration from one end of the room to the other, there was no pattern there. Colors and grains varied wildly. In her land, boards were smoothed, polished. Floors were carpeted, walls were lacquered, and blankets were woven of fine woolens.

Even smells, in this uncertain environment, were unexpectedly diverse. Sometimes the air in her secluded second-floor chamber was scented with apple smells, and sometimes with a spicy pine. She looked to the little fire which snuggled gleefully into the depths of the darkened hearth. Next to it, a disarrangement of various woods were piled offhandedly; bundled, she supposed, according to some sort of classification. Never mind that those gay little packets promised an unending individuality in their very personalized incandescences; they did not produce *home* fires.

In her land, fires were lit only on damp wintery days, to take the chill off a rainy December morn. By June, the weather was warm. By June, trees and shrubs were heavy with pure and perfect promise. Here, in these ragged mountains of northern New York State, the first blush of June brought only cold, damp mornings and long-wished-for sightings of occasional virgin growth. Underfoot, moss, newly shed of snow, glistened darkly in the shadows of the lofting pines. The surprise appearance of an early crocus here in this slow-yielding land was a wonder to be profoundly cherished. Never mind that the anticipation of such wonders only deepened one's enjoyment of them; this unkempt, unchallenged land was not home.

The door of her room swung open, at first hesitantly. Seeing that Velvet was awake and about, the intruder burst cheerily into her musings. "Sure it's a glorious morn, lass," the newcomer exulted. "I've brought your breakfast." She rustled into the room, setting down the heavily laden tray, swinging the water kettle over the low fire, brushing the draperies aside. Velvet sighed. As always, when the vibrant Hanna entered her life, Velvet's day was begun.

Following a much too heavy breakfast of eggs, flapjacks,

15

and wheat muffins, which Velvet found vulgar but nevertheless deliciously satisfying every morning, she began her day's toilette. This small amenity, which other ladies of this region seemed not to follow, was something that Velvet had not been able to forgo. Hanna, the household's only servant, had allowed that it was "a lady's prerogative" and one in which she would happily take part. She had become, in a way, Velvet's personal maid. For an indentured baker's daughter from the slums of Londonderry, Hanna felt this was a soaring elevation in her status. Velvet found the young woman's candid admiration refreshing, and welcomed their morning chats.

Beyond that, Hanna was an astonishingly accomplished coiffeuse. And while this achievement seemed unimportant to others hereabouts, to Velvet, with her unruly mane of dark, luster-struck curls, it was a talent of some consequence.

"You've got the prettiest hair in the world, Miss Velvet," Hanna marveled, as she often did when she brushed and tucked the remarkable tresses. "Sure it's like black water on the darkest of nights, after the moon comes up and streaks it with golden ribbons. It's amazin'; wondrous is what it is," she concluded in awed summation.

Velvet laughed. "You are so good for me, Hanna," she said. "Mammy Jane calls it 'Devil's hair.' "

"Well, it surely isn't 'Devil's hair' to me," Hanna rejoined, blessing herself hastily, "and this Mammy Jane person has no right to say so."

"Mammy can say anything she wishes to"—Velvet giggled—"no matter how unseemly, or seemingly undiplomatic. Mammy's just the nerviest old thing in the whole world." Velvet paused. Her manner became serious, subdued. Hanna knew what to expect. Not a day went by that the dear child did not express an aching homesickness. Hanna understood such things. She paused in her work and patted Velvet's shoulder. The girl's small face, reflected in the glass, crumpled. Hanna sat next to her on the wooden bench.

"Now, Miss Velvet," she soothed.

"Well, I can't help it, Hanna," Velvet sniffled. Tears came

16

slowly, dampening her heavy lashes. She allowed her head to fall on Hanna's sturdy shoulder. "I know I'm being foolish. I know I've got to stop this nonsense; breaking into big wet, sobs every time my home is mentioned." Velvet swiped impatiently at her little nose. "But I just can't seem to conquer this lonely, empty feeling I get from time to time." She raised her eyes and regarded the Irish woman solemnly. "Don't you ever miss your home?"

Hanna nodded. "Sure and I miss it terribly, Miss Velvet," she answered. "But I've learned some things since I sailed from Belfast six years ago. I've learned that you've got to have faith in *yourself*. Home doesn't necessarily have to be a place, Miss Velvet. Home is a feelin', it's a safe and comfortable, soft feelin' you get right here." Hanna touched her stomach. "And here." She touched her heart. "In a way, I suppose it comes with growin' up . . . or bein' comfortable with yourself." She smiled fondly. "It's hard to explain, darlin', but you'll find it out for yourself. You've only been here a scant few weeks. Why the snow wasn't even melted away when you arrived. It takes time to get to know a place."

Velvet acknowledged with a nod that Hanna was right. "I know Mother and Pa were only trying to protect me when they sent me north, but I don't think either of them realized how much I'd miss them."

"Of course you miss them, but that's natural. You're little more than a babe," said Hanna brightly.

Velvet scowled darkly, for the moment forgetting her sorrow. "I am not a baby, Hanna," she retorted. "I'm eighteen years old. Mother was married by that time, and had a babe of her own, for heaven's sake!"

The Irish woman laughed, relieved to see Velvet's spirit restored. "Sure and so might you be married someday soon." She stood and reapplied her deft touch to Velvet's remarkable hair. Cocking her head mischievously, Hanna reminded Velvet of the party that very afternoon. "There'll be all sorts of handsome young men there," she coaxed.

Velvet lifted a nonchalant shoulder. "All those Yankee boys are alike," she sniffed, applying a dampened cloth to her reddened nose. "I don't like them."

Hanna laughed. "Give the laddies a chance, Miss Velvet." She stabbed a pin into a thick curl and added the embellishment of a silk tiger lily. "They surely like you."

Velvet turned in vexation. "Oh, they like me well enough," she said, glaring petulantly at Hanna. "They want to be with me, but they don't know how to act in the company of a lady. They're so . . . so unrefined. They tease and frolic and talk about their witless war till I just want to scream. If I've managed to impress those boys at all, it's a wonder—a sheer wonder," she finished resentfully.

"Now, not a bit, Miss Velvet," Hanna assured her. "Sure and you're so pretty and so feminine, they couldn't help but be impressed. 'Tis only that the Northern boys aren't trained up like your lads back home. You have to help them—teach them." Hanna's gaze turned sober. For all her assurances to the contrary, she had watched Velvet's social energy with some concern, had, in fact, mentioned it to Mrs. Duffy. That good woman had agreed that Velvet's flirtatiousness with the unsophisticated Northern boys was something that warranted concern. She had stopped short of admonishing the girl outright. How could she begin to explain that behavior fully accepted and even embraced in one society was frowned upon—and perhaps even dangerous—in another. In the end, both women decided to trust the natural shyness of the lads who surrounded Velvet, and her own innocence. Velvet, after all, was just entertaining the lads hereabouts, Hanna acknowledged. In any event, the boys would be leaving soon and the danger, if any, would be eliminated.

Hanna produced from a nearby chest a light cotton frock of palest peach. "Step in, darlin'," she ordered gently. "And if you plan on walkin' today, don't be forgettin' your parasol. The sun is comin' through, and it's bound to be a heavenly day."

Velvet felt warmth spread through her as she smiled at Hanna's command. She dutifully plucked her parasol from the stand before leaving her room. It was comforting to have someone she cared for caring for her. Perhaps the dear Irish woman was right. Perhaps home was a feeling and not a place.

18

Hanna was right about another thing, too, Velvet mused as she made her way down the post-and-rail stairway. The Northern boys needed to be *taught* to act like gentlemen. Perhaps, she thought resolutely, if the Northern girls acted more like ladies, there wouldn't be such a problem.

In the airy kitchen, Velvet's Aunt Yvonne and her pretty daughters, Nicole and Juliette, worked side by side. They carefully latticed pie crusts, turned marinating meat, and sorted berries. Their work continued uninterrupted at Velvet's appearance. It was tacitly understood that the girl's lack of expertise in the kitchen was not due to laziness but to inexperience. Though, when she had first arrived, they had fully expected that she would provide another hand to help in the endless daily chores, they had quickly observed the differences between themselves and her. While their fingers deftly worked bread batters, and boned fish, Velvet's seemed to be less than adept ornaments. She played the ancient pianoforte in the parlor well enough, and her delicate needlework was competent, though hardly utilitarian. What good, they wondered, were her few talents? Velvet had, in the beginning, gamely attempted to do what seemed expected of her. She watched, with valiant patience, as her Aunt Yvonne had debrained and gutted a roaming hog that had been shot and dragged bleeding and sweating into the kitchen. Later, Velvet was found wretching uncontrollably in the frost-crusted garden.

"What is it, child!" her aunt Yvonne had exclaimed, seeing the girl doubled over amid the tangle of empty vines. "And you without a shawl," the woman had admonished. Velvet had lifted woeful, red-stained eyes to her aunt.

"I . . . I'm sorry," she'd gasped.

"Was it the pig?" her aunt asked gently. Velvet nodded in resignation. "Have you never seen an animal slaughtered before?" the woman inquired incredulously. Velvet shook her head miserably. "But who does your rendering at home?" the older woman had asked.

Velvet glanced up at her aunt. "I . . . I don't know. . . ." she'd said vaguely, pitifully. "Perhaps . . . Quamina?" she had offered. "He's the Guinea slave . . . I suppose he does

19

it." It was then that Yvonne Duffy had realized the extent of the child's innocence of the simplest basics of everyday life. After ushering Velvet inside and tucking her into a warm bed, Yvonne had gone to her daughters.

"We must be patient with the girl," she'd said gravely. "We must not expect too much of her." The petite and sturdy Canadian woman had shaken her head later when in the company of her husband. "I shall never understand how my sister has managed to raise such a daughter," she'd confided. "Honestly, Andrew, I couldn't believe it. There she was, poor baby, huddled in the garden, sick as you please — and all because of a silly dead hog." Her husband glanced up from his book. His weathered face crinkled in the firelight that set the small parlor aglow.

"That's what your good sister gets, Vonnie, for marrying a Southern laddie," he'd chided. As always, when that point was made, Yvonne smiled, eyed the big, healthy, shirt-sleeved man rocking at her side, and agreed that she'd certainly got the best of the two husbands.

After that, Yvonne and her daughters had come to a kind of reconciliation with Velvet's shortcomings. It was not, after all, the girl's fault that she'd been so poorly trained up. The fault lay in an indolence fostered by her environment.

Yvonne Duffy regarded her niece now in sympathy. There really was no place for her among these accomplished, busy women. She wiped her hands on a berry-stained apron. "Do you want to help, darling?" she asked kindly.

"Oh, could I?" Velvet asked, praying that yet another stinking hog was not about to appear.

The older woman nodded assertively. "You certainly can." She reached above her for a basket that hung from a low beam. "We'll need every flower you can find for the tables." She smiled. "You probably have the most difficult job of all of us," she assured her niece. "Flowers are not so easily come by this time of year." The youngest of the Duffy girls perked her own smile.

"May I go with her, Mama?" she asked. Juliette Duffy had not only become reconciled to Velvet's ineptitude, she had

20

come to adore it. Velvet represented to the impressionable sixteen-year-old all that a lady should be. She followed the older girl whenever the opportunity arose. Yvonne regarded Juliette warily. Ordinarily, she would discourage such frivolous pursuits, but as she'd just that moment expounded on the difficulty of Velvet's task, she decided to allow a lapse in the child's discipline. Yvonne indicated, with gentle resignation, that the two young women should be off.

"Get whatever you can for decoration, girls," she called after them. "This is, after all, a party."

Shawls draped over tender shoulders, the two young ladies began their early summer search.

"We might try Doriel's Pond for flowers," Juliette remarked excitedly as they walked from the house. She eyed Velvet's little cashmere shawl admiringly. Her own, a huge, heavy homespun wool, seemed drab by comparison. Everything about everyone seemed drab next to the resplendent Velvet, the younger girl thought disconsolately. But, she reminded herself, she was on an errand with this remarkable, perfect pattern for all womanhood—the standard by which all women must ultimately judge themselves—and, on this gloriously clear June day, Juliette must take pleasure in that. She must enjoy this exalted moment to the fullest. She took Velvet's hand, noting the encouraging smile that curved the older girl's lips, and led her along a fir-shadowed path. "There are always pretty things at Doriel's," she said gaily. "It's the sunniest place in the Adirondack forest."

Whether or not Doriel's Pond was the sunniest place, thought Velvet, it certainly seemed the busiest place. As the girls quietly approached the water's edge, spruce grouse and Lincoln's sparrows nested busily while water shrews frantically skimmed the surface of the little moss-covered lake. Grassy plants along the shoreline rippled in the light breeze.

"We're lucky for the wind," Juliette assured Velvet sagely. "Otherwise we'd have to contend with the black flies."

The girls bent to their task in this rich, luxuriant fragment of the magnificent glacial woodland. Doggedly they hunted and at last found early wild violets, trillium, and berry blossoms, creating color for their bouquet. The blue-

21

green foliage of the hemlock, the silver of the balsam and the red of the Adirondack spruce yielded a complimentary bed. When their basket was plump with the hard-won wildflowers and decorative ferns and foliage, the young women sat beneath a stately, sprawling beech, its wide branches dipping almost to the water and offering them a private shady niche in which to rest. Together, they did what young women do very well; they shared secret and, up to now, silent thoughts.

Her legs folded beneath her, Juliette listened wide-gazed as Velvet told her of the young man she'd met yesterday, embellishing the tale prettily.

"He is modest, quiet-spoken, and gallant," Velvet assured her young cousin. "He is, without a doubt, a gentleman."

"What's his name?" Juliette breathed, caught up in the romance of the thrilling encounter.

"His name is J. Eliot Cutter," Velvet proclaimed proudly. She noted the sudden intake of Juliette's breath, the quick excitement of recognition, and, finally, the reluctant dip of the girl's lashes. "Do you know him?" Velvet asked.

"Everyone knows him," Juliette murmured. She glanced up at her beloved ideal. "Mr. Cutter is . . . very well known hereabouts." Juliette glanced away, and Velvet's winged brows drew together in puzzlement.

"Is there something I ought to know about J. Eliot Cutter?" Velvet asked. When the younger girl did not answer, fiercely studied instead a grazing white-tailed doe at the water's edge, Velvet placed delicate hands on her shoulders. Turning the girl gently, she said, "What is it, Juliette?"

"It . . . it's nothing," the girl insisted, her eyes lowered determinedly.

"I think you're hiding something," Velvet said with equal determination. When Juliette remained steadfastly silent, she added pettishly, "Don't tell me then; see if I mind. I hope Mr. Cutter does retain some sort of deep secret. I rather enjoy a man who is haunted by romantic presences." She laughed lightly. "Have you read the Brontës or Lady Lamb? They create such wonderful, dark-browed heroes, just filled with mystery and . . ."

Juliette shook her blond curls resolutely. "You wouldn't like that in real life, cousin," she said softly.

"Of course I would," Velvet asserted. "And anyway," she added with a piquant smile, "there isn't much chance of me finding out whether I'd like it or not. What man in these parts—or any parts, for that matter—could possibly have the poetical secrets of a Heathcliff or a Glenarvon?"

Juliette quirked her brows in puzzlement.

"For heaven's sake, dear child," said Velvet impatiently, "don't you even read romances?"

"We don't get much time to read," Juliette said guiltily.

"Well, you should make time," Velvet asserted sagely. "Then you'd find out a few things about men." Her young cousin eyed Velvet uncertainly. Already she was adjusting her shawl, opening her parasol, preparing to leave their shady niche. She placed her hand hesitantly on Velvet's arm.

"From books?" she asked, needing to know what Velvet knew about men.

Velvet glanced at her. "Of course," she said. "Everything I know about men, I've learned from books. For instance, you can tell exactly what they're thinking just by looking at their faces." She settled herself once again in the thick, soft ground cover. "If a man's eyes just stay on you—on your face, your eyes, your lips—while you're talking, you know he's enthralled with what you're telling him. If his eyes wander, you need to flutter your fan or twirl your parasol or drop your glove, or do something to get his attention back to where it ought to be—on you. And then you need to say something extremely clever so he continues to pay attention to you."

"But I don't know anything clever to say," Juliette moaned, thinking of the sturdy Jason whom she would love, that very afternoon, to impress with her own cleverness. "Besides," she added with a sigh, "the men seem so distracted these days."

"Of course they're distracted," Velvet agreed. "That's why you have to be *particularly* clever. You must do whatever you can to take their attention from their dreary war. And if all else fails," she added with a small, indifferent shrug, "you need to be particularly overwhelming in your flirtatiousness.

23

You just have to bowl them over with your femininity. Men are always impressed by helplessness; they always think they have to protect you."

"From what?" asked the practical Juliette.

Velvet expelled a breath. "You're not supposed to worry about *that*," she declared. "For heaven's sake, Juliette, do I have to tell you everything? Can't you think these things up for yourself?" Velvet immediately regretted her impatience with the chastised girl. She touched her cousin's arm and smiled encouragingly. "Watch me," she said gently. Velvet stood and snapped out her parasol. She placed it over one slender shoulder and held it lightly with both her hands, twirling it airily. She let her shawl drip down so that her shoulders were bared, and she tilted her head. Her lips curved into a carefully arranged smile. "Why, Mr. Cutter," she began, with an exaggerated sweetness in her voice, "how divine of you to come." She regarded the rapt Juliette gravely. "That's how you begin. You make them think your life begins with their arrival." Velvet strolled out into the sunny clearing, followed by her deeply attentive cousin. "Now," Velvet instructed, "you have to make them think you just can't wait to hear what they have to say. That's important." She looked up at her tall, imagined companion, and flicked her lashes. "Just what is it you do, Mr. Cutter," she asked in a syrupy tone. Glancing back at Juliette, she warned, "Now he'll say something silly like he works in a bank, or he runs a plantation, or . . . something, but you don't really have to pay attention to that. What you have to do is get his attention on you. You can say 'Oh, my, how interesting,' or 'I declare, if that isn't the most fascinating thing I've ever heard,' just anything like that. Then," she continued, "you can say, 'I've always wanted to see the inside of a bank, Mr. Cutter.' Men love to show off about their work. They'll just go on and on about it—if you let them." She arched an eyebrow at her cousin. "You have to nip that right in the bud," she asserted. "Use their work to precipitate an outing, if you have to, but don't let it get out of hand. Right in the middle of one of their drawn-out explanations, you can say something like, 'Oh, I seem to have taken on a chill, Mr. Cutter.' " She glanced sharply at Juliette. "See how I've changed the subject and made myself seem frail and vulnerable all at the same time?" she asked. "Right away, he'll want to protect me. If you do it right, he'll take a moment to lift your shawl, or, if it's in the evening, he may even offer his coat. That's always so romantic. Now watch me." Velvet trembled prettily. "You're just as gallant as you can be, Mr. Cutter," she said, lowering her lashes shyly. "Whatever would I do, poor me, without your tender care?"

Juliette could not repress the giggle that bubbled suddenly to her lips. Velvet offered a sharp glare. "Do you want to learn, cousin, or don't you?" she inquired loftily.

"Oh, yes, I do," Juliette answered, her mirth not quite restrained. "It's just . . . it's all so . . . *funny,*" she burst out at last. Velvet found a small smile curving her own lips.

"It isn't one bit funny," she admonished. "It's quite serious." Her own laughter threatened as she watched young Juliette's merriment. "There is just no hope for you, my girl," she said finally through her own giggles. Juliette wiped at her laugh-teared eyes.

"I'm sorry," she gasped. "I just can't see myself . . . with Jason . . ." she added, her laughter returning. She attempted several times to catch her breath. Velvet's bright glee merged with that of her cousin's, and both girls found themselves supporting each other as they reeled with laughter.

"Well, I suppose it *is* funny," Velvet acknowledged when they'd regained their composure. "But it works."

Juliette's laughter subsided, and she regarded her cousin thoughtfully. "To what end?" she asked finally.

"To what end?" Velvet repeated dumbly.

"I mean, *why* do we do it?" Juliette persisted. Velvet shrugged a delicate shoulder.

"I don't know," she said simply. "I suppose we do it to keep from being bored."

"But, I mean," her cousin went on, "what is our purpose; what do we want from them?"

Velvet lifted her parasol and twirled it reflectively. "I suppose we want . . . attention . . . and . . . consideration."

25

She glanced at Juliette. "I'm not sure exactly what we want," she admitted. "But I'll tell you this; once you get a man drooling over you, he won't ignore you, and there's something to be said for that." She laughed lightly. "That's the way it is between men and women. We have to make them fall helplessly, hopelessly in love with us. But," she warned, "we must never fall in love with them." Juliette eyed her uncertainly. Assimilating all that her older, wiser cousin had told her was not easy. She picked up the basket of flowers and foliage and placed it thoughtfully over her arm.

"But what if we do fall in love with them?" she asked, "I mean accidentally, of course."

"That's very dangerous," Velvet said gravely. She took Juliette's arm, and the two girls began their stroll back to the Duffy spread. "I suppose, if we do fall in love, it might be best not to show it," she mused aloud.

"But shouldn't we love our husbands?" the younger girl asked hesitantly.

"Marriage has nothing to do with love," Velvet said incredulously as they walked. "Marriage is something to be gotten through." She eyed her young cousin doubtfully. "Didn't your mother ever tell you what you have to *do* when you're married," she asked breathlessly. Juliette shook her head. "Well, I can't tell you," Velvet explained ominously, "because, I'm not exactly sure what it is myself, but Mother says it's just simply awful. Ask your mother," she finished, "but, for heaven's sake, don't mention I brought up the subject."

The voices of the two young women faded. Only the sounds of the forest creatures remained to filter through the breezy clearing. To the lone figure watching the departing girls, those sounds were cherished, the voices an intrusion. Eyes the color of a chilly Adirondack pool narrowed as they watched the trim forms, blocked by a frothy, twirling parasol, disappear into the trees. The eyes glinted in amusement. Velvet's little cousin was not the only woman who would benefit by a lesson on men this day.

26

Chapter Three

The Duffy house was a monument to order, except for that little bastion of chaos that was Velvet's room. Try as she might Hanna Clark could not keep it in order when Velvet was preparing herself for an important occasion. An 'important occasion' included any dinner, any gathering of people—including the immediate family—and the stopping by of a peddler or the local doctor, an outing of any sort. Even a trip to the general store in Cranberry Creek sent Velvet flying to her wardrobe in search of the perfect gown. She agonized over which jewels would be best suited to that particular event. Hanna had sighed inwardly and often over Velvet's fretful changes of costume and worried applications of ornament to each ensemble. There was no point in explaining to the girl that comfort and practicality were the only measures of a costume's appropriateness hereabouts. Velvet made so much of looking pretty. Hanna smiled as she surveyed the clutter of gowns, petticoats, shoes and chemises. In fact, the plain-thinking Hanna rather enjoyed the girl's tendency toward frippery. Dealing with her over the past few weeks had been like having her very own porcelain doll to dress, to decorate, to arrange in pretty poses. And Velvet knew how to pose. She stood now before a tall mirror and regarded her reflected image critically. She lifted her chin and flipped her skirt pointedly. Noting Hanna's attention, she repeated the action.

"I just can't decide which underskirt to wear," she pouted. "Do you prefer the green, or the pink?" Hanna surveyed the light, pale cream of Velvet's India muslin frock. Her consideration was careful and cautious, for she understood how important her advice would be to the girl. The tiny rows of piping which bordered the neckline and hem were of soft, verdant silk, and the little self-belt and ruffled sleeves were appliquéd in the same green with touches of palest rose. Hanna made her decision.

"I think . . ." she narrowed her eyes and rubbed a reflective finger over her chin, "you should wear the . . . green," she finally proclaimed. Velvet turned once again to her own reflection. Repeating the flipping action, she smiled.

"You're absolutely right, Hanna," she said joyfully. "The green will be perfect." She tilted her gaze piquantly. "I was hoping you'd say that." She laughed. The two women bent to the task of positioning the skirt over the wide hoop beneath Velvet's gown. The taffeta rustled and snapped gaily, adding a festive music to Velvet's further preparation as she made her way from jewel case to hat box to glove basket. "I just want to look pretty this afternoon," she insisted, quite obviously understating her goal. Hanna's smile deepened as she followed the girl, retrieved discarded adornments, offered suggestions, and generally supported Velvet in her efforts. Hanna noted her frenzy, and while every prelude to every event in Velvet's life seemed frenzied, there was a difference — a resolve — this day that Hanna had not, up to now, encountered.

"Sure and I've a feelin' there's somethin' you haven't told me, darlin'," the woman said airily, for she and Velvet had become most open together. Hanna felt she could probe. She regarded Velvet keenly. That young lady glanced over her shoulder as she tested the effect of rose glass — beaded eardrops against her gown.

"Have you?" she asked offhandedly. Hanna nodded shortly and smiled, offering Velvet the opportunity to confide in her. "If you must know," Velvet said through a small curve of her lips, "I will be expecting a guest today."

"I knew it," Hanna declared. "A lady doesn't go to such lengths for just anybody."

Velvet suppressed a giggle. "He isn't just anybody," she said. As Hanna continued to fill her arms with discarded underthings, Velvet turned back to her mirror. "He's just the most chivalrous old thing," she said wistfully as she attached the eardrops. "His name is J. Eliot Cutter, and —" Velvet

28

noted Hanna's quick, audible intake of breath and turned. "Do you know him?" she asked.

A long moment passed before Hanna spoke. Velvet's brow creased in puzzlement as the woman continued her work with new resolve. At the girl's silence, Hanna hazarded a speculative glance in her direction. "The eardrops are perfect," the Irish woman said with forced brightness.

"And what about J. Eliot Cutter?" Velvet said archly. "Is he less than perfect?" When Hanna did not answer, Velvet persisted. "I had the same reaction when I mentioned his name to Juliette this morning." Velvet turned fully to face the older woman. Hands on hips, she asked firmly, "What is it about that man's name that sets everyone to gasping?"

Hanna straightened slowly, her arms draped with lacy garments. "I was only surprised he was back up north," she said, attempting offhandedness. Her voice was measured, and Velvet offered a skeptical glare. "That's all, darlin'," Hanna insisted. She regained her composure and smiled.

"Are you telling me that Mr. Cutter is from the South?" Velvet asked.

Hanna shook her head. "I don't know where he's from," she said lightly. "He comes and goes. It was only . . . I was surprised to hear he's back."

"You do know him then," Velvet stated, her voice betraying her bemusement.

"Of course I know him." Hanna laughed. "Everybody knows Mr. J. Eliot Cutter." The woman's words were, Velvet perceived, delivered in tones that were lighter, airier, more heavily brogued than they'd ever been. Though Velvet did not consider herself an expert on the subtleties of human voice, she could tell that Hanna Clark was hiding something. Velvet did consider herself an expert at one thing; getting men to talk about themselves. This afternoon, she would discover the mystery, whatever it might be, that surrounded J. Eliot Cutter. And she would meet the mystery head-on—at its source.

Three o'clock passed without significant notation. The

guests had arrived early, as always, and the party was well under way by the time that fateful hour was struck. Velvet achieved the dream of every young woman of her acquaintance; she was the belle of the ball. Though the picnic was hardly a 'ball' or even a true party by Southern standards, it was well-attended, and gay by any standards. Velvet passed among the guests, garnering their attention and, she noted with satisfaction, their admiration. She had captured the hearts of the Adirondack mountain gentry as efficiently as she'd captured the hearts of her beloved Virginians. Velvet attempted to remain humble as the plain-speaking Northern women complimented her delicate gown.

"I don't imagine this old thing is even in style anymore," she confided to the tall, raw-boned Mrs. William Chapman-White. "I had a letter from Mother last week, and do you know what she told me?" The lady shook her head mutely, waiting in awe for the revelation. "She told me," Velvet said confidentially, "that some of the ladies back home are not even wearing hoops anymore." Mrs. Chapman-White's gray brows drew together in fascinated concern. Though she herself had never even seen a hoop, she knew what she knew about the proprieties of fashion. She read *Godey's Lady's Book* often enough—never mind that the copies were several months, and sometimes a year, old by the time they reached the Adirondack Mountain country—to know that this was a significant fashion trend. And even Mrs. Chapman-White, dressed as she was in raw, colorless cotton, could appreciate a fashion trend. She gazed approvingly at Velvet, deciding that the girl's gown was perfectly suited to this occasion at least.

"Don't you mind," encouraged Mrs. Chapman-White, patting the girl's arm. "You look lovely." She smiled gently, wistfully. "You're like a delicate breath of gentility in these rough environs."

Velvet received the woman's approval with a sweetly dimpled smile. "Why, thank you," she responded graciously, as though Mrs. Chapman-White's approval was what she lived for. Then she fluttered on with apparent reluctance to her next guest—her next compliment.

30

Through the drifting sunlight of the late afternoon, Velvet's thoughts turned occasionally to the absent Mr. Cutter. Where could he be? she wondered as she glanced down the path that led from the woodland to the house. Fortunately, though she anticipated his arrival with some small impatience, her heart did not cry out as it had in the past cried out for the arrival of, for instance, the elegant and doting Mr. Brett Whitney of Richmond. That fierce, soul-stimulating expectancy was reserved, in the depths of her heart, for only Mr. Whitney. Velvet recalled him now with a keen twinge of longing.

At her last ball, her farewell to her home, she had danced with Mr. Whitney and wondered, held in his strong arms, if she ought to allow him to kiss her. She wanted Mr. Whitney to kiss her, but he hadn't even tried. Her fate had been essentially decided by this abiding deference to Southern convention, Velvet mused inwardly. If he had tried to kiss her, and if she'd allowed such a liberty, Mr. Whitney might have been forced, by the dictates of custom, to offer at least an engagement. As it stood now, Velvet had no promise of assured male companionship when she returned home. Naturally, the thought struck no terror in her heart, as it might strike terror into the hearts of her acquaintances. She thought immediately of Morgana Carleton, her most relentless rival back home.

The brandy-haired Morgana had been sent to the little city of Albany, New York at the start of the war, and was attending classes at the Female Academy there. While Velvet had quite a substantial male following at home, as did Morgana, that girl had no hope of meeting men at the academy. Here, there was all sorts of charming male diversion. Unfortunately, that diversion would not be lasting very much longer. Within a few days, the young men would all be leaving—heading for soldierhood, for glory, for some silly male concept of honor. Crude as they were, they had afforded Velvet at least a temporary opportunity to exercise her well-honed powers of coquetry. And, though her Aunt Yvonne had advised her vaguely against stimulating their Yankee blood, and had forewarned some oblique and dire

31

consequence of such behavior, Velvet could not help but take pleasure in the knowledge that the lads quite simply adored her. She dallied, with a small inward smile, over their attempts to gain her favor. Young Cain Gifford had only just offered her a plate of sweets—and had been deeply heartsore when she'd accepted the one offered by Bobby Van Campen instead. Never mind, thought Velvet, she would favor the downhearted Cain later, at the dance. She'd played this stratagem so often at home. She fondly recalled her young suitors, the Virginia lads who fell over each other to win her attention. There was Will Sutter, who owned the Live Oaks near Brandy Station, and there was Andrew Davis, who boasted that he was fourth cousin to President Jefferson Davis, and there were the Calhoun brothers . . . . Her thoughts trailed off.

Velvet ruminated on how happy she was capable of making her young men—and how sad. Her power over them seemed remarkable to her, though she accepted that power with grace. She reminded herself contentedly that she was never unkind, only benignly authoritative. She could not, after all, allow them just any liberty. The blond and bubbly Josiah Keller had only yesterday attempted to hold her hand. She had reminded him quite sternly that this was a privilege a girl did not render lightly. Josiah had been immediately apologetic. He had understood, for all his coarse Northern boldness, that certain refinements in his behavior were expected where Velvet McBride was concerned. Velvet allowed a kindly smile to curve her lips. Tonight—if Josiah behaved himself in other ways—she might just allow that little intimacy. She would see. The evening held promise.

Even now, several boys accompanied her as she sat in the bower of a budding shadbush, its abundant limbs nodding in the afternoon breezes. Velvet had promised each of the lads a dance, and she listened as they argued for the first and the last. How sweet they all are, she thought idly. How pleasurable it will be to nestle in their strong young arms and be twirled in the dance. Velvet's pleasant anticipation of the evening to come was not without its bittersweet moments. For all their deference to her, for all their worship of her, none of those boys compared to the polished Mr. Whitney . . . Brett. She'd called him "Brett" that night, her last night in Virginia, and had secretly promised herself to him with all the poetic abandon of her adolescent heart. The first thing she would do when she returned to Sweet Briar Hill would be to make it quite clear to Mr. Whitney that—if he were still the gentleman of her memory—she would allow that liberty, that kiss, that would bind them in a promise of marital harmony forever. Apparently, she must make it *very* clear to Mr. Whitney, she thought, her brow arching in unconscious determination, for he was nothing if not a true Southern gentleman. His unrelenting courtesy, his veneration of her, his insistent civility were flattering, but . . . well . . . monotonous. Velvet resolved that, if necessary, she would aid the very honorable Mr. Whitney in overcoming his courtly diffidence. After all, if one must be married to someone, it was best that someone be at least courtly. In the meantime, she would make the most of her current resources. She would enjoy the time left to her in the company of these Northern boys. And after them, there would be J. Eliot Cutter.

The taming of Mr. Cutter would take some exertion on her part, but Velvet was confident of her abilities. The rough and, from what she could recall, rather uncivil gentleman would probably prove to be the least problematic of all her challenges. He at least had a foundation of gallantry with which she could work. And, most importantly, he was not a soldier. Most importantly, Mr. Cutter would not be running off to that burdensome war.

Velvet was lost in her reflections when she heard a shout of welcome from her Uncle Duff. The big man moved with a hurried, wide-gaited grace, despite a limp which was the residue of a logging accident, toward a horse and rider. Instantly, Velvet recognized the figure of J. Eliot Cutter. The two men met on the path to the house and stood talking for several moments before they proceeded to the party. Velvet straightened, fluffed her dark curls and graced her devoted coterie with a smile, managing with her flirtatious energy to increase their devotion almost to zealotry. Pretending she'd not seen J. Eliot approach, she gave a warm and studied attention to the young men who surrounded her. She fluttered her fan, laughed delicately and purposefully at their jokes and waited in earnest for J. Eliot to notice her popularity. Glancing surreptitiously in his direction, she was bemused to note that his attention seemed to be everywhere but on her. She watched with widened eyes as he greeted her Aunt Yvonne with warm-spirited hugs, Juliette with tweaks of the girl's dimpled chin. Even the usually sullen Nicole was not immune to the glowing affection that seemed to characterize this apparent homecoming.

In contrast, the young men in Velvet's company took note of the new arrival with scornful disdain.

"There's Cutter," said one beneath his breath.

"The cowardly wretch dares to show his face here," snarled another. Velvet regarded the young man quizzically.

"What makes Mr. Cutter a 'cowardly wretch'?" she asked, just the least offended by the appellation.

"I . . . I'm sorry, Velvet," the youth said sheepishly, quickly correcting his unguarded reaction. "I shouldn't have made my feelings known that way."

Velvet arched a brow and did not notice the derisive laughter that was directed at the focus of her attention. She continued to question him. "Why do you boys disdain Mr. Cutter?" she inquired doggedly.

"Because," said one courageous gallant as he straightened, "he refuses to wear the uniform of his country."

Velvet rolled her eyes. "Is that all?" she retorted.

The young men regarded her incredulously. "Is that all?" one of them blurted. "Why every manjack in these parts is preparing to fight the good fight. How can we forgive a young and healthy buck who won't?"

"*You* may not be able to forgive such a one, but I can," she said coolly. She stood abruptly and snapped out her skirts. "I had the same argument with some boys yesterday. I am sworn, you're all alike. Do you think going to war is the only respectable occupation for a man?" Velvet's wide, challenging regard flashed with aquamarine fire. Before any of them could answer, she twirled away, her hooped skirts, like a wide bell, fairly nudging the lads off their balance. "Quite frankly, I prefer the company of a man who doesn't need to flaunt his masculinity," she commented haughtily as she swept off.

Levelly targeting her prey, Velvet made her way toward the newly arrived guest. If he would not notice her on his own, she would be forced to command his attention. Her skirts swaying, she moved like a breeze-tossed blossom through the guests. Speaking to one or the other of the ladies and gentlemen she passed, she made sure to keep a veiled scrutiny upon Mr. Cutter. *Ah,* she thought with satisfaction, as she at last noted his narrow gaze upon her. She must now be very sure to make the most of her advantage. She placed her closed fan to her delicate lips and laughed modestly as Mr. Gifford, Cain's father, complimented her shyly.

"Oh, sir," she said, her smile pointedly engaging, "how you do go on." Mr. Gifford laughed roguishly, proud of his ability to still assert his masculine charms and fascinate a lady such as Miss McBride. Velvet lifted her lacy shawl over one shoulder and then allowed it to slide demurely down her arm. "You mustn't toy with a poor little Southern drab like me. You sophisticated Northerners are all alike," she bubbled. "You just go on and on with your clever compliments. How am I to know whether you really mean them or not?" She sighed wistfully and cocked her gaze. "I'd just give anything in the world to meet a really *sincere* gentleman." Mr. Gifford's brows lifted and he meant to lean forward to assure this delicate, and easily bruised, flower of femininity that he was indeed sincere in his compliments. Before he could, however, a large shadow passed between them. J. Eliot Cutter stood nearby. He bowed curtly and allowed a small smile to etch his lips. Velvet was appropriately disconcerted at his "unexpected" appearance.

"Forgive me," Cutter said evenly, "but I could not help overhear your exchange with Mr. Gifford. I am so sorry you feel that way Miss . . ."

"McBride," Velvet said, only a hint of annoyance in her tone. How could the oaf have forgotten her name already?

35

She hid her momentary irritation and fluttered her lashes and her fan coyly. "I am sure I need have no fears where Mr. Gifford is concerned," she murmured, gracing Cain's father with a benevolent smile. He hastened to assure her that her observation was correct. "But one hears so many compliments," she continued with exaggerated desolation, "how is one to know which are true?"

"One only needs to consider the focus of the compliment, dear Miss McBride," said Mr. Gifford earnestly.

"You are too kind, sir," Velvet demurred. Her tilted blue gaze drifted to Cutter. She waited expectantly for his repudiation of her concerns, but no encouragement was offered. Again, Velvet thought aggravatedly, she would have to take the initiative. She lifted her chin. "But how can a poor girl know that all men are as forthright as you, Mr. Gifford?" she said, her voice tinged with challenge. There was a pause as the older man attempted to collect himself and offer an appropriate response. At last Cutter spoke.

"As a rule," he said evenly, "men respond to women in kind. If the . . . 'poor girl,' as you say, is forthright, she can usually count on an honest response from the gentleman."

Mr. Gifford laughed uncomfortably. "Now, now, Cutter," he said in a conciliatory tone, "we must take into consideration the . . . the *expected* elements of coquetry that endear us to our feminine counterparts. It's a fact they wouldn't be nearly so enchanting to us if they were just . . . well . . . like us." He patted Cutter's shoulder companionably. "It's all a game, after all, my boy," he chuckled softly.

"Games can be fun," Cutter allowed, "but games ought to be left to the nursery. When we grow up, time becomes too precious to waste on . . . games." The time had come, Mr. Gifford decided, for him to return to the more straight-spoken comforts of Mrs. Gifford. He would leave this younger, and obviously uninitiated, buck to the strategies of the talented female Miss McBride. Oh, but Cutter had a great deal to learn, Gifford thought delightedly as he moved off.

Velvet made a studied inspection of her challenge. He was not wearing his spectacles today, and he seemed less bookish than he had the day before, though he was still no polished gentleman. She looked up and down this rather rough-cut specimen of manhood. Inspected the dark glisten of curls that fell in profusion over the tanned forehead, the wide, muscled shoulders sheathed in a thin cotton shirt, the broad chest, bound by a well-worn leather vest, the long, hard thighs. Oh, yes, he was worth the effort the taming would take. Her green-blue gaze lifted to his keen, silvery one. She knew a sudden, inexplicable tingle of . . . something. She averted her eyes quickly, too quickly she remonstrated herself. He would think her an unapproachable twit—the way Lisa Mae Bloomer was thought of at home. Velvet must compose herself. What was that sensation she'd experienced while looking into those remarkable, uncivil eyes? She'd felt cold, or . . . or . . . hot . . . or something. She shook off the inexpressible and lifted her gaze once again. Again that odd, unsettling rush thrilled up from her middle. Again, she turned away. It was ridiculous, she thought, this suddenly acquired inability to look a man in the eye. But then Cutter was no ordinary man. Velvet perceived that even in her innocence, though she could not define her perception.

"Do you know something," she said on a breath, "you are a most unusual gentleman, J. Eliot Cutter."

"In what way?" he asked lazily.

"In every way possible," Velvet said, her composure returning by degrees. "For one thing, you are on the verge of trying my patience to the bone." His regard did not waver, and Velvet continued in her most practiced tone of feigned affrontery. "I distinctly recall instructing you to call me Velvet," she said. "You can't seem to remember my name, and that is most insulting."

"Forgive me, Miss . . ."

"McBride—*Velvet!*" she blurted in her consternation. Then, reining in her sudden, unguarded frustration, Velvet regarded Cutter evenly. "You're mocking me," she pouted.

"Am I?" Cutter asked, his lips twitching in amusement.

"Yes, and it isn't fair of you," she said petulantly. Turning and snapping her skirts, she started away from him, fully hoping, if not fully expecting, he would follow. He did. Velvet felt a relieved satisfaction. "I'm only trying to be

37

friendly," she added, tilting him a wounded glance.

"I'm sorry," he said softly. They walked in silence for several seconds, she assessing the sincerity of his conversion and he impassive.

"Besides that," Velvet asserted softly, "you're late. I distinctly remember telling you the picnic was at three." She watched as Cutter nodded, conceding his indifference to her instruction.

"I had business to attend," he said with maddening calm. Velvet's lips tightened and she raised a delicately winged brow.

"And," she added putting a final emphasis on her disapproval, "I strongly suggested you accommodate your clothing to this festive occasion." She swept a delicate hand, indicating the neatly turned-out assemblage. "These people don't have much, but they do try to present themselves as well as they can under the circumstances."

"You're absolutely right," Cutter said. Velvet abruptly turned and regarded him suspiciously. Cutter splayed a bronzed hand. "Believe me, I understand your concern. This is a festive occasion. We may be the last civilians any of these boys see for a long time. We owe it to them to send them off with happy images to sustain them. Beyond that," he conceded, "we need to show them how deeply we respect their efforts by dressing up for the occasion of their sendoff."

"Th-that's right," Velevet said uncertainly. Only yesterday, Cutter and the newly uniformed soldiers had been at each others throats. What, Velvet wondered, had inspired such a change in his attitude, if not theirs. It was probably that ridiculous male sense of fraternity, she thought derisively. As though reading her thoughts, Cutter laughed and quickly explained his posture.

"I do respect these lads," he said, "and their cause, though we often seem to disagree on a personal level. The only reason I am not joining them in their good fight is because my work here is so important." He held Velvet in a hooded gaze. "Would you like to hear about my work?" he asked.

"Why . . . naturally, J. Eliot," she said, averting her eyes once again from that odd, distinctly uncourtly, boldness in

38

his. She wondered if Juliette was watching, and what her reaction was to this sudden turnabout. Only that morning, Velvet had instructed her young cousin that men loved being questioned about their work, and now, here was J. Eliot Cutter bringing up that very subject. He really wasn't so "unusual" a man, after all, thought Velvet smugly. She placed her little hand in the crook of his elbow as they once again began to walk.

"These mountains are remarkable in so many ways," he began softly.

Velvet nodded. "The forest seems almost primeval in its beauty," she agreed.

"Ah," said Cutter, "but that is the very crux of its magic. The Adirondack forest is, in the scheme of things, very young, not at all old. It only seems ancient. It was formed, possibly, as recently as twenty million years ago. These mountains are a rebirth, if you will, of very old basement rock that was created in Precambrian times, and was originally igneous. It has changed so over the millenia that it is now classified as metamorphic rock."

Velvet smiled blankly.

Cutter continued. "Because of that profound metamorphosis, some scientists are not fully convinced the original form was igneous, but my theory stands currently as the prevailing one. Naturally, you can see why I am constantly defending my position, and why I must continue my relentless research."

"Naturally," Velvet responded after a slight pause. She had not been sure that he'd finished speaking. She'd not understood a word of what he'd said, and she decided this jabbering about his work and igneous rock and Precambrian time had gone quite far enough. She trembled delicately and glanced at Cutter. "It seems, as soon as the sun sets these days, the air turns cool," she observed. He quickly lifted her shawl to her shoulders. "Thank you," she murmured with a small, grateful smile, and gazed with a determined helplessness up into his pewter scrutiny. She felt a sudden, true chill and once again turned uncertainly away. Every time she looked at him, he seemed to be studying her. Why is he doing that? she wondered. She was no rock or plant. Nevertheless, she consoled herself, things between them seemed to be going very well. If only Juliette were here to see the success Velvet was having with this rough, untrained mountain man. She stood with him now, preparing to carry out the next phase of her carefully constructed seduction. But suddenly she was aware of a darkening of his regard, a hardening intensity in his gaze.

"You know," he said huskily, "your eyes remind me of labradorite crystals. They seem to sparkle with an inner fire."

Velvet felt an arcing thrill of satisfaction. The compliment, awkward as it was, proved his interest in her as explicitly as any gesture he might have made, and it explained the odd intensity of his gaze. The unbred oaf was smitten with her, she exulted. He was a singular man, and it followed that his response to her would be as singular as he. He would not drool and slobber over her, as the younger boys had done. He would not flutter and flush boyishly. He was as clumsily inept as any man who found himself helplessly in love, but he was infinitely more restrained. Cutter went on. "Labradorite, as you must know, is one of the feldspars, a class of rock-forming minerals. It was named after Labrador, where Moravian missionaries discovered it around 1775. . . ."

"How fascinating," Velvet said hastily. "I should love to see a sample sometime." As she had predicted, J. Eliot Cutter would be the least problematic of her triumphs. He was quite simply dazzled by her. She must make the most of that.

"I have some at my cabin," Cutter was saying, "but the best specimens are found along the river bed in Lewis County."

"Is that far?" asked Velvet, her wide gaze becoming even wider in anticipation of an outing.

Cutter hid a glinting amusement. "It is." His tone was casual, though his keen gaze remained steady. "But the trip could be made in . . . oh, a week or two."

"Velvet looked away. "I see," she said, thinking rapidly.

"Well . . . but . . . there must be much to see nearby."

"There is," Cutter responded evenly. "Anorthosite; both black and white. It is *the* Adirondack rock."

"Yes . . . well . . . wouldn't that be fun to explore," Velvet said, mustering excitement and taking a few steps away from him.

"You don't know what fun is," Cutter said, following her enthusiastically, "until you've seen Mount Marcy at sunrise. There you have the finest example of black anorthosite in the world. The trip to Mount Marcy can be made in just a few days." In his apparent excitement, he touched her slim shoulder with a large rough hand. She suddenly shivered, and he glanced down at her. "Anything wrong?" he inquired politely. "Are you cold again?"

"Heaven's no," Velvet said, forcing a lightness she did not feel. She moved away from him once again and waved at the rapidly cooling air with her fan. Was the lout really so dull witted? Could he not even understand her purpose? By now, most men would have suggested an afternoon outing. They would have begged to call on her. But Cutter was not "most men," she reminded herself. So far, he had suggested only outings that would take them on days-long journeys. She must lead him into more manageable territory. He had mentioned his cabin. Naturally, she could not go there, but perhaps she could suggest he bring his samples over to her uncle's house. She turned to face him, and a sugared smile curved her lips. "You live nearby?" she asked.

Cutter nodded lazily. "I have a cabin up at Doriel's Pond," he said.

"Why, then we're practically neighbors," Velvet said breathlessly, apparently overwhelmed by the happenstance. "Isn't that just too remarkable?" Cutter merely watched her, and Velvet felt her words, so inviting, so invested with communicative promise, were now hanging uselessly between them.

At that moment, and with mercifully perfect timing, Velvet's Aunt Yvonne moved toward the couple. "Everyone's going inside," she called brightly. "Supper will be laid and the fiddler will be here any minute." She herded

41

of them, along with several other young people, into the house for the evening's festivities.

A reprieve, Velvet thought gratefully. She must get this situation back under control. She placed her hand on Cutter's politely proffered arm and offered a vigorous smile. She had never met a more dense male. He seemed impossibly crude, impossibly bookish, impossibly laconic. The only thing that gave him any apparent pleasure was the anticipation of the sight of Mount Marcy at sunrise. J. Eliot Cutter was, quite simply, boring. The revelation gave her pause. She cocked a hidden glance in his direction and wondered if her first assessment had been correct. She wondered if, in fact, J. Eliot Cutter would prove worth the taming, after all. Well, she mused with a small sigh, she must at least make the effort. In a very few days, he would be the only eligible male within miles of Northville, New York. She must attempt to make herself at least as attractive to him as a clump of black anorthosite. He was already infatuated with her, she reasoned. Why not encourage that? If anyone could do it, Velvet resolved, she could.

Chapter Four

For the latter part of the evening, Hanna had done wonders with Velvet's mass of black, gold-struck curls. She had spent more than an hour lifting and twining the silken tresses into a luminous array of moonlit waves. She had weaved into them a garland of crystalline beads. Velvet's gown was of the softest night-green organza, with tiny sequins sewn into the voluminous skirt and bodice. Delicate ripples of shirred black silk ornamented the wrist-length sleeves and the hem. The neckline was elegantly rounded and deep enough that the gentle mounding of her creamy breasts was visible over a dark rim of piping. Velvet stood now at the bottom of the stairs, at the entrance to the parlor, accepting the approval of the guests, and waited impatiently for Cutter to notice her entrance.

She eyed him brazenly as he socialized with several men, and ignored her. The oaf has an odd way of showing his interest, she reflected peevishly. Arranging the froth of netting that caressed her shoulders, she murmured excuses to her admirers and made her way with determination across the parlor. Velvet decided that she must do something, yet again, to rouse his attention. This whole campaign to kindle the adoration of such a dim-witted bumpkin seemed hardly worth the effort. And yet, Velvet determined, she really had little choice in the matter. She was a young woman who thrived on male courtesies, and Cutter would soon be the only eligible male in the vicinity. It is ludicrous, she thought hotly, that I must consistently take the initiative. This unpolished roughneck hardly deserved her attention, and in other circumstances she would not have bothered with him. Back home, in Virginia, he would not have caused a feminine heart to flutter—particularly her own. But Velvet was not at home, and she could surely encourage whatever paucity of charms he might have to offer. She was, after all, a practiced coquette. She wended her bell-skirted way through the milling guests. As was usual, she was accompanied by a covey of resolutely worshipful young men.

Cutter stood, wide-shouldered, before the blazing hearth, his tousle of jet curls falling recklessly over his forehead, his silver gaze crinkling in humor. His oblivion to her was at an end, she resolved. She impatiently rebuffed the attempts of her companions to gain her notice. At last, standing before Cutter, she smiled purposefully. Her blue-green regard raked him with barely concealed reproof.

"Why, J. Eliot," she purred beneath the din of conversation, "isn't it time we continued our little talk?"

Cutter eyed her dispassionately. "Oh, yes. Miss . . ."

"McBride," Velvet said flatly.

"Miss McBride," Cutter responded lazily.

"Your memory astounds me, sir," she said, waving her fan near the rounded ripeness of her bosom. "And here I thought you were merely toying with me. You really can't remember my name, can you, J. Eliot," she stated with forced lightness. She pursed her lips and wrinkled her brow in a question. "We were having such a fascinating discussion of your work before. Mightn't we continue it before the evening is over?" Velvet glanced beneath her lashes to where Juliette was standing in the steady embrace of her beau, Jason. She hoped her young cousin was paying attention. "I was thinking, we might take a stroll," she continued, her eyes drifting back to Cutter. Velvet's gaze took in his tall form. "Wouldn't that be ever so much fun?" she asked fluttering her lashes.

"Actually," J. Eliot said evenly, "I was discussing my theories with these good people." He indicated, with a lift of his eyes, the assemblage who had gathered to converse with him. Velvet looked to several of the gentlemen, and her smile deepened.

"Oh, I'm sure they would forgive you . . ." Her voice trailed off. The men nodded deferentially, but before any of them could respond, Cutter's words stung the overheated air of the small parlor.

"But I would not forgive myself," he said slowly.

Velvet offered a quick, curious perusal of her challenge. Did the man's lack of sophistication where women were concerned never end? Surely, he realized that he could not possibly refuse her very public invitation. Her smile was tolerant. "Oh, I think you could forgive yourself . . . eventually, don't you, J. Eliot?" she prodded amiably. She placed her small hand in the crook of his arm and gently tugged. "You will excuse us, gentlemen?" she said in dismissal as she started out. Velvet was both startled and annoyed when Cutter did not move. She glanced at him and her gaze darkened perceptibly. "Shall we go?" she stated with a sugared smile.

"I think not," Cutter said quietly. Velvet's jaw dropped and her green-blue gaze widened.

"I . . . I . . ." She quickly reined in her embarrassment. "I'm sure you have mistaken me, J. Eliot," she said evenly, and perhaps just a bit too stridently. "I wish you to accompany me . . . for a stroll." Her smile had left her eyes, but her lips remained curved icily. "Shall we go?" she said once again. Heads turned. Conversation stopped.

"If you truly wish a stroll," Cutter said into the silence, amusement tingeing his tone, "you might ask one of these hearty lads to accompany you." He lifted his gaze and eyed the coterie of young men surrounding Velvet. "They, at least, seem most anxious to please." The sudden quick intake of her breath drew his eyes to Velvet's deep bodice and the luminous swell of her breasts. He smiled fully, as he slowly raised his gaze. "If it is . . . something else you crave, Miss . . . McBride—wasn't it?—I can accommodate you in just a few moments—after my discussion with these men." With the words, he turned from her, giving Velvet a full view of his wide, muscular back, and continued his conversation as before. Velvet waggled her fan wildly, and attempted to believe what she'd just heard. The others who were gathered in the room made a great show of resuming their own conversations, but many nervous coughs and a great deal of throat clearing could be detected.

As hot waves of embarrassment welled up from some

45

unknown source, Velvet's humiliation became complete. She noted that her blush was, for nearly the first time in her young life, a true one. She had feigned the phenomenon often enough to the delight of many young men, but the actuality of it appalled her. Embarrassment—true embarrassment—was no demure posture. Embarrassment, Velvet discovered in the unkindest way of all, hurt.

Abruptly, before she had time to pray for a hole to open in the parlor floor, one into which she could crawl, she felt herself swept into strong masculine arms. Unexpectedly, at that precise moment, the fiddle began to squawl a rhapsodic prelude to a joyous dance tune.

Andrew Duffy bounced his niece out onto the hastily cleared floor. "We hired old Everet," he shouted to the standers-by, "and by jingo, we'd best use him up!" He laughed heartily as the other guests, grateful for the diversion, joined in. Clapping and stamping of feet and general merriment overshadowed the first few dreadful moments of Velvet's shame. She glanced up at her uncle as they danced, and her thanks were in her eyes. "You're welcome," he whispered gently as he danced them to the far perimeters of the room. He led her to a quiet chair, and there they sat for a few moments while Velvet composed herself. "You really ought to say thanks to your Aunt Vonnie," he said, his eyes twinkling kindly. "It was her idea." Velvet nodded and made a feeble attempt at a smile.

"Oh, Uncle Duff," she said at last, "I just think I'd better get some air." The man nodded in understanding. He watched as his niece made her way among the dancing firelit shadows to the front door of the house.

"Is she all right?" asked Yvonne Duffy softly, as she approached her husband.

Andrew shook his head helplessly. "Wish I knew, Vonnie," he answered. "A real shame what happened, though."

His wife nodded. "I've tried to tell her, love," she said forlornly, "but she doesn't seem to understand."

"In any event, the child needs some time to herself," Andrew said shortly. "Let's get supper on, so those lads that are always following her don't get the idea she needs consoling."

Yvonne nodded, and a twinkle of a smile touched her lips. "They'll want to do that," she said softly. "That girl is more popular than Hanna's muskrat pie." Her expression immediately became grave. "It was bound to happen, one way or another," she murmured. "She just doesn't seem to understand."

Velvet did not understand. As she stepped out into the cool softness of the June night, she reflected that nothing made sense to her. One moment she was everyone's sweetheart, and the next moment, she was a laughing stock. How had it happened? Her gaze narrowed as she traversed the pebble-strewn terrain outside the house. It happened, she reminded herself, because that blackguard Cutter had engineered it. No. She hastily amended the direction of her thoughts. He was not clever enough to have deliberately humiliated her in that way. And why would he? On the other hand, his response to her, that cold reference to the possibility that she was seeking in him something other than companionship, was nothing if not calculated. Velvet stopped abruptly. Could he have deliberately baited her? Impossible, she reflected. Yet a sudden chill slithered ominously up her spine. If he had done that, if he had masterminded such a terrible seduction, he was nothing more than a lowly cad. Velvet's eyes widened with the unspeakable possibility. Her mother had told her of such men. They led a girl to believe they harbored deep feelings for her, but they were after *only one thing*. What that "one thing" was had remained unspoken by Alicia McBride, but Velvet understood it to be something painful and ugly that only husbands were allowed to do to their wives. Apparently, the dreadful thing brought the men great pleasure. Velvet sniffed derisively. Men were always allowed their great, private pleasures in this world. Anyway, Velvet reasoned, dismissing that possibility, J. Eliot Cutter seemed to want nothing to do with her. His purpose seemed to be only her complete humiliation. But why? Her winged brows drew together in a delicate frown.

She sat heavily on the outstretched arm of a fallen pine,

and her eyes swept the star-crusted night. The whole incident confused her, nettled her as nothing else had ever done. How could her judgement have so inexplicably deserted her? Who was this man Cutter, and what were his motives? He is, Velvet told herself, merely a stupid, Northern clod. It was obvious he'd had no breeding, at least in the area of how to treat a lady. As for his motive, she pooh-poohed any dark justification for his actions. The man was too dull witted to harbor intelligent sources of aversion; he probably disliked her because she was from the South—and there was that silly war. Well, she disliked him right back, and her reason had nothing to do with cultural bias. J. Eliot Cutter was a boorish nincompoop. He was not worth one more second of Velvet's consideration, and she would let him know that.

She stood in a resolute rustle of organza. She must get back to that party before her absence became awkward. When she did get back, she would make it a point to curtail any speculation concerning her departure. She would dismiss any hint of discomfort on her part over what she would describe as a silly misunderstanding. She would be gay and animated. And she would ignore the detestable Cutter as noticeably as she possibly could. Let the imbecile enjoy the folly of his prejudice; he'd soon find himself spurned by all for his abhorrent treatment of her. Her determination kindled, she brushed at her curls, snapped out her skirts, and turned to make her way back to the house. Her progress was almost immediately impeded by a tall, unyielding figure on the tree-shadowed path. She stopped abruptly and surveyed the silhouette.

"Who is it?" she asked, though she knew only too well what the answer would be. Reining in her trepidation, she lifted her chin as the dark form answered.

"Cutter." The word sent shivers of loathing, and only a little fear, through her heart. She took a few steps toward him, her gaze steadily lifting. In the starlight, as she neared him, his own eyes took on the translucence of silvered glass.

"Let me pass," she breathed, attempting to keep any hint of weakness from her voice. Cutter did not move. Velvet attempted to step around him, but his towering form merely blocked her way with a casual sidestep. Velvet looked up. "I said, let me pass," she gritted out.

"When I'm ready," he rejoined easily.

"I shall scream," Velvet assured him. She could not actually see the smile, but she perceived it lurking in the gray depths of his keen regard. "Dammit, sir," she ground out, "is it your intention to make fools of both of us? Haven't you had your fill; hasn't your thirst for blood been slaked?" The perceived smile deepened as Cutter pushed his soft hat to the back of his tousled head.

"You mentioned a stroll," he said.

Velvet's lips formed an incredulous and soundless "O" and her eyes widened. "How dare you taunt me with my own words," she finally gasped.

"I dare, dear improbable little coquette, because I find you far more alluring than even you imagine yourself to be." His tones were husky and touched with amusement. Velvet had no idea what her reaction ought to be. She was sure she'd been insulted, though, and she was tired of this arrogant swagger's insults.

"I insist you let me by," she said at last. "I don't like you. And I have no interest in anything you have to say to me." She made a decisive move to pass him, but her attempt was thwarted. Cutter grasped her arms and snapped her to him. Helpless, truly helpless for the first time in her life, Velvet merely gaped up at him. He held her pressed against the hard expanse of his chest. As before, he seemed to study her. There was no amusement in his regard now. The star-shot night closed in. Velvet felt herself reel. "I shall faint," she gasped softly.

"No, you won't," Cutter rasped. "You won't faint, and you won't break." But Velvet thought she might break beneath the banded steel of Cutter's sudden embrace. Her breath came in sobs. His big hand cupped the back of her head. His mouth, so hard, so demanding descended upon hers. She felt the yielding pliancy of her lips twisted against the demanding hunger of his. She struggled against the assault and against her own disbelief. Squealing wildly, she writhed against his power. For her efforts, she was merely held

49

captive, commanded to meld to the hard length of his body. His lips were like stone against the softness of her innocence. She'd never known such aggression in a man. That her first kiss should be like this . . . As the world turned dark with Velvet's horror, she felt herself set away, unceremoniously cast from the encompassing, uncompromising steel of his embrace. He gazed down at her. Her knees would not support her, and she realized that she was still held, though less demandingly. She grasped at his broad chest for support, and his arms came around her waist. His silver gaze caught the starlight and again Velvet saw amusement glinting there. She found her strength returning as anger took hold. *How dare he find any of this amusing!* She mustered her own power and thrust herself away from him.

"You blackguard!" she shrilled. Her white hand swung up in the dark and connected with a resounding slap against the bronze of his jaw. Cutter barely flinched, as though he'd been expecting the response, but Velvet was too filled with righteous indignation to notice his reaction. "You're one of those men Mother warned me about," she raged on. "You want only one thing!" She swung her arm again in a stinging arc, but this time Cutter's rough hand snapped up and he caught her slender wrist in a viselike grip.

"Your mother was right," he grated. He drew Velvet unrelentingly to him until she was once again captive of the commanding power of his hunger. "I want only one thing of you. I want that silly Southern belle simper wiped off your beautiful face. I want you warm and womanly beneath me. And I shall have you, make no mistake." His breath came, hot and hoarse. Velvet felt feathers of lingering fury give way inexplicably to another sensation entirely. Her flesh thrilled with fiery shivers. Her lips parted as she licked at them, unaware that the gesture lit them with the luster of the star-frosted night. "Oh, yes," Cutter growled, *"I shall have you,* and soon. I am not a patient man, Velvet McBride." He paused. "You see, I do know your name." A fleeting glimmer touched his gray gaze. "I know your name well."

"And I know yours, Cutter." She gasped out the last word, denying, with all the passion of her innocent heart, the unwanted turmoil of unexpected need in her soul.

"And so you do," Cutter said after pause. "And so you do." With calculated languor, he released her. Velvet rubbed at her bruised wrist, her eyes never leaving his.

"I shall tell you one thing, *Mr.* Cutter," she ground out, "you shall never have what you want—never. I shall molder in the blistering flames of hell before I give you that."

"I can always . . . take it," he said evenly.

Velvet's chin snapped up. Her eyes blazed star-captured fire. "Yes," she challenged. "I concede that you are stronger than I."

"Do you also concede," he asked coldly, "that if I should happen to lose my patience, there would be no help for you? There would be nothing on earth that could stop me." His last words, delivered menacingly, caused Velvet's heart to tilt wildly. She took a quick, tripping breath. He stepped toward her. "You do know it, don't you, Velvet?" he said almost gently. She nodded, swallowing, licking at the moist bud of her lips. Her blood raced.

"I know it," she breathed. "But I tell you this," she went on hurriedly, splaying a hand against his muscled chest, "there would be no pleasure in it for you, I promise." She noted the glitter of insolent amusement that tinged his gaze. Wrath and fear congealed in her breast. "I would fight you, Cutter," she gasped out. "I would fight you with every last ounce of my strength."

"And you would lose," he said through a small smile. He cupped her delicate chin in his rough hand. Velvet's impulse was to jerk away from his touch, but she checked her impulse, knowing, conceding—for now—his physical superiority. Cutter seemed to perceive her inner struggle and his regard lightened with what might have been admiration. She was nothing if not an intelligent minx, he acknowledged. "But that isn't the way I want you," he said finally. His gaze hooded. "You know that, too, don't you?" Velvet could only nod. Some barely reasoned instinct told her that Cutter was offering unimagined mutual pleasure. She could not move, could not think. She only felt. From some unexplored source, her woman's soul sent waves of knowing acceptance. This is the way it must be between man and woman. The unfocused, unfamiliar inclination insinuated itself in the very core of her perception. It was unwelcome, for she knew that she hated Cutter. At last, she twisted from him.

"I don't want it to be that way," she whispered. "Not with you." Cutter took her white shoulders and, for all his roughness, turned her tenderly to face him.

"But it will be that way," he said softly. "And with me."

"No," she breathed, her eyes lifting to his.

"Yes," he answered. Velvet's blue-green gaze became lustrous with star-glistened tears. Cutter could see the terror that welled in her heart. "Don't be afraid," he whispered hoarsely. "You were made for love, Velvet. Don't you know that? You were made for me to love." She shook her head. He smiled. "Well you were," he assured her. He drew her into a protective embrace. "You posture and pose and affect a disinclination to the real woman in your soul, but I know she exists. I have felt her there since the first moment I saw you."

In the pine-scented warmth of his embrace, Velvet knew the first moment of security she'd felt since leaving her home. She nestled in the comfort of that protection, until, abruptly, the words Cutter had just said pierced the mind-softening layer of sensate emotion that had captured her brain. She jerked away from him and looked up into his startled perusal.

"Posturing?" she asked him. "Posing?" she demanded. Cutter, unwilling to relinquish their warm moment together, pulled her back into his arms, but she snapped away from him. "I want to know exactly what you meant by those last words," she shot out.

Cutter raised a dark brow. Then, rethinking the impulse to drag her back into his embrace, he hooked his thumbs into his belt loops and his broad shoulders stiffened. "What . . . exactly . . . did you want to know about them, Velvet?" he asked lazily.

"Oh, just everything," she retorted, folding her slender arms across her breast.

52

Cutter's lips tightened into a grim line. "I meant what I said," he answered slowly. He had already apprised this mercurial wench of his lack of patience; why did she continue to fight him? He had to allow that it was her perceived lack of passivity that had seduced him in the first place. A smile of appreciation twitched at the corners of his mouth. Oh, but she was an adorable vixen. "You *do* posture and pose," he said fondly. "You flirt your beautiful little behind — and I only imagine that it is beautiful, though I fully intend to see it for myself very soon — underneath those skirts until the poor lads who dog your heels are drunk with adolescent desire. And still you tease and taunt them. You'd faint if any one of them took you seriously."

"I would not faint," she stated, her winged brow snapping up.

Cutter laughed. "I concede my error," he said knowingly. Velvet stiffened. "*They* would faint if you took *them* seriously," he amended. "The point is," he went on, chuckling, "not one of you knows what you really want. You play at seduction." He watched as Velvet received his evaluation with an indignant gasp. "It's true," he continued. "It's a Southern tradition, and because of your beauty, and may I add your remarkable training and talent, our boys have been lured into it. Let me tell you something about yourself, Miss McBride of Sweet Briar Hill, I have been flirted with and fondled by the best of your Southern belle sisters, and I find you a most gifted little vamp. But," he said, his silver regard darkening to slate, "I am no boy." His arm snaked out and he caught her to him. "I know exactly what I want," he grated, "and, like it or not, you will give it to me." Velvet wrenched herself free of the confinement of his arms, and, unexpectedly, he allowed her her freedom. She stumbled backward. Twirling her skirts stormily, she spun away from him.

"Don't count on it, *Mr.* Cutter," she spat out. "I will tease and taunt anyone I please to the end of my days, and I'll posture and pose till I die, and, like it or not, Mr. Cutter, you will never know whether I am serious or not!" Hiking up the bell of her hoop-skirted gown, Velvet marched away 'from him toward the house. Cutter could not restrain the wide smile that lit his tanned face.

"Velvet," he called after her, and she turned, glancing toward him.

"What is it?" she asked impatiently.

"Your plantation is aptly named, love. You are the sweetest little briar of a woman I have ever met." He saluted her lazily and turned, making his way to his own cabin down the road.

As Velvet stamped up onto the front steps of the house, she heard the strains of the final song of the evening. The fiddler was being accompanied on the pianoforte by Nicole. Everyone was standing in a circle as Velvet entered. They did not notice her as she made her way into the parlor. They did not welcome her into their circle. The young men in blue were receiving their final farewell as the soft, sweet, sad voices of their parents and friends melded lovingly with the words Francis Scott Key set to "To Anacreon in Heaven."

Slowly, quietly, Velvet climbed the stairs to her bedroom. She did not wish to interrupt the solemnity of the moment, and she would have been hard pressed to explain her absence—had anyone thought to ask her about it.

"He's his own man," said Hanna cautiously as she rolled back Velvet's bedcovers, fluffing them busily as she did so. "Sure, and he'd be as like to cuff ya as to kiss ya."

Yvonne Duffy had joined the two women in Velvet's bedchamber, and she nodded, affirming Hanna Clark's words as she built up the fire. Both women eyed the outraged Velvet and then each other warily.

"He doesn't deserve to *live!*" the girl shrilled. She tore at her dress, ignoring Hanna's attempts to assist her in removing it. "He doesn't deserve to draw breath! He doesn't deserve to *exist! Damn his hide to hell!*" Velvet tossed her ravaged gown to the floor near the hearth. It was saved from the dancing fire by Hanna's hasty retrieval.

"Now, now," the Irish woman said soothingly, "no man is all that bad. . . ."

"Not that bad?" Velvet rejoined explosively. "Uncle Duff ought to call the blackguard out for this. Do you know what he did to me tonight?" Indeed Hanna knew, or thought she did. Within seconds of the incident, Cutter's rude response to Velvet's flirtation had reached the kitchen. And Hanna understood the girl's embarrassment, but her reaction far exceeded the expected response. "He humiliated me!" Velvet railed. She plucked wildly at her hairpins, hurling them recklessly across the room. "That Northern lowlife debased me! I could kill him!" Suddenly, with the words, tears popped into Velvet's eyes. Her wide gaze became feverish with anger and frustrated hurt. Naturally, she had not been able to tell her aunt and Hanna everything that had happened. It was all too embarrassing. As far as either of them knew Cutter had only verbally insulted her. She looked back and forth between them, deciding whether or not to reveal the true source of her anger. At last, her face crumpled. She could never tell these good women of her shame, of Cutter's rough handling of her, of his vile insinuations. She could never tell them—or anyone—of that secret part of her that wanted him. She sat heavily on her rocking chair and doubled over, heaving great, defeated sobs.

"There, child," said her Aunt Yvonne, moving to her. She lowered herself onto her knees before the girl and held her.

"Will Uncle Duff call him out for it?" Velvet asked faintly, pitiably.

Yvonne looked quickly at the Irish woman. "Please get us some tea, Hanna," she said gently.

"Glad to, Mrs. Duffy," Hanna answered, and quickly exited the room. She hastened down the narrow stairway. Much as she admired Mr. J. Eliot Cutter for his good work, she could not suppress the impulse to strangle the insensitive lout. She made sure to give Mr. Duffy a scorching glare, which he noted with some puzzlement, as he sat, smoking his pipe in the kitchen and awaiting his wife. *Men!* Hanna asserted in silent derision, as she noisily prepared the tea.

Upstairs, Yvonne had gotten Velvet into bed. Sitting near her, the older woman had tucked in the covers, offered handkerchiefs, and swathed the child's forehead with cold cloths. It was all she could do. After all, Mr. Cutter had not laid hands on her. Yvonne Duffy wondered, as Hanna had, at Velvet's extreme reaction to a rather simple case of boorish behavior. She could not very well insist that her husband challenge Mr. Cutter to a duel merely because he'd spoiled the party for Velvet. Still, she reflected, this might just be the time to reaffirm some advice she'd offered in the past. Yvonne Duffy squared her shoulders. Her niece was badly in need of an education where men like J. Eliot Cutter were concerned.

"You know, darling," she began hesitantly, for she did not want the child's wrath to be rearoused, "sometimes we take for granted that men will act in certain ways, but men — certain men — react in ways that frustrate . . . and frighten us. They don't mean to be unkind, mind you."

Velvet sniffed loudly and swiped at her reddened nose. "If you're speaking of J. Eliot Cutter, Aunt Vonnie," she muttered, "you needn't try to defend his actions. I shall never — ever — forgive him."

"I know that," Yvonne said softly, patting her niece's hand, "but maybe if you understood —"

"I understand that *Mr. Cutter,*" she said the name bitingly, "is the meanest, the most dull-witted, cravenest beast I have ever had the displeasure to meet." Her eyes glistened with tearful anger as she raised them to her aunt. "I am aware that he appears to be a friend to this family — I saw how you all greeted him so warmly this afternoon — but, I beg you not to defend him to me."

"I wouldn't think to defend him, darling," the older woman said kindly. "What he did was indefensible, and I won't forgive him, I promise you, but I must say that your Uncle Duff is not about to challenge the man to a duel because of a . . . misunderstanding."

"How can you call it merely that?" Velvet demanded incredulously.

"I call it that because that is what it is," said Yvonne firmly.

Velvet's gaze widened. Suddenly, recalling that her aunt had no idea of what had transpired after Velvet had left the party, the girl sighed. "Then there is no protection for me at all, Aunt Vonnie. I am at the mercy of brutes," she said simply. The girl's sincerity—her honest dread—sent a wave of sympathy through Yvonne Duffy. Southern sensibilities were so very different from those hereabouts.

"Let me try to explain," she said with a kind smile. She watched as Velvet leaned back resignedly on her pillows and accepted the tea which Hanna had just brought in. The Irish woman settled into the rocking chair and listened closely. Yvonne Duffy had not expected an audience. She glanced dubiously at the servant. "You see," she said at last, "in the South everybody courts everybody. I mean, in a certain sense, you all seem to be acting parts."

"Like Mr. Tyrone." Hanna bubbled reminiscently, her interest roused. "My dad took me to see him in 'The Soul of Wit' at the Narthex Theatre when I was a girl. I'll never forget how handsome he was . . . how virile . . . how . . ." Yvonne lifted an admonishing brow in her direction and Hanna restrained her enthusiasm. "Go on, Mrs. Duffy," she said solemnly.

"Well," Yvonne continued, "here in the North, we do things differently. Courting is . . . well . . . courting. We haven't time for drawn-out rituals. And when we like someone . . . we simply act . . . well, nice to them."

"I act nice," rejoined Velvet, once more on the verge of tears.

"Of course you do, darling," her aunt responded hastily. She looked to Hanna, but the Irish woman merely shrugged helplessly. Yvonne turned back to Velvet and began again. "When *you* act nice, you appear to be . . . more nice than is, strictly speaking, necessary. You act as though you're . . . well . . . courting." Yvonne Duffy had stated her case rather lamely, she felt. She'd had this same argument with her sister, Velvet's mother, when she'd visited her and her new husband at Sweet Briar Hill, and, though she'd put the whole situation a bit more succinctly to Alicia, she'd been equally unsuccessful. Yvonne sighed. "Look at it this way, darling," she said gently, "it isn't necessary to act as though you've fallen in love with every man you meet."

57

"The boys don't seem to mind the way I act toward them," said Velvet petulantly, her defenses keen as she recalled Cutter's assumption of a passionate nature lurking somewhere deep within her.

"I think they rather enjoy it," smiled Yvonne, "but the fact is, they are still boys. They're flattered by your attentions, naturally. But boys grow up to be men, and men . . ." Again Yvonne sought Hanna's aid.

"Men are men," stated Hanna. "They'll take advantage when they can. They get wrong ideas, my girl," she said knowingly. "They might assume you're willing to . . . to . . ."

Velvet winced. That was exactly what Cutter had assumed.

"But, naturally, we know differently," Yvonne interjected hastily. "We know it's just your way. It's only that if you are to live up here successfully, you need to amend your ways."

"Are you saying Mr. Cutter's brutality was my fault?" asked Velvet incredulously, once again ignoring the fact that she and her aunt were discussing two very different situations.

"Not exactly," sighed Yvonne. "I suppose, in a way, we might guess that Mr. Cutter thought you were being . . . well . . . immodest." She watched as her niece's eyes widened and then suddenly filled with tears. "He thought you were . . . *perhaps* he thought you were . . . tempting him." The sturdy little Canadian woman stood abruptly and licked at her lips. She was not used to discussing in detail such unseemly matters. Why, she'd not even mentioned these things to her own daughters. Naturally, in the uncompromising environment of this rugged land, there was no need to speak of the fripperies of behavior. People had no time for such silliness. People here, in this hard wilderness, fell in love, married, had children, and died. They rarely considered such subtleties of human intercourse as flirtation. She upbraided her sister silently for raising her daughter in such a careless fashion. Surely, Alicia had not been raised that way. Their hard Canadian childhood had not prepared either of the two sisters for a life of drawn-out rituals, of

58

long, indolent days and indulgent inactivity. That was the atmosphere to which Alicia had been led by that devil-may-care bounder from the South. Too much money and too much time were the villains. Yvonne glanced guiltily at her stricken niece. Poor child. She had no way of understanding the evils to which she had been bred. None of this was really her fault. The older woman rubbed her hands together disconsolately. How could she begin to remedy a lifetime of misteaching. She sighed. "I know it is hard to understand, darling," she said softly, "but some men — and that would apparently include the likes of Mr. Cutter — ought to be left alone."

Velvet's eyes were glazed with question. Perhaps, in some way, Yvonne Duffy might be able to help her understand what had taken place between Cutter and her, and why. "Is he so different from other men?" she asked.

"I think he is," Yvonne answered. "He cannot be trusted to behave in expected ways." She returned to Velvet's side and sat, once again, on the edge of the bed. "He is a different breed of man from those you've known. It might be best," she said as she smoothed the riot of curls that lay damp on her niece's troubled brow, "if, before you treat men quite so . . . intimately, you get to know them. We are not a courtly people," Yvonne sighed. "We are not given to insincere mannerisms or affectations. We haven't the time." She smiled sadly. "I am sorry to be so indelicate, child. Still, you need to know these things." She paused, hesitating to go on, but knowing that she must continue to be honest. "I have done you a great disservice, you know." Velvet looked at her questioningly. "It's true," stated her aunt. "I should have told you this before — when you first arrived. I should have explained that things are different here. Men are different. I suppose I simply trusted time to teach you what you needed to know, or maybe I just assumed that eventually you would fit in."

Velvet lowered her lashes, and they were wet with tears. Yvonne Duffy felt a sharp twinge of pain for this vulnerable, wounded child. She was young and alone for the first time in a strange land, with people, she could not begin to understand, and she had been deeply hurt. It was no one's fault, really, and yet Yvonne felt deep regret that she'd not addressed this problem before. She glanced at Hanna who was having her own struggle with tears. Gesturing to the Irish woman, Yvonne rose and drew the covers over Velvet's shoulders. Quietly, the two women lowered the bedside lamp, banked the dancing hearthfire and left the room.

In the dark silence that followed their departure, Velvet did battle with the questions that assailed her. Was life— were people—really so different here in the North? Was she really such a misfit? Was her behavior perceived as "insincere"? It did not seem possible. And yet the same had been said of her by J. Eliot Cutter. The name sliced through her consciousness, shredded her confidence, brought her bolting upright in the darkness. She sat amid the tangle of her quilts. The glitter of the dying fire reflected in her green-blue gaze, she conjured up his image. Tall, wide-shouldered, cold-eyed, he stood before her. She tore mentally at the derisive sneer that etched the granite of his lips. With her nails, she raked the arrogant jaw. She ravaged the broad chest, rending flesh from muscle. A silent scream raged up from her breast as he stood, laughing, contemptuous, knowing her most carefully kept secret. Her hatred flared. But the hatred was stirred from its centrality by something else. Another emotion seethed within her, seared her heart, pounced at her senses. Velvet felt the pang of deep longing. She had never known such aching need. The vision of Cutter changed. His jet curls caught the radiance of the stars, his bronzed, muscled flesh reflected their sheen. He moved toward her, his virile power warm against her soul. She did not want that image. She must exorcize it. She lunged into the empty blackness before her and fell into the tousle of covers at the foot of her bed. Clutching at a deep, writhing outrage she began to sob. Velvet McBride surrendered, in that heart-crushing moment, to the darkest anxiety she'd ever known.

Chapter Five

The men were leaving. They marched carelessly, waving, the bright blue wool of their new uniforms shimmering in the sun, the brass of their buttons and buckles flashing pridefully. They were heading south to fight a war. Long reckless lines of them—sons of loggers and storekeepers, sons of farmers, sons of teachers and preachers—trod the pebbled roads toward an unfathomable destiny. Boots shined by careful mothers that morning were already dusted with Adirondack powder. It would be washed away one day soon, in the rains and mud of a faraway land—a land that had, up to now, existed only in their imaginations. Cain Gifford and Bobby Van Campen, Eddie Chapman-White, and Jason Amsterdam were among them. They were plain lads, working lads, the products of strong and simple moral teachings. They did not yet know about war, and so their leave-taking was a spirited one, optimistic, joyously filled with the anticipation of adventure.

Velvet watched from her window the jaunty progress that summer of 1862. Parting the light curtains, she waved sadly, unseen by the departing soldiers. She had intended to be there at their leave-taking, dressed in her finest, but she'd not had the courage. She'd not had the heart. She had seen virtually no one since the night of her humiliation at the hands of J. Eliot Cutter. She had no idea how any of the boys felt about his rough verbal handling of her. Perhaps they applauded his scorn—thought she'd had it coming. Perhaps they, too, believed she had behaved immodestly. She had not dared to find out. Of course, none of the boys knew of the private confrontation between Cutter and herself. And that was just as well. Velvet did not want to face the possibility that they, too, believed she hid some dark, disgraceful passion. She needed to recover her dignity before she could again face the rigors of courtship. For better or worse, she had the luxury of time. It would be, according to all reports, many weeks, and some said months, before she saw any of the boys again. They were leaving. She envied them. She glanced over at the midnight blue silk gown that now lay in idle disarrangement on her bed. The daintily laced canezou had slid onto the rough flooring. She moved to it and lifted it, fingering the delicate folds of its front. Slowly she paced back to the window, holding the frail garment to her breast. Velvet gazed across the lusterless panorama afforded her from her second-floor chamber. Those boys were going home — to her home.

She looked down and watched the tender parting of Jason and Juliette. His tall form leaned down from his horse. Juliette handed up a quilt she'd made and Jason took it, laying it fondly across his saddle. He touched her cheek and she curved her head into his large hand. Her tears were visible, even from where Velvet stood now. Go with him, Juliette, Velvet pleaded silently. If you love him stay with him.

If only Velvet had heeded her own advice. If only she'd fought harder against her parents' command, she might well be, right now, in the company of Mr. Brett Whitney of Richmond. Even if he was a soldier now, even if he'd been caught up in the misguided zealotry that was carrying these boys away, Velvet would be with him, she resolved. And she resolved another thing, too. If she ever had another chance with Mr. Whitney, she would see to it that his stolid Southern reticence was broken. She would make it clear to Mr. Brett Whitney that she was available to him. Velvet's flirting days were over. She wanted the comfort of one man — and that man was Brett Whitney. He was her kind; he understood her. He could never take her coquetry for anything else. He could never find it in his gentleman's heart to think of her as anything but a lady, and to treat her accordingly.

And it would not be long before she would have her chance, she thought, rousing herself to cheerfulness. Drawing her shoulders back, she recalled her mother's parting words: "We shall see you back at Sweet Briar Hill before the magnolias have bloomed quite properly." The magnolias were blooming now, Velvet decided with sudden hope. Today, this very day, she would write her mother a letter and beg to be allowed to come home.

Velvet scrambled for paper and pen. She sat down at her little writing secretary and scrawled a note. Oh, it would be so easy, she entreated. She could take a carriage and even, perhaps, catch up with the boys who'd just left. They could escort her south. And she could ask Juliette to accompany her. And Juliette could be with Jason, and she could live at Sweet Briar Hill while Jason and the other boys fought their silly war, and there could be a ball in her honor and barbecues every Saturday, and Mammy Jane could tell her stories, and Juliette would get to know the sweet, gay life of a proper Southern lady. And wouldn't it be wonderful!

And best of all, best of all, Velvet thought joyously, clutching the finished letter to her breast, she would see Mr. Whitney again, and Mr. Whitney would ask her to marry him and she would be safe.

She quickly placed the letter in an envelope and addressed it. Then, at last, she called for Hanna. Velvet's morning toilette was begun with more enthusiasm than Hanna had seen in several days.

"It's foolish," said Nicole quietly.

"I have to agree," Yvonne affirmed.

Juliette scowled darkly at her sister and then altered her expression to one of sweet pleading as she regarded her mother. "But, Mama," she entreated, "I could be such good company to Velvet. It seems only right that someone accompany her. Why shouldn't it be me?" The family was gathered for the evening meal. All month the talk had been of the expected invitation to Sweet Briar Hill that Juliette would receive any day now. Andrew Duffy eyed his family doubtfully. He'd allowed the talk to go on too long. He cut into a loaf of wheat bread and cleared his throat.

"I don't think it's necessary to come to any decisions right now," he said a bit more harshly than he'd intended.

"But *why* not come to a decision, Pa?" Juliette entreated. "If we make up our minds now, then Velvet and I can be ready when the letter comes."

"It should be here any day," Velvet said confidently. She ladled bacon gravy on her roasted potato and smiled sweetly at her uncle. Andrew Duffy's eyes were downcast. He concentrated fiercely on the slab of pork that lay on his plate. He was not eating well these days. He was not sleeping well either.

"Actually, Andrew," said his wife, "it might be best to make our decision. Alicia ought to be responding to Velvet's letter soon, and—"

"You're all fools," stated Nicole. She flung her napkin onto the table and stood abruptly, knocking back her wooden chair. As it rocked, dangerously close to falling, everyone gaped at her. "Well, you are fools," she repeated. "To even consider sending Juliette to such a place is madness." Her eyes glittered in the lamplight. "Do you want her under the influence of godless Southerners? Do you want to see her taken in by people who keep other people as slaves? For the love of God, think about what she'd be exposed to."

Velvet's eyes widened, and Yvonne Duffy attempted a soothing interjection. So far, she'd managed to keep politics away from her table. Before she could say anything, Andrew spoke.

"Calm down, daughter," he said sternly. "Your cousin and her family are not demons."

"Demons are what they are, Pa," Nicole retorted.

"Why would you say such a thing?" Velvet gasped.

The girl rounded on her cousin. "I say it because that's what you are, Miss Velvet McBride of Brandy Station, Virginia—Miss Sugar-coated Southern Belle, flaunting her hoop-skirted innocence and her baubles. You are swine, and I don't blame Mr. Cutter one damned bit for what he did. Why, a man like that, a man of such noble ideals should never have to put up with—"

"That's enough!" roared Andrew Duffy, as he, too, stood. His big fist rammed the table. His elder daughter spun to face him, her lip curled derisively. "Don't say another word, daughter," he warned. "Not one more word will we hear from you, miss." His eyes were hard. No one in the family had ever seen them so hard. Even Nicole's outrage withered at the sight. The room became silent. Only the crackling of the fire broke the stillness. When Andrew spoke again, his tone was quiet and rigid with control. "There is no sense in our discussing this further." He targeted Velvet and his eyes softened. "You'll not be going home, girl, not for a very long time," he said evenly. Velvet stared at him as though mesmerized. Her uncle continued. "There's been a terrible campaign, seen days of fighting around your home."

"My . . . home?" Velvet asked in a childlike voice. Andrew nodded.

"It's a real war now, girl," he said almost gently. "It's no longer a fight between gunboats and shore batteries. Civilians are being routed from their homes, being captured and killed by otherwise decent young men." He shook his head sadly. "That's what happens in a real war."

Yvonne bowed her head. "Thank God I have no sons," she intoned. It was a genuine prayer.

"But . . . Sweet Briar Hill?" asked Velvet, her tone reluctant, pleading, her eyes glazed with tears. Andrew merely shook his head.

"We'll not know for a while, I'm afraid. Your 'Stonewall' Jackson's in the Shanandoah Valley, but Banks has him outnumbered three to one. There's fighting in Williamsburg, Fair Oaks, Mechanicsville, and Richmond." He noted with some annoyance that his elder daughter eyed her cousin triumphantly. "I'll not have dissension in this house," he cautioned. But Velvet perceived nothing of the exchange. She pushed herself from the table.

"Excuse me, please," she said in a whisper. "I . . . I need some air." A hush fell over the family as, seemingly in a stupor, Velvet left the room. Yvonne Duffy eyed her husband as he sat down.

"Are you sure of this, Andrew?" she asked. "Are real people—families—involved in this contention?"

"I am," he answered shortly.

"Of course they are," Nicole retorted. "What did you expect?"

"Then I'll never get to Sweet Briar Hill," Juliette pouted. Suddenly she lifted her soft brown eyes and they were wide with frightened questions. "Jason," she breathed. "Oh, what if he's there?"

"Our boys were headed down to Kentucky and Tennessee," said her father. He looked hastily to his wife.

"Don't you worry, child." Yvonne Duffy patted her daughter's hand soothingly. "Jason will be fine," she said with forced lightness. "He's strong as a young bull."

"Besides," Nicole said sullenly, sitting back down, "he hasn't even had time to get down there yet." Juliette eyed her gratefully. Nicole offered a reluctant smile, and shrugged nonchalantly, as though dismissing any danger to Juliette's young beau. She targeted her dinner and determinedly began to eat. She ignored, for the most part, her father's stern perusal. She knew, as did they all, that she had been wrong to bring her strong feelings to the table. Up to now, Nicole had avoided airing her passionate opinions on the reasons for this terrible war. She wondered how much longer it would be possible to do so.

Each day, her cousin exemplified to her what the war was all about. Each day, Nicole's aversion to Velvet's lifestyle grew stronger. That girl still held, even in this bastion of Yankee morality, to behaviors that could be engendered only by an evil, though, mercifully, dying culture.

Still, for the time being, while she lived here, Velvet McBride must be endured. It would not be easy, Nicole reflected as she attempted to eat and to rein in her contempt for that insipid, sugar-coated symbol of man's inhumanity to man.

Chapter Six

Richmond . . . Richmond . . . Richmond. The word pounded in her veins each time Velvet's heart pulsed. With each pulsation, the image of Mr. Brett Whitney flared in her mind. With his soft, moonlit curls, his deeply set green eyes, his firm chin, he haunted her soul. If there was fighting in Richmond, surely the gallant Mr. Whitney was involved.

Velvet's uncle had not been sure if Brandy Station had been touched by the war. She consoled herself that her home might still be safe. Of course it was; it could be nothing else. She had to believe that. She had to believe that a letter might come any day now, and she would be allowed to go home, to see it for herself. She could bring Mr. Whitney there, and tend to him if he was hurt in the war. *But he must not be hurt in the war.* He must remain always as he'd been the last time she'd seen him—elegantly confident, smiling, courtly. *Oh, Mr. Whitney . . . Brett, please be safe.* Velvet must write to her mother again. She must be sure that everyone was safe. Her eyes scanned the empty velvet of the dark night sky. Why had there been no word from home in over a month? she wondered. But letters took time. Her mother was always so punctual in her correspondence, though.

Velvet's eyes stung with the onslaught of hot tears. Confusion, frustration, and abject helplessness were the spur of her sudden retreat into lamentation. She had not allowed herself to lose hope in over a month. She must not indulge such weakness now. She must be optimistic. But how could she remain optimistic when unknowable horrors threatened her home and loved ones? What is out there? she wondered, as she peered up into the moonless sky. What does the future hold? That vast and limitless ebony void was all the future Velvet could conjure. Her mind swirled with empty possibility. She must not think. She would go mad with thinking. She must act.

J. Eliot Cutter had gone south again, they'd told her, probably on some silly geological excursion. She'd not seen him in weeks. He would be back soon—maybe. And when he did come back, Velvet would seek him out, though the idea brought sudden shivers of revulsion slithering along her spine, and she would insist on information about her homeland. She would not allow evasion. She would gather her courage and confront the slavering oaf—no matter the cost to her dignity. For she knew only too well that in the most secret recesses of her soul, she shared with him a potentially devouring passion. He knew it, too. She shuddered. She must not let the disgrace of that knowledge mar her resolve. She must shake off any aversion she felt to seeing him again, any dread of what seeing him might arouse in her. She must know what was happening at home.

She swiped impatiently at her tears. Velvet knew she must resist the impulse to hide from Cutter, at any rate. He was, after all, a friend to the Duffy family. If seeing him meant repressing those ugly, disreputable impulses that haunted her—and they had done so—then repress them she would. She would simply have to find a way to dispel that base and foul element in her otherwise refined nature. If it could not be dispelled, it must be suffered, it must be borne. And Velvet had certainly borne, unwillingly, the burden of her hidden passion. Though she was able to regulate her conscious thoughts, she could not control her dreams. In those, Cutter raged unrestrainedly, ravishing her soul with unconquerable power. Velvet would awaken suddenly, her flesh sheened with perspiration, her heart thudding against the panic of inexplicable rapture. She wiped now at her moist brow, and shook herself from the memory of those impure dreams. She must not succumb to their siren's call, no matter the sense of enchantment, the thrills of wonder and awe they produced in her vulnerable, sleeping heart. She must fight those impulses, those degrading, controlling . . . voluptuous impulses. She dared not allow them space in her consciousness, for once indulged, they threatened to dominate. This was her curse, Velvet determined, and it must be battled.

Good women — refined women — did not feel such swelling sensations. They left bestial instincts to the men.

Velvet had wandered far from the Duffy house, she noted. She stood now beneath a tall white pine. Dry needles under her feet prickled quietly. Her heart tripped as she realized she was completely alone in this dark wilderness — or so she hoped.

The shape, silhouetted against the black, twining figurations of the forest, barely moved. Its hunched and shadowed form might have been a tree trunk, or a shrubless hillock. Velvet reined in the sudden impulse to run. She was tired of fighting demons. She leaned back, resting herself against the bole of the tree, and then slid down along its scabby bark, unmindful of possible damage to her delicate frock, to sit on the floor of the forest. She saw, through waves of silent resignation, the roughness of the terrain that surrounded her. How different home would be. Her family would have gathered by now, in the evening breezes, on the wide porch to sip cider and converse in the softness of the night. There would be moonlight on rolling lawns, and the sound of children's songs. The only sound here was the chirrup of lonely crickets. Are they lonely? Velvet wondered. They have each other. They are among their own kind.

Another sound caught her attention. Something was moving in the thicket, rustling the underbrush. Velvet's eyes widened and caught the sudden emergence of moonlight through a cloud cover as she glanced around her. There was nothing, only silvered shadow. She slowly pushed herself up along the bole of the tree, listening. The sound came again. It was heightened by the sudden silence of the crickets. Velvet, too, stopped, waited. There was no sound. Her eyes scanned the darkness. There! It moved! It was watching her! She shuddered, her mouth suddenly going dry. Is it an animal? she wondered. She placed delicate fingertips to her lips, stifling a scream. The silhouette broke up into several pieces, scattering the moonlight, filling the darkness with noise. The forest seemed to close in on her, towering pines forming a black ceiling that lowered menacingly. The scream raged up. Velvet felt the heat of bodies upon her, a big hand over her mouth. The scream died with her breath. Silence reigned.

Only the soft crack of a fire and a comforting dimness of light greeted her upon her awakening. Velvet slowly unclosed her eyes. She might have been in her own room, but she was not, she suddenly realized. The palette beneath her was hard. It lay over a rough earthen floor. She sat up suddenly. Several people surrounded her, women, black-skinned, turbaned. Her gaze widened.

"Who are you?" she breathed.

One of the women placed a fingertip over her lips. "Please speak quietly," she said. Her voice was like warm honey and Velvet suddenly felt no fear.

"Who are you?" she repeated in a whisper. No one spoke. For a fleeting second, Velvet wondered if she'd been transported home. A flutter of familiarity rose in her breast. This might have been the slave quarters at Sweet Briar Hill. She'd visited Mammy Jane's daughter there once. "Where am I?" she asked, awed by the improbable, but apparently possible transmittal. Again, no one spoke. "Am I in Virginia?" she asked hopefully. The first woman smiled. A second joined her. Chuckles, soft, smothered, were heard round the circle. Velvet felt a vague sting of annoyance. "Am I in the South?" she asked, a little more sharply than she'd intended.

"Take your ease, child," said one of the women calmly. "You'll find out soon enough."

"But am I in the South?" Velvet insisted.

"Not hardly," said another woman smiling softly.

"Thank the Lord," intoned the first woman, bowing her head. She looked up at Velvet. Her eyes shone silkily in the firelight. "Won't you just try to sit quietly until he gets here?" she asked gently. "We don't want to hurt you." Velvet's finely winged brow shot up.

"Hurt me!" she demanded. "Don't you dare speak like that

70

to me, young woman!" Velvet's outburst was greeted with a wild outpouring of shushing sounds, and she quickly amended her volume, if not her tone. "Well, just you watch your language," she admonished. Taking in the earnest faces, Velvet folded her arms across her breast and glared defiantly at her captors. "You could all be punished for this, you know," she stated, careful to keep her voice to a whisper. The truth was, she wanted no one whipped at her provocation, but these women were behaving shamefully. "You'd better explain to me what this is all about," she said tartly, "before you all get into real trouble."

"I suppose," said the first woman, shaking her head ruefully, "we're already in trouble, missy. I don't imagine we could get into much more."

"Well, I should think not," Velvet said with certainty. Then her brow wrinkled slowly in a puzzled frown. "What have you done?" she asked.

"You mean, aside from taking you prisoner?" asked the woman.

"Am I your . . . prisoner?" Velvet gaped.

All the women laughed softly. "No," said one through her mirth. "At least not for long."

Velvet puzzled this over in her mind. It would be easy enough to escape these women. They held no weapons. Hunkering in a circle around her, smiling, communicating, they seemed completely unthreatening. The first woman waved long, elegant fingers toward Velvet.

"Not to worry, missy," she said. "He'll be here soon. He'll take care of you."

"He?" Velvet asked, more puzzled than ever.

The woman merely nodded, her smile growing broader, more enigmatic. "Let me get you some water," she said gently. "You must be scared blue." She stood and moved away, returning with a tin cup. "Water's all we've got," she said almost apologetically. Velvet sipped slowly, regarding the women over the rim of the cup. The water was tepid, but she swallowed it gratefully. These girls were kindly but dimwitted, she reflected. They could not seem to get anything straight. Was this "he" they spoke of their overseer, their father, their master? She must discover where she was, who they were and who "he" was. Most importantly, she must discover their purpose. She handed the woman the empty cup. Before the woman could take it, the door to the little cabin burst open.

Several dark-skinned men entered, leading the way for the tall figure who followed them. Velvet gasped involuntarily. There before her, filling the doorway of the little cabin, stood the man she hated most in the world — J. Eliot Cutter. She drew in her breath with involuntary suddenness. He stood before her as he had in her mind's eye — tall, hands on hips, jet curls falling recklessly over his forehead, his cold eyes raking her. Velvet flinched as hot waves of shame overwhelmed her. His silver-sharp gaze narrowed in a mockery of a smile as he seemed to sense her humiliation. She felt the flush of anger rise from her breast. She rose to face him.

"What is going on here, Mr. Cutter?" she demanded.

His smile became lazy, offhanded. "So this is the danger you spoke of," he said, glancing at one of the men.

Velvet's outrage flared. How dare the oaf ignore her question? "I repeat, Mr. Cutter," she hissed, "what is going on here?"

He regarded her once again and hung his thumbs onto his belt loops. "What are you doing here, Velvet?"

"It is Miss McBride to you, and I can assure you it's not my choice to be here," Velvet snapped. "And wipe that silly grin off your face."

"Sorry," he said nonchalantly, his smile unwavering.

"If you don't explain this to me, Cutter," she railed, "and very quickly, I am going to see to it that you are hauled into court for kidnapping!"

Cutter raised his dark brows. "Kidnapping?" he asked, barely containing the mirth that bubbled from his broad chest.

"Laugh now, you brigand," Velvet growled, "for it will be your very last chance to do so at my expense. I will see you locked up for the rest of your life." She spun, snapping her skirts, and bolted from the cabin. Soothing the worried urgency of the people gathered there, Cutter took a resigned breath and followed her out into the warm darkness.

In a very few seconds, he caught up with her. Tangled in the sinewy undergrowth of witch-hobble that grew in patches in the Adirondack forest, the fallen Velvet struggled wildly amid heaps of crinoline underskirts and hoops. Cutter could not help but laugh openly, boisterously at her predicament. Velvet glared up at him in the moonlight.

"You could at least help me get untangled," she spat.

He sobered suddenly. "What?" he asked with mock incredulity. "And have you go directly to the sheriff to have me arrested?" he asked. "Now, why would I want to do that?"

Velvet's gaze narrowed. She swiped a fallen tress of moonstruck hair from her pinkened cheek. Her breast heaved beneath the perspiration-darkened cloth of her bodice. Cutter took in the struggling vision appreciatively. "All right," Velvet breathed, "I won't have you arrested."

"How can I be sure?" Cutter asked, unwilling to disencumber the captured vixen quite so easily. She looked . . . well, adorable . . . lying there, her cheeks flushed, her hair tousled, her eyes—those incredible eyes—flashing, glittering with inner fire. He leaned down, from the waist, and held his soft hat to his chest. "I would be a fool," he purred, "to just let you go off without extracting some kind of promise from you, my dear delectable Velvet."

"Miss McBride to you," Velvet shrieked. Cutter straightened and regarded her dubiously. "All right," she said at last, attempting to project an outward calm, "I *promise.* Now, help me up!"

Cutter repressed a smile as he lowered himself to one knee. Almost tenderly he reached into the dark tangle of vines. He found a trim ankle, held it in his large hand just a bit too long, and then extracted it slowly from the snarled undergrowth. "During the Revolutionary War, I'm told, our boys were able to escape into these mountains while the British were repeatedly tripped up by this very bush," he said, lifting her.

"I don't want to hear another word about war," she snapped. She flicked at her skirts, pulling them from the deep jumble of brush and vines. "I just want to go home," she finished. Righted on firmer ground, and steadily on her feet, she looked up at Cutter. His gray gaze caught the shimmer of the moon, and overpowered her for the moment. "I just want to go home," she repeated softly. "I thought I was home, for a while." She paused. "I'm not, am I? I'm right back where I started." He was very close to her. His dark form blotting out the moonlight. They might have been one silhouette.

"I'm sorry," Cutter said huskily. He knew she must be very homesick. He was sorry the situation had raised her hopes. He was equally sorry that she'd discovered the secret of the Duffy spread. Cutter shook his head. Recalling who she was, this daughter of the old South, and who he was, he abruptly altered his tone. "I'll take you back to your uncle," he said curtly.

Velvet's brows quirked. "What is this all about?" she asked earnestly.

Cutter studied her a few more seconds. His decision made, he said, "I'll take you home." As they walked, carefully now, he supporting her, she hanging onto his strong arm, he wondered if he dared tell her. What would her reaction be? How would she handle such a revelation? If she chose to attempt to reveal the secret, she might very well end up a watched prisoner—he would see to that—kidnapped, as she'd said. He must leave it to Andrew Duffy to decide. Cutter was sure the man had not told his niece the truth of the situation. Maybe it was time.

Chapter Seven

"But why would you do such a thing, Uncle Duff?" Velvet's wide gaze was stricken. "You could all end up in jail, or worse; don't you know that?" Yvonne Duffy sat very close to her on the small sofa. Cutter turned away to study the nuances of the purling hearthfire, his jaw clenched, his tanned brow darkly furrowed. Nicole eyed her cousin with derision.

"Why do you think we do it, you stupid child?" she said sourly.

"I . . . I don't know." Velvet answered, honestly bewildered.

Nicole uttered a sharp, impatient exhalation. "Do you imagine they *want* to be slaves?" she asked, leaning close to the girl. Velvet flinched at her cousin's aggressive intolerance.

"Now, daughter . . ." Andrew Duffy began.

Nicole targeted him angrily. "Why do you coddle her?" she demanded. Velvet turned uncomprehendingly to her aunt.

"Please, Aunt Vonnie," she begged, "explain it to me again."

Yvonne Duffy looked forlornly into her niece's eyes. How could she explain that all Velvet had been taught, from the time she was a babe, was wrong? She'd already tried explaining certain things, pointing out flaws in the girl's behavior, and done a poor job of it, she recalled. She looked helplessly to her husband. That man, sitting uncomfortably in his large chair before the fire, glanced at Cutter. The younger man drew slowly on a small cheroot. He exhaled, dropping the cigar into the fire, then turned to Velvet. His pewter gaze impaled her.

"Your aunt and uncle run what is known as a 'safe house,'" he said. "People of color come here from the South to escape prosecution as runaway slaves. They know that your aunt and uncle, and all those who live in this house," he continued pointedly, "will be sympathetic to their flight. This is one link in the chain known as the Underground Railroad."

"I've heard of it," Velvet said softly. "I just never knew what it was. And I thought it was . . . well . . . underground." Cutter could barely suppress his own impatience. Was the girl really so innocent? "What I do not understand," she went on, "is why? I mean it's . . ."—here Velvet's voice lowered to an earnest whisper—*"treason."*

Velvet looked at all the people who had gathered in the small, low-ceilinged parlor. Hanna was there and Juliette. That girl regarded her cousin sympathetically, but with the same odd blankness as the others. Why didn't they understand her question? It was a simple one.

Nicole had thrown up her hands and moved to the other side of the room, where she stood tapping her foot. "I cannot believe you are that dense," she said coldly.

"I am not dense, Nicole," answered Velvet, beginning to feel just a twinge of anger. She stood and moved to the girl. "I am trying to understand something. I don't think anyone should be faulted for that." Velvet turned to face the rest of the gathering. "I'm surely sorry if I am causing you all frustration, but I can't imagine why anyone would decide, voluntarily, to break the law. Besides that, I cannot understand why those people would choose to leave a beautiful home in the South to travel to this cold Northern wilderness. Why, even in July, you have to have a fire to ward off the chill of the cool nights." She swept out her small hand and indicated the little fire. "It just doesn't make any sense." She stopped abruptly and placed her fingertips delicately over her lips. "Please forgive me," she said softly. "I'm not criticizing, you understand." Lowering her eyes, she went on. "It's only that I'm confused. Why would those people choose to leave a perfectly lovely environment where they're cared for and protected?" She lifted her gaze and looked around the room.

"Perhaps they're less than satisfied with the Southern brand of *protection*," Nicole said bitterly.

Velvet regarded her coolly. "I have never heard one breath of dissatisfaction among the workers—at least not at Sweet Briar Hill," she said defiantly. "They all seem so happy; always singing, laughing. They're so cheerful, you'd just swear they hadn't a care in the world." Lifting her small chin in challenge, Velvet continued. "Naturally, I have heard of some discontented darkies." She glanced at each of the gathered company. "Haven't we all," she said with a small shrug. "But those are few and far between. And Pa says, it's just bad breeding that does it." She folded her hands primly before her, satisfied that she had proved her case.

Cutter moved to her slowly. Standing over her, he seemed to weigh the sincerity of her words. At last he spoke. "Do you really believe what you've just said?" he asked.

"Of course I do," Velvet answered, gazing up into his narrowed perusal. She wondered why everyone called *her* dense. Cutter lifted his eyes and regarded Nicole steadily. "Get Mary Ann," he commanded softly.

"Are you sure?" the young woman inquired worriedly. Cutter nodded. Reluctantly, and not before she received her father's consent, Nicole Duffy left the house.

Velvet looked up at Cutter. Confusion warred with impatience in her wide green-blue gaze. "What is it you intend to do, Mr. Cutter?" she asked.

"I intend to educate you, Miss McBride," he said. Velvet could not help the small wave of satisfaction that rose in her breast. It was just about time the oaf addressed her properly. She raised an elegant brow.

"Educate me, indeed," she said obliquely.

"Yes, educate you," he growled. "Your ignorance requires either education, or a sound beating." He grasped her shoulders in his big hands. Yvonne Duffy winced as the girl snapped to a sudden fearful attention. She understood Cutter's impatience, but sympathized with her niece's lack of awareness on the subject. It stemmed, after all, from what she'd been taught. She looked quickly to her husband. An-

77

drew rose from his chair, and it was only his calming intervention that checked the younger man's ire.

"Relax, son," he said gently, placing a roughened hand on Cutter's wide shoulder. "The child will learn soon enough."

Reluctantly, Cutter released her. " 'The child,' " he intoned, "had better learn." His gaze held her as forcibly as had his hands. "Has it never occurred to you," he asked tightly, "that the singing you hear, and the laughing are only a veneer? Has it never occurred to you that we human beings are remarkable creatures who attempt to make our lives bearable even when we are in darkest pain?"

Velvet's chin lifted. The challenge in her eyes met Cutter's brazenly. "I know about pain," she gritted.

Cutter was silent for a long moment. "Do you?" he finally inquired.

"Yes," Velvet shot back. "I know about making life bearable for oneself, Mr. Cutter, and I know, dammit to hell, about putting superficial polish on an ugly wound. I'm not stupid, Mr. Cutter; I'm only unacquainted with your logic on this particular subject."

"Yes," Cutter said quietly. "And that you will discover soon."

Andrew watched the couple for a moment, assessing that the danger had passed — or had just begun for them. Finally, he patted his stomach and searched the room for something. "Wasn't there some of that pie left over from supper?" he asked, targeting a suddenly attentive Hanna. That woman smiled knowingly and left for the kitchen. So the old man had regained his appetite, she reflected fondly. Thank God! It had been the subject of much concern among the women of the house, that Andrew Duffy had not been eating as well as a man of his spirit and energy ought to eat. Maybe now that Velvet knew the truth of this household, the old fellow might relax some. Hanna reentered the parlor with a tray, but her progress was halted at the seriousness of the confrontation she perceived.

"Tell her," Cutter said softly to the young, honey-skinned woman who stood just inside the door. "Tell Miss McBride about your life in the South." Velvet remembered the woman

78

from the cabin and watched her carefully as Cutter again prodded her. "How did you come to be there?" he said kindly. "Begin with that. Tell her all of it."

The young woman looked at Cutter quickly and then turned back to Velvet. Mary Ann started her narrative softly. "I came to be in the South because that's where I was born," she said. "I was a slave, the daughter of a slave, the granddaughter of a slave. A hundred years ago, the captain of a sailing ship kidnapped my great-grandmother and carried her across the ocean from her African home to a crowded wharf in Baltimore. He sold her to the highest bidder in an auction. Her children and her children's children and their children belonged to master, as surely as did his cows and pigs." Her words were like a litany, and Velvet listened raptly. "I live . . . lived" the woman continued steadily, "on a plantation, in a hut, with eleven other slaves. Since I was very young, I've gotten up before the sun to light the fires in the big house. Every day of my life I have swept, dusted, peeled potatoes, and plucked chickens. I washed the clothes for the master's family, and then hung them to dry. I scrubbed floors in the master's house, and carried messages between the master and his overseer. In the hot season, I crawled along the rows of tobacco plants with the other women and picked fat green hornworms from the underside of the leaves. And I shucked corn . . . until my hands were raw." With the last words, her voice dropped to a whisper. She glanced apologetically at those gathered in the room. She had not intended to introduce a personal observation, only to state the facts. She regarded Velvet once again. "I have a family," she continued. "I have a husband and children, but when I was sold—" Her voice broke momentarily before she went on. "When I was sold a year ago," she said, her tone steady, "I lost track of them." Her chin lifted in what Velvet recognized as her own gesture of defiance. "I came north to begin a new life. I don't want to be owned by master anymore." The last statement was made simply, with quiet strength. Velvet found it difficult to imagine that this gallant woman might be any one of the workers from Sweet Briar Hill saying these same words, but, as she reflected on the work they did, she conceded that she might be.

Perhaps they were given too many responsibilities, she mused, as she studied the woman's face. Velvet's father and his friends contended that the workers would not labor, except when forced to; but this vital woman did not appear to be averse to work. And there were days, set aside, when there was no work at all. She recalled gay outings with the younger girls when they all went crabbing, or walking in the woods. Those days were few, she reflected, but they did occur. The girls at Sweet Briar Hill were not overworked, as far as Velvet knew.

There was, of course, the matter of the separation from her family. At Sweet Briar Hill, such a thing could never happen. The workers were encouraged to have families, and they were never sold off separately. Still, Velvet recalled once having heard Mammy Jane's daughter speak longingly of a young man at a neighboring plantation. But the elder McBrides had decided that fellow was "trouble," and Mammy Jane had agreed that her daughter ought to stick to the boys at home. Velvet could remember her consoling the girl. But, if they had been married — and marriage ceremonies were monthly and sometimes weekly occurrences at Sweet Briar Hill — they would never have been separated.

Reluctantly Velvet's thoughts turned to that most disconcerting question of belonging to someone — belonging to them, as surely as did their cows and their pigs, Mary Ann had said. Velvet felt a shudder of revulsion slither along her spine. Is that really how the workers feel? she wondered. Surely, Mammy Jane . . . She could never feel as this woman felt. And yet . . .

It seemed impossible to Velvet that all these years she had been party to the violation of another's . . . what? Dignity? It had never occurred to her that the workers had, or even thought of, that. And yet, this woman stood before her now, chin raised, voice soft and confident, face aglow with pride. Velvet could not speak. She did not understand the tumult suddenly roiling inside her. She lowered her gaze. The family and Hanna and Cutter and Mary Ann seemed to watch for her reaction. Velvet did not know what it should be, and she felt vaguely frustrated that she did not.

What did they want of her? She slowly sat down on the small sofa. Her Aunt Yvonne put tentatively an arm around Velvet's shoulders.

"Take a moment, darling," the older woman said gently. "You cannot be expected to absorb all this immediately." Yvonne Duffy raised a brow, almost surreptitiously, in Hanna's direction. That good woman recognized the signal and broke the silence.

"Wouldn't you all like some pie?" she said, her voice purposefully cheery. Andrew Duffy nodded.

He stood and led Nicole and Mary Ann and a reluctant Juliette to the table. The younger girl glanced fervently at her beautiful and bewildered ideal as Cutter stopped before her.

"You realize," he said tersely, "that what has happened here tonight must never leave this house." Velvet nodded hesitantly. "There's death in the bargain, if it does," he intoned menacingly. Velvet lowered her eyes against his regard.

"I understand," she murmured. Cutter watched her carefully, and Velvet felt a rising resentment that he would imagine her endangering the lives of her family. She glared up at him, her wide gaze snapping in the golden firelight. "I *understand*, Mr. Cutter," she said bitingly. "No matter how I may feel about all this, I could never put those I love in jeopardy. You may count on my silence."

The vixen had better understand, he reflected silently as he stood over her, his fists clenched. On this matter, there could be no claim of innocence, no hedging on grounds of cultural naiveté. The girl was in the North now; daughter of the South or no daughter of the South, she must live by the ordinances of this uncompromising land.

Juliette had hung back and she now approached the couple. Glancing nervously at Cutter, she slid onto the sofa near her cousin.

"You see," she said, her tone steady and soft, as much an appeasement of Cutter's obvious anger as it was a soothing emollient to Velvet's resentment, "some of us . . . some people here in the North think the law is wrong." She looked again at Cutter, begging him with the gentleness of her appeal to be patient with the volatile Velvet. He turned away and stood apart from the two girls, a muscle in his jaw working tautly. Juliette continued. "And one day very soon, we expect the law to be changed." She glanced at her sister who stood regarding the two younger girls somberly. "We all know you are a kind person, darling Velvet," she said pointedly. "We all know you have never personally enslaved anyone." Juliette turned her regard back fully on her cousin. "But, for some of us, you represent that 'master' Mary Ann spoke about."

"But I don't 'own' anybody," Velvet responded earnestly.

Juliette smiled kindly. "In a way, you do," she answered.

"You reap the benefits of ownership," Nicole interjected with a harshness that caught everyone's attention. She looked around the room defiantly. "Don't glare at me," she snapped. "This sugar-tongued miss is as guilty as any one of those bloated Southern patriarchs. She is the shame of this country, just as surely as if she'd captained a slave ship herself."

Juliette made a move to stand, but Velvet placed her hand on the younger girl's shoulder. The room seethed to silence as, watching Nicole, she slowly rose. The two elder cousins faced each other.

"It is true I don't understand your willingness to break the law," Velvet said quietly, "And it is true that I don't understand completely the opposition you feel toward what I have always considered a harmless and even benevolent custom, but"—here Velvet paused and eyed all the people in the room—"I will not be held accountable for the sins of my fathers—if they have committed sins." Velvet faced Mary Ann fully, and her next words were only for her. "I'm sorry," she said softly. "I am sorry you have been forced to endanger yourself in the name of freedom. I promise you," she continued, raising her right hand solemnly, "I never dreamed you, or any of your people, felt oppressed by me or any of my people. If it is ever within my power to right that wrong, I shall do it." Velvet lowered her hand and took a step toward

Nicole. "I am going to try my best, cousin, to rectify and to reestablish our relationship. If you try as hard as I intend to, we shall have no problem." She glanced at Cutter. Lifting her chin, she said, "As I told you, sir, you may depend upon my silence."

At last Velvet faced her aunt and uncle. She went to each of them and embraced them. Then she moved to Juliette and held the girl in her arms. "I love you, little cousin," she said into her ear. "And I really will try to understand." Velvet glanced at Hanna and offered a small smile. Without further words, she moved from the room and made her way to her chamber.

"I'll go to her," said Yvonne Duffy once Velvet had left the room.

"Let me," said Cutter. His eyes had not left the departing Velvet. Yvonne looked to Andrew quickly, but her husband merely nodded.

"Do it, lad," he said shortly, ignoring the audible protests of the women. "Be easy," the older man warned Cutter. "You've already determined that words won't break the girl, but I won't see her insulted by you again." Cutter turned and strode from the parlor.

"Are you insane, Andrew?" protested Yvonne in an incredulous whisper.

"I don't think so," her husband responded laconically.

"But, Pa—" Juliette began.

Hanna opened her mouth to offer an uncharacteristic remonstrance of her own, but Andrew Duffy quieted them all with a wave of his hand and a knowing laugh.

"The boy'll do fine," he said.

"But what about Velvet?" Juliette wailed.

"Trust your Pa," her father said easily as he made himself comfortable in his chair. Andrew Duffy looked for all the world as if he had a secret. What that secret might be, Yvonne Duffy reflected anxiously as she brought her husband his pipe, was anyone's guess.

Only Nicole, escorting Mary Ann from the house, seemed to understand her father's design, and for a very quick, unguarded moment, she hated him for it.

Upstairs, Velvet reclined on her bed. She had not bothered to light the lamp. The melancholy, moonstruck darkness of her room comforted her. Hers was not a mood enhanced by light. She did not know—or care, right now—if she would ever assimilate all that she had been told. Somehow, everything she'd ever believed had taken on an unsavory aspect. Her attitudes toward men and people in general seemed inappropriate now. Her faith in her very way of life had been shattered. And there was Cutter. She closed her eyes tightly against the image conjured by his name. He was the deepest mystery of all to her. Was he lover or demon? She had, over the past weeks, reconciled herself to the hard-fought truth that he roused in her something of which she wanted no part. But it was part of her—this hungry, angry need. The question was: after tonight, did he want her? She tossed her head restively. If he still wanted her—was still impatient for her to come to him—would she be willing? Velvet had heard a great deal about dignity, about choice this night. Was it possible that any of what Mary Ann had said related to Velvet? She moaned softly in the darkness. She wanted not to think, not to wonder, not to plan. She wanted to sleep. She wanted to forget. She wanted to go back to a time when she was young, careless; a time when life was simple, sunny, tender. She wanted home.

The knock at the door of her chamber was oddly severe—not Hanna's bright tap. Velvet sat up quickly.

"Who is it?" she asked tremulously, for her heart prophesied the response.

"Cutter." The word was expected, but not welcomed. Velvet stood slowly.

"What do you want?" she asked, making the attempt at least to sound sure and strong. The door swung open and Velvet's gaze widened as Cutter filled the aperture. "How dare you!" She gasped.

"I have your uncle's permission," he said.

"This is my chamber," Velvet retorted. "Uncle Duff has no right to . . ." Her protest died as she watched Cutter step inside the room and close the door behind him. "You

84

can't—"

"I can," he said quietly. He moved toward her, and Velvet backed away, watching him warily. "I only want to talk—for now."

"I'm not ready to talk to anyone," Velvet answered, more sure of herself when she considered that even the unspeakable Cutter would not dare to attack her here.

"We have a great deal to talk about, and, ready or not, you will tell me what you're feeling, Velvet," he directed softly, still moving toward her.

"Why do you want to know?" she rejoined. "What do you care about what I'm feeling?"

"I am attempting to penetrate that aristocratic little brain of yours," he said, his patience at the snapping point. "I find it hard to believe that you've never considered the feelings of those people you tyrannize."

"Tyrannize?" she gaped. "Why, I've never tyrannized anyone in my life. The workers at Sweet Briar Hill are my friends, Mr. Cutter. There's not a man, woman, or child among them whom I wouldn't trust with my very life. I know every one of them by name, for heaven's sake. I never thought about their feelings, because I never considered they were owned—by me or anyone else. It never occurred to me." Velvet's indignation rose and fell with mercurial quickness. "But, I intend to do some thinking about it now, I can tell you that, Mr. Cutter. You may depend on it," she finished, her voice nearly a whisper. Cutter's gaze narrowed. A sudden rush of realization overtook him. Velvet was telling the truth. She had to be. Even this tinsel-hearted little bauble could not pretend such impassioned sincerity. Cutter had sensed from the beginning that, beneath the moonlight and magnolia hypocrisy of her behavior, there lurked a woman. Now he was sure of it.

"If, as you say, I am an unusual man, Velvet McBride, then you are a most unusual woman," he intoned.

Her breath caught as she saw the transformation in his eyes. She swallowed several times. Cutter's inexorable presence filled her vision—and her soul. She found herself backed to the rough log wall. He was very close to her; his

85

warmth, his manly radiance had haunted her dreams, and now he was here. She looked hastily away from the dark silver of his gaze, lowering her lashes so that the thick silk of them fanned in a tangled fringe over her flush-pinkened cheeks. "Leave me alone," she whispered.

"You don't really want that, do you, Velvet?" he said huskily.

"Yes," she breathed. "Yes." Her gaze lifted, and in the shadowed luster of the moonlight, her eyes were blue satin, melting with appeal. "Don't you understand?" she asked. "Don't you understand that tonight has been the final blow for me? Every day since I arrived here, I have been made aware, one way or another, that I don't fit in. I don't belong here." She placed a small white hand on his hard chest as much to push him away as to hold him there. "Don't you know how awkward I feel? I have been living a life that has no consequence here. I've been guided by convictions that seem suddenly trivial, even cruel." Her head fell back against the wall, the slim white column of her throat blue-veined and invitingly vulnerable in the moonlight. Cutter saw the first dewy tears appear on her lashes. "If I could make you understand," she whispered. "I am alone in this. I have discovered truths about my upbringing — truths about myself — that I can barely believe. Oh, Cutter," she breathed, and a soft, rueful laugh budded from her lips. "And I was going to educate all of you." Her tears came fully now, lustrous rivulets cascading down her cheeks. Cutter reached up and, with a rough fingertip, brushed at the warm rills.

"You are not alone in this," he said gently. "I can help."

Velvet gazed into the depths of his tender regard. "But you are at least part of the problem," she murmured. "Perhaps you are the biggest part. Who can I talk to about you? Whose counsel can I seek regarding my shameful feelings toward you?" She drew herself from him and paced the room, swiping impatiently at her tears. "And what of this latest information? How sympathetic are you to my sensibilities? Everyone, including you, watched me tonight as though I were an alien. I suppose," she said, lowering herself onto her bed, "I am." Cutter moved to her, realizing that she

86

was being as honest and as open as she'd ever been in her life. He felt a wave of sympathy and swelling warmth that unsettled him. He stood over her, looking down at her bowed head, wanting in ways he'd not experienced before to protect her. He touched a moonstruck curl that fell unheeded onto the cream of her shoulder.

"I would try to understand," he said huskily.

Velvet glanced up at him and smiled sadly.

"Would you, Cutter?" she asked. "Would you, really?" He nodded. "I was right," Velvet murmured. "You are a most unusual gentleman." She glanced away. "But you have your own reasons. I fear you would exact a terrible price for your . . . understanding."

"Price," Cutter said evenly, suddenly wary.

"Yes," Velvet answered as she stood and faced him. His brow lifted, and his gaze darkened. "You," she continued softly, "would use me as surely as Mary Ann has been used."

"That isn't true," Cutter answered. His lips became a rigid line, and Velvet placed delicate fingertips over them.

"It is true," she said simply. "For your protection, for your . . . kindness, I would be your slave."

Cutter swung away from her. Ramming his big fists into the pockets of his trousers, he stood for a long moment not looking at her. Perhaps he'd been wrong about the minx. She was as practiced a little manipulator as he'd first assessed her to be. One minute she was all starshine and wounded virtue, and the next she was prickling with unexpected barbs. What he should do—what he should have done long ago—was take her in his arms and compel that brambled tongue to silence. Instead he remained rigidly aware that, if he acted now, he might do something for which they would both be sorry. "You, Miss McBride," he grated finally, "have a damned odd way of looking at relationships."

"Is that what you proposed to me that night in the forest?" she asked evenly. "Did you suggest a . . . 'relationship,' Cutter?" When he did not answer, she went on. "I think not. Yours was not the language of *relationship*. You spoke of submission—my submission." Velvet's voice grew stronger, as her resolve deepened. "Tonight you spoke of my ignorance. Well, you were right. I have been dependent on traditions inspired by ignorance. You could help me to learn the sham of those traditions, it's true, but then I would be learning your truths. I would be dependent on your point of view. I have no desire to pass from one dependency to another. Oh, I shall become educated, as you said, but my education will be on my terms. I will learn about Mary Ann and her people; I will learn about me, and about you; I will learn about how I need to behave in this Northern wilderness in order that I may survive here. I will learn all those things, but I will learn them for myself." Cutter swung abruptly to face her. He seemed to rein in some barely suppressed impulse. His muscles taut, his gaze thunderous, he held her in the grip of that potentially deadly energy.

"I have said I am not a patient man, Velvet," he intoned, his eyes hooding. "But I have proven to have more patience than I imagined where you are concerned. Whether you are the wronged, oh-so-innocent flower of the South or the conniving bitch makes little difference to me. I want you, and I'll have you. This business tonight changes nothing. Learn what you must, but I will be waiting when you are ready for a . . . higher education."

Velvet lowered her eyes quickly, recoiling from the potency of his regard. That day at the picnic she had sensed the virile seduction she now perceived. She had feared it the night in the forest. As she had promised herself so many times over the past few weeks, she must find a way to live with what she knew existed between them. But, Velvet resolved, she must deal with his power over her on her own terms. Whether or not Cutter was the one would be her choice. Velvet resigned herself to the fact that he would remain in her soul forever. She would dream of him, and in her dreams she would cling to that heart-crushing need for him. She might even surrender to that need one day, but in the end she would control her own destiny. Velvet knew that at once. She lifted her gaze, unafraid now. "As I said, Cutter," she offered, her tones clear, steady, "I concede your physical superiority. But if I succumb to you as you want me to do, it will be my decision."

A slow, easy smile creased the hard line of Cutter's jaw. "Don't be too sure of that, Miss McBride," he said. "Surrender has an odd way of legitimizing itself. It just seems, at times, to be the right thing to do."

The lines had been drawn. Velvet and Cutter faced each other squarely, he—for the moment—reining in his might, she accepting it and knowing that, for the first time in her life, she was guided by her own instincts and not by those of a stagnant and crippling discipline which no longer applied to her—at least not as long as she remained in this foreign land.

It would not be easy, she determined, to break from long-practiced conventions, but if she were to survive she must try. She must disavow old behaviors; learn new ones. And she must start immediately. She had no choice but to be realistic. The North was not home, and she could no longer pretend it was. Cutter had said it himself; time was too precious to waste on games.

Chapter Eight

Summer heat and humidity had settled over the Adirondack Mountains. Only the cool, ice blue ponds that pocked the landscape held relief. Juliette and Velvet waded in them daily. The bouncing yellow of the younger woman's curls glittered in the sunlight as they removed their stockings and shoes and stepped expectantly into the water at Doriel's.

"It's freezing!" Juliette shrieked joyously. Velvet smiled, watching her, and dabbed her toes indifferently into the pond. For weeks Velvet had felt like a prisoner in her uncle's home. The family had been generally tactful, but they had watched her, nonetheless, to see what her reaction would be to the news that the Duffy household was a haven for run-away slaves. Though she was not entirely comfortable with her new enlightenment, Velvet realized that she had learned a valuable lesson.

She had made an effort to speak with Mary Ann before she and her companions were escorted by Cutter to their camp at North Elba. The woman was exceptional, to be sure. Mary Ann did not understand her purpose in life to be subservience, though that was all she'd ever known. It was possible then for people to deviate from the dictates of their upbringing; if Velvet had learned nothing else that summer, she had learned that. Mary Ann spoke of the fact that she hoped one day to be reunited with her family. When she left, Velvet wished her well, and promised that, once she got back to Sweet Briar Hill, she would look into that very situation. She would have to be discreet, she worried; she was not sure that her father and mother—and especially their politically influential friends—were quite as enlightened as she.

The summer had brought more than an education to Velvet. It had brought a deeper animosity toward her from

90

her cousin Nicole. Though there had been no overt bitterness between them, Velvet had long ago abandoned any hope of their becoming friends. Velvet had made more than her share of conciliatory gestures toward Nicole, but to no avail. That young woman was fiercely dedicated to her cause — and, it appeared, to J. Eliot Cutter. She spoke of him constantly, praised him extravagantly, and never missed an opportunity to refer to their growing kinship — where it concerned their cause, of course. Of all the mistrust Velvet encountered within the family, Nicole's was the most vitriolic and the most unrelenting.

Velvet's first few letters home, after the revelation, were gently checked by her Aunt Yvonne. The older woman merely wanted to verify, she said, that Velvet had not inadvertently mentioned the Underground Railroad. That, in fact, was the last thing Velvet wanted to mention. Her letters were bald pleas to her parents that she be allowed to come home. But each time she wrote, her very good reasons why she ought to be allowed to return to the South were roundly ignored. Optimistic letters arrived each week from Sweet Briar Hill — the plantation had not been touched — but they strongly stated that Velvet must stay exactly where she was.

Velvet, nevertheless, continued to write and to plead, and each time she wrote, Nicole insisted that her letters be censored. Long after Yvonne Duffy had ceased to do so, Nicole continued to inspect her cousin's mail. Velvet felt badgered and mistrusted due to this supervision. And she felt sure that J. Eliot Cutter was at the bottom of Nicole's antipathy, though she had not seen Cutter for weeks.

Velvet had suffered many hours of soul-searching self-examination since the night she'd discovered the runaways. Cutter's physical absence had given her the luxury of time, though, she reflected, he was never truly absent. Her dreams continued to be haunted by his presence. Her heart was haunted by the specter of his power over her. She attempted to divert herself from the compulsion of her need, but she was reminded of it every hour of every day by ungovernable thoughts of him.

She and Juliette walked toward the house after their exercise, and found the front yard crowded with men. Andrew Duffy was already hiring loggers for the long winter ahead. Velvet scanned the assemblage beneath the concealment of her veiled lashes. She quickly checked recently disavowed but not forgotten instincts, and walked past the men, her eyes lowered, her face impassive. Their jovial appreciation of the two young women went, apparently, unnoticed.

Velvet and Juliette headed directly to the lines strung at the back of the house and removed the day's laundry from them. Hefting baskets of sun-dried clothing and linens, they made their way across the yard. Juliette cheerfully admonished the several dogs that frolicked in their path as they walked, reminding them that Velvet was not used to dealing with such menial, heavy work and their exuberance at the same time. She eyed her older cousin with pride. Velvet had advised everyone in the household that she no longer wished to be excused from the labors expected of the other women. She had much to learn, she told them, and though great patience needed to be exercised by all, Velvet was an eager student, if not a gifted one.

Over the summer, she had learned the nuances of polishing the silverware, dusting the mantelpieces and window frames, and mending the carpets. She followed the tolerant Hanna relentlessly, asking questions, and at last, with the enthusiasm of the newly initiated, advising.

Velvet had even worked in the kitchen. Though that room held terrible memories for her—she still was not able to face the roaming hogs—she did manage to lace an entirely acceptable pie crust. One night, she promised the family, she would endeavor to create an entire dinner on her own. Tonight might just be the night, she thought with determination as she and Juliette climbed the back steps to the kitchen. She eyed her young cousin tentatively. Perhaps Velvet would try the idea out on the patient Juliette before she approached Aunt Vonnie or Hanna with the proposal.

Once inside the house, Velvet noted that Nicole stood rigidly in the parlor. She watched from the window the proceedings outside.

"Sometimes Pa is so stupid," Nicole groused at the girls'

entrance. Both young women glanced at her with puzzlement. She cocked her brow. "I just mean," she said, replacing the light curtain, "that some of those boys are bound to want to tour the spread."

"You mean they'll want to inspect the premises before they decide to work here?" Juliette giggled.

"Exactly," Nicole affirmed sullenly.

"I don't think any of those boys gives a ding dang where they are," Juliette said, dismissing her sister's concerns. "They just want the job. As long as they get their dozen eggs a man every morning, and their ninety cents every night, they'll be happy."

Nicole moved toward her menacingly. "You don't seem to understand that we have visitors," she said with emphatic significance. "Mr. Cutter has just returned from a long excursion south, and he's returned with friends."

"Those boys wouldn't tell," Juliette said with ingenuous sincerity. "I would lay you odds that every one of them voted Union. I would also lay odds that every one of them got our Uncle Abe elected president last year." She glanced quickly, guiltily at Velvet. "Oh, I'm sorry, Velvet," she said. "I know you don't think of Mr. Lincoln as president, but here in the North . . ."

Velvet touched the girl's arm. "It's all right, Juliette," she said. She glanced, smiling, at Nicole and saw in that woman's regard a stinging disapproval. Attempting nevertheless, once again to soothe her cousin's disfavor, she said, "I have no interest whatsoever in politics, I assure you both." Her calm certainty was only momentarily suspended by the knowledge that Cutter was now very near. Velvet believed, however, that she hid that irresolution very well.

Nicole studied her with a jaundiced smile. "Don't you?" she said bitingly.

"Not in the least," Velvet responded with as much nonchalance as she could muster.

"That's good to hear," Nicole retorted. "Mr. Cutter and I will be working together on a campaign within the next couple of months to assure our Negro brothers and sisters their freedom, and we certainly wouldn't appreciate interference from you." Her tone held a combination of contempt and triumph.

Velvet stared at her older cousin, bewildered, incredulous. How could Nicole imagine that she would have any interest in seeing such a project undermined? It didn't make sense. On the other hand, nothing really made sense where Nicole was concerned. And, once again, her cousin seemed to be holding Cutter up as an inflammatory banner. Nicole's relationship with him, her apparent closeness to him where it concerned their cause, gave her some sort of perception of victory. Velvet had no idea what victory there was to be had in this, unless . . .

"You needn't concern yourself, Nicole," Velvet said before her thoughts had an opportunity to take hold. "I repeat that I have no interest in politics."

"She's told you that a hundred times," Juliette said impatiently. "Why won't you believe her?" She turned to the parlor table and began furiously to pull the dry laundry from her basket and fold it. The smell of sunshine and fresh mountain air cut through the dampness and heat, but even that pleasant intrusion did not lighten the atmosphere of the room. "Honestly, Nicole, sometimes you aggravate the life out of me," Juliette grumbled. "Can't you just, for heaven's sake, be friendly with your own cousin?"

Nicole's cold regard did not waver. It raked Velvet with it's intensity. "It's bad enough I have to live with this foul slave breeder, I don't have to like her. And I do not have to trust her."

"Slave breeder!" Velvet gaped. "In God's name, Nicole—"

"How can you say such a thing!" Juliette's brown eyes widened in disbelief. In all her sixteen years, she had never known her sister to speak so abusively. She looked hastily toward Velvet and saw a decisive change in her appearance. After the first flush of disbelief, there appeared a certain understanding, a sudden knowing insight. Juliette flinched. What sort of a life could they have in this house if her cousin ceased to make conciliatory gestures toward Nicole? If those two strong-willed women became enemies, life would be hell. She ran to Velvet. "She . . . she didn't mean it . . . she really

94

didn't," Juliette stammered.

"Yes, she did," Velvet said, her face rigid. "Oh yes, she did." Nicole raised her chin. "What I want to know, cousin," Velvet continued quietly, "is why you persist in your headstrong resentment of me. It seems impossible at this point that you could question my loyalty to this family."

"Why is that so impossible?" asked Nicole coolly.

"Because I've given you no reason," answered Velvet. "So I must conclude there is some other reason for your animosity."

Nicole's posture sagged just perceptibly enough to be noticed. "What other reason could there be?" she inquired. When Velvet did not answer, she went on. "Don't think for one minute you're fooling me with your sudden and, as far as I'm concerned, unexplained eagerness to learn our ways. This monumental effort on your part to shed your gentry-bred affectations, to 'understand' as you say the Northern sensibilities, doesn't impress me one bit. And, may I add, it will not impress anyone else—including Mr. J. Eliot Cutter." She targeted her younger sister. "How the rest of you have managed to be fooled by this little gewgaw is beyond me," she said haughtily. "Mr. Cutter and I see right through her." At once, Velvet understood her cousin's ruthless hostility. It was jealousy and nothing more.

In other circumstances Velvet might have found the prospect of her cousin's competition exhilarating. In this case, because they lived together in the same house, because they were cousins, and because the prize was Cutter, the thought of a contest brought her no pleasure. The stakes were too high, Velvet realized in a sudden rush of comprehension. As yet, however, the "stakes" had not been explored or explained. She watched rigidly as her cousin stalked from the room.

"Oh, Lord," Juliette moaned, moving to the sofa. She sat heavily, and then glanced up at Velvet. "You really must not give up on Nicole," she said softly. "You really must continue to try." Juliette felt her apprehension grow when Velvet did not respond. "Velvet, dear," she said, attempting to penetrate the barrier of her cousin's intense concentration.

Velvet eyed her cousin, noting with a start that Juliette had been trying to gain her attention. She felt a surge of sympathy at noting her woeful expression. Juliette appreciated peace. She wanted no contention in her life. Velvet forced a small smile.

"Don't worry," she said gently. "Everything will work out." Indeed, Velvet resolved, everything would work out. She intended to see that it did. This disaffection between her cousin and herself could not go on. Velvet knew its source, and at the source was where she was bound to end it.

Velvet carried the lantern high. She was not anxious to get trapped again in the witch-hobble that had made her last departure from Cutter so ungraceful. She tread slowly and carefully over the rough terrain, over the projecting arms of fallen, moss-shrouded pines, over low twining shrubs that grew along the wilderness paths. Night creatures, by their sudden silence, announced her passage, and she was sure that Cutter would be aware of her coming. Let it be, she thought. She was not in the business of ambush this night. She wanted only a straight forward talk with the man. She intended to apprise him of the fact that Nicole was in love with him. And she intended to make it clear to him that if he had encouraged the girl in any way whatsoever, he must, as a gentleman, either make good on his obligations to her or tell her frankly that he had no interest in her. Velvet's musings were interrupted by the realization that, even to her, her reasoning sounded lame. Who was she, after all, to admonish a man like Cutter concerning his dalliances? It had even occurred to her that her motives for visiting him lay elsewhere.

Nevertheless, Velvet had planned the confrontation very well. She had waited until supper was over and the house asleep. She wanted no interference from anyone. She must face Cutter alone; there must be no extraneous talk. She would tell him exactly how she felt and then she would leave—or so, in her fantasy, she imagined.

To facilitate her journey through the forest, Velvet had abandoned her petticoats, and put on a light cotton frock. Its filmy skirts wrapped themselves around her unstockinged legs as she moved through the vegetation. She had made no attempt to be fashionable tonight. The truth was, she did not care how she looked. It was not her intention to attempt to impress Cutter; she'd already tried that, she recalled ruefully, and look where it had gotten her. Tonight she wanted him to concentrate only on her words—for they were important words—and not on her appearance.

The night was clear and star-struck, and Velvet kept her course toward Doriel's pond. It was near there, Juliette had pointed out, that Cutter lived. His cabin would not be difficult to spot. As she reached the water's edge, Velvet lowered the lamp, and placed it on a spot of level ground. She gazed out over the night landscape. Woods, dark and towering, cast a quivering, breeze-softened silhouette against the sky.

There has to be a path, she reasoned as she began a slow circle along the forest's edge. Quietly, carefully, she peered into each Stygian fissure in the barrier of the trees. An owl hooted in the beech tree that overhung the water. Velvet started, composed herself, and began to search again. She treaded as unerringly as she could, searched the dark recesses assiduously, and finally made a complete circle of the pond without a glimpse of Cutter's home.

"Damn," she muttered.

"My, my," said a voice nearby. "Where would a gentle daughter of the South learn such language?" Velvet's attention became riveted. It was Cutter. She peered into the surrounding darkness. She saw nothing.

"Is it you, Mr. Cutter?" she demanded, her confidence waning when no answer came. "I said, is it you, sir?" Her eyes ranged the silent, star-shadowed landscape. "It had better be you, J. Eliot," she insisted darkly. "I am sick and tired of being scared."

Suddenly, he was there before her, his gray eyes catching the starshine. Velvet gazed up at him, relief and annoyance doing battle in her expression. Neither of them spoke until at last he said huskily, "It's me."

In the stillness that followed his appearance, Velvet did not think about the reason she was there. It had ceased to exist.

97

Time had ceased to exist. Her only reality was now, this very moment, this enchanted moment. Tall, darkly looming like a pine tree, he stood so near her. Unlike a tree, he exuded masculine warmth, suppleness, sinewed power. Velvet dragged her regard from the tanned face, shadowed in the dark. She must remember . . . she must keep to the point . . . she must . . .

His big hands clasped her shoulders. He drew her toward his hard chest. Holding her there, he looked down on her, and very slowly she raised her eyes to his. She knew he would kiss her, and this time the kiss would not be born of cruelty. This time the kiss would be born of need. She lowered her lashes, accepting the inevitable. In her dreams, it had been this way between them.

Their lips were very close, so close, in fact, she could feel the touch of his like a feathery breath upon her own. Her eyes opened. In their depths, her soul burned. At last, at long last, with tantalizing tenderness, his mouth caressed hers. Yielding to the hungry insistence of his tongue, her lips parted.

Velvet felt herself drawn beyond the earth's pull into a misted fantasy. She felt no specific sensation; her body was one with his. He consumed her. Eagerly, powerfully he drew her into him. His breath, his caress, his whispered endearments transformed her. She had no will.

He lifted her. She felt herself carried on the soft night breezes. Her head fell back over the column of his muscled arm. His lips feathered hot kisses along her neck, her shoulders, her breasts. Nothing mattered now; not time, nor place, nor reason. He lay with her somewhere, somewhere wonderful. She opened herself to his command. A yearning heat filled her. His hands, so big and rough, ravaged her flesh tenderly. His mouth, so cruel, so hard, plundered her most secret treasures; grazed upon the sweet bud of her resistance. The confinement of her clothing was torn away soundlessly, mindlessly. Velvet writhed beneath the voluptuous assault. She could not think, did not want to think. She could only feel. Throbbing pleasure encloaked her, took the place of her cotton frock. He was her raiment. He arrayed her in silken

98

rapture.

Velvet had never imagined such joy. Her innocent soul sang with illusive ecstasy. Like the sun sparkling on a pool, he was over her. She quivered beneath the heat of his intent.

"I want you," he rasped.

"Yes, oh, yes," she breathed. He lifted her, in one powerful motion, to him, and Velvet suddenly cried out, startled by the unexpected pain. His lips came down on hers, and she wriggled against his restraint.

"Let me love you," he growled.

"No!" Velvet screamed, twisting from the piercing agony of his thrust.

"Yes," he said. This, then, was the old Cutter. This was the cruel, arrogant Cutter she had come to hate. She attempted to tear away from him, but he held her hard against him. Her body tensed as, once again, the weapon of his will pierced her soft flesh. A scream raged up from her breast. Once again he covered her mouth with his hot, demanding kisses, compelling her to silence—to silent agony.

Velvet managed to unleash pounding blows against him, but her efforts were nothing to his savage resolve. At last, he pinned her arms and she was helpless beneath him. She could do nothing more than yield to the brutality that was Cutter.

"It will go better for you, if you do not fight it," he urged hoarsely. The words took on their own horrible significance. Velvet knew he spoke the truth. But she must fight it; she could not surrender passively to his bestial abuse. She twisted mightily, and managed a certain freedom. For an instant, their eyes locked, their wills collided. Green-blue fire met a silver torrent—and the fire was deluged.

"No," she breathed into the abyss.

"Yes." It was the last word, the last sound Velvet recognized. She was swept into a tidal flood of sensate delirium. She did not know what was happening to her. The pain throbbed to quivering nonexistence. It was replaced by a tingling flush, a rippling, liquid fever of need, of insatiable hunger. A sudden heat, pungent and pleasurable, over-whelmed her. She felt—or believed she felt—a powerful undertow of unimaginable warmth. The pull of that eddying rapture was insistent, puissant, irresistible. Velvet knew she was dying — or dead — or had never been. Reality ceased in one sudden surge of joyous surrender. Release shattered the darkness, shuddered to the surface of her being.

Substance toyed with consciousness as rapture ebbed. Cutter's hands soothed her flesh, his heart pounded at her breast, his breath swathed her soul. "Forgive me," he said against her ear.

"Oh, no," she whispered, as she held him to her. "Oh, no. There is no need for forgiveness here." Her hands explored the instrument of her abandonment. With feather touches, she sought the rippling muscles beneath perspiration-sheened flesh, the hard buttocks, the perfect hollows and swells of his body. Her fingertips ranged the manly form. He lifted himself, taking his weight onto his muscled arms. Once again, he seemed to study her, the liquid silver of his opaline scrutiny exploring her as she was exploring him.

He brushed at the tangled curls that clung to her cheek. "Velvet," he said softly, and the word was a breath. He rolled onto his back and drew her with him to lie pressed against the lean length of him. A cool coverlet billowed up and blanketed her against the receding heat of ecstasy.

In that dark, nested seclusion, Velvet gave in to slumber — dreamless slumber for the first time in many weeks.

Chapter Nine

The morning came softly to the little cabin that stood in the forest near Doriel's Pond. Dawn shadows lightened the interiors slowly, casting pearly fingers over the snugly sheltered inhabitants. Velvet awakened reluctantly. The aroma of coffee, the sizzle of bacon, the sun-warmed air nudged her to consciousness, but did not offer the comfort extended by the cozy cradle of her sleep. It had been the first true rest, the first respite from her wrathful dreams, she'd had in a very long time. She stretched, awaking, remembering her sleep, remembering the cool luxury of oblivion. Her soft yawn caught the attention of someone just outside the room. He parted the light curtain that separated them, and Velvet's sleepy gaze widened. Her lips, midyawn, gaped in a perfect expression of surprise.

"Cutter," she gasped. Dragging the coverlet to her breast, she slid her knees up in protection of her unguarded nakedness. "How dare you!" she raged. "Get out."

His smile was slow and appreciative. He placed his hands on his narrow hips, and stood, his feet solidly apart, in the archway. His unshirted chest swelled with laughter. Velvet cocked her gaze incredulously. In her sleep-softened nest, her hair poufed and tousled wildly about face and shoulders, her lips budded in question, she was to him as beautiful, as alluring, as dangerously tempting as any woman had ever been.

"Oh, Velvet," he said at last, "you are magnificent. You are temptress and gamin, cherub and siren wrapped up in one adorable bundle." He moved to her, his bare feet taking the rough flooring like a cat's. "I am a most fortunate man," he breathed as he sat near her on the bed. He brushed at the aurora of a flaxen-streaked curl that fell sweetly on the swelling mound of her breast. She stiffened. Cutter raised an amused brow. "The time for demure pretensions is over, sweet," he observed wryly.

Awareness had come to Velvet in an abrupt stroke of startled disbelief. She watched Cutter as he leaned, questing with his tongue and rough fingertips beneath the protection of her blanket. She rigidly held to that defense against him. "Stop," she whispered, the effect of his probing already rendering her breathless. He seemed not to hear her. His tongue, insistent and seductive, enticed the tender flesh at her throat as he grasped a handful of her tangled mane. Her head fell back. Velvet moaned softly. Cutter's arm snaked out and he caught her to him, flattening her breasts against the fur of his hard chest. His lips took hers. Velvet knew the same sudden swell of hungry warmth rising in her as she had known the night before.

"There will be no pain this time," Cutter said at her gasping protest. His hot breath consumed her.

"Cutter," she breathed suddenly. The urgency in her tone gave him pause. He looked up, and then his eyes darted to where her attention was riveted, at some point over his shoulder.

In the doorway between the two small rooms of the cabin stood an irate Nicole. Cutter released Velvet slowly. He stood and turned to the scowling woman.

"Did you wish to see me?" he inquired darkly.

Nicole did not answer immediately. Instead, she took a moment to coldly survey the scene before her. There was no mistaking its significance. Her eyes drifted back to Cutter, and her mood seemed to change perceptibly. She raked her fingers through her soft, dark blond curls. "You have certainly had us fooled, Mr. Cutter," she said with a small smile. "One day you are the scholarly geologist, the next you are the noble humanitarian, risking your life for your fellow human beings. Now we find that you have hidden yet another identity." Her gaze became hooded. "We find, Mr. Cutter, that you are little more than a rutting bull when it comes to the elegant Miss McBride." She glanced coolly at Velvet. "For shame, cousin," she said in a mockery of reproach.

"Miss Duffy," Cutter began, his impatience clear in his tone, "what did you—"

"I'm leaving now, Mr. Cutter," Nicole interjected sharply. She turned abruptly to leave. As abruptly, she turned back. "Oh, by the way," she said, tipping them both a piquant smile, "Pa would like to see the two of you up at the house." She ambled from the cabin. "Don't keep him waiting," she called lightly as she stepped outside.

Velvet sat dumbstruck on Cutter's tousled bed. Not only had she done the unpardonable, but now, apparently, her family was aware of the whole sordid exploit. She swung her legs over the edge of the bed and, holding the sheet to her breast, searched wildly for her clothes. Cutter glanced back at her. She regarded him truculently.

"You might help me find my gown," she snapped. Cutter turned with maddening languor. He moved to where her frock from the night before lay rumpled on the floor. With one finger, he lifted it. Velvet gaped at the ragged tatter of cotton. "Is that all that's left?" she cried.

"I'm afraid so," Cutter said. Velvet's gaze darkened at the amusement she perceived in his tone.

"Well, I shall just have to make do," she said, snatching it from him. Keeping her back to his relentless and deliberate examination of her, Velvet pulled the gown over her head. She looked down, once it was in place, and wailed piteously. "It's ruined, Cutter." At his chuckle, she rounded on him. "How dare you, sir!" she gritted.

His mirth, as it rumbled from his broad chest, filled the room. "Velvet. Oh, Velvet," he said, shaking his head. "You are ever the gently bred little pretender." His raven curls fell boyishly over his forehead, as he moved to take her into his embrace.

"How can you laugh?" she railed, struggling away from him. Not quite succeeding in her bid for freedom, she faced him squarely. "You are infuriating!" she wailed. "And, *Mr. Cutter*, you are *no gentleman!*" She lifted a winged brow and her little chin, as though she had, with those particular words, delivered him a verbal death blow.

Cutter's laughter only deepened, and he drew her more

103

closely into his embrace. "You are right, milady," he said softly. He felt the first tears of her frustration and mortification seep through the down that covered his chest. He drew away from her, and cupped her head in his large hand. Looking down at the aquamarine glaze of her anguish, his heart swelled with melting tenderness.

"What are we going to do?" she moaned.

"I don't know," he answered softly. "But whatever our punishment, Velvet McBride, I will consider the sin well worth the price."

"What is Nicole to you?" she asked suddenly.

Cutter's brow lifted. "What is she to me?" he repeated blankly.

"Yes," Velvet answered. "I need to know that, Cutter. No matter what happens, I need to know how you feel toward her."

Cutter shrugged. "I don't know exactly what you mean," he said.

Velvet drew away from him, unable to look into his eyes as she asked her next question. "Have you . . . I mean, have you and she . . . ?" She rubbed her hands together disconsolately. "I need to know if you ever . . . with her . . ."

Cutter's initial bewilderment was abruptly dispelled. "If we ever made love?" he asked, realizing what Velvet's discomposure was about.

"Oh, of course not," Velvet retorted with impatience. "Nicole would never do such a thing. She's a decent young woman."

"And so are you," Cutter stated evenly. Velvet glanced wretchedly up at him. He moved to her and took her shoulders, turning her to him. "Velvet," he said gently, "you have done nothing but follow your heart."

"I've followed the basest of my instincts," she rejoined.

Cutter did not resist the impulse to shake her.

"Stop it," he commanded. "For the love of God, Velvet, will you diminish yourself because you surrendered to the most womanly part of you? What happened between us was meant to happen. You knew it and so did I."

"I didn't want it to," she wailed softly. "Not with you."

Cutter released her abruptly. He turned from her, tucking his thumbs into his belt loops. His proud shoulders were hunched, his head bowed.

Velvet realized her error. "I didn't mean it that way," she amended. She placed her small white hand on the bronze barrier of his muscled back. He shrugged away from her.

"Forget it," he muttered. At last, stiffly, he strode across the small room and reached into a chest. Drawing out a pair of trousers and a shirt, he tossed them to her. "Put these on," he said harshly. He took one last, long look at the luminous splendor of pale flesh barely concealed by tatters of filmy cotton. In the streaming morning sunlight, she might have been an angel fallen to earth, given into his protection. But he reminded himself that Velvet McBride was no angel. Her viperous tongue might lash out at any time to wound the one who dared attempt to hold her close. Woe to him who took that precious opaline jewel to his heart; prismatic glass would rip that heart to shreds. Cutter drew a regretful breath; his gaze narrowed. He would guard his own heart fiercely, savagely if necessary.

"If you are still interested, Velvet," he said huskily, "there has never been anything except a mutual belief in a valued cause between Nicole and me. She is a most dedicated woman, and I respect her for that. I always shall." He turned abruptly and left the room.

Chapter Ten

The sun rose quickly over the tall pines that shadowed the wooded path back to the Duffy house. And it is the *Duffy* house, Velvet reminded herself forlornly. She had never fit into it. No matter how hard she had tried, she had remained a guest there — a pampered guest at times. But those salad days were over. And perhaps it was just as well. Even Velvet's best efforts to insinuate herself into the everyday mold of the household had resulted in her being merely tolerated. She was a gross failure, it seemed, at anything but self-indulgence.

She trudged with Cutter over the tangled brush of the roadway, knowing these might be their last moments together. That was probably just as well, too. Tomorrow, Andrew Duffy would send her south just as surely as the sun rose, and Velvet could begin anew the life to which she was best suited. She could go back to live among people who understood her, and whom she understood. At last, she could return to a comfortable existence where there were no ambiguities of behavior — as there were here.

At home, work was done by workers. Women acted like women; they flirted and posed and lured handsome fellows into marriage. Men acted like men; they were appropriately and amiably lured — and deferential. She glanced pettishly up at Cutter through the veil of her lashes. Striding next to her, he was so tall, so unperturbed, so . . . so . . . uncaring. He was so unlike anyone she'd known in Virginia. Why, the men with whom she'd been acquainted would never have seduced her the way Cutter had. Seduction was left to the women. Men, at home, didn't dare show their corrupt, debauched selves to decent women. They took their lustful instincts to other sorts. Velvet flinched at that thought.

Guiltily, she made a hasty, silent prayer that she might be forgiven for her weakness. It would never happen again, she promised. Unused to lengthy communication with the Deity, or piously indulgent raptures of self-blame, Velvet turned her guilt immediately into resentment of Cutter. He got what he wanted, she reflected acerbically. And now, she would get what she had wanted, practically from the moment she'd arrived in this hellish wilderness. Velvet lifted her chin against a sudden uncertainty. She had wanted to go home, she reminded herself firmly, since her first day at the Duffy's.

If she was very fortunate, her Uncle Duff would be discreet about the circumstances of her dismissal from his home, and no one would ever know of her disgrace. She would take up her life as before. War or no war, her mother most likely still ran a gay and lively household. There would be balls and barbecues — and lots and lots of boys. Even if the male population had taken to soldiering, they were surely given holidays. And when they were, Velvet and Sweet Briar Hill would be awaiting them.

Velvet wondered wryly whether her flirting instincts could still be depended upon. She'd not used them in months. She reassured herself that she'd never really forgotten her womanly powers — they'd merely been held in suspension since she'd come to this odd and unconforming environment. She looked up, once again, at Cutter. Actually, she recalled pettishly, it was he who had changed her life. Velvet had been making the best of a less than comfortable situation until Cutter had invaded her peace. He had barged his way into a perfectly tranquil, harmonious meeting of two very different cultures, had bullied his own design onto that harmony and shattered it. Thank God, Velvet concluded, she would not be playing defenseless lamb to his lascivious wolf again.

She thought fondly of Mr. Whitney — Brett. He would never have dared to treat her so cavalierly. Mr. Whitney was grateful for the slightest offering, the most selective display of affection. Mr. Whitney was a gentleman. And when Velvet was at last back home, she would be certain to let Mr. Whitney know how deeply she appreciated his restraint.

From the mouth of the passage through the forest, Velvet

heard a hoarse shout. Her eyes narrowed against the morning sunlight, and she recognized her younger cousin.

"Velvet!" the girl gasped as she ran toward the couple. "Oh, Velvet!" She made her way down the path, avoiding the outcropping underbrush. "Oh, darling Velvet," Juliette breathed as she reached the two of them. She clasped her cousin's arm and tucked it possessively into her own. "Pa's pretty calm." She gulped out the words. "But Nicole's acting like an outraged Canada lynx." Swallowing hard, she continued as they walked. "Mama's taking it all in stride, as far as anyone can tell. Hanna took to her bed, of course, good Catholic girl that she is."

Velvet halted their progress abruptly. "How did everyone find out?" she asked.

Juliette offered a woeful glance. "It wasn't hard," she blurted. Then, hastily amending her attitude, she looked quickly at Cutter and back to her cousin. "Everyone kind of suspected, when you weren't in your bed this morning," she said kindly, "but Nicole confirmed it later." Juliette swallowed again, attempting to make her story intelligible. She wanted desperately to give her dear Velvet the benefit of preparation for what she was about to face. "It's going to be a trial for you, but you must try to stay calm. Actually," she continued, lowering her voice discreetly, "you needn't admit to anything. You could just say you got lost . . . or . . . or something." She patted her cousin's arm with a confidence she could only pretend to possess. As they continued to walk toward the house, she kept up a steady din of chatter. Velvet was apprised that Nicole wanted her shipped south, but that Yvonne Duffy had suggested the Female Academy in Albany. Velvet shuddered at that prospect. To be isolated in a tiny industrial town in the north, with the likes of Morgana Carleton as her only link to home, appalled her. "There is the tiniest possibility you'll be allowed to stay," Juliette intoned, lowering her voice so that only Velvet could hear. She glanced nervously at Cutter, but he seemed to take no interest in their conversation. "Perhaps, Mr. Cutter will have to leave," she whispered in conclusion.

The three people had reached the front door of the Duffy

house. All of them stopped before it. Velvet and Juliette stood in a kind of awed stupor, until finally, Cutter took Velvet's arm and, with that same rigid air of restraint he'd been displaying all morning, led her into the house. Juliette, releasing her cousin reluctantly, followed them.

Andrew Duffy sat in his chair by the hearth with an air of perplexing insouciance. Yvonne Duffy sat on the sofa and twisted a handkerchief relentlessly. Only Nicole displayed any real animation. She paced the little room, hands on her hips. Her pacing stopped abruptly at her cousin's entrance.

"Well," she said mockingly, as she eyed Velvet, "the princess has finally deigned to end her royal seclusion." Nicole turned, with a significant tilt of her head, to her father. That man merely watched Cutter and Velvet as they placed themselves uneasily before him.

"Have you anything to say for yourselves?" he asked.

"It isn't at all what you're thinking, Uncle Duff," Velvet began. Andrew Duffy silenced her with an unhurried, rather blatant appraisal. She realized how hollow her words must sound to the older man. She looked down on her apparel — if you could even call it that. She'd pulled on a pair of Cutter's trousers and rolled them up at the ankles. Bunching one of his much-too-large shirts beneath the waistband, she'd secured it with a leather belt which she'd tied, out of necessity, rather than buckled. Her hair was piled carelessly and pinned, with hasty disregard to fashion, atop her head. Even now, great masses of it threatened to tumble from their confinement. She sighed audibly.

"What am I thinking, girl?" Andrew said evenly.

Velvet sighed once again. She could not bring herself to lie to this dear and distinguished relative, but — just perhaps — she could bend the truth a bit. "You're probably thinking what anyone would think," she said tentatively. "I mean, you're probably wondering how it happens that I was in this man's cabin, and you're probably wondering what I was doing there." She glanced up at Cutter. Her gaze narrowed resentfully. Why wasn't the oaf saying anything? He was merely standing there, silently, aloofly, as though none of this had anything whatsoever to do with him. Velvet turned her regard back on her uncle. Apparently, she must handle this situation by herself. "Things aren't always as they seem, Uncle Duff," she said firmly.

"And this particular . . . 'thing'," said Andrew, rising and circling the two of them, "is this one of those 'things' that are not as they seem?" He placed his hands behind his back and rocked casually on the balls of his feet. Cutter faced him finally. The two men were of a height. Velvet nervously watched the dark silver of Cutter's perusal as it took in the older man. At last, she thought, he is going to intervene. But what would he say? What does it matter? she reflected with quick relief; Cutter was going to defend them.

"No," said Cutter at last, "it is not." Velvet felt her mouth gape open in disbelief. He could not possibly have said the words!

"Why, whatever do you mean, Mr. Cutter?" she gasped without thinking. "Of course it is! It is, Uncle Duff," she babbled wildly. "It's just one of those silly circumstances one finds oneself in that isn't anything like it seems." She attempted a casual laugh, but the sound that emerged was something more hysterical. "You all know how it is," she appealed, her comradely smile sweeping over the people in the room, "one minute you're safely going about your own business, and the next you're embroiled in some ungodly catastrophe! Oh, it's all so *silly*," she rambled. "It's happened to all of us at one time or another. You all are just going to laugh and laugh when you hear how it came about. She watched with beguiling anticipation the stony faces around her, waiting for them to soften, praying she might suddenly be graced with a "silly" story with which to entertain them. Unfortunately, no such inspiration came. Velvet was abashed by the sudden realization that they all knew the truth—they were not buying, even for a second, her frenetic attempts to parry their awareness. It isn't fair, she railed inwardly. If something like this had happened at home—though something quite like this could never happen at home—everyone would have had the delicacy of nature to at least allow her to advance her lie. These Northerners have absolutely no tact, she decided. And the most tactless of them all was her supposed ally in this. She glared at Cutter. Oh, what wouldn't she say to him before she was shipped south. For the moment, however, she must concentrate on accepting the inevitable censure of the family. She lifted her small chin and swatted impatiently at a fallen tress of her hair. "All right," she said quietly, "it's true."

Nicole might have been given a Christmas package. Her triumphant exhalation caused everyone to look her way. "I knew it," she exulted, smiling broadly.

"So did we all, Nicole," Juliette groused. She offered her sister a dark scowl. "You can't blame our dear Velvet for—"

"Yes I can," Nicole hissed. "I blame her for everything."

"Now, girls," said Yvonne Duffy quickly, thankful to have a concern other than the thorny one posed by her niece. This kind of trouble, she reflected regretfully, guiltily, had not been unexpected. Perhaps it was best that the girl be sent down to Albany. At least, except for a few old pedagogues, there were no men at the Female Academy. She sighed. She would miss the child deeply. But there seemed no alternative. If Andrew took her advice, that's where Velvet would go.

The question was, of course, how would they explain the unexpected move to Alicia. Yvonne's sister would not take kindly to the knowledge that her only daughter had been violated under the noses of her trusted aunt and uncle. Oh, it is too much, Yvonne thought wretchedly. The handkerchief twisted wildly in her work-roughened hands. If only they could all just ignore what had happened, allow Velvet to stay on and hope that she and Mr. Cutter would behave themselves from now on. But Andrew was a hard man when his mind was set on something. She'd made that suggestion to him tentatively, but he'd glared at her. "Ignore it?" he'd roared. "We will not ignore it, woman!" And that had been his last word, until now. He eyed the couple with a keen sort of interest.

"So," he said finally, and did not speak again for several seconds. He paced again, his wide-legged carriage giving his gait a gentle, rolling movement. Velvet watched, mesmerized, the slight limp, the powerful arms folded behind him, the hard, bright blue of his intense stare. She wondered what dreadful things he was thinking of her. She waited, mustering her composure, for the terrible judgement. "Lord, Lord, Lord, girl," he said quietly, "this is about the worst thing as ever's happened on my spread." Velvet's head bowed. Shame rose up to pinken her cheeks.

"Just tell her she's as good as dearly departed, Pa," Nicole said impatiently. Her eagerness was stilled by her father's squinting perusal.

Yvonne gave her daughter an admonishing look of her own, then faced her niece unhappily. "We don't want to lose you, dear," she said soothingly. "You know how fond we all are of you."

Velvet nodded dejectedly, not looking at anyone. "I know, Aunt Vonnie," she murmured. Velvet was only a little irritated by her cousin's obvious enjoyment of her debasement.

"Vonnie has suggested," Andrew said, "that you might enjoy a term or two at the Female Academy." Velvet lifted her eyes quickly.

"Oh, Uncle," she breathed. "I wouldn't enjoy that at all!" One of the reasons Velvet had been shipped up here to Northville was because she'd fought so vehemently with her parents against the alternative of the Female Academy. She dared not do battle with her uncle, however. In the first place, she had no idea of the breadth and depth of his rage against her. And, in the second place, she must remember that she'd caused him great embarrassment. For now, she would have to depend on a gentle appeal—a humble one, to be sure—in the hope that, like most men, her uncle could be coerced from his determination. "Can't you think of something else?" she pleaded.

"I say," Nicole offered harshly, "we send her right back to Virginia." Again, she caught the grim flicker of her father's anger. "Well, it's only right." She defended herself hotly. "She's their problem, not ours." Velvet eyed her cousin obliquely. Mingled with her shame was the hot spark of irritation. She understood why Nicole wished to be rid of her, but Velvet was becoming increasingly aware of the injustice of her situation. She was, after all, only one half of this miserable disgrace. Holding her tongue, for now, she glanced at Cutter. His posture was one of total dispassion. She might've expected such disinterest, such blatant indifference from the scoundrel, but that awareness did not ease her impulse to jog his culpability. Velvet wanted him guilty, begging her uncle's forgiveness, shamefaced, morose. But Cutter was none of those. He stood, leaning now at the mantelpiece, his arms folded across his wide chest, watching them all.

". . . but, naturally, at the academy," her aunt was saying, "the child would be spared the horrors of the war. You were saying yourself, Andrew, that Virginia was taking the brunt of the fighting these days, that so many boys had been transported to Manassas, and that—"

"Nevertheless," Nicole interrupted, "she ought to go home where she belongs to face her shame."

"Oh, for heaven's sake, Nicole," Juliette said sharply, "will you insist we sew a red 'A' to her bodice, in the manner of Mr. Hawthorne's heroine?" Here she smiled at Velvet. "You see, we do read occasionally, cousin."

Nicole shot her sister a withering glare. "A red 'A' would be little enough punishment for the lusting baggage," she grated. "She deserves much worse, flaunting herself shamelessly before this poor—"

"How dare you, cousin!" Velvet exclaimed. She could contain her wrath no longer. "How dare you call me names. How dare you blame me *alone* for this. I did not take him by force, you know. Mr. Cutter had a thing or two to say about it." Velvet paused only long enough to catch her breath, but before she could go on, Andrew Duffy interjected.

"I agree," he said very quietly. The softness of his tone, the intensity of his proclamation brought all attention upon him. He regarded his family soberly. "Velvet is right," he continued. "She alone must not bear responsibility for what happened between these two people; that is, of course, unless she did take Mr. Cutter by force." His glance drifted to Cutter. "Did she, son?" he asked.

The two men shared what might have been perceived as a moment of roguish amusement had the subject been less serious.

113

"No," Cutter answered. Velvet noted the elusively sly glint in Cutter's silver gaze, but decided quickly that she was only imagining such a thing. He wouldn't dare take this scandal lightly—and certainly her uncle wouldn't. She looked back to Andrew Duffy, hopefully. At last someone was taking her side. Everyone awaited his next words.

"In that case," Andrew said, "we must consider that Velvet and J. Eliot Cutter are equally guilty of transgression. It follows," he continued, "that they must suffer equal reparation." He paused significantly. "It is my judgement that Velvet and Mr. Cutter become man and wife."

The gasps, the sudden expostulations, the horror he noted on Velvet's face caused Andrew Duffy not one moment of irresolution. He stood firmly before his family.

"Pa," Nicole railed, "you can't mean it!"

"Andrew, the child needs her mother here, her father's permission," implored Yvonne.

"I've made my decision," Andrew thundered. He targeted them all, impaling them with the bright blue of his glower. "I'll hear no more about it." The uncharacteristic authority in his tone preceded hastily swallowed protests. Each woman stared at Andrew dumbly, each harbored her own private conviction concerning the verdict, and at last each realized it was immutable.

Chapter Eleven

Hanna Clark might have been presiding over a Maytime revel in the emerald hills surrounding her native Londonderry. But it wasn't May, and the hills weren't green, and this was northern New York State. She bustled merrily in and out of the summer kitchen, shooing horseflies with her apron, overseeing the preparation of festive cakes — and humming. The tables had been laid outside, beneath the shimmering September sky, with pristine linen cloths and the family's finest silver. Guests were gathered, the littlest ones among them racing to hide under the tables, laughing gleefully as they frolicked with the several frisky dogs, while their parents shifted stiffly in their Sunday clothes, drank hard cider, and hailed their neighbors. Hanna was happily, exultantly, and victoriously in charge.

In the little chamber on the second floor of the Duffy house, no such revelry was evident. Dismal labor was being done there.

"Pull, Juliette," gasped Velvet hoarsely. The younger cousin drew mightily on the corset strings as Velvet held pitilessly to the straining bedpost. "Why isn't . . . Hanna up here . . . doing her job?" she gritted.

"She's . . . downstairs . . . enjoying her . . . victory," Juliette clenched out. "If it wasn't . . . for her . . ."

"We'd have had . . . a simple . . . civil . . . ceremony," Velvet finished. She was finding articulation difficult, and deemed the occlusion of her corset to be at last appropriate. "Now . . . tie it," she panted. Juliette, still grasping rigorously onto the laces, glanced wide-gazed at her cousin.

"How?" she wailed. "It's as tight as I can make it, and if I let go to tie it —"

"Wrap it around first." Velvet's groaning order gave her cousin pause.

"Shall I really?" she asked dubiously.

"Yes!" Velvet commanded. "This is the most important day of my life," she asserted in labored tones, "and I damn well intend to have a sixteen-inch waist for it." Obediently her cousin made the attempt to follow her orders. Raw and stinging, fingers slipping, Juliette exerted her most gallant effort. It was not until Yvonne entered the room, however, and hastily put her hand to the operation that the monumental effect was achieved. "There," Velvet said in panting satisfaction as she smoothed her rigid bodice.

"There what!" Juliette exclaimed. "You'll die for sure from lack of breath."

Velvet offered a preemptive smile. "Would that really be such a terrible alternative?" she asked.

"Now, darling," admonished her aunt as she shook out the white satin underskirt that Velvet was to wear, "we've been through all this. You agreed that you would suffer this day with as much grace as you could possibly muster." Velvet frowned, more in reproof of herself than anything else.

"I know it, Aunt Vonnie," she said quietly, "and I'm sorry." She had agreed, after all, to make her best attempt at a cheerful, or at least not scowling, acceptance of this terrible consequence of her weakness. She had damned herself a thousand times over the past three days. She had cursed herself with unflinching severity. Much as she blamed Cutter for what had happened between them, she took full responsibility for her part in it. And now she must pay the price. Her folly had been her downfall, and her dark, secret passions had led her to her destiny. What the future held for her and Cutter was undetermined. For now—for this day—their wedding day—Velvet must accommodate herself to the present. She glanced from her window.

Hanna was as jubilantly tyrannical as any cateress might have been. It was her day more than Velvet's it seemed. With the authority of a field marshal, she was lining up the guests for the wedding march, instructing the skinny, dark-coated preacher as to where he must stand and tossing orders to the hired girls. She placed Cutter, Velvet noted,

116

with especial surveillance.

He'd arrived only moments ago, and he stood, at Hanna's exacting command, beneath a bower of white chrysanthemums which were twined delicately into the overarching limbs of a budding apple tree. The effect, Velvet noted reluctantly, was magnificent. Against the bright azure of the late summer sky, the green of the large leaves, the pink of the apple-blossom buds, and the alabaster of the mums exhibited themselves with unconscious splendor. Nature, in all its glorious opulence—and Hanna, with her insistence that a formal religious ceremony be held—had provided Velvet with a most perfect landscape for her wedding.

Only Cutter, she observed wryly, seemed out of place. In his borrowed, broad-collared, black frock coat and white neckcloth, he might have been a figure out of a Parisian fashion catalogue. He shifted uncomfortably in the stiff trousers, and tugged self-consciously at the stock. His actions caused Velvet to experience a spontaneous surge of delight. She had no idea from where that gratification stemmed, and immediately checked her crueler instincts, but she turned with new vigor to her aunt and cousin who hurriedly adorned her for her fateful moment.

"Well," Hanna sighed after the last guest had departed, "it wasn't a Catholic wedding, but it was, faith, a pretty one—and well worth the toil." She was humming again. Carrying trays of dirty dishes to the summer-kitchen garden for washing, she seemed totally unconcerned with the night's work that lay ahead of her. In fact, Yvonne Duffy remarked to her husband, Hanna seemed to be looking forward to it.

"Well, she got what she wanted," Andrew observed comfortably as he sipped at a final tankard of whiskey. "That dear creature wouldn't have rested if Velvet hadn't agreed to the religious ceremony." He settled deeper into his chair and lifted his tired feet, resting them on the table.

"And you, love?" his wife asked. He offered her a quick, puzzled glance. "Did you get what you wanted?" She sat down across from him, resting her chin piquantly in one hand. A small, knowing smile curved her lips. In the dark, Andrew studied her.

"If you mean," he intoned, "was I glad to see them married; my answer is yes." Yvonne tilted her luminous brown gaze. "Shoot, woman," Andrew said softly, "anyone can see those two are as crazy in love as a pair of loons."

"For shame, Andrew," she reproved him gently. At the inquiring lift of his graying brow, she laughed. "You fashion yourself after a judgmental deity, banishing those two children from your garden, but you are, in truth, a sentimental old matchmaker."

"I haven't fooled you a bit, have I?" He chuckled.

"Oh, you did at first," Yvonne admitted, "but the way you danced and caroused and acted the doting father today, it wasn't hard to see that you took full credit for this union."

"Is that so disreputable of me?" he asked in mock indignation. Yvonne Duffy reached across the table to lovingly pat her husband's big hand.

"It is not," she said tenderly. "It's downright sweet."

Andrew regarded her dubiously. He'd never perceived himself as . . . "sweet". However, he reflected with a slow-coming sense of satisfaction as he sipped his whiskey, if his darling Vonnie thought him sweet, then sweet he was.

Juliette lovingly smoothed the tissue paper as she packed away her gown. Up to today, it had been her Sunday gown, a simple swirling-skirted taffeta in shades of palest green. Today had become her most perfect remembrance of Velvet's wedding—the most perfectly beautiful wedding she'd ever seen. Her mind replayed the glorious moment of Velvet's walk down the rose-strewn path to the apple tree where the radiantly handsome Mr. Cutter had waited. In her gown of ivory organza and her headpiece of wildflowers, set off by her cascading bouquet of larkspur and slender willow boughs, Velvet had been the grandest bride the world had ever known. Juliette rhapsodized now, remembering the wedded couple's kiss. How could she ever forget that sublimest of moments when the two most glamorous, elegant, lustrous people she'd ever met became one. Holding her own bouquet of wild thyme and baby's breath to her, she lay back on her quilt and envisioned the moment when she and Jason would follow their path. Everything for them would be exactly the same. She looked out of her window at the star-frosted night.

Beneath that wide panorama, that luminous vision of late-summer splendor, Velvet and her new husband were nestled somewhere, loving each other. For them, Juliette was certain, this night would be, as their day had been, perfect.

Boxes, trunks, baskets, and valises had been trundled down to Cutter's cabin. They lined the walls to the ceiling; they shifted obstinately beneath his feet as he attempted to move among them; their luxurious contents burst out and tumbled into chaotic disarray as he attempted to relocate them. Tissue paper flew as Velvet unpacked.

"I can't do this alone, Cutter," she complained bitterly as she ripped into yet another amorphous jumble of lacy things. Cutter could not begin to imagine her need for the unfamiliar and, to him, inexplicable garments.

"I was going to make coffee," he muttered.

"Coffee! How can you think about coffee," Velvet ranted, "when I have a million things to organize. My undergarments alone are going to take all night." She scooped a pile of frothy somethings into her arms, and glanced around the tiny, crowded room. "Have you another bureau?" she asked. Cutter merely stared at her.

"No," he said finally.

"Well, what am I supposed to do with these?" she demanded. "For heaven's sake, Cutter, I'm not asking for the moon, all I want is a little space, a tiny accommodation. I don't think that's asking too much."

Cutter took a calming breath. Drawing back his wide shoulders, he hooked his thumbs into his belt loops and regarded her through hooded lids. All evening, since they'd arrived from the wedding, he had held his tongue, girded his temper, reined in his impatience. He must continue to do so, he cautioned himself. "I agree," he said with distant tolerance. "It is just that I haven't any more space."

Velvet lifted an elegant brow. "You're patronizing me again," she retorted. "All evening, it's been like that. Don't think I haven't noticed it. Don't think for one minute, sir, that you are going to get away with it, either."

"And don't *you* think, madam," he grated, "that you are going to get away with—" Cutter stopped suddenly. He realized that he had been about to match her, barb for barb. He teetered on the edge of rage. Noting, however, that the storm of her blue-green gaze matched precisely the turbulence roiling in his stomach, he stiffened. Holding himself firm against what he knew would be a violent outpouring of fury, he took another tack. "Velvet," he said evenly, "do you think we might continue your unpacking tomorrow? We've had a most tiring day."

"If it has been tiring for you, Mr. Cutter," she shot back, "perhaps you should just lie down and go to sleep. I can finish my unpacking alone."

"I would love to lie down and go to sleep," he said with excessive civility, "but the bed is piled with your gaudy finery."

Velvet's eyes narrowed. Abruptly, she dropped her filmy load onto the floor. She turned to the bed and, with one wrathful sweep of her arm, cleared it. "The bed is yours," she snapped. Hiking her wide skirts, she attempted to make her way past him to the other room. Cutter jerked her to an ungentle stop.

"The bed is ours," he growled.

"Not tonight," she stated haughtily. "*You're* too tired." She moved to pass him again. Again, her retreat was roughly halted.

"Don't you see what you're doing?" he ground out.

"I don't see anything, except that my new husband is an insulting savage," she retorted. She wrenched away from him. Cutter's arm whipped out and caught her, dragging her to his hard chest. "Leave me alone," she screamed.

He grasped a clump of her thick hair and jerked her

head back. Holding her helpless against him, he glared down into her eyes. "Savage or not, madam," he said, "I am your husband. That means, *madam*, we share a marital bed."

Ignoring the warnings in the dark silver tempest of his gaze, Velvet gritted out, "I did not want this marriage, sir."

"Nevertheless," he grated, "it is done. You are my wife. Do not for one second of your life forget that." He released her abruptly, dispassionately. Turning away from her and unbuttoning his shirt, he said evenly, "Now take off your clothes and get into bed. I will, by the gods, have my wedding night."

Velvet gasped audibly. "How dare you, sir!" Cutter rounded on her so suddenly that she nearly lost her balance. Velvet believed for the first time in her life a man would strike her. She girded herself, flinching as little as possible, for the blow. It did not come. She opened her eyes cautiously.

Cutter stood rigidly before her, his shirt falling away from his darkly matted chest. The manly expanse looming before her reminded Velvet that he could, if he wanted to, render her senseless. Her chin lifted in defiance. Finally Cutter spoke. "I won't hit you, Velvet," he said roughly. "But I probably should. I should establish a few ground rules."

"Are we to have a marriage or a boxing match?" she rejoined.

"I don't know which," he answered. He raked her with a cold regard. "I shall tell you this, though, there is one rule that you may, as of this moment, consider nonnegotiable."

"And what is that?" she said lifting a defiant brow.

"You are never to refuse me my husbandly rights. And don't say," he continued, cutting off her next response, " 'how dare you, sir!' I dare because that's as it must be between a man and his wife. And that is how it will be between you and me." He reached out and pulled her to him. "You can have it any way you want, Velvet," he ground out. His eyes flashed liquid fire. "You can be what a woman is supposed to be to her husband, or you can fight

121

me. If you fight me, you will lose." Velvet wrenched away from him, but he snapped her back to face him. He lowered his lips to hers, and took her in a fierce, burning kiss. Sweeping her up into his strong arms, he carried her to the bed.

Velvet felt herself tossed onto the mattress. She bounced to her knees, intending to escape Cutter's brutality. He grasped her hair and dragged her down, covering her writhing struggle with the steel of his hard length. She gasped as he ravaged her with bruising kisses.

"No!" she raged, as he fiercely tore the bodice of her gown. She was exposed from breast to belly to his naked savagery. Her struggle was as nothing compared to the ferocity of his intent. Mindlessly, she fought him, wildly she lashed out; but he would not be stopped. He pinned her arms and straddled her. His animal strength defeated her. With one swift thrust, he entered her most treasured, guarded place, tearing away her most sacred choice. She cried out and he paused deliberately, looking down at her. His eyes flared with a silver fire.

"This, then, is the choice you make when you refuse me. Think about it, love," he growled. Her breath caught as, abruptly, he released her wrists. She might have twisted away from him, but he dragged her into a steely embrace. She could not move.

His mouth came down on hers. Her jaw clenched against his blazing kiss. Her body tensed against the hands that ranged her flesh. "Call it rape or seduction, Cutter," she gasped, "it is all one."

"We shall see," he ground out. With practiced determination, he arched her to him, opening her to the hot hunger of enticement. Her body writhed against a sudden, swelling response as Cutter tortured her flesh with stunning probings, stirred her soul with knowing explorations. Blood pounded to flush her cheeks, to inflame the kernel of her woman's need. Liquid pulsations melted the last whispers of her resistance. She moaned beneath the teasing torment of his hands and tongue, and lifted her arms, entwining them around the strong column of his neck. Her breasts, her belly, her woman's essence were consumed in the fire of his relentless power.

"Oh, Cutter," she gasped raggedly. "I do want you." She opened herself, flowering to the throbbing heat of his man's sun, blossoming in the dew-burst of her own surging will. He took her then, with a completeness that immersed them both in a flood tide of elemental currents. Their rapture billowed, crested, culminated in the shuddering maelstrom of their mutual need.

Nesting deep in the hollows of repletion, Velvet felt the warmth of her gratification ebb slowly. Rivulets of realization ran suddenly cold in her veins. *What had she done!* She felt dashed on the rocks of reality, torn to shreds on the icy arrogance of Cutter's will. Her body stiffened in his arms, and Cutter knew, immediately, that he had won, and that Velvet despised both herself and him for that victory.

As he rolled away from her, he recalled his threat to her. He had cautioned her that if she fought him she would lose. She would always lose, he reflected, but so would he.

In the darkness, Velvet turned her back to him — the sweating, panting, hairy brute. Her wedding night, she thought derisively as she curved herself into a tight, protective ball. It should have been the most perfect blending of two young souls. She looked out of the window above the bed. It allowed the luminous night to enter the room.

The starshine bathed them both in silver light, softening the contours of their marriage bed. It gazed down on the two young people who did not succumb to its sleep-inviting softness for a very long time.

Chapter Twelve

Sunday afternoon dinners with the Duffys had become a ritual for Velvet and Cutter. Each week they trudged the pathway from their tiny cabin to the main house preparing themselves for the various attitudes which would greet them. Juliette was invariably ecstatic to see them, believing giddily, as she did, that they were the most romantic of couples. The truth was, though a certain peace existed between them, and even at times affection, they had not come to complete terms with their relationship. Velvet was unsettled and frankly frightened of Cutter's power over her, and Cutter was keenly aware of her resistance. Her resistance angered him at times, or sent him into black, somber reflection — but it did not deter him. Resistant or not, Velvet was his wife, and he would not be denied his rights as a husband. Thus, a certain ambivalence, an uneasiness that could not be shed, clouded the handsome, newly wedded couple.

They were met by Hanna with motherly concern; they looked thin, she often observed. Were they getting enough sunshine, enough exercise? Yvonne Duffy wrapped packages of food and pies for them to take back to the cabin, and Andrew greeted them with avuncular good humor. It was only Nicole Duffy who did not welcome them enthusiastically. She made her disapproval of their union and of them clear. At table she was either cold or snide. Her attitude caused discomfort for all, especially Velvet. For she knew, only too well, that Nicole's observations were terribly, horribly true.

"How is the happy couple?" Nicole would inquire with sneering contempt. "Yours is a marriage not made in heaven, but on the Duffy spread. I wonder if that makes a difference in a relationship." On a particular Sunday in the fall, she remarked caustically, "Shotgun weddings have always seemed to me to be the stuff of which ironies are made. The patriarchs enforce them to ensure a secure future for the offending couple, but how can that couple possibly be secure knowing that neither of them really intended the marriage to happen." She shook her head in a mocking display of lamentation. "I don't know about anyone else, but I prefer old-fashioned romance to coercion, especially where something as sacred as marriage is concerned."

Hanna, at that moment serving a bowlful of gravy, was hard pressed not to dump it into the young woman's lap. Juliette eyed her sister narrowly. Andrew and Yvonne exchanged surreptitious glances.

Velvet, deciding for the moment at least to defend her marriage, speculated, "On the other hand, cousin, haven't some of the most romantic marriages in history been products of . . . coercion of one sort or another?"

"For instance?" Nicole challenged.

"It is well known that Napoleon I married Madame Josephine de Beauharnais when he was only a First Consul. He was told by his advisors that the marriage would profit him most significantly. And I might mention that it did."

"He later divorced her, as I recall, cousin, and married the younger and sweeter Austrian archduchess," Nicole countered triumphantly, "whom it was said he had really wanted to marry from the start."

"I am also thinking of Henry Plantagenet and his lovely Eleanor of Aquitaine," Velvet parried.

Nicole smiled. "He jailed her, if I'm not mistaken, for the better part of their marriage, extending her imprisonment because he was enamored of the extraordinary Alys."

"What about Mr. Aaron Burr's daughter, Theodosia? She and Mr. Alston were forced to marry—"

"And she died quite young—*quite horribly young*—on his steamy Southern plantation, which she, incidentally, abhorred." Nicole sat back and patted her lips with her napkin. She exhaled a deep sigh of satisfaction. "It would seem, cousin," she said obliquely, "that your examples of enforced romantic liaisons merely support my observation that such marriages can only end most tragically."

"Well," Juliette stated with certainty, "that's not going to be the case with Velvet and Mr. Cutter." She eyed the couple, tilting them a reassuring smile. "I just know their marriage is bound for a happy ending."

Velvet smiled back weakly. She had no choice but to accept her younger cousin's optimism, she could certainly not depend on history to support her claim that enforced marriages could also be sound ones. Apparently, she reflected, glancing at her husband, she could also not depend on him.

Cutter, as always, regarded Nicole's barbs with dispassion. He was rising now from the table. He and Andrew were adjourning to the parlor where they would enjoy their after-dinner drink. They stood before the mantel, casually discussing whatever it was men discussed, while the women helped Hanna clear the table.

"You do think everything will be fine between you, don't you?" asked Juliette as she walked to the kitchen carrying dishes and linens.

Velvet, eyeing the men and transporting her own burden, shrugged one shoulder. "One can never be sure, little cousin," she answered, "but I'll tell you this." She glanced around, searching for Nicole. That young woman had already made her way to the kitchen. "I'll do more than my best, if for no other reason than to prove your sister wrong." Both women giggled conspiratorially.

Once the dinner dishes had been washed, the women joined Cutter and Andrew Duffy in the parlor. The late afternoon and evening were passed pleasantly enough with conversation. Velvet was enjoined to entertain the family with several remembered pieces on the pianoforte. Her music was enhanced by Juliette's pretty alto voice and even, at one point, Andrew's base and Cutter's clear baritone. Her own well-trained soprano completed the quartet. Hanna and Yvonne formed a particularly appreciative audience. Nicole had excused herself early, much to everyone's relief, and the family enjoyed their Sunday together. It was soon after Hanna offered a light supper that Velvet and Cutter departed, as they always did, for their cabin. Nicole made an appearance long enough to remind Cutter that a political meeting was to be held in Cranberry Creek the next night. She admonished him that, as a citizen leader, he above all others must be there. He merely nodded and escorted Velvet from the house into the cool of the autumn night.

Woodsmoke and the scent of moist earth filled the air. Velvet walked confidently, her arm snuggled in Cutter's. With him, as always, she felt safe in the snarled, ensnaring environs of the pine forest.

"What is your meeting about?" she asked after they had walked for some moments.

"We hope to see to it that a certain law is issued," he said curtly.

"What law?" Velvet persisted. He looked down at her and cocked his brow. She had never been very much interested in his activities before. In fact, on the occasions when he'd left the house in the evenings, she'd seemed glad to be rid of him. She'd not asked questions, nor even inquired as to his destination. Even when he'd taken his last trip south, and Velvet had gone up to live at the Duffy house for a week, she had not questioned either his reason or his objective.

"What makes you so curious tonight?" Cutter asked. Velvet merely shrugged. She did not know why she'd asked him the question. She knew she was not, in fact, curious about Cutter's politics—even where they involved Nicole. She did not deem her cousin a threat to her marriage. Cutter rarely spoke of the woman, and, despite her dire predictions concerning them, Velvet realized that she was not the enemy. If there was an enemy to their marriage, she realized intuitively, it was something between the two of them—or something that was not between the two of them.

"I just wanted to know," she said quietly, still wondering at her own curiosity.

"If you must know," Cutter answered, "we are lobbying Mr. Lincoln with petitions and letters. We hope he will issue what will be known as an Emancipation Proclamation. If he does, it will cause a most violent reaction from the South."

"It sounds serious," Velvet murmured.

"It is," Cutter replied. "It could mean the end of . . ." His voice trailed off, and Velvet looked up quickly.

"The end of what?" she asked.

"The end of many things," Cutter said lamely. He knew that it would mean the end of the life Velvet had known, the end of the genteel, refined elegance that had characterized the South. Cutter wanted this proclamation because he knew it would end the bitter custom that enslaved human beings to other human beings. But he realized, as others did not, that it would pave the way for the industrialization and exploitation of that gentle world and its equally gentle people. He perceived, as others did not, that beneath the horror of slavery there was another element, personified by Velvet. He glanced at her now, her dark, flaxen-streaked curls glistening beneath the September moon. This woman was no tyrant, and there were others like her. There was a whole generation of quiet, courteous Southerners who had no perception of slavery as it really was. It was those people, that generation of mild-minded sons and daughters of the old South, who would be ravaged by this law. And the law would come, he reflected. Lincoln would have to be a fool not to issue it — and Mr. Abraham Lincoln was no fool.

They entered the cabin reluctantly; neither of them quite willing to end their unaccustomed intimacy. The cool, scented night was behind them as Cutter shut the door, built up the fire, and sat down to his small desk cluttered with rocks and writings. As always, Velvet busied herself with tidying the cabin; it was always in need of tidying. She removed her gown and slipped into a soft night robe. Fluffing goose-down pillows behind her, she reclined on the bed with one of her favorite books; a volume by the scandalous French writer Madame Dudevant who called herself George Sand, which Velvet's mother had sent. For reasons unknown to her, Velvet could not concentrate on the poetic language, the unconventional ideals which usually titillated and enlightened her. Tonight, for some reason, she felt unfocused, vaguely disoriented. She looked up to catch her husband in the next room in a familiar posture. As always in the evening, he was hunched over his writings, the silver gleam of his spectacles catching the lamp-light. She watched him for long moments. The ebony of his curls, in his concentration, fell over his bronzed forehead in glistening, boyish abandon. His broad shoulders shifted occasionally beneath the confinement of his cotton shirt.

Velvet rose and thought to close the curtain that separated the two rooms, but instead, for some reason, she moved into the larger room. Stepping softly, she went to the window over the small sofa and pushed it open. Glancing up, Cutter offered a half-smile. He, too, was glad of the sudden soft coolness that wafted into the cabin.

"It's warm." Velvet tendered the words offhandedly, but she gazed at her husband with a certain unexplained hope of approval.

"Yes," he said quietly, perhaps sensing her need.

"Maybe I'll open the window over the bed as well," she offered. Cutter nodded. He wondered, as he so often had over the past weeks, at this little change in her attitude. These eddying, shifts of mood were an enigma to him. Like flashes of liquid sunlight on stormy days, they signified a certain possibility; the possibility that one day there could be between them a certain peace, a certain bright hope. But he would not pin his optimism too blindly on these quicksilver moments. Velvet was still the mercurial creature he had married. The sharpness of her tongue still wounded him. The acrimony of her indifference still had the power to bruise him. He slid his glasses down from the bridge of his nose and looked over them.

"You are full of surprises tonight, love," he intoned.

"Am I," she said, lifting her chin. "I don't think it should come as such a surprise that I am warm on a warm night, Cutter."

"That's not the surprise," he answered her. "That's not the surprise at all." He pushed back his chair slowly, raising himself. He faced her, his broad shoulders drawn back. Between them there was the heavy, expectant dread that had haunted their evenings since their wedding night. They both knew that the lovemaking would come, as it always did, at Cutter's insistence; hard, intense, sometimes offering pleasure, most times leaving them empty and unfulfilled. Cutter hooked his thumbs into his belt loops. "This new attitude is most appealing," he said huskily.

"I don't know what you mean," she said, laughing lightly. Even to herself she sounded giddy and uncertain. "I declare, if you aren't the most odd-talking husband in the whole world," she went on. "My attitude is just the same—just exactly the same—as it's always been."

Cutter said nothing, but he slid off his spectacles and slid them onto the desk behind him. He moved toward her and touched a tumbled curl that framed the ivory shimmer of her neck. His rough fingertip moved tenderly down the curve of her shoulder to rest on the swell of her breast above her nightgown.

"No, it isn't," he said at last. "There is a softness about you tonight, a yearning perhaps"—his voice lifted questioningly— "that I've not seen before."

She tilted her gaze. "A yearning for you?" she murmured.

"Yes," he answered on a breath. Velvet felt the hot turbulence of sudden and unexplained hunger fill her. It was very much like her dream-clouded ecstasies of long ago. She had succumbed to those hungers, she had surrendered to Cutter's siren call, and her heart told her that she must again. Her thoughts raced to their wedding night and to all the nights— the weeks of nights—that had followed. Resentment for the debasement those nights represented warred with recollections of the rare times when Cutter had aroused in her those yielding moments of aching need. In that flash of an instant as he touched her, as his warm breath enfolded her, thoughts and emotions battled wildly within her. She looked at him, up into the melting silver of his gaze, and in that moment her heart hardened.

"I suppose," she said evenly, "I was very much disturbed by my cousin's talk today. I always am, Cutter. It doesn't seem to bother you in the least."

He cocked a smile. "Oh, Velvet," he said gently, "you mustn't let Nicole upset you. Though, if it leads to this sort of sweet change, then—"

"There is no change," Velvet said archly, "and you mustn't think it. What there is, Cutter, is a determination to prove Nicole wrong." Her words hung in the air between them, and Cutter's brow furrowed in question. Velvet removed his hand

130

from her breast, and shrugged one shoulder gingerly. "I am determined to be a perfect wife to you," she said without emotion. "I will not fight you again." She lowered her gaze at his silence, and then raised it as quickly. "Though a proper Southern gentleman would not think to impose his attentions on his wife, you apparently have another code of behavior altogether. I accept that." She lifted her chin. Her eyes, in the golden lamplight, were polished turquoise. "Do what you will with me, Cutter," she said resolutely.

Cutter's mouth became a grim line. "I see," he intoned. After a pause, he said, "Is that what you think a perfect wife is suppose to be?"

Velvet's gaze cocked. "Of course," she answered. Her sincerity could not be questioned. "In other circumstances, at home in Virginia I would be the perfect hostess. I would entrance your influential friends with my charms. I would put on perfect dinners and perfect balls, I would run a perfect household for you. And I would have your babies," she continued, lowering her gaze once again.

"In that, at least," said Cutter with grim amusement, "we Northern barbarians agree with our genteel Southern brothers."

"Yes," Velvet conceded quietly. "But," she said, lifting her gaze, "in that alone. The men of my acquaintance would not think to merely pleasure themselves with their own wives; decent women held a more elevated position in their lives. We are a different breed, Cutter. But I won't go into that. I believe I have come to terms with what you expect of me, of what I must do if I am to survive here. I really do want our marriage to work," she finished earnestly. "Divorce would be unthinkable."

Cutter stood over her, gazing down on her. He could barely credit her innocence of anything that resembled reality. Checking his irritation, he realized that Velvet had her own reality, her own truths, learned at her mother's knee. For the moment, at least, he must succumb to that reality. Velvet was trying so hard, he realized, to bring what she'd learned while in the North together with what had been ingrained in her from her youth. As in all things, Velvet was an eager student.

No matter that her learning was slow, often tentative, more often uneasily faulty, she was making the attempt. For that she was to be admired. And, in many ways, Cutter did admire her. She was a good little soldier, he thought fondly. He hid a tender smile. Intuitively, he knew that in her determination, she would not appreciate his making light of her efforts.

"Where shall we start?" he asked seriously.

"With tonight," Velvet answered. Judiciously, she placed her arms around his neck. She closed her eyes, and lifted her face to him. "You may kiss me," she said resolutely. Cutter's hard gaze drifted over the opaline perfection of her skin. When he did not respond immediately to her invitation, Velvet's eyes snapped open. "Don't you want to kiss me?" she asked, dismayed.

"Oh, yes," Cutter replied laconically.

"Well, then," she said, once again closing her eyes and offering her lips to him. Again, he merely stood before her. Her eyes unclosed slowly. "Isn't this what you wanted?" she inquired tartly.

"Not quite," Cutter said evenly.

"Oh, for heaven's sake, Cutter," she said, jerking away from him. "What *do* you want then?"

"Let me show you," he answered huskily. He swept her suddenly up into his arms, and gazed down on her. Uncertain and decidedly leery, she felt herself transported to the smaller room in the cabin. He lowered her onto the thick folds of the bed cover. Slowly he unbuttoned his shirt. Rhapsodically, she watched as he removed it, baring the dark matting of his muscular chest. The virile expanse of him came toward her, and she felt that familiar heat of unexplained hunger writhe beneath her flesh. Cutter lowered himself next to her, and she felt the weight of him and the warmth of him next to her. He took her into his embrace, simply holding her next to him. Velvet felt tension slowly ebb as he stroked her. Soft words caressing her, moist breath seeping into her soul, she realized that same enrapturing pleasure that she had known their first time together. But this time, Velvet was perfectly aware of what was happening to her. This time, the dream faded. This time, reality took hold. His feathered kisses were real. His

132

tongue tickled and enticed her flesh to tingling ripeness. She felt a liquid awareness of him in the middle of her stomach, and it reached tentacled fingers out to touch and tease her.

Cutter's hands and mouth ranged her neck and breasts and shoulders and belly, pleasuring her with tender pressures, tantalizing abrasions, teasing nips and sucks. She moaned softly, longing to feel him fully against her. He lifted her in one strong arm and slowly, rapturously slowly, he removed her gown. Her own fingers, unguided went to the fastenings of his trousers. Impatiently, she pulled at them, drawing them apart, releasing to her yielding desire that wholly perfect instrument of his manhood. Cutter assisted her, pushing at his trousers while holding her and continuing to take her flesh with demanding kisses. He drew her to him, the hardness of his hunger tauntingly close to the core of her womanly need. Velvet arched to him, taking full pleasure in the consequences of her acquiescence.

The dream was real. She breathed in his manly scent. She tasted with her own mouth the manly feast of him. She touched and teased his bronzed flesh with her fingers, as he, aware that her hunger was nearing its peak, brought her to her fullest awakening.

Velvet felt the first fiery bursts of unbridled want. Her nails raked Cutter's hard back, her teeth bit into his flesh. He lifted himself over her. In the dim lamplight, he was like a polished bronze statue over her, but Velvet knew he was a man. She knew he could gratify that searing need. She lifted herself to him, opening wholly to his command. She shuddered wildly at the thrust that penetrated her desire, intensifying it, liquifying it so that it melted to all parts of her. Her body heated, as Cutter's silver gaze fused her awareness to frenzied elemental realization. Nothing would ever be the same between them — nothing. In this, at least, they were one. Pleasure, heightened to rapturous ecstasy united them, welded them, unified them into one soul. The throbbing euphoria of their union lifted them beyond earthly boundaries and they felt themselves transported. Touching the voluptuously golden light of self-awareness, they were ravished by the heat of their perfect Elysian paradise. The pungent sweetness of their pulsing harmony throbbed to shattering completion as, together, Velvet and Cutter touched the sun.

Velvet heard Cutter's hoarse groan. She clutched him to her, her own quickening senses, like butterfly wings, flitting and fluttering between darkness and light. For that fierce, searing moment, he was her and she was him. No egos, no separate minds came to interrupt the grandeur of that unity that made them more than one. Holding together they emerged from that perfect blending of lighted star and earthly awareness to float protected, the music of the night encloaking them, in each others arms.

"Oh, Cutter," she breathed as he held her in the nested sphere of his embrace. "I will be the perfect wife to you." He gazed down at her, his smile tender.

"My Velvet," he intoned. "You are."

Long hours passed as Velvet listened to her husband's even breathing, and fought sleep. She did not want to sleep, she did not want to lose this night, this moment of purest marital bliss. She watched him, the cadent rise and falling of his chest. John Eliot, the preacher had said. "Wilt thou, John Eliot Cutter, take Velvet Elizabeth McBride . . . ?" John . . . Johnny . . . Jack. John and Velvet. Velvet and John. Mr. and Mrs. Cutter; the perfect couple. At last sleep, and love-lit dreams, did come for Mrs. Cutter—the perfect Mrs. Cutter, at last.

Chapter Thirteen

"Dammit, Velvet, I will hear no more of it," Cutter bawled. The cup he'd hurled against the wall shattered stingingly, and Velvet flinched against sharded missiles.

"Oh, yes you will, Cutter," she shrieked. "Oh, yes you will. I will bother and nag you about this to my dying day."

"Your dying day," he growled, grabbing her shoulders and snapping her to him, "may come sooner than you imagine, madam, if you persist."

Velvet jerked from his grasp, and grabbed a fireplace poker. Flinging it, barely missing her husband, across the room, she shrilled, "Don't think you can manhandle me, sir." The near miss startled them both into sudden silence. "I am not asking much, Cutter," Velvet finally gasped out, her breath coming raggedly.

"You are asking a great deal," he rasped, "and I want an end to it."

"Mother sent me this catalogue, and I demand that I be allowed to order from it." She held the little pamphlet aloft. "Damien Archambault is the finest designer in Paris. He offers a collection to American women once in a decade, Cutter! For heaven's sake, do you want me to miss out on it?" As Cutter smiled tightly, Velvet's regard darkened and she placed her hands on her hips. "Don't you dare find this amusing," she warned. "Oh, I know you tend to dismiss the importance I place on clothing, but I have given up every other luxury in the world, and I won't give up that."

"Velvet," Cutter said, hiding his smile and making a poor attempt to sound reasonable, "you have more clothes — gowns and gloves and petticoats — than you will ever need. Why order more?"

"In the first place, Cutter," she said rigidly, "this is Damien Archambault we are discussing. In the second place, everything I have is old. My clothes are patched and mended; they're not in style. I'm ashamed to be seen in them. In any case," she finished haughtily, "the first place should be reason enough."

"You are not ordering a one-hundred-dollar gown from that catalogue," Cutter rejoined, his patience snapping. "And I don't give a good goddamn who designed it."

"Mother said that Pa would pay for it," Velvet retorted, knowing this would—as it always did—enrage Cutter. But he was not enraged this time. Instead, his expression seemed one of pity, or gloom, or . . . something. Velvet's brow quirked.

"Your Pa is not going to be paying for much of anything these days, Velvet," Cutter said quietly, "and not for a long time."

"What are you talking about? Pa's a rich man."

"Nobody's 'rich' anymore, love, nobody—not in the South, at any rate."

Velvet knew a sudden dread. "Has Pa lost all his money . . . or something?" she asked in awe.

Cutter shook his head sadly. "Money is not the issue, Velvet." He looked into her wide, stricken gaze. "Oh, love," he said softly, moving to her.

"What is it, Cutter?" she demanded breathlessly. "You are just scaring me to death."

"I know," he said kindly as he took her into his embrace. "There is more than enough money in the South," he added. "Women bring their money to market in baskets—and take their food home in their pocketbooks."

"I don't understand," Velvet wailed softly.

"It's hard to imagine," Cutter said, holding her. "It's very hard—especially for people in the South who have always depended upon trade for their wealth. The South sends its cotton and tobacco north, and in return the North sends tools, machinery, and weapons to the South. That's how it's been for decades, but now that trade has been cut off by the war. Southerners were ill prepared for this war, Velvet. They had no idea what it would cost them in terms of the necessities of life. Everything is at a premium now. With all their wealth, people just cannot buy things, because there's nothing to buy."

"But surely Damien Archambault would take my father's money," she said, hope lifting her tone.

"Damien Archambault would be a fool to take your father's money, love. The Confederate dollar will be worthless when this war is over; it will be more worthless than it is even now." He looked down into her eyes and tried to smile. "The only thing Monsieur Archambault would be able to do with your father's money is make a dress with it. Now wouldn't that be an innovation—a paper dress."

Velvet drew away from him. She was in no mood for whimsical speculation. "I still don't understand, Cutter," she said quietly.

"I know," he answered. "I know." He realized that Velvet would not understand until she saw for herself that the legacy of her forefathers—the Southern aristocracy, "the flower" of American culture—had been doomed by Southern arrogance. He dropped his regard. They had grit, the Southerners, but they had from the start taken the path of least resistance. While the North had operated on a grander scale—developing industries and trade with foreign countries—the people of the South had utilized their huge landholdings and their rediscovery of a primitive invention—chattel slavery—to insulate and isolate themselves from the real world. This provincialism could go on for only so long. It had gone on, in fact, for as long as it could, and now it was over—or nearly over—and what would be left, all too soon, would be the ashes of a great burning pride.

Velvet rubbed her hands together disconsolately. "If things are so bad at home," she said uncertainly, "I should be there." She glanced quickly at Cutter. She saw that his jaw had set obstinately. "This is no time for your husbandly doggedness, Cutter," she stated impatiently. "On

137

your next trip south, I'm going to be with you."

"I've told you before, love," he said quietly, but with deep, unyielding significance, "your place is here. You are my wife now; this is your home. *This* is your place."

"Oh, dammit, Cutter, how can you be so stubborn?"

"You come up with a new reason for going south every week, love," he answered. "I've told you that one day when this war is over," he added pointedly, "we'll visit your parents. In the meantime, get used to staying where you belong."

"But I *don't* belong here," she cried. "Haven't you been able to see that? It's painfully obvious that I'm still an outsider. The women gawk at me, the men are scared to death of me. Aunt Vonnie and the rest of the Duffys—excepting of course for Nicole, who hates me—are my only friends."

"You've got me," Cutter said, offering a broad grin.

"You!" Velvet's voice was heavy with irony. "You're no friend to me, Cutter. You're never here—and when you are, you're hunched over your desk with those damned rocks of yours."

Cutter winced. This sharp-tongued minx still had the power to inflict painful injury. He hooked his thumbs in his belt loops and drew back his shoulders. "You're talking about my work, Velvet."

"Your work," she said dismissively. "You send reports up to that university and they send you back just enough money for you to buy more paper and ink. What kind of 'work' is that? You don't even get paid for your other 'work.' Everything you do for your precious cause, you do at your own expense—at my expense, Cutter. I am sick of it." She sat down heavily on the small sofa and kicked out at a ramshackle foot stool. It rocked and waddled across the small room until it finally fell, one of its rickety legs splintering and thunking dolefully onto the rough flooring. They both watched, awed by the little spectacle of ruin. "I didn't mean to do that," she said petulantly. "I didn't mean to wreck your furniture. Lord knows—"

"It's your furniture, Velvet," Cutter said softly. "And

138

maybe that's the point. Maybe you haven't yet come to the conclusion that this is your home, and everything in it is yours." She looked up, an oblique and sly smile tilting her lips.

"Including you, Cutter?" she asked.

"Including me," he acknowledged.

"That's the difference between us," she said tartly as she rose. She made her way into the smaller room of the cabin in a puff of satin skirts.

"What do you mean by that, Velvet?" he asked, his tone dangerous. Velvet did not heed the danger.

"Just what I said." She slipped her dress over her head, and stepped out of her petticoat. "You say you're my husband—my friend. You profess great heaps of love for me. But I haven't seen any evidence of it." She stood with her back to him, in only her corset and shimmies, brushing her hair slowly, deliberately, before the newly installed standing mirror. "When I profess something, I give my all. I said I was going to be the perfect wife to you, and you must admit, I am." She glanced over her shoulder, expecting his affirmation. When it did not come, she turned, in a blaze of righteous anger. "Well, I am," she shot out. When he did not answer, she continued. "I am, too, the perfect wife," she railed. "Don't you dare deny it." Cutter merely watched her. "You are saying more," she grated, "with your silence than you ever could with words, Cutter." She glared across the half-curtained archway. "Are you telling me I'm *not* the perfect wife?" she asked incredulously. "Don't I lie down on that bed every night and let myself be slobbered over without saying one single word. Do I protest? Do I complain?"

"Do you enjoy it?" Cutter asked lazily. Velvet lifted her little chin.

"Maybe I do and maybe I don't, but that's hardly the point."

"What is the point?"

"The *point* is, I do it for you," Velvet said haughtily, "because I am trying my level best to be a perfect wife. I do it because I know that's what you want."

139

Cutter stepped toward her and leaned on the door jamb, his broad shoulders and towering height filling the aperture. He raked her with a scathing perusal. She stood there before him, her cheeks pinkened with defiance, her raven curls pale streaked and tousled about her face and shoulders, her eyes flashing a satiny, aquatic luster. "I was under the impression," he said quietly, "that you wanted it, too, love."

Velvet began to spy the danger. "What I wanted, Cutter," she said, turning from him and shrugging hastily into her dressing gown, "was to show you — and everyone else, including my cousin — that an enforced marriage was not necessarily an unhappy one."

"Because, if you don't want it," he continued as if she had not spoken, "I could take my . . . 'slobbering' elsewhere." Velvet turned quickly to glance at him and then as quickly turned away. She began to brush rebelliously at her hair.

"If someone else would please you more," she said sharply, "then do so. If that's what you want, John Eliot Cutter, that's what you may have. I won't fight you on that, either. I am determined to be a *perfect* wife." Cutter moved further into the room. Velvet saw his reflected image behind her in the mirror. She hesitated her brushing chores long enough for him to perceive an uncertainty. *Damn!* she reflected inwardly. The warmth of him, that masculine-scented heat enfolded her. Cutter's big hands came around and cupped her breasts, his thumbs teasing the response he knew would come. Her head rolled back onto his hard chest. "Oh, Cutter," she breathed.

"You were made for love, Velvet," he said huskily. "Why do you deny it so?" With tantalizing slowness, he drew off her robe. In the mirror, she saw revealed the lushness of her figure. Above her corset, her breasts mounded, blue-veined, shuddering against the luxurious rapture of Cutter's caress. Her tiny waist, made tinier by the corset laces, curved to a ripe fullness at her hips. Her flesh strained against fragile lace, and Velvet knew that she was

140

lost. Languidly, Cutter undid her corset, sliding it away to reveal the ripened peaks of her desire. He dropped to one knee and drew down her bloomers, petal soft against her skin. She stepped from them without thought. Her long, slender legs sheathed only in silken hose, she watched mesmerized as Cutter knelt before her. His muscular arms holding her to him, he took her flesh in agonizing kisses, tormenting her most secret places with his tongue and teeth. Her breath tore raggedly from her. "Do you want it, love?" he asked, his mouth ravaging her. Velvet felt the first liquid bursts of fiery hunger overwhelm her.

"Yes, oh, yes," she gasped. "I do, Cutter. I do." He raised himself slowly and lifted her into his arms. He gazed down at her as she arched herself to his command.

"And no more talk of . . . slobbering?" he asked, only a hint of amusement apparent in his tone.

"Never," she breathed.

"Then, you shall have your wish, princess," he said, moving to the bed. He set her down on it, and she felt his weight and heat follow. Velvet felt no prick of annoyance, as she should have at his practiced manipulation of her. She melted into his ravishing embrace.

He took her with easy confidence, with demanding tenderness, with enthralling command. It was only a long time after, as she lay in his muscled embrace, replete, fully blossomed, that the first vague hint of uncertainty entered her thoughts. She ran her fingers lazily over the dark fur of his chest.

Offering him a piquant perusal, she murmured, "You've done it to me again."

"Done what?" he asked hoarsely, enjoying his own unhurried moment of perfect gratification. When she did not answer immediately, he looked down at her as she rested in the bronzed nest of his caress. "Done what, princess?" he repeated.

"Made me want to . . . to . . ." She sat up impatiently. "Oh, you know, Cutter," she blurted out. "Once again, you have made me want to . . . love you," she finished with an embarrassed mutter. Cutter's gaze glinted in amusement.

"Is that so bad?" he asked, his smile deepening as her consternation grew.

"Of course it is," she said earnestly. "Don't you know that at home I would be considered a loose woman?" Cutter laughed fully now. "Make sport if you will," Velvet reproved, "but I'm quite serious." She drew herself out of the bed, pulling the blankets with her. "A decent woman isn't supposed to like . . . that sort of thing." She wrapped herself in the tangle of bed coverings and went to the hearth. Cutter watched appreciatively as she bent to build up the fire, noting that, in the process, her behind peeked out perkily from its confinement. She pushed at the water kettle, swinging it over the newly kindled flames, and turned back to her husband. Noting exactly where his gaze was riveted, she wrapped herself more tightly. "Honestly, Cutter," she said disgustedly, "you're just as lascivious as you can be—and with your own wife! When we do go south, you must promise me you won't tell anyone," she huffed. Cutter sprung from the bed.

"I'll give you lascivious, princess," he said, lunging for her. In the tumble of bedclothes, Velvet could not keep her balance and she plunged, Cutter twisting and taking their fall, onto the rough floor. They rolled about wildly, laughing and wrestling, until the bedding—but for one thin sheet—fell away; then Cutter lifted her over one powerful shoulder, and naked except for the dubious protection of the patched swath of linen, Velvet was swept out into the other room, through the door and outside.

"No, Cutter!" she shrieked. "John Eliot Cutter, you take me back inside. You're just depraved, sir."

"We noble savages enjoy making love in the great outdoors," he said as he smacked her backside and continued his progress. Velvet's shrieks and laughter covered the sound of several horses crashing through the brush. It was only after they were surrounded that the couple noticed they were not alone in the "great outdoors."

Cutter stopped short, and Velvet commented that at last he'd come to his senses. Noting his sudden intake of breath, she glanced awkwardly over her shoulder, seeing, to her absolute horror, what he was seeing.

"Mr. Cutter, sir," one of the men said hesitantly. "Hello, sir," said another. "Pleasant day," offered another man.

"Mighty pleasant," Cutter replied easily. Velvet cringed wildly, though she did not attempt to free herself. Better to stay just exactly as she was, she reflected; perhaps she might go unnoticed.

"How do, ma'am," said a fourth man, tipping his hat respectfully, if a bit uncertainly.

"How do," Velvet muttered flatly. She drew the sheet more tightly around her bottom.

"Any particular reason you boys have stopped by?" Cutter asked genially. "Not that you need a reason, of course."

Oh, dammit, Cutter, Velvet railed silently. *Will you stop being so almighty sociable!*

"We thought you'd want to be first to know, sir," one of the men said excitedly, "so we rode up first thing."

"Uncle Abe has done it! He's gone and done it for us, Mr. Cutter."

"He's gone and issued that Emancipation Proclamation we've been hoping for, sir," the first man exclaimed.

Velvet was not prepared for the whoop Cutter let out. He threw her into the air, and very nearly didn't catch her as she dropped like a stone. Then, grabbing her, he swung her in an exuberant dance, twirling and lifting her over the pebbled ground. She nearly lost what little protection she had against the not completely averted, awestruck gazes of their guests.

"Congratulations to all of us!" Cutter exulted before he realized Velvet's discomfort. Hastily, he reined in his excitement and placed her, with delicate and exaggerated chivalry, behind him. His smiles matching those of the assembled men, he said, "Boys, I'd offer you a drink, but you can see, I'm kind of indisposed. Get yourselves up to the Duffy house and tell Andrew. I'll be up in two shakes of a bobcat's tail." He waved, as the men rode off, then turned enthusiastically to Velvet, but was immediately cowed by her withering glare. Arms folded pointedly over her breasts, she eyed him wrathfully.

143

"How could you," she seethed. "How *could* you!" In those three words, her voice reached a shrill crescendo. She turned on her heel and stormed into the cabin, dragging her sheet and her hard-held dignity behind her. Cutter knew, as surely as he knew that Adirondack crustal rock contained iron ore, that he would have to live with this day for a very long time.

Chapter Fourteen

Velvet sewed, as she always did on Tuesdays and Thursdays, with her Aunt Vonnie and Juliette at the main house. Her stitches were becoming more utile and less decorative, she sighed inwardly. She supposed that was as it should be—as it must be for an Adirondack woman. She settled deeper into her heavy woolen shawl and dreamed of lighter moments, of stitching carelessly with Mammy Jane before the dancing log fire in the sitting room at Sweet Briar Hill. By this time winter would have settled over Brandy Station, as it had over Northville, New York, but it would be, by far, a more gentle winter. She glanced out of the frosty window at the icicles that had formed on the eaves of the house. They hung like angry, jagged teeth against an angry winter landscape, harsh and chill, and menacing. Velvet shuddered against the cold that suddenly invaded her soul.

"Are you all right, child?" Yvonne Duffy asked gently.

"I'm fine, Aunt Vonnie," she said vaguely. "I was just thinking. . . ." Her voice trailed off. Yvonne and her daughter exchanged glances.

"I'm going to get some tea," Juliette said with forced cheerfulness. She and her mother shared another concerned glance as the younger girl left the room.

Yvonne Duffy slowly dropped her sewing into her lap. "A mountain winter is hard on a woman," she offered softly.

Velvet managed a small smile. "Every winter everywhere is hard," she said, hoping to alleviate her aunt's worry. "I'm doing just fine."

"You know something?" Yvonne said brightly. "You really are." Velvet looked at her in puzzled surprise. The older woman nodded her head with certainty. "You are doing much better than I did my first winter. Now up in

Canada we were rather used to harsh winters, but I don't think anything could have prepared me for the awesome loneliness I felt that first winter here." She smiled in sad remembrance. "It's one thing to live out a hard winter, it's another to envision a hard life.

"Your mother and I were born in the little town of Deschênes, outside of Toronto. The town was named after my grandfather who founded the first settlement there, and we were the town's first family. Oh my, Alicia and I were what you might call debutantes up there. Well, naturally your mother, marrying a wealthy Southern boy, went right into a pampered life, but I had set my cap for Andrew Duffy." She laughed softly. "I wanted that man, and I didn't care what it took to get him. I didn't even care that I'd end up the weathered old bag of bones that I am." She waved long fingers at Velvet's protest, and smiled deeply. "It's true," she said, "and I don't give a skunk's hind end about it. I love my life. It's a hard life, but as long as Andrew's in it, it's a beautiful one."

"What makes it beautiful, Aunt Vonnie?" Velvet asked earnestly.

The older woman regarded her questioningly. "Don't you know, darling?" she said. Velvet shook her head. "Oh, my," said Yvonne Duffy. "I'm not sure myself." Both women laughed. "I suppose," said the aunt dreamily, "it has to do with liking someone. It has to do with liking that person better than anyone else, and wanting to be with them. It has to do with sharing your life — with sharing every part of yourself. Yes," she said at last, "it's liking and sharing."

"Hanna says to remind you, tomorrow is fish cleaning day," Juliette said as she came into the room with the tea tray. Velvet groaned audibly. How she hated fish-cleaning day. She hated her fish-cleaning lessons almost as much as she hated her hearth-emptying exercises. This learning to become a homemaker was as distasteful a process as anything Velvet had ever done. She wrinkled her nose. "I'm sorry to be the bearer of bad tidings." Juliette laughed as she handed Velvet a cup. Velvet took it gratefully and wrapped her stiff fingers around the hot surface. Actually,

Juliette admired her cousin as much as she'd ever admired anyone in her life. Her admiration soared as Velvet's abiding dedication to her chores had grown. It was not that Juliette particularly admired good housekeeping, but she did admire determination. And no one was more determined than her cousin. No one, in her experience, worked harder or tried more diligently to accomplish something. In her romantic dreams, the sixteen-year-old Juliette imagined Velvet doing all of this for the handsome J. Eliot Cutter. She could not have known that Velvet felt she had little choice in the matter. She had become increasingly uncomfortable with running to her aunt and Hanna each time she was unsure of something. She'd become increasingly uneasy over their gifts of food. Velvet was nothing if not independent. And now especially, during the long, painfully cold months of the Adirondack winter, trips up to the main house were tedious and, most importantly, noticeable. She had counted six pairs of footprints on the snowy path through the woods one day, evidence of her six trips up to the house for advice or warmer blankets or clothes, or for some other reasons. She had resolutely brushed out the footprints, and decided that day that she would learn once and for all how to do things for herself. She had realized that her earlier forays into the art of housewifery were mere frolicsome preambles to the real thing.

Velvet had learned to wash clothes in water melted from snow and heated laboriously over the fire. She'd learned to fashion mittens from rabbit skins, and to dress and stew the little animals from which the skins were stolen. And tomorrow, once again, she would practice cleaning a fish; she'd already learned the art of ice fishing. She recalled with humor her journey with Cutter to the center of Doriel's Pond to fish through the ice. Checking herself hastily, she remembered, too, that she'd been less than happy with the results. Cutter had tried to show her how to clean the slimy wall-eyed pike they'd caught, but her revulsion along with his impatience had impelled the whole affair to a nasty end. They had fought dismally . . . and made up as they always did, going to bed—without their supper that night.

Velvet sniffed, and rubbed a roughened fingertip beneath her nose. She did not wish to remember *that*. She looked up ruefully at her relatives.

"I suppose the next thing I'll be doing is gutting a roaming hog." She managed a small laugh. Her aunt and her cousin watched her appreciatively. All three women knew, as did Velvet, that, indeed, might be the next step in her education.

"Just worry about the fish for now," Juliette said brightly. They all laughed.

At that moment, a hard, impassioned rap shook the heavy front door.

"Now who could that be?" Yvonne wondered aloud. Hanna made her way into the parlor and waved the woman back into her seat.

"I'll be getting it," she said, wiping her busy hands on her ever-present apron, "though I can't imagine who it could be with the men all up at the logging site." She opened the door and a chill wind raced through the already cold house.

"Mrs. Duffy?" the man inquired without introducing himself.

Hanna stepped back and indicated Yvonne who rose hastily.

"What is it, young man?" she asked, stepping from the parlor into the reception area.

"I got a youngster out here, says he belongs hereabouts." The man jerked a heavy thumb over his shoulder toward the road outside. "Says his house is farther on up the road, but he wants to be let off here. I just wanted to make sure it's okay."

Juliette and Velvet stood. "Who is it?" the younger woman asked.

Yvonne leaned toward the man and looked around him. She could see nothing but the great sleigh outside, its team prancing silently in the thick snow. She looked questioningly at the visitor.

"Says his name's Amsterdam. Jason Amsterdam. You ladies know him?"

Juliette's eyes widened. A gasp, and then a shriek, rose

148

from her breast. "Jason!" she cried, and started for the door. The man stopped her urgently.

"Let me bring the boy in." His tone belied the aggression in his manner. He looked down at the smiling girl. Juliette's smile faded as she saw a solemnity in the man's look that presaged something other than the happy homecoming she had immediately envisioned.

"What is it?" she breathed out. "Is everything all right?"

Yvonne went to her daughter.

"Was Jason hurt?" Velvet asked, stepping to her cousin, and placing her arm around her slim shoulders.

"I'll get him," the man said quietly. He turned then, leaving the women standing in the icy chill. They watched as, slowly, painfully, he drew the young Jason from the interior of the carriage. "Take it easy now, son," the man said, his words deadened in the frost-heavy air.

He walked with the limping Jason up to the house. Hot tears glazed Juliette's eyes as she saw the crumpled, weakened figure make his way, with the assistance of the stranger, along the path. "Oh, Jason," she whispered. She stepped from the door. The other women did not stop her; nor did the man, as she placed her arm beneath Jason's splinted elbow and brought him the rest of the way inside. The man stood apart, as did the women, as the young couple made their way into the parlor. Without words, the driver retraced his steps back to the sleigh. He gave a cursory nod to the three women at the doorway, then snapped his team to a start. Silently, the door was closed. Without speaking, the women moved to the parlor. They watched as Juliette tenderly unwrapped Jason's muffler, as she looked with aching love into his face, as at last, painfully, Jason smiled.

"I'm finally home," he said softly.

"Those smarmy Southerners ought to pay dearly for this," Nicole railed.

Juliette glanced woefully at her sister. "Please keep your voice down," she said worriedly. "This is the first time he's slept since he arrived." The family had gathered at the table. With Jason tucked securely in bed, his parents informed of his arrival and expected at any moment, he had at last slipped into a troubled sleep. Hanna had shooed everyone from the room, advising that Jason ought to be left alone for a change. She would keep a caring eye on him, she said, while the family ate their dinner. She came down the stairs now, to hear the exchange between the sisters.

"And he is sleeping," she stated firmly. With a significant look toward Nicole, she added, "And it's sure the sleep'll be doing him more good than the promise of revenge."

Nicole eyed the woman narrowly. "You're getting snippier and snippier every day, Hanna Clark," she said truculently.

"And that's the truth," Hanna conceded cheerily. "Maybe it's because me indenture's almost up." She made her way back to the kitchen, and returned to the family in time to serve the dessert course.

"Nothing like your raisin pie, old girl," said Andrew Duffy. He cast an oblique glance at Cutter. "I hope you've made an extra one; this boy's eating like he's never seen food." Everyone laughed, and eyed Cutter slyly.

He offered a self-deprecatory grin. "I suppose," he said, accepting a huge chunk of pie, "I'm just not used to all this physical labor, Duff." Cutter had, at the beginning of the logging season, accepted a job with Andrew Duffy at his logging site.

Nicole glared at Velvet. "If you weren't married to this spoiled descendant of the Southern aristocracy, you might be able to carry on your real work and not have to worry about making money."

Juliette snorted. "Oh, for heaven's sake, Nicole," she said derisively, "does Velvet look like an aristocrat?"

Nicole managed a tight smile. "Actually, little sister, she doesn't," she remarked snidely. "What *have* you done to yourself, cousin?"

Velvet flinched inwardly, but made an outward show of defiance. Lifting her little chin, she said, in her best regal tone, "Why, I can't imagine what you mean, Nicole sugar. I believe my clothes, designed by that world famous couturier, Monsieur John Eliot Cutter, are the most original one could find." She pulled her deerskin vest, made for her by her husband at the beginning of the season, tighter across her uncorseted bosom. "And my hair was designed by the finest barber in the world, Monsieur 'Mountain Blow!' " She gave the name her most practiced French enunciation, and haughtily patted her tousled curls which were lifted heavily, with no bow to style; to the top of her head. "Now my shoes," she went on, lifting a bearskin-booted foot. . . .

"Make sport if you will," Nicole said through the uproarious laughter, "but you look like a tempest-tossed waif!"

"And what would you expect me to look like, cousin," Velvet rejoined hotly, "A breeze-tossed flower, in this ungodly wilderness?" The exchange had taken on a hard edge which the family noted uncomfortably. Cutter regarded Velvet, through the uneasy silence that followed, with what might have been admiration. Velvet noted his look but shrugged it off. She knew the truth. She looked awful—just as her cousin had, in her barbed way, pointed out. In Cutter's pants, cut off and rolled and his shirts, stuffed into any available opening, she looked no better than the trashy squatter women back home. Velvet was a disgrace, and she knew it, but she was damned if she would let Nicole know she knew it. She smiled sweetly, and regarded her cousin through veiled lashes. "You just wait till I get my gown from Monsieur Archambault," she said. The family made a great show of clearing throats and pushing plates away. It was well known that Velvet and Cutter had battled mightily on this very subject. Cutter must have conceded defeat, Andrew reflected wryly. He could not know that, for Cutter, the battle was lost before it was begun on that day in front of his cabin, when he'd made the foolish decision to be impetuous, when news of the Emancipation Proclamation had come.

A keen, pained groan came down the stairs. Everyone lurched from their seats.

"It's Jason," Juliette cried, starting with everyone else for the stairs. Hanna was there in an instant.

"Let the girl go to him," she commanded. "The rest of you, get to the parlor. I've got some elderberry wine to serve with the coffee." When the family did not respond immediately, she snapped, "Now get!" Obediently, they retired to the parlor, and only Juliette was allowed to attend the fallen Jason.

The family talked quietly, as they drank their coffee, and listened for sounds from upstairs. Jason's papers had said that he had been wounded, shot in the arm, at the Battle of Fredericksburg, Virginia. Lying in a hospital, he had contracted diphtheria. He still had remnants of the raging fever which had made him incoherent and hallucinative. There was no treatment for the disease, and it was decided by the doctors in the South that he should be sent home as soon as the fever had abated. Their best advice, according to the documents that had accompanied him, was to bathe him regularly with cool water, keep him comfortable, and force as much liquid down him as he could bear. This the family had been doing. The doctor had been sent for, and he had shaken his head mournfully. This was the result he was seeing more and more these days. A terrible rampage of disease was the scourge of Northern boys living and fighting and starving in the humid Southern climate. Unaccustomed as they were to the differences in climate and food, the boys were succumbing more to disease than to the ravages of battle. The young and vibrant Jason had endured both.

Later in the evening, Velvet listened silently as Jason's father spoke with Cutter and Andrew Duffy. The other women had accompanied Mrs. Amsterdam to the sickroom, while the men had remained below. Velvet had, after her initial visit to Jason, decided that all the company he was enduring, as Hanna had pointed out, did him no good. She had excused herself to sit in the parlor with the men.

"You know," Cutter was saying, "you men cannot think to go on with this forever."

"Once a reformer, always a reformer," Mr. Amsterdam commented genially.

"But it's true, George," Andrew put in. "What Cutter says is quite true. The trees can only last so long. Eventually, we will both have to exercise some conservation measures."

George Amsterdam nodded ruefully, and looked down into his wine glass. "Try to convince the other loggers of that, Duff," he said softly. "It'll be me and thee—and of course Mr. Cutter," he added, raising his glass in an amiable toast to the younger man, "against all of them."

Cutter accepted the toast with a nod. "They must be made to understand," he said, "that we are now cutting down trees at the rate of nearly ten thousand a year. The Adirondack forest cannot endure such exploitation."

"And yet," Andrew said dolefully, "it will be exploited, if not by the likes of George and me, then by others. The need is great, boy. Lumber is a vital resource in this country. Every roof is made from wooden shingles. Furniture, clocks, buckets, baskets, the plow, the harrow, the pipes for leading water are all made of wood. Wagons, bridges, fences, and most roads are made of wood. Now this is all to say nothing about the growing pulp industry, and the fact that those vests you and your wife are wearing were tanned by means of the tannin in the hemlock bark." Velvet found herself surprised by Andrew's reference to her. She looked up, but realized that he was not speaking to her or, for that matter, about her. Andrew went on. "Do you realize, it takes an acre of forest a day to keep a large iron furnace going with charcoal? Why there are nearly four thousand sawmills on the Hudson River alone."

Velvet's nose wrinkled. As always, the men were deep in a conversation that only they understood. They would exclude her, even though she was sitting right here in their company. It was the way with men. She looked up longingly toward the staircase. Even if the women were here, she decided, she would be in no better company. She didn't enjoy their talk of sewing and cooking and keeping their houses dry. She was doing what they did, all right, but she surely did not wish to discuss it. Where do I fit in? she wondered idly. Life was much less complex when all she had to worry about was getting the men's attention. She could do that easily enough, she reflected slyly. Checking her wicked instincts, however, she merely sipped at her coffee and waited for the evening to end—or for some encouraging word of Jason to reach the parlor.

The women came down the stairs, talking, deciding about the young man's further care. Velvet could see the relieved look in Juliette's eyes when it was determined that Jason should remain at the Duffy house, as it was closer to the doctor in Cranberry Creek. Hanna and Juliette would be the primary care givers, and that suited Juliette just fine. Velvet took her hand as she entered the parlor.

"I must admit to a certain selfish motivation for wishing him well," the older girl said gently. "As soon as he's able, I would love to talk with him about Virginia."

Juliette patted Velvet's hand. "I know about 'selfish motivations,' cousin." She giggled. "I want him well, too."

"And he will be well very soon," said Yvonne Duffy consolingly. "He's a strong lad."

"That he is," affirmed Mrs. Amsterdam as she was helped into her coat. "We'll be by tomorrow, Yvonne," she said. "And thank you—all of you. My sweet boy could not be in better hands."

Velvet and Cutter said good night soon afterward, and made their way through the soft, sparkling winter night to their cabin.

Chapter Fifteen

The winter had melted into an uncertain spring before Jason was allowed to join the family in the parlor. On that day, near the end of April, the Duffys and Velvet and Cutter had met with the joyous Amsterdams to welcome him from his sickbed. He weakly descended the stairs, while the families saluted him with spring wine. His voice, which he had used rarely since the winter, came hoarsely.

"Thank you all," he managed. He offered a sweeping, if unsteady, bow, and was immediately dizzy. He was necessarily, and ruefully, helped to a chair by a reproving Juliette.

"You will be the shame of this house, Jason Amsterdam," she scolded. "If you don't allow yourself to recover fully, everyone will say we didn't do our job properly."

"But you have," Mrs. Amsterdam said softly. "I cannot thank you all enough." She smiled around the room. "Yvonne has taken care of my son as if he were her own," she said. "Look at the lovely robe and slippers she made him. And Andrew. You've been the finest surrogate father a young gentleman could have."

George Amsterdam toasted Andrew warmly. "If it couldn't be me with him all these months," he said, "I'm glad it was you, Duff."

"And Velvet, dear Velvet," said Mrs. Amsterdam going to the girl and embracing her. "Jason tells me you've spent hours reading to him. I can't thank you enough for his newly awakened love of Shakespeare." She laughed.

Jason regarded the younger woman wryly. "I had little choice in the matter," he said hoarsely. "I was a captive audience."

Everyone enjoyed the lad's returning sense of humor.

"But it was Hanna's beaver stew that did the trick," Mrs. Amsterdam laughed. "No one makes it like you, Miss Clark." Hanna beamed.

"It was a pleasure, Mrs. Amsterdam, for such a worthy boy."

Cutter noted the sheaf of papers in Jason's hands. "What have you got there, son?" he asked.

"Oh," Juliette said, running to Jason, "these are his drawings." She lifted the large representations and held them up for all to see. "I've written to *Harper's* about them, and they want to see them," Juliette went on brightly. "They're pictures of the war." One by one, the drawings made the circuit of the room. One by one, the realistic depictions of devastation passed before Velvet's gaze. The ruins of the bridge at Lackburn's Ford, the evacuation of Manassas Junction, the occupation and burning of Norfolk lay before her disbelieving eyes. The caring Juliette realized her mistake too late. She felt a surge of regret when she saw the horror in her cousin's face. Hastily, she gathered up the pictures. "Isn't it silly" — she laughed uncomfortably — "people wanting to see pictures of something so awful?" By that time, the room had become silent. Jason bowed his head, knowing that the depictions were nothing — only pale imitations of the reality.

Velvet's voice came clearly, and hollowly, through the quiet. "Mother writes that people take picnic baskets to the battle scenes, and watch them from a safe distance."

"It's true," Jason acknowledged in his soft murmur. "There is both fascination and revulsion in people's view of war — or any catastrophe. It is not my intention to exploit that double perception, however. I believe the reality ought to be brought home to people. Perhaps the next time humanity thinks to make war, others will look at these pictures and remember — and think again." Tears glistened in his sad gaze. Jason was remembering.

Velvet went to him and tenderly touched his freshly shaven, young cheek. "It is truly horrible, isn't it?" she said, her words as much a revelation for her as an observation.

"Yes," Jason said quietly.

Velvet seemed to gaze into a far distance. "I didn't know." She turned slowly to Cutter. "I'm going south," she said simply. Cutter watched her retreat from the house. In him there was no remonstrance, no repudiation. His wife had the quiet dignity, at that moment, of a suffering animal. He felt his throat tighten, and he turned from the awed and questioning faces in the room. He knew, at that moment, that he and Velvet would be going south.

Spring burst gloriously on the Adirondack Mountains that June of 1863. Sunlight, glittering and innocent, shone through the moist canopy of the trees, drying the rain-swelled, pine-needled floor of the wilderness. As glacial till raged down jagged mountain slopes in the melting warmth, plump mosses cushioned the thin-soiled rock. Shadbushes blossomed early, and heavily. Ferns emerged and flaunted their feathery new growth. Streams, released from winter's icy confinement, burbled and sparkled exuberantly over stair steps of rock-strewn earth. Deer, rabbits, squirrels, and woodchucks fed on the soft, juicy flowers of the deciduous trees, while birds flitted about through the pines, singing their springtime song. The lushly foliated wood burst each day with new life. It was no time, Cutter thought restively, to leave the Adirondack forest. But, leave it he must.

He had never seen his wife so determined. She had spoken of going south before, but never to the extent that she had talked of it that winter. The whole, long, harsh, chilled season, she had planned their leave-taking with the certainty of one who had made a decision. Cutter realized that no amount of dissuasion would stop her. If he chose not to accompany her, Velvet would make the trip alone. But, naturally, he could not allow such a thing. As she sat before the fire in the evenings, he eavesdropped on her plans, casually glancing at her lists, asking seemingly idle questions, and he understood how ill-equipped she was to make such a journey. The fact that she had been determined to leave Northville before the spring thaw had given him his first glimpse of her unrealistic thinking on the subject. Cutter had managed to talk her into waiting till the spring before undertaking the journey. He argued, reasonably, that roads were often impassable, inns were often closed to travelers during the more inclement months of the winter because of icing conditions on the paths leading to them, and shortages of food. Innkeepers, he explained, were likely to close their doors and their larders to guests in deference to their families.

Velvet had listened tolerantly to his discouragement and decided that he was right—about the timing of her trip. Cutter was less successful when he attempted to dissuade her on other grounds. What could she possibly do? he asked her. What use could she be to her family? She would be another worry to them. She was sent north, in the first place, so her parents might be easy in their minds over her. Velvet had lifted her chin on more than one occasion, and had informed Cutter that if he saw so many negative elements in her decision, he was perfectly free to remain in Northville. She was going south.

Cutter stood now in the debris of the logging site. Strewn shards of bark and fallen twigs would be gathered by the cleanup crew as night fell. Their work was just beginning; Cutter's was at an end. Andrew Duffy approached him ruefully.

"She's still determined?" he asked.

"She is," Cutter answered, as he received his final ninety cents. "Thank you, Duff," he added quietly. "This job has been a real blessing to both Velvet and me." Andrew smiled knowingly, a twinkle of amusement in his pale eyes.

"Well," he said finally, checking his impulse to comment on the exigencies of marrying a woman with expensive tastes, "you've been a blessing to me. You're the damnedest worker I've ever had." He placed a heavy arm around Cutter's shoulders. "You've got a job next year, if you want one." Cutter returned his smile.

158

"You may not want me, Duff," he said. "Remember, I'm a reformer. I'll be on you and all the loggers up here about conservation."

"We'll appreciate your insight, boy," Andrew said solemnly. "We don't want the trees to run out either." He watched as Cutter doffed his wide-brimmed hat and strode off through the forest. "We'll be by tomorrow morning to see you off," he called out.

Cutter approached the cabin with a growing sense of dread. He saw what he had feared; the cleared area around the front door was scattered with luggage. Baskets, boxes, and trunks were heaped in uncertain piles. A low groan emanated from his throat. "Oh, Lord," he said, reining in immediately, the impulse to reprove his wife on yet another thoughtless design. He wondered how she could imagine that it would be possible to carry this excessive amount of baggage, but thought it best to simply apprise her of their itinerary.

"I think I mentioned," he said quietly as Velvet stepped from the cabin, "that we will be traveling by horse to Albany." Velvet nodded brightly and held out a sun-dried towel to him.

"Yes," she acknowledged simply.

Cutter paused, thinking as he ducked his face and head into the water barrel. He emerged from the cold water, his skin and hair glistening in the low, glowing sunlight.

"We cannot," he said very softly, "take all this with us." To his surprise, Velvet was laughing.

"For heaven's sake, Cutter," she said, her hands on her hips, "I know that."

Cutter cocked an uncertain brow.

"This is all," she continued, sweeping a hand out to include the strewn luggage, "going up to the main house. You don't think I'm intending to leave my precious things *here*, do you? I've asked Aunt Vonnie to store them for me." She shook her head, and offered a sorrowfully reproving smile. "Do you think I'm a dolt? I may not know a lot of things according to your standards, John Cutter, but I do

159

know how much a pack horse can be expected to carry. Now dry yourself, and come in to supper," she said, turning back to the cabin. "You look awfully silly, standing there dripping wet—and with your mouth open."

Cutter watched as she stepped—rather smugly, he thought—from his view. He closed his mouth pointedly, and slowly wiped at his dripping face and hair. Would he ever come to understand this minx he'd married? He doubted it. Her variety never ceased to amaze him.

The scent of woodsmoke and frying venison steaks at last entered his consciousness. Here was yet another example of Velvet's remarkable transition. From a spoiled, uncompromising Southern aristocrat, she'd emerged as a paragon among Adirondack women. With an interior wince, Cutter realized that she had developed her skills more out of a fierce desire for independence than out of any great love of him, but that made the transition no less extraordinary. He wondered, as he moved inside, anticipating yet another exemplary meal, what the move back to the South—temporary though it may be—would bring about in Velvet's behavior. He wondered, too, what they would find there.

The war had become the North's principal business, by this time. The Union soldiers were the best-clothed and equipped army in history. President Lincoln had declared that the Confederates were "rebels" rather than "belligerent" in this conflict. This fine point in international law made the conflict a rebellion—a "family fight" —rather than a full-fledged war, and neutral nations were discouraged, by law, from giving aid to the South. While the North was receiving arms, munitions, and supplies of all kinds from abroad, European nations were significantly stymied in offering aid, trade, or correspondence to the South.

Equally important was the fact that the South was slowly being cut off from all other areas of the country. Lincoln's government had taken possession of all railroads and telegraph lines, effectively cutting off communication and transportation so vital to the far-flung armies of the Confederacy.

Before going to bed that night, Cutter checked his smooth-bore musket carefully. Though he was not used to conversing with the Deity, he made a silent prayer that he and Velvet would not have to fight their way to Sweet Briar Hill.

Chapter Sixteen

Hanna had put up several jars of lichen jelly, and Juliette had made little pillows stuffed with the aromatic needles of the balsam fir.

"Tell your mother and father that those little pillows are said to be very healthful," she said as she handed up the package prepared for the McBrides. "You just sniff the odor of the balsam, and you'll feel much better." Velvet smiled down at her little cousin. She would miss the girl's bright optimism deeply. She leaned down from her saddle to give Juliette one last hug.

Yvonne Duffy offered her own souvenir of the Adirondack Mountains in several jars of sugar maple syrup. She also handed Velvet a letter for Alicia. Andrew Duffy made his own contribution to Velvet and Cutter's journey. He slipped the younger man a small sack of coins.

"Take care of each other," he said softly, watching the two as they at last spurred their horses and took leave of the Duffy spread. Jason stood apart and waved as the couple rode off. No amount of admonition had had the power to stop Velvet from this folly, he reflected sadly. She would have to see the destruction for herself, if she was to believe it.

Only Nicole was not there to say goodbye. She had shown up long enough that morning to consider Velvet's traveling costume and wonder snidely what her Southern belle friends would think of her "outfit" of Cutter's rolled-up trousers, cut-off shirt and wide-brimmed deer hide hat. Perhaps it gave the unfortunately bitter Nicole some pleasure to imagine her cousin in rags. But Velvet had other plans. She did not bother to mention that she'd packed suitable clothing for when she and Cutter were out of the wilderness.

Lovingly, she had smoothed the Archambault creation and a riding frock over the top of their packed things. They would be heading into Albany within a few days to catch a train south, and Velvet would be forced by conscience to contact her friend Morgana Carleton there. She did not intend to greet Morgana in Cutter's chopped-off raiment. Velvet would make very certain to take the little industrial town—and Morgana Carleton—by storm, in her Damien Archambault gown.

For the time being, she must be content with practicality. She and Cutter would be riding over wilderness trails, and fine and delicate fabrics had no place here. They would be heading down along the Sacandaga River, through marshlands, and for the most part through uncleared territory to the little village of Fish House which would be their first stop for the night. Velvet had hoped to visit the little town of Mayfield where, it was said, they had a string quartet that played the music of Wolfgang Amadeus Mozart, but Cutter had told her that their route would not accommodate such a deviation even for one so illustrious as Herr Mozart. Velvet had pouted and had informed Cutter that if a cultural oasis bloomed in the Adirondack wilderness, she wanted to experience it. Cutter promised that when they returned he would surely take her there.

When they returned. The words echoed in Velvet's thoughts. As they rode now, on this refulgent spring morning, she wondered whether she would be willing to return to this uncompromising wilderness. Here she had heard the horrifying cry of the timber wolf on full-mooned nights. She had seen the high, jagged peaks of unconquerable mountains of rock. She had felt the icy arctic winds of an Adirondack winter. Here, she had experienced, as nowhere in her life, the stern depths of nature's darkest power; a nightmare world, savage, gnarled, devouring. She glanced quickly at Cutter. She had also experienced here a certain growth of feeling—for both the land, and for her husband. What was it, she wondered, that would draw her back to this place, to these fierce and unyielding mountains? Would it be that inexplicable response to something she had not yet begun to understand? In truth, Velvet doubted such a thing. Secretly, in her most private moments, Velvet still ached for the gently patterned ways to which she'd been bred. Even as she and Cutter traversed the sun-brightened channels that twisted through the forest, Velvet longed for home. Once they reached Sweet Briar Hill, she doubted that she would ever again leave it.

The little trickle that was the Sacandaga River wound into the village of Batchellerville on the second day of their journey. Cutter greeted people he had known, and introduced Velvet. Friendly faces beamed bright welcomes as the couple passed through. They stopped for lunch at a little inn near the edge of town, and Velvet enjoyed the house specialty, caribou steaks. She complimented the proprietress warmly before she and Cutter left.

Their journey, this second day, would take them farther than they'd traveled on their first day. Cutter had wanted to measure Velvet's stamina, and, finding it worthy of the most seasoned veteran of Adirondack travel, he decided they would be able to cover more ground than he had at first believed. It was well into dusk before Velvet complained.

"Cutter," she said, her lips forming a thin line from weariness and chafing, repressed dissatisfaction, "is it necessary that we make the entire trip to Virginia in one day?"

He glanced at her. "Did you say something, princess?" he asked.

"I did," she replied tightly. "I was just curious as to whether or not you intend on stopping tonight. Or did you plan on going straight through to Sweet Briar Hill?" The last sentence was said sweetly, but with more than a hint of displeasure. Cutter smiled easily.

"We'll be stopping in Hagaman, at the house of an old friend of mine," he said, as they continued to ride. "I had actually planned this part of the trip to take two days, but since you responded so well the first day, I thought we might be able to—"

"Remind me," Velvet interrupted sullenly, "not to respond quite so conveniently to your brand of torture in the days to come."

Cutter laughed, leading them even farther into the darkness of the falling night.

The moon sprung out of the black, star-clustered night as the little town of Hagaman lit the horizon. A few houses, yellow-lit against the dark, greeted the weary couple, but it was a church building to which Cutter led them. A lofty steeple rose ghostly pale in the moonlight. Velvet eyed the steeple, and then her husband uncertainly.

"Are we going to church?" she asked in a whisper. Cutter shook his head and smiled. He pointed to the church roster. It read: The Rev. Dr. Taylor, minister.

At that moment, a greeting was called from a small house on a slope behind the church. Velvet could make out the figure of a man carrying a lantern approaching.

"What can I do for you folks?" the man greeted them. As he came nearer, Cutter swung from his horse.

"It's me, Cutter," he called out, with a wave of his arm. The lantern went down quickly, and the man began to run down the sloping hillside and into Cutter's hearty embrace.

"Why, John Cutter," the man cried joyfully. "How in the blazing hell are you, lad?"

Cutter turned to Velvet. "Meet the Very Reverend Harmon Taylor," he said, smiling roguishly. From the height of her mount, Velvet looked down on the little frock-coated gentleman in dismay.

"How . . . how do you do, Dr. Taylor," she managed, and offered her hand. Harmon Taylor took it with exuberant warmth, nearly managing, in the bargain, to dislodge Velvet from her saddle.

"You must be that adorable little wife John has told me so much about," he said cheerfully. "If you're not," he added with a rakish wink, "I've got the subject for my sermon next Sunday."

"This is," Cutter assured him, "*Mrs*. John Eliot Cutter." As he assisted Velvet to the much anticipated, and clearly welcomed, ground, he said, "We need a room, Harmon. Can you spare one?"

"I can spare several," Taylor said jovially, as he led them up to the house, "but, to be quite frank, John, I hadn't expected such a request from you since the proclamation was issued. Didn't expect to see you hereabouts." In almost the same breath, Harmon Taylor called to his wife, "John Cutter's here, Emmie. Light the lights, old girl, and pour out a tankard of ale for the boy."

In the yellow-lit doorway there appeared a heavyset woman, her hair netted, her face warm in greeting. She held out thick arms at the trio's approach.

"Johnny Cutter," she called. "You just get your behind up here, and let me hug you! Oh, it's been too long." The woman bustled Velvet and Cutter into the house. "Cool tonight—cold, really. Got a nice fire to warm you. I just put on a pot of water for tea. Get yourselves in here now, right into the parlor." She turned at last to Velvet. "You're the sweet little Velvet Johnny talks about all the time," she said, surveying her guest, and continuing her flow of welcome. "Now you just take a load off. Sit down right here and tell me all about yourself. I've been just dying to meet you." She looked up, still smiling, at her husband. "Get us all something, Harmon, love. What would you like, honeypot?" she said to Velvet.

"Tea will be fine," Velvet answered in the quick silence that followed.

"Tea for me, too, Harm," the woman said, then addressing Velvet once again, she added, "You wouldn't like a little something stronger?" Velvet shook her head. "Then tea it is. We'll save that old devil moonshine for another day." She laughed. "Oh, by the way, I'm the Very Reverend *Mrs*. Taylor; Emmie to my friends." Once again Velvet offered her hand uncertainly, and Mrs. Taylor shook it enthusiastically. "Sit down, Johnny," she ordered. Cutter did so. Emmie turned back to Velvet. "Now tell me all about yourself." Velvet was not quite sure if it was now time for her to speak. She waited for a moment to see whether or not her hostess was truly finished.

When the older woman continued smiling silently, Velvet decided that it was, indeed, her turn to talk. "I'm from the South," she blurted for lack of forethought on the subject.

"Are you?" the woman asked with interest.

Velvet nodded. "My parents sent me north when the war started." The Very Reverend Mrs. Taylor proved to be as exuberant a listener as she was a conversationalist. Velvet found herself telling the interested and warm-hearted Emmie everything she could think of about herself. "And then Cutter and I were married," she finished, eliminating, naturally, the details which necessitated the marriage.

"Why, that's a grand story," Emmie Taylor exulted. "Can you imagine, Harm, the two of them meeting up here like that, and falling in love and all?"

Harmon Taylor nodded indulgently. "It is a grand story, sweetheart," he said to his wife. "And any kin to the Duffys is a friend to this house," he added warmly. He glanced at Cutter. "We've heard only wonderful things about that family." He stood. "Let's get these two fed, love," he said to Emmie. "Help me in the kitchen. I've taken care of the horses, John. You two go and freshen up. Take your old room." Cutter led Velvet upstairs, as the older couple retired to the kitchen to fix their supper.

It was very late before Cutter and Velvet finally got to bed. Stories had been exchanged, laughter shared. Velvet had been apprised that the Taylor home had been, like the Duffys', a safehouse in the Underground Railroad. It was this connection, and the older couple's natural warmth, that had led Cutter to stop here for the night. And Velvet was deeply pleased they had. The bed, thickly covered with downy blankets, looked warm and inviting.

"Ow," she moaned, as she at last felt the resulting sting of the day's ride. Up to that point, she realized, she must have been numb. "Oh, Cutter," she implored, "you'd better help me." He was at her side in a moment. Together, they peeled the trousers from her aching bottom. Cutter lifted her, and swept her to the bed, laying her gently into the thick folds. There would be no demanding of his husbandly rights this night, he resolved.

They lay together in the moonlit dark, Velvet moaning piteously from time to time, and Cutter damning himself a thousand times for keeping such a grueling pace. Tomorrow, he vowed silently, they would not ride more than twenty miles—less, if Velvet's tender behind demanded it. In any event, the trip was, Cutter consoled himself, going well. They would be in Albany within the next few days, and then it would be on to New York City, and south. He was right to have insisted they wait until spring was firmly upon the land before they started out. It made the trip so much less complicated.

Chapter Seventeen

The little city of Albany, New York, its Dutch origins plain in its architecture, spread out beneath Velvet and Cutter as they watered their horses in the great trough atop Pinkster Hill. Fairytale buildings, with their high-ridged roofs and "step" gables facing the street, a picturesque church, its twin towers lofting against the misty skyline of the Helderberg Mountains, and, to the east, glimpses of the brawling Hudson River dotted with steamboats bespoke a social fabric dominated by pride in ancestry and vitality of spirit. The orderly grid system, by which the streets of the city were arranged, allowed a view of the riverfront, which seemed to teem with bustling life.

Velvet sat her horse rigidly. "I wonder where the Female Academy is?" she said tremulously. Cutter tilted her a smile.

"We could go right on through," he offered. "We don't have to see your friend." Velvet shot him a hopeful glance. Her expression as quickly changed to one of rueful acceptance and then resolve.

"No," she said firmly, lifting her chin. "If the Carletons ever got wind of the fact that I was in Albany and didn't visit Morgana, why, there is no telling what they'd do. They would cut the McBrides from every season here to Sunday. Mother would be so embarrassed. And Pa depends so on Mr. Carleton's nasty old sloops to get our tobacco north; I simply couldn't risk offending the family." Cutter said nothing. His lips formed a grim line. He could not bring himself to assure Velvet that Mr. Carleton's "nasty old sloops" were probably sideling idly in Richmond Harbor at that moment — and they would be doing so for a long time to come. She would know, all too soon, the truth of how life

169

in the South had changed. Instead, he snapped his horse to attention.

"If I remember correctly," he said, "the academy is on North Pearl Street. Shall we go?" he asked as he spurred his mount. The sudden, horrified protest that emanated from Velvet's lips caused him to jerk the reins, and bring the startled animal to a wheeling halt. "What is it?" he asked.

"Cutter," Velvet groaned incredulously, "you don't expect me to greet Morgana Carleton for the first time in nearly two years looking like this, do you? How can you be such an oaf? It'll take me at least twenty-four hours—and maybe more—to ready myself for such a confrontation!"

Cutter had not thought of this. He checked any exasperation he might have been tempted to feel, and recalled the Velvet McBride he'd first met. Meticulous in her dress, rabidly deliberate in her grooming, the Velvet of his memory quickly evaporated with the reality of what he now beheld. The snippet before him, garbed in worn trousers shiny from travel, an oversized shirt, begrimed and hinting at the odors of long days on the road, was by no means the delicately scented flower of the South. He smiled. How the mountains—and marriage to him—had changed her. The sweet bow of her lips pouted in the shadow of the wide-brimmed hat she wore mashed over her wildly curling, upswept mane. Her eyes, wide, flashing a turquoise challenge, offered both a plea and a command.

"Let's find ourselves a hotel," Cutter said softly. Velvet's grateful smile was his reward as he led them down the hill to the best hotel in Albany, New York.

The lobby of Stanwix Hall on Broadway was not a tranquil place that warm spring evening, as Velvet had hoped it would be. Instead, the swank hotel seemed to throb with sophisticated life, soft laughter, and effortless refinement. Velvet kept her eyes firmly on the finely patterned Brussels carpet as she entered. As she and Cutter checked in, receiving skeptical looks from the clerk, women in smart gowns brushed by on the arms of distinguished gentlemen. Velvet had hoped to make an anonymous entrance into Albany society, but somewhere high above the domed roof of the elegant building, the fates, with sinister glee, were weaving the ironic threads of a terrible web. Velvet shuddered involuntarily, and Cutter placed a protective arm around her slim shoulders.

"It just *couldn't* be! I am sworn, it just couldn't *be!*" The voice, melodious and sweetly resonant, rose to the arching ceilings of the lobby, above the din of elegant humanity below. Velvet recognized it in one horror-filled, disbelieving moment, and stiffened. "Well, it is! It is; I *knew* it." The copper-haired Morgana swept across the room, and stood, in all her exquisitely gowned and groomed glory before her old acquaintance. "Velvet McBride! If you aren't a sight for sore eyes!"

"Morgana," Velvet blurted on a woebegone breath, "I wanted to freshen up before I called on you."

A syrupy laugh bubbled up from Morgana's jewel-swathed throat. "Now, don't you be a ninny. You look just fine!" She lifted a fluttering gaze to Velvet's companion. "And so does your friend," she said, her tones softening to a purr.

"My friend," Velvet responded blankly. She glanced at Cutter, as though seeing him for the first time. Her shame at their disreputable appearance knew no bounds. How pitiful she and Cutter must look, he unshaven, travel-grimed—and she . . . Velvet shuddered once again in the warm scented air, not allowing herself to think further about her disgrace. Her gaze drifted to Morgana's side where a polished gentleman stood, smiling in deep condescension. Velvet looked back at Cutter, sadly; spiritlessly comparing the two. "This is my husband," she finally acknowledged, in abject defeat, "J. Eliot Cutter." The young man looked first surprised and then delighted. His hand shot out.

"John Cutter," he exclaimed. "This is indeed an honor, sir!"

Cutter merely nodded, accepting the man's greeting. Within moments, Velvet realized that others were gathering close to meet the apparently famous John Cutter. She felt herself pushed, prodded, and jabbed as smiling, murmuring humanity crowded in. Both she and Morgana stared in awed bewilderment.

"Who is he?" Morgana breathed.

"I have no idea," Velvet blurted out, then quickly shot her old friend a glance. "I mean . . . well, naturally, I know who he is. He's my husband."

Morgana lifted a finely etched brow. "I know that," she snapped. "*That* is certainly no reason for this unadulterated display of worship." She looked hastily at her bedraggled little friend, and smiled sweetly, recalling her manners. "You'll forgive my lapse," she amended in an altered tone. "I just mean, he must be someone famous."

"He *must* be," Velvet agreed on a breath. At that moment, a gentleman took her hand and shook it heartily.

"And you must be Mrs. Cutter," he observed. "Now this really is a pleasure." He glanced over his shoulder and called out, "Everybody, here's John's wife!" Velvet's eyes widened at the sudden and inexplicable attention she was receiving.

"Thank you," she murmured a dozen times as she accepted praise. Her bewildered gaze at last lifted to Cutter and he politely and firmly made their excuses. Leading her behind a deeply solicitous bellboy, he made their way through the crowd, up the staircase, and to their room.

Once inside the elaborately adorned hotel suite, Velvet collapsed onto a padded sofa, and looked in astonishment at her husband. She took long, calming breaths. "What in the flaming hell is going on?" she finally asked. Cutter offered a shrug of his broad shoulders and a guilty smile.

"I had no idea, princess," he said earnestly.

"Of what!" Velvet demanded. "You had no idea of what, for heaven's sake?"

"I suppose," he answered quietly, "that I am not unknown in this city."

" 'Not unknown,' " Velvet gaped as she stood and paced the bright patterned carpet. "You are positively lionized."

Cutter nodded in concession. "I imagine it has to do with my work in the Underground Railroad," he said.

"I thought you people were supposed to be be *anonymous!*"

she rejoined indignantly. "Do you think I would have come into the city looking like this," she railed, "had I known that we were going to be inundated with attention?" She took a resentful swipe at her indecorous apparel.

Cutter took her shoulders in an attempt to calm her, but she jerked away. "Listen to me," he said, raking his fingers through his tousle of jet curls, "since the proclamation, I've heard that some of us have become celebrities. I'd no idea that—"

"Well, I just want to thank you very much, J. Eliot Cutter," Velvet shrilled tightly, "for what may prove to be the most humiliating day of my entire life." At that moment an insistent rap was heard at the door.

"Hurry, and let me in," came the muffled voice. "This stupid bellboy said I couldn't see you." A thunk was heard as though someone had been hit. A groan and another thunk came from behind the closed door. Velvet hurried to answer it. "They said I couldn't come up," Morgana said haughtily as she swept into the room. "That little ferret-faced swine tried to stop me!" The beleaguered hotel employee stood in the dim corridor, holding his left eye protectively.

"I told her she shouldn't . . . but she barged right past me," he stammered. Cutter quickly placed a coin in his palm and assured him that he'd done his job well. Closing the door, he turned back to see his wife—his resentfully bitter wife of a moment ago—smiling dewily at Morgana Carleton.

"Of course we'll join you," Velvet was saying, her voice oozing cordiality. "Why, that would be ever so much fun. Now, you must give us an opportunity to freshen up. We'll meet you and Eben down in the dining room." She glanced sweetly at Cutter. "Morgana and her friend Eben Conway have invited us to a late supper, darling. Isn't that ever so sweet of them?"

"Sweet," Cutter acknowledged curtly. He watched as Morgana was led to the door and skillfully deposited in the hallway.

"We'll see you in an hour," Velvet said, and waved cheerily.

She swung the door closed and leaned on it. "This is the worst thing that's ever happened to me," she intoned, her teeth clenched. Then, closing her eyes, Velvet took a long breath. It was almost as if she were preparing for battle, Cutter reflected in wonder. He was not far from wrong.

Within minutes, the valet and maid service had been summoned. A bath had been drawn. Velvet flew about the room, tossing orders, her wet curls flying, her dressing gown flapping. The Archambault creation was extracted from its tissue; matching satin shoes, a jewel case, and gloves were searched out and dug from the several packs that now lay scattered about the room. The maid was instructed assiduously in the dressing of Velvet's hair, while the befuddled, ordinarily efficient valet was warned, as he shaved Cutter nervously, that one nick to Cutter's jaw would cost him his job. At last, Velvet stood before her reflected image in the standing mirror. The fine, golden fabric of the gown shimmered in the low lamplight. She pushed discontentedly at her upswept, flaxen-streaked curls, and at last pulled one dark tress down to lie sweetly against the cream of her bared shoulder. She glared at the results.

"It will have to do," she snapped. Then, pinching at her cheeks until they were coral-colored, she curved her lips into a smiling bow, and turned to the now neatly dressed Cutter. "What do you think?" she demanded through her smile.

Cutter felt his breath desert him. He had not seen Velvet so meticulously beautiful in months. Her gown—the Archambault creation—was of a deep gold netting, its many satin underskirts replacing a hoop. The sleeves, falling in full, draping folds from the deep neckline, reached to a point at her slim wrists. At her neck was a double strand of emeralds that met in one heart-shaped stone at the base of her throat. Her eyes picked up the gems' green to glimmer the deepest aqua Cutter had ever seen. In their translucent depths, however, he perceived a determination and a hardness of spirit that belied her outward beauty, and he turned away.

"You look beautiful," he said tightly. Not quite satisfied, Velvet turned back to the mirror. It was only upon a second inspection that she decided she was ready to face their public.

"Give me my gloves," she said to the maid, and the girl brought them. Of the palest ivory lace, they would not completely hide the destruction of Velvet's hands, but they would mask it. "And it only took two hours," she said derisively as she slipped them on.

Together, she and Cutter descended the stairs. In the lobby, the milling crowd once again greeted the handsome couple. They made their way to the dining room, where they were welcomed effusively by the waiting Morgana and her friend, Eben Conway.

Eben, with his drooping black mustache and snapping black eyes, was so handsome, Velvet noted, as to be almost pretty. He swept his arm out as the couple arrived, and the parade of service began. Champagne was brought, and crab canapés. Delicately sauced capons were offered for the main course. Velvet had not dined on such elegant fare in almost two years. Her eyes widened, though she maintained a studied, smiling reserve, at each new offering.

". . . and tomorrow is the fair," Morgana was saying. "There'll be the shadbake in LaFayette Park, of course."

"I happen to be president of the Hudson River Shad Fishermen's Association," Eben said with expansive modesty, "and we are sponsoring the event. It should prove quite a colorful occasion. The receipts will, naturally, go to the relief of the families of our fighting men." The table seemed to suddenly go silent, as it occurred to Velvet to ask the obvious question. Why, she wondered, is the young, and apparently vital Mr. Conway here, and not off fighting? Old restraints, manners long unused but not forgotten, checked her curiosity.

"What is a shadbake?" she inquired politely, with unfelt interest.

"Oh, now," said Eben, warming to his subject, "that is something—a cherished custom in these parts—that must be experienced to be appreciated." Though the custom

175

needed the experiential element, according to Mr. Conway, he went on to explain it anyway. "Well before the crowd arrives, the cooks have gathered plenty of hard wood—it makes the best embers—and cleaned hundreds of the fish. The wood is ignited early in the day to get rid of most of the smoke and to form a good bed of red-hot coals about twenty feet long and a yard across. The halves of shad are pegged onto inch-thick oak boards about the size of a child's writing tablet. Across the fillets are draped two or three slices of lean bacon. As soon as the guests arrive, the planks are set around the bed of coals, tilted just enough to keep the fish from slipping off. The intense heat reflected from the fire sets the bacon to sizzling and the fat bastes the fillets. Every once in a while the boards are upended to brown the fish evenly. Over another bed of embers roe is cooking in shallow skillets. The meal commences with fish chowder, but as soon as the bowls are removed, the shad and roe are served, sometimes with a salad and sometimes with corn on the cob." Mr. Conway laughed indulgently. "Anyone who doesn't beg a second helping doesn't deserve to go to a shadbake," he finished exuberantly.

"Then we shall be sure to ask for a second helping," Velvet said brightly as she glanced at her husband. Cutter, she noted, was gazing intently at Eben Conway. His glinting regard was not the least indulgent, or cordial. Velvet wondered if he could possibly be jealous of the young man, and drew her hand from beneath his. She realized that his hand had, on several occasions throughout the conversation, landed upon hers, and she wondered whether the gesture was inadvertent or not. She patted her lips with her linen napkin, and surveyed Morgana through veiled lashes. That woman seemed not to notice anything untoward. She was already extolling the joyous possibilities of fair day.

"We'll go over to Swan Street first thing in the morning," she planned, "and get my carriage at the livery stable. Then we can pop in on the academy—you'll naturally want to see it," she said to Velvet. "After that we'll go on to the park. We'll have such *fun!*" Morgana had not changed, Velvet thought with an inward chuckle. Everything to her was "fun." Velvet reflected contentedly that it was good to be with someone who reminded her of what life had been like before the unyielding Adirondacks—and Cutter—had entered her soul.

It was long after midnight before Cutter and Velvet bade good night to the exuberant Morgana and the prideful Eben Conway. For Velvet it had been a fateful evening. She had almost forgotten how glorious life could be.

In their room, Cutter undressed in silence. Velvet eyed him surreptitiously as she bent to her own nightly toilette. Never again would she allow herself to become so seedy that she was ashamed to greet her friends. People—smart, sophisticated people—like Eben and Morgana reminded her of what counted in life. She lay her emeralds in their padded case, and ran her fingertips over them lovingly before closing it. She glanced again at her husband. His sullenness irritated her, especially when she was so content.

"What *is* the matter with you?" she demanded at last, impatiently, as she drew the pins from her hair. Her wild tousle of gold-streaked curls flew in ringlets about her face and shoulders. In the flickering lamplight, her form curved in misty outlines beneath the film of her nightdress. Cutter watched her from his prone position on the bed. Velvet paced the room, putting her things away. "You hardly said a word all night," she groused.

Cutter placed his hands behind his head, and attempted to concentrate on the lushness of his wife's deliciously female aspect, and not on her words—on her snappish attitude. He was finding it difficult to separate the one from the other. A quiet petrification had begun in him. He did not know exactly when it had begun, or what had begun to cause it, but as he watched Velvet now, he knew deeply that something in him was being lost, or supplanted by a growing asperity. He must discover that within them both which had given them some measure of success in their marriage.

"Come to bed," he said tersely.

Velvet shot him a look, hesitated, and then said lightly, "In a minute. I don't want this gown getting wrinkled, I may have to wear it again. If we plan to stay here for any length of time, I may have to—"

Cutter lunged from the bed and caught her in a stinging grasp. "I said," he repeated, "come to bed." His voice was dark and deeply, dangerously quiet. Velvet's breath caught, and her eyes widened as she looked uncertainly into his. His own gaze was narrow, glinting shards of silver in the lamplight. The expanse of his bronzed nakedness caused her to flinch imperceptibly. So this was how it was to be between them, she thought. Her chin lifted, and her eyes shot lucent blue-green sparks. The easy camaraderie that had been between them was apparently gone. Gone were the swelling tides of heated need each time bedtime approached. All right, she reflected, let it be so. Even though they had never had a real marriage, one founded on a great mutual love, their mutual physical attraction had been enough to merge their souls. They had been happy for a time. But that was apparently over. For a time they had existed on a narrow plain, vacillating between love and hate for each other, and leaning toward a certain love. Apparently, tonight they'd stepped out of that misted limbo, and into a concrete sphere. Where would this step lead? she wondered. Hate was not the antithesis of love, Velvet reminded herself; apathy was. And apathy was what she felt at this moment toward her husband.

"As you wish," she said finally, veiling her gaze. Avoiding the urge to jerk away from him, Velvet glanced down at Cutter's big hand where it gripped her upper arm. She looked back up at him. Neither of them moved. The potential for violence between them was great. Neither wished to empower that possibility. Someday—and very soon, too—it would, most certainly, come. It seethed ominously between them like heat-swelled tinder, needing only the spark of an angry word to ignite it. When that happened, the ensuing rage of the conflagration would either destroy or purify the couple.

At last, Cutter loosened his hold, and Velvet moved silently to the bed. She lay down, waiting. Cutter blew out the lamps and moved to stand over her in the moonlight. The manly fur of him shone dark and glistening against the

178

lighter expanse of his muscled form.

"Take off your gown," he said evenly. Velvet did so, and felt her nakedness scrutinized. "Now lie back." Again, Velvet obeyed. She felt tiny prickles of embarrassment and rage tingle along her flesh. She felt another thing, too. As Cutter lay down next to her and began a practiced exploration of her body, she felt deep shame. Her flesh responded to his teasing touches, though her mind railed against them. Her heart pounded a rampaging crescendo as, with his tongue, he tantalized, to a ripe bud of desire, her darkest resistance. She felt the first waves of warming hunger shudder up from her belly. They swelled, growing hot beneath her flesh, encompassing her heart and mind and, at last, her soul. Velvet arched to—and against—the tongues of liquid passion that melted her endurance. With a pleading moan, she drew Cutter's lips to her own, and held him in a demanding kiss. But he delayed her sought-for release. With mocking languor, he taunted her desire. Plucking and nibbling, like a preying beast savagely torturing its victim, he explored greedily the deepest recesses of her need. A hoarse cry raged up from Velvet's breast.

"Oh, please, Cutter," she gasped as a piercing hunger erupted and shattered inside her. "I cannot bear it." Ferociously, without sweet words, he lifted her to him and, raging took the sweet, hot swells of her desire. Penetrating the flow of her passion, thrusting against the tide of her desire, he took her, and left her limp and trembling against the throbbing sheen of his furred chest.

Sated, though somehow not quite satisfied, Velvet lay in the darkness—nearly alone. She heard Cutter's rasping breath beside her, felt his warmth and weight against her in the bed, but she sensed that neither of them had truly experienced fulfillment. The perfumed night crept in through an open window, and Velvet felt an inexplicable loneliness. This was not the tender lovemaking of the Adirondacks. Here were not the gentle aftermoments of sweet words and caressing touches that she had experienced in the past. Something had changed for them. The night's gentle warmth was no consolation. Between Cutter and

Velvet there was a coldness she had not known. At their worst together, they had at least shared a certain fiery reluctance to be drawn to each other; they had at least shared that. Now there seemed to be nothing between them. A hollow, empty space separated husband and wife, though they shared the intimate confines of a marital bed.

Disconsolate, somehow uncertain, but deeply resolute, Velvet shifted against the stiff sheets and turned away from her husband. If this was how he wanted their life to be, then Velvet would not protest. Cutter had made his decision. She would forbear until they reached Sweet Briar Hill. Once home, she would not be dependent on him, she could make her own decisions as to their future—*her* future.

Drowsily, Velvet watched, through the lightly curtained window, the mirror of the moon drift lazily in the soft sky. Each day she was closer to home. As the moon drifted, Velvet accompanied it, across the darkness to Sweet Briar Hill.

Chapter Eighteen

The city of Albany was washed in the rosy glow of newly blossomed tulips and pinks. Crowds of finely dressed citizens milled along the narrow streets, displacing the warm, fragrant morning air with the human breezes of joyful activity. The auction in Academy Park roused the interest of most passersby, and Morgana ordered Eben Conway to halt the carriage beside the iron fence surrounding it.

Men were bidding furiously as the four people entered the park. A hush settled over the crowd. "Going to Mr. Gerrit Smith, for one thousand dollars. Going!" proclaimed the auctioneer. "Gone! Sold to Mr. Smith for one thousand dollars!" The victorious buyer stepped up onto the platform. He turned to look into the crowd as he accepted his purchase. His smiling eyes stopped suddenly, seeming to pinpoint a spot very near Velvet. She glanced around, saw nothing that would draw the man's attention, and then looked back at him.

"This is a most auspicious occasion," Mr. Smith said, his voice flowing with pride and gratitude. "I have purchased the first draft of what might be said to be the most important document in this nation's history — Mr. Lincoln's Emancipation Proclamation." His smile was now riveted just behind and just above Velvet's shoulder. Before she could calculate an awareness of his intent, Mr. Smith's words bore down on her. "The man who helped make it possible is with us today, fellow Albanians. I give you Mr. John Eliot Cutter!" The crowd roared its approval, and Cutter was forged, by the exuberant will of the people, to the podium. He stood there, his head modestly bowed. Mr. Smith shook his hand. Others forged up to the platform's edge. Cutter extended his greeting to everyone. Everyone, it seemed, wished to touch, wished to congratulate, wished to be close to Velvet's husband.

Velvet felt herself swept to his side. Together, not quite understanding the adulation they were receiving, they greeted their admirers.

"I fear," Eben Conway admonished them later as they sat around a table, nibbling at the last of their picnic feast, "you will not receive the same sort of reception in Virginia that you have enjoyed in Albany."

"That is a magnificent understatement." Cutter smiled ruefully. Velvet eyed him, not quite certain that all that had happened that morning had not been a dream. She looked to the others. Morgana's face still reflected a kind of awe, as it had most of the day. Her wide eyes had targeted Cutter from the first moment his name was mentioned, and had not left him. Velvet felt a tingle of resentment.

"Well, really," she said wryly, "that may be a blessing. We are not, after all, celebrities."

Eben Conway laughed. "Here in Albany you are, or at least Mr. Cutter is."

"Then it's probably best we leave Albany as soon as possible," Velvet rejoined.

In her own right, she would not have minded today's attention. She would not even have minded the fact that it was Cutter who inspired such adulation—as long as, appropriately gowned in her newly purchased fawn velvet traveling frock, and groomed, she could be at his side. What seemed to gnaw at her was this inexplicable hero worship suddenly developed by the ordinarily unflappable Morgana. Morgana was always extravagantly dewy around men, but she was always in control. With Cutter, today, she was uncharacteristically, and most unattractively, ungainly in her admiration. Her clumsy words of praise came tentatively; her gestures toward him were awkward. This was not the Morgana Carleton who had inflamed, who had unashamedly captivated every young male within a fifty-mile radius of her amber gaze. Velvet turned away from the disgustingly fascinated Morgana.

"I think we should leave today," she said shortly.

"Leave today?" Morgana cried. "Oh, but you can't possibly!" Velvet's eyes narrowed. Morgana smiled lamely. "I just meant . . . well, you haven't *done* anything yet."

Eben Conway lifted a brow, and offered Morgana a patronizing glance. "These good people haven't come to Albany to sightsee," he said quietly.

"That's right," Velvet said, with a dismissive shrug. "We only stopped here to greet you, Morgana. And it was only at my insistence that we did." She looked at Cutter, a challenge hardening her turquoise glare. He said nothing, to Velvet's frustration. "We ought to leave today, don't you think?" she persisted. As though roused from deep contemplation, Cutter looked at her. "We ought to be leaving," Velvet repeated.

"If you wish," Cutter said shortly.

"If *I* wish," Velvet demanded. "You were the one who—"

Cutter stood abruptly. "I hope the three of you will excuse me," he said curtly. He made a short bow, and stepped from the table. "You'll see that Velvet gets back to the hotel, Mr. Conway?"

Eben nodded.

"Thank you," Cutter said, and strode quickly away, his shoulders wide and taut against any objection.

Velvet glanced in embarrassed outrage at her companions; then, managing a sweet though decidedly weak smile, she said, "There's no reason why we must end our fun. Won't the two of you show me the rest of the city?"

Eben Conway smiled an aristocrat's smile. "Let's be on our way." He stood, waiting for the women, in their sudden discomfort, to rise and adjust themselves to an altered mood of false enthusiasm, and watched the departing Cutter. His smile faded. Hardly a word had passed between the two of them, and yet there was something about J. Eliot Cutter that disconcerted him.

The public room of Stanwix Hall glinted in the low lamplight of several elegant brass sconces. Eben Conway sat at his usual table with the usual party of hangers-on, and watched in detached fascination the activity—or rather, the lack of activity—of the lone patron at the bar. J. Eliot Cutter had been there upon Conway's arrival, after he'd seen the ladies home, and had remained there now for at least an hour. Cutter's drinking was determined. A man who drank steadily, unwaveringly, was not drinking for pleasure. Conway excused himself at last, and made his way to a stool beside Cutter. He ordered a whiskey for himself and one for Cutter. That man merely nodded an obligatory thanks.

"Gerrit Smith certainly got himself a prize today," Conway said after a pause. Cutter nodded once again. He sipped at his drink. Eben Conway smiled companionably. "The old fellow owns quite a bit of property up where you come from." Again Cutter nodded. "Like to get my hands on some of that," Conway said.

"I doubt you'd put it to the good use Mr. Smith's put it to," Cutter said.

"I don't understand," Conway replied carefully.

"I think you do," Cutter answered. "Mr. Gerrit Smith has for years offered his land up north for the use of the Underground Railroad. Mr. Gerrit Smith puts his money where his patriotism is."

"I see," Eben Conway replied. "So you don't think much of my—what you might call—lack of patriotism."

"You bet I don't," Cutter answered. He turned on his stool, and lifted the drink Eben Conway had bought him. Holding it aloft between them, he asked, "Would you call yourself a conscientious objector, Mr. Conway?"

"That's what I call myself," Eben Conway said quietly.

"And because the draft act allows you to hire a substitute soldier for yourself, you feel your . . . conscience has been assuaged?" Cutter asked.

"I do."

Slowly, deliberately, Cutter turned the glass and emptied the contents onto the polished surface of the bar. "That's why we call this 'a rich man's war and a poor man's fight,' Mr. Conway."

"I hadn't heard that," Eben Conway said, watching Cutter. He sensed real violence in the man's dispassion. Even the careful way in which he poured out the whiskey had an element of savagery inherent in it. "You'll forgive me, Mr. Cutter," Conway said haltingly, needing, despite the element of danger, to defend himself, "but some of us put on different sorts of uniforms—just as you have." Conway realized immediately his mistake. He looked away from Cutter. The quiet darkening of the man's gaze sent thrills of dread through him. "Forgive me, once again," Conway said softly. "I have no desire to diminish your contribution to this cause. I know you have fought the good fight in more ways than I could ever take credit for." He stared tight-lipped at the mirrored wall behind the bar. "You don't seem to realize that some of us—at least we consider ourselves to be so—are truly conscience-ridden over this conflict." He glanced quickly at his companion. "We stay at home and try to raise money for the widows and orphans of the war. You might have noticed several of my associates passing through the crowd collecting money. We ask one dollar from every citizen of this city. That's all. If every person gave one dollar, no woman or child would have to go to bed hungry." He paused, his polish, for the moment, dulled. "Try not to judge us too harshly," he said softly. "We are not cowards . . . some of us. We cannot be held responsible for the frauds that have been perpetrated in the name of this system. We did not write the law. If it serves us . . ." His voice trailed off. He lifted an eyebrow and looked at Cutter directly. "You cannot look into my head, Mr. Cutter. You cannot look into my heart—as I cannot look into yours. We do things of which we are not always proud. Haven't you, Mr. Cutter, done things of which you might not boast in a public room?"

Cutter turned slowly, after a moment, on his stool. His arms resting in front of him, he kept his narrow gaze on the darkly mirrored wall, and ordered yet another drink for himself. Finally, Eben Conway finished his whiskey, and stood.

"Your wife tells me you are leaving tomorrow," he said, offering his hand. Cutter did not take it. "Goodbye, Mr.

185

Cutter," said Eben Conway, and moved back to his table.

Velvet paced the hotel room tensely. She could no more have stopped Morgana Carleton than she could have stopped the steamboat that would take them south in the morning.

"I'm going," Morgana was saying, "and that's all there is to it." Velvet had arranged for the tickets for her and Cutter, and had realized with a sickening frustration that Morgana was building to a rationale that would carry her south as well. Before Velvet had finished purchasing her own tickets, Morgana was as well as on her way. Now she was here. In a froth of yellow taffeta, she sat on the small sofa, explaining her decision. "I've bought the ticket, and I'm going with you; I'm every bit as noble as you are Velvet McBride . . . I mean, of course," she corrected herself with a sweet smile, "Cutter." But Velvet knew that Morgana's slip of the tongue was no mistake. It was not altruism that motivated her.

Velvet tilted a glance at her friend. "Morgana dear," she said, her voice dripping concern, "it's true we have no idea what we'll find at the end of our journey, and you may call me noble if you wish, but quite honestly, I left that godforsaken Adirondack wilderness because I simply couldn't stand it another minute." She sat next to Morgana and took her hands. "Please believe me, I have no fears for our homeland. It will probably be just as we left it, but I only suggest that . . . well . . . some change might have taken place in our absence. We've been gone over two years, and you know what can happen in such a long time. There is simply no reason for you to leave this lovely city right now, to involve yourself in God knows what unpleasantness; I'm quite prepared to write you if you're needed."

"That won't be necessary, Velvet darling," said Morgana, a smile stubbornly affixed to her lips, "I'll be right there with you." She stood and brushed out her wide skirts. Moving to the mirror and adjusting her plumed bonnet, she continued. "We'll take the packet to New York, just as you and John planned, then we'll travel by train to Virginia. It'll be such a lovely trip." Velvet found herself inexplicably resentful of the way Morgana seemed to verbally caress the word "John." She stood, realizing that no amount of dissuasion was going to change Morgana's mind. Once the woman had chosen her prey, she was like a blue-tick hound in her determination. Morgana swept into her cloak, and splayed a hand at Velvet's look of consternation. "I won't be one teeny bit of trouble," she said, "you'll see. The luxury of a steamboat journey ought to be a most welcome prospect for you. Lord knows, you and John can do with a bit of luxury for a change." She eyed Velvet's patched night dress with an extravagance of sorrow. "You are such a pitiful sight these days, poor Velvet. Except for that charming little gold frock, and, of course, the lovely traveling gown, you seem a perfect little waif." She kissed the air in the general direction of Velvet's left cheek. "We must stay in New York for at least a week—I insist upon at least that, or maybe more—and get you some clothes." She pulled on her gloves. "We'll have you looking like the lady you are in no time. Mr. Brett Whitney is not going to see you like this if I have anything to say about it." Morgana smiled ruefully. "Now get a good night's sleep," she said solicitously, "you seem so tense tonight." Waving cheerily, having delivered her happy message, she swept from the room.

Velvet stared incredulously after her. *Charming little gold frock?* she railed inwardly. How dare the vixen refer to an original Archambault as a "charming little gold frock"? How dare Morgana decide their travel plans? How dare she call Velvet a waif? How dare she . . . For the first time in a very long while Velvet recalled not only Morgana's style and sophistication but her deviousness as well. Morgana Carleton was a master of innuendo. Velvet had forgotten the woman's shrewish powers. She had forgotten the power of gossip, on which Morgana had created her reputation. At home, during their growing-up years, Velvet remembered with a shudder that Morgana had left a trail of shattered reputations and intentionally interrupted possibilities. She had mentioned Mr. Brett Whitney, and had made reference to the fact that there might still be something between Velvet and him. Velvet's eyes widened. She wondered what the unscrupulous Morgana had planned. She would do anything to gain Cutter's notice. She might even dredge up an old infatuation just to arouse Cutter's suspicion and cause him to turn to Morgana herself for comfort. Velvet's fingertips went involuntarily to her lips. Nothing was beyond Morgana Carleton when she wanted something; and she wanted Cutter. Panic came to Velvet in a tilting rush. She moved with unsteady haste to the window to open it and breathe in the perfumed air of burgeoning summer. She must remain calm; she must think this out.

For the first time, Velvet found herself the object of — not party to — Morgana's cruelty. For the first time, Velvet understood the cutting twist of the woman's venomous capabilities. Velvet held herself rigid. She must think; she must reason this out. She was, after all, no insipid little victim. Velvet was not without her own resources. Though she'd never resorted to cruelty . . . really, Velvet had her own store of pugnacious gristle. She had always been a fighter . . . when the necessity arose. She'd done, throughout her life, what was necessary. Short of being impolite, Velvet had known exactly how to handle sly whispers and grating insults alike. Morgana Carleton, she resolved, had met her match. If she wished to take on the challenge of her life, she'd certainly chosen the correct field on which to do battle.

Velvet must think this situation through. Like the shifting lights of an opal, her thoughts darted from Morgana to Cutter. Had he responded to Morgana's flirtations, and caused this unexpected glitch in their life? She moved about the room, thinking, waiting for him to arrive, deciding whether or not to accuse him of such complicity. In truth, as the night wore on, as her fierce anticipation waned, Velvet realized that Cutter had not responded to Morgana. Morgana was quite simply a willful girl, she was quite simply infatuated with Cutter's celebrity, his status as a hero, and she was doing what spoiled, bored young belles did. Morgana wanted an adventure. And she wanted an adventure at the expense of Velvet's happy marriage. The suddenly conjured image made Velvet wince. *Happy marriage?* Velvet and Cutter's marriage had never been "happy" by anyone's standards. And yet, there was—or had been—something between them that had seemed worth exploring. Once, perhaps, she might have termed their relationship . . . almost happy. Up there in their tiny cabin, for a brief luminescent time, there had seemed a chance for them. Isolated in their snow-drifted world of mountains and quiet grandeur, they were, in many ways, content.

Velvet's memory drifted in silence to a time of snowy, twilit days, when she would await Cutter's arrival, when she would be building the cook fire. She recalled the deep, tired contentment of wintery nights when they were warm by their fire, he studying his rocks, his spectacles studiously perched on his nose. She found herself smiling, enjoying the serenity of her recollections. One day, perhaps, they might again find that . . . intimacy that had existed between them.

At once, the door exploded. The room darkened as Cutter bore down on her. Velvet had no time to imagine why he lunged in that odd, aggressive fashion toward her. His hard silver gaze was thunderous, wild with tempestuous hunger. He grabbed her to him, and she gasped against the hard snap of her body to his. She tried to scream, but his mouth came down to take hers in a brutal kiss. She writhed against him, but his arms were like steel bands, holding her within his savage assault. Velvet could barely breathe. She knew, in a horrible, heart-clenching moment of realization, that he was going to take her without love. He had done the terrible raging thing before, but always he'd allowed her the dignity of her own desires. Now there was nothing for her. She would merely be brutalized. He threw her onto their bed. Her breath caught as she determined to fight him. But there was no margin for denial. He was upon her. He tore her nightdress from her body, rending it to tatters. His hard fingers grasped fragments of her hair, and he snapped her head back, laying bare her flesh to his savagery.

She felt she would die. Arms flailing, Velvet fought to

189

survive, but she was helpless against his charge. With pounding dispatch, he tore at her, rending her defenses useless. A ragged scream tore from the deepest recesses of her outrage. Teeth clenched, soul aflame, she battled the assault.

When he was through, when his lust had been sated, when he at last let her go, Velvet lay still. Her breath came in drags of relief. Too quickly, too horribly quickly, he was asleep. Velvet shifted, her heart pounding. He did not move. He would not wake. She raised herself from the bed. Wrapping herself in a coverlet, she moved slowly, resolutely, to a chair. As she sat, swathed in the cover, beginning to shiver beneath its warmth, Velvet knew what had happened. Cutter had gotten himself drunk. Her face, as she watched him now in his besotted sleep, became rigid.

No, she thought icily, there would never be a time for them now. *Not ever.* Still, Morgana would not have him. Velvet would fight them both — and she would win.

Chapter Nineteen

They had been nearly three days in New York City. Arriving aboard the steamboat *Clermont*, a "floating palace" which offered the most opulent of accommodations. Plush sofas and well-padded chairs, ornately appointed saloons and elegant company were among the amenities that made the twenty-four-hour trip down the Hudson memorable — and difficult to relinquish, for at least two of the travelers, once they had reached New York. But, if the journey was abundantly comfortable for Velvet, and richly appealing, the city itself was more than that. It was a wonderland, a kaleidoscope of colorful citizenry dashing about thronged streets glittery with effervescent life. Velvet had seen it only once, from the windows of a private carriage on her trip north two years before. This time, she was to truly experience the legendary metropolis. Morgana, having secured a sizable "loan" from Eben Conway, had squired Velvet from shop to shop. She'd brightly taken the initiative, and, though at first reluctant, Velvet had succumbed to the heady enticement of Parisian laces and Oriental silks that were displayed by the perspicacious New York merchants. Too, Velvet had seen how the zeal of her buying ignited Cutter's anger.

"We cannot afford this insanity," Cutter had thundered.

"Morgana's only loaning me the money. Pa'll pay her back as soon as we get to Sweet Briar Hill," she'd rejoined.

" 'Pa'," Cutter had grated, "has about as much chance of paying back your debts as I do."

"Pa's a rich man," Velvet had said archly. "Besides, I can't be bothered with your grim forebodings. If I were to succumb to your depression of the past weeks, I would be as gloomy a traveling companion as you've turned out to be." Cutter had, characteristically, slammed from the room.

No mention had been made in all this time of their last night together in Albany. Rigidly silent on the subject, Velvet wondered if Cutter even remembered it. He had been deeply angry for a very long time. Velvet barely recalled the Cutter of their Adirondack days — the cockily assured, the confident and cavalier Cutter who had swept her into his arms and into his bed with equal nonchalance. In a very subtle way — a way indefinable to her — Velvet missed that bold and spirited male who might, in earlier days, have apologized briefly for his untender handling of her, and then taken her with the arch-browed certainty that she would, once again, receive him, finally, seeking her own pleasure. Velvet was a little awed by her own yearning for that arrogant Cutter. She wondered at such a weakness in herself. She'd always, like Morgana, been in total control of such yearnings.

She entered their hotel room now, laden like a steamship plowing the waters of the mighty Hudson River, her arms full of boxes, sacks, and tissue-wrapped finery. She laid out the lavish array on the bed, and threw off her light cloak. As she stepped to the mirror to remove her bonnet, she noted, in the shadows beyond the afternoon light spilling into the room, Cutter's slouched figure. Drunk again, she railed inwardly. But Cutter was not drunk.

He moved toward her slowly, deliberately. Velvet stiffened, her fingers awkwardly removed the pins from her bonnet. She offered him only the slightest notice. It was best not to encourage an encounter between them, she assured herself. She turned crisply from the mirror, and headed back toward her packages, but Cutter's big hand shot out and captured her arm. He swung her to face him.

"I'm leaving," he said quietly, his mouth a grim line.

"What are you talking about?" Velvet gaped. "You're doing no such thing. You have to accompany Morgana and me to Sweet —"

Cutter snapped her to him. "Listen to me very closely," he grated. "I'm leaving today. Don't say another word." He paused, his silver gaze above her darkening to a thunderous pewter. "Don't you know I could kill you? Doesn't it frighten you?" Velvet felt her heart tilt at the intensity of his words, at the horrible innuendo. She arched a dark brow, her teeth clenched in defiance, her anger taking precedence over her trepidation.

"No man has ever frightened me," she ground out.

"No?" Cutter asked, a smile beginning to form. Very slowly, he untensed his grasp. "No?" he asked again.

MORE PASSION AND ADVENTURE AWAIT... YOUR TRIP TO A BIG ADVENTUROUS WORLD BEGINS WHEN YOU ACCEPT YOUR FIRST 4 NOVELS ABSOLUTELY *FREE*
(AN $18.00 VALUE)

Accept your Free gift and start to experience more of the passion and adventure you like in a historical romance novel. Each Zebra novel is filled with proud men, spirited women and tempestuous love that you'll remember long after you turn the last page.

Zebra Historical Romances are the finest novels of their kind. They are written by authors who really know how to weave tales of romance and adventure in the historical settings you love. You'll feel like you've actually gone back in time with the thrilling stories that each Zebra novel offers.

GET YOUR FREE GIFT WITH THE START OF YOUR HOME SUBSCRIPTION

Our readers tell us that these books sell out very fast in book stores and often they miss the newest titles. So Zebra has made arrangements for you to receive the four newest novels published each month.

You'll be guaranteed that you'll never miss a title, and home delivery is so convenient. And to show you just how easy it is to get Zebra Historical Romances, we'll send you your first 4 books absolutely FREE! Our gift to you just for trying our home subscription service.

BIG SAVINGS AND FREE HOME DELIVERY

Each month, you'll receive the four newest titles as soon as they are published. You'll probably receive them even before the bookstores do. What's more, you may preview these exciting novels free for 10 days. If you like them as much as we think you will, just pay the low preferred subscriber's price of just $3.75 each. *You'll save $3.00 each month off the publisher's price.* AND, your savings are even greater because there are never any shipping, handling or other hidden charges—FREE Home Delivery. Of course you can return any shipment within 10 days for full credit, no questions asked. There is no minimum number of books you must buy.

4 FREE BOOKS

TO GET YOUR 4 FREE BOOKS WORTH $18.00 —MAIL IN THE FREE BOOK CERTIFICATE T O D A Y

Fill in the Free Book Certificate below, and we'll send your FREE BOOKS to you as soon as we receive it.

If the certificate is missing below, write to: Zebra Home Subscription Service, Inc., P.O. Box 5214, 120 Brighton Road, Clifton, New Jersey 07015-5214.

FREE BOOK CERTIFICATE

4 FREE BOOKS

ZEBRA HOME SUBSCRIPTION SERVICE, INC.

YES! Please start my subscription to Zebra Historical Romances and send me my first 4 books absolutely FREE. I understand that each month I may preview four new Zebra Historical Romances free for 10 days. If I'm not satisfied with them, I may return the four books within 10 days and owe nothing. Otherwise, I will pay the low preferred subscriber's price of just $3.75 each; a total of $15.00, *a savings off the publisher's price of $3.00.* I may return any shipment and I may cancel this subscription at any time. There is no obligation to buy any shipment and there are no shipping, handling or other hidden charges. Regardless of what I decide, the four free books are mine to keep.

NAME

ADDRESS _____ APT

CITY _____ STATE _____ ZIP

( )
TELEPHONE

SIGNATURE _____ (if under 18, parent or guardian must sign)

Terms, offer and prices subject to change without notice. Subscription subject to acceptance by Zebra Books. Zebra Books reserves the right to reject any order or cancel any subscription.   069002

"No," Velvet snapped. She twisted away from him. "You've always underestimated me, J. Eliot," she said, stepping toward the opposite side of the room, thinking quickly. Her eyes keenly assessed the distance between herself and the door. Cutter, for the moment, stood dangerously in the way of escape. She must attempt to divert the dark turn of the conversation. Tilting her gaze, she continued. "You were convinced from the first time we met that I'd just fallen off the turnip wagon. Well, you were wrong then, and you're wrong now. I'm not afraid of you."

Cutter's smile deepened. His eyes, as he moved toward her, held a brilliance Velvet had not seen for a very long time. His unshaven face still shone bronze beneath the dark stubble, and Velvet felt the familiar heat began to swell.

"You weren't afraid of me that last night in Albany?" he said lazily. Velvet's heart lurched, bitterness overtaking any passion she might have experienced at that moment. She knew, if he wanted to, he could take her again at any moment, without love. He stopped his advance. He was so near she could feel the heat of him, his manliness penetrated the layers of her clothing to veil her naked flesh with hungry stirrings. Emotions warring, Velvet turned away.

"So you do remember," she said softly. Cutter nodded. Velvet's turquoise gaze lifted. "I hate you for it," she said.

Again, Cutter nodded, but the smile vanished. "I hate myself," he answered. "But it doesn't change what happened. If I stayed with you, it would happen again." An involuntary shudder ravaged Velvet's spine. Before she could respond, Cutter grabbed her. His big hand cradling her head, he held her to him. She struggled, and was immediately stilled, admittedly terrified by some terrible force that both unified and disjoined them. Isolated for an eternity in that lifeless and yet vivid moment of absolute awareness, the couple clung together. Cutter drew back Velvet's head, and his mouth came down on hers in a shattering kiss.

Outraged and uncomprehending, Velvet watched as Cutter, without further words, strode from the room. She sat numbly on the bed amidst her gathered, newly purchased finery. Fingering laces, delicate silks, and polished cottons, she attempted in some tactile way to recapture the lost sensibility of Cutter's presence. She felt only a deep hollowness. The possibility of his leaving had never entered her mind.

Had hours passed—minutes, days?—before Velvet heard the knock on the door? Without benefit of invitation, Morgana bubbled into the room.

"Oh, but you haven't even begun to prepare yourself," she scolded. Velvet's eyes stared vacantly toward her. "But this is intolerable, darling Velvet," the woman went on as she moved briskly about the room lighting lamps against the gathering dark. Grabbing up paraphernalia, choosing and discarding various items, Morgana continued. "Ring for the maid immediately! For heaven's sake, we have less than twenty minutes to meet him."

Velvet's brows drew together. "Who?" she asked faintly.

"Damien Archambault, for heaven's sake," Morgana stated firmly. "How *could* you have forgotten, you ninny. I made the arrangements this morning." She arched a cinnamon-colored brow in Velvet's direction. "Oh, you really are too lamentably dense for words. Now get into the damned dress," she directed, "before I strip you naked, and dress you myself." When Velvet did not move, Morgana tilted her a questing look. "I suppose Cutter is going to be conspicuously absent tonight," she determined. "That's what this is all about, isn't it? You told him about the dinner with Damien, and he refused to join us." Morgana plucked Velvet's Archambault original from the armoire, and brushed at the voluminous skirts. "Well, you and I will be so effervescent that Damien will never notice we're bereft of a fourth. Now put this on," she demanded. Velvet stood slowly, and began to undress.

"Cutter's gone," she murmured.

"Gone?" questioned Morgana wryly. "You mean he's off on another binge?" She lifted the gown briskly and brought it down over Velvet's head. "Don't you worry, honey," she said, "once we get him down to Brandy Station, we'll clean him up."

"I mean," Velvet said, as she turned and allowed Morgana to fasten the dress, "Cutter is gone. He's left me." She turned briefly, to see the expected look of satisfaction in Morgana's eyes. A moment of silence thrilled through the air between the two women. Morgana stepped away, averting her gaze.

"Has he?" she said thoughtfully. "Has he, really?"

"Yes," Velvet affirmed. She moved to the dressing table and removed the pearls she'd worn that day, replacing them with the

194

emeralds. The cold, brilliant sparkle of the gems glared back at her from the mirror's reflected image. Winking slyly in the lamplight, they seemed a sculpted chain of dispassion that penetrated the white flesh of Velvet's throat to score the deepest recesses of her heart with a cold passion. No longer hollow, Velvet received that icy fullness gratefully. She turned toward Morgana. "I don't know where he is, or if he'll ever come back," she said.

The other woman looked at her quickly. "But he must come back," she said, "if for no other reason than to divorce you." Velvet's gaze narrowed, and Morgana altered her tone. "I mean, of course, we'll . . . you'll see him again. Once we reach Virginia, you can write to him. He'll probably just return to that awful mountain range where you met him, and you can write to him there, demand that he come south so you can divorce him. A husband owes that to his wife." Morgana stopped abruptly. She lifted a wine silk draped shoulder. "Personally," she said offhandedly, "I think you'll be better off without him. He's no Mr. Brett Whitney, in any case."

Velvet watched Morgana steadily. "Oh, I will write to Cutter, Morgana. And I will demand he come south. But I have no intention of divorcing him, and I'll never give him a divorce should he seek one."

Morgana pursed her lips as a smile threatened. "You may have no choice, darling Velvet," she murmured. Velvet knew exactly what Morgana was planning. Already, her mind was most assuredly awhirl with the gossip she would spread about Velvet and Brett Whitney. Oh, Morgana is a clever girl, Velvet conceded.

"And why would I have no choice?" she asked sweetly.

"Well," Morgana said lightly, "who can tell, honey? Who can ever say what the future holds?"

"I can," Velvet said quietly.

"Can you?" asked Morgana. Velvet nodded.

"You see, Morgana, I hold the key to the future—Cutter's and my future."

"Do you?" Morgana said snidely.

"Yes," answered Velvet. "You see . . . I carry our child."

Chapter Twenty

"You make great distinctions, Miss Carleton," said Damien Archambault modestly in his French-accented English.

Morgana laughed lightly. "But they are significant ones, *monsieur*. The French use of lace, as opposed to the German, is masterful." The man offered a cocked grin, and Morgana patted his hand. "Now you must admit, your point lace is point-device, particularly as compared to Herr Schnaubel's. I shall not discuss it further." She turned to Velvet. "Don't you agree, dear Velvet?"

Startled, Velvet glanced wide-gazed at her dinner companions. "Of course," she answered with false enthusiasm. She had no idea what she'd been asked. Her earlier admission to Morgana had come as a revelation to both of them. Velvet had not admitted her condition even to herself. She had not dared. The first time she'd missed her woman's flow, she'd attributed it to the hard Adirondack spring—or something of that nature. She'd fully expected it to return. But now it had been two months, and she was certain the absence indicated that she carried a child. It was not, for her, at this time, a happy indication. She'd made the disclosure insolently, with full knowledge of what such information would do to Morgana's plots. Now, fully admitted, it haunted her.

Velvet was apparently a woman alone. She had no resources, no protection, little money. Cutter had left her with what remained of the gold with which they had started their journey, and Velvet prayed it was enough to insure her fare home. Home, Velvet reflected. Where was home? Without Cutter to define her world, she must begin to create her own definition. For once and all—and especially now—Velvet needed to become a complete person, not dependent on father or husband or uncle for her completeness. For the sake of the babe growing within her, she must identify with only herself, and become prepared to wel-

196

come her child to a "home" defined by its mother. Velvet closed her eyes against the suddenly overwhelming responsibility. Her energy would fail her, she was sure. If she could only reach Sweet Briar Hill, she could begin to gather her strength. There, she'd been certain and strong. It was only within the last two years—only since she'd known Cutter—that she had become hesitating, frightened, searching. She had been courageous at Sweet Briar Hill—and she would be again. Cutter, the Adirondack Mountains, the so-called truths revealed there had weakened her. She would go back to her beginnings. She would gather her energy. She would become, for her child, a whole person.

Her thoughts elsewhere, she smiled vacantly toward Monsieur Archambault as he touched her hand with his pudgy, neatly manicured fingers. The gold pinky ring he wore caught her attention, and Velvet wondered for a fleeting second how much the ring cost—how much it could be sold for.

"I meant to make it clear to you," he said in faltering, but sincere English, "how vastly you compliment my design, Mrs. Cutter. You say you acquired your gown through one of my catalogues?"

Velvet nodded, smiling, recalling the battle that had preceded the purchase. "My mother sent me the catalogue from Virginia," she said.

"I am deeply . . . honored," Archambault answered gallantly. "The color is . . . apropos . . . appropriate for you. More than that," he amended with a smile, "the gold is so like the . . . high . . . gleams?"

"Lights," interjected Morgana drily.

"Ah, yes, . . . lights. Light gleams." He laughed. "How charming."

'Highlights,' Morgana said, her impatience with the man's praise of Velvet clear.

"Highlights," repeated the Frenchman, "of your hair." All three people laughed, Morgana with more volume than was absolutely necessary. She led the conversation adroitly from Velvet's remarkable tresses.

"You really must come south very soon, Monsieur Archambault," she said seductively. "We would be so happy to entertain a man of your distinction and wit—to say nothing of your . . .

197

beaux yeux."

"Someday," answered Monsieur Archambault, "I would love to be entertained by you, Miss Carleton. Your South is the most remarkable of places; the most *romantique.* Your New Orleans reminds me of the left bank in my city of lights. Someday you will take me south, and my *réciprocité* will be a trip to Paris."

"There is no reason to wait, *monsieur,*" said Morgana energetically. "Travel with us." She glanced at Velvet. "That would be all right, wouldn't it, dear Velvet?" she asked. Without waiting for an answer, she grasped an astonished Monsieur Archambault by his sleeve. "Oh, say you'll come. We'll have such fun!"

"But, Mademoiselle Carleton, you cannot be serious."

"I was never more serious . . . Damien," countered Morgana.

"It is madness to think of it," Damien Archambault burst out. "You cannot truly consider traveling south now. I cannot have it!" Both Velvet and Morgana were stunned to silence by the man's vehement objection.

"If it's the war you're speaking of . . ." offered Velvet haltingly.

"Mais oui!" the man declared. *"Destruction est partout, partout, partout."* He waved his arms wildly in all directions.

"En anglais, monsieur," entreated Velvet, attempting to make sense of the man's frenzy. "What did you say about destruction?"

"It is everywhere, madame. I have been there. You must not think to go."

Velvet's heart quickened. She had nearly forgotten her reason for making this trip in the first place. Jason's pictures flared in her mind's eye. His remembered images of charred bridges, ravaged farms, and the desolate skeletons of grand old houses overwhelmed her so that she saw nothing but those haunting visions. The elegant laughter of the other restaurant patrons dimmed. Velvet heard only the screams of the dying, and saw bodies everywhere.

"Excuse me," she said, as she pushed herself from the table. "I'm . . . unwell." She raced, covering her mouth, from the room. If her departure was unceremonious, she decided, the alternative was more so. Stomach lurching, Velvet leaned her forehead against the cool stone of a nearby building, and ungracefully forfeited her dinner.

"You okay, lady?" asked a voice. The inquiry was repeated

several times before Velvet allowed herself to turn around to face it.

"I'm . . . fine," she said, forcing a small and ineffective, smile. She prayed in silent humiliation that the Samaritan would simply take her word and leave her, but he did not.

"Can I see you home?" he asked. "The streets aren't safe at this time of night."

"No," she said, with uncharacteristic sharpness, "I'll find my way." She began to walk, at first slowly, obliquely, toward some contrived destination. Actually, she could not imagine where she was in relation to her hotel. The night world seemed blurred before her. Before she could gather her wits, she must get away from the do-gooder. She could not bear to face anyone. She made her way past him, hurling herself along the cobblestoned street. Her benefactor kept a brisk and puzzled pace alongside her.

"Where do you live?" he asked.

"The Wellington," she shot back. "Leave me alone."

"The Wellington's back that way," he mentioned hesitantly, following her. "I'll take you there, miss."

Velvet stopped and turned abruptly. "Can't you see, I . . . I'm embarrassed? I've just lost my supper in the middle of a strange city. Won't you . . . ?" At once, perhaps because of the quick movement, the sudden rise of her temper, Velvet felt the world turn gelatinous beneath her feet. It swung and swelled so that her balance failed her. She groped for something to keep her steady, but all she could find was the soft wool of the young man's coat. Grasping it, she watched the lights of the city swoop to dimness, and then there was nothing.

She heard the young man before she saw him. "I think she's waking up," he was saying.

Velvet unclosed her eyes very slowly. Focus was difficult, but she forced her consciousness to accept the fact of the stranger hovering above her. "Who are you?" she demanded softly.

"He's just a dear young fellow, is all," the familiar voice declared. Morgana. "If it wasn't for him picking you up from that gutter, I might've never seen you again." Her perfect oval of a face swam above Velvet, the lavish riot of her red curls a comforting sight. "Now you just keep this on your forehead, you silly thing." A cool cloth was clamped onto Velvet's brow. "How could you think to go running off like that? You ought to be ashamed."

Velvet struggled to sit up, to explain herself, but she was promptly shoved back onto the bed. Perhaps it is just as well, she thought. It would be too humiliating to try to explain to Morgana her earlier departure. "Who is he?" she asked.

The young man bowed over her. "My name is Erastus Winthrop, ma'am," he said. "And I'm happy to be of service." The man—he was a boy, really—was grinning broadly. His clean-shaven face sported deep, likable dimples in each cheek. A blond tousle of down drifted up as he bowed, and then lay feathered over his forehead. Velvet could not hold back the smile that curved her lips. She held up her hand.

"Happy to meet you, Erastus," she whispered. The boy winked confidentially as he shook her hand.

"This city is so big and noisy, everybody feels a little bit faint on first seeing it," he offered.

"You live here, darling?" asked Morgana from somewhere in the room. No matter how young they were, Velvet thought, Morgana was out to charm them.

"Not for long, miss," returned the young man. With a last quick, secretive smile in Velvet's direction, he turned away. "I'm heading south tomorrow."

"Are you?" said Morgana. "Well you'd better mind those plans, young sir. We've just had it on very good authority that there is terrible trouble down there. I strongly suggest you amend your itinerary."

"I'm afraid I haven't much choice," said Erastus.

Velvet drew off the cloth, and sat up awkwardly. "Are you in the army?" she asked.

The young man bowed his head. "It's a pity and a shame, ain't it?" he said softly. "I hadn't thought to go, and I want both you fine ladies to know I got nothing against my Southern brothers personally, but . . . yes, ma'am, I'm in the army. I'll tell you the truth, it would suit me just fine if Mr. Lincoln and Mr. Davis were to just fight this thing through, man to man, and not get the rest of us involved."

Velvet licked at her lips, and Erastus came immediately with a cup of water. After she had sipped, she said gently, "you're just a boy."

"I'm near sixteen," he said with a cocked smile. "You sound just like my ma." Morgana lifted a sly brow in Velvet's direction.

"I can assure you," Velvet returned, "I am not, by any means, old enough to be your ma."

"I know that, ma'am," the boy laughed. "What I meant was, she always tells me I'm just a boy. Well, she got to looking at me a bit differently when I handed her the three hundred dollars." Both women eyed him quizzically. "Three hundred dollars is what I got from Mr. Delaney to take his place in the army, don't you see," he explained. "I came down from Stony Point last week to sell the chickens from home, like I do every month, and I wasn't off the boat five minutes when this fellow, Mr. Delaney, comes up to me. He offered me three hundred dollars if I'd be here in the city today to answer his draft call. Naturally, I took the money. We're poor folk, don't you know, and that kind of money doesn't fall into our laps every day." Erastus lowered his gaze. "I know I sound kind of mercenary, but my daddy hasn't been around for years, and when your family's hungry, you'll do just about anything." Velvet hesitantly handed him the cup. He took it, and smiled. "Now, don't you ladies go worrying about me. I'll be fine. At least I talk the language — a little less genteelly than your Southern gentlemen, I'll grant," he added with a smile. "Most of your substitutes are foreigners, right off the boat. Now that's a sorry state to be in. Just get off the boat, somebody hands you three hundred dollars, and you go off to fight a war in a land you've barely heard about. But what are you going to do when that kind of money just falls in your lap? Most people don't see it's like their whole lives, don't you know."

Velvet nodded. She'd learned recently what it was like not to have money. She wondered if she wouldn't have done the very same thing under the same circumstances.

"Have you any idea of your destination?" she asked reluctantly.

The young man nodded. "Gettysburg, Pennsylvania," he said softly. Velvet's heart lurched. Thank God, it is not Virginia, she exulted, and then immediately amended her joy.

"We wish you well, Erastus," she said quickly. She smiled.

"You might wish us the same. We're headed for Virginia. Brandy Station." The young man seemed to become visibly pale. "What is it?" Velvet asked.

"Nothing, ma'am," he said quickly. He glanced at Morgana, who was watching him intently.

"If you've heard something," that woman said archly, "you'd better tell us."

"It's our home, you see," Velvet said urgently.

If possible, the lad paled even further. "News is spotty up to Stony Point," he said. "We don't get it like they do here. I wouldn't've heard anything if it weren't for my being here in the city today. I ain't even sure it's true, but . . ."

"But, what," Velvet demanded, clutching the boy's sleeve. When he did not answer immediately, she sat up fully, and faced him. "You must tell us what you know, Erastus," she said.

The boy ducked his head. "It's only that . . . well, I heard . . . well, the other boys was saying today we was lucky not to have been sent to Virginia. There's — as I hear it, don't you know — but it is just hearsay —"

"What!" Velvet nearly screamed.

"There's been fighting there, real vicious fighting," Erastus finally conceded. "That place where you said."

"Brandy Station?" asked Morgana, her amber gaze wide and fear-struck. "You can't mean it?" Erastus, his terrible message conveyed, simply nodded. "Well, that does it, we are not leaving New York City."

Velvet, ignoring the jolt to her weakened stomach and the dull pounding inside her head, jumped from the bed. "Oh, yes we are," she exclaimed. "And we are leaving tonight." She raced to the armoire and flung it open. She dragged from it her pack, along with several garments of indeterminate usefulness. Stuffing clothes, shoes, shawls, jewelry, and anything else that happened to be within reach into the overburdened canvas, Velvet informed Morgana that she could go or stay, or do anything else she pleased.

"But, surely, you can't think to continue south. That would be folly," Morgana declared. "And you *certainly* can't think to go alone, you silly twit."

"Silly twit that I am," Velvet shot back, "that is exactly what I

202

intend to do."

"But how will you get there?" For the first time in Velvet's memory, Morgana was completely unhinged. Even her infatuation with Cutter had not left her this befuddled. Velvet smiled. Despite her own frenzied sense of urgency, she was enjoying this.

"I'll take the train as we planned, Morgana dear." She continued her packing. Neither woman was paying the slightest attention to young Erastus, who was, by now, frantically attempting to get their attention.

"But, ma'am," he kept saying. At last Velvet turned to him.

"What is it?" she snapped.

"You can't."

"*What* can't I?" Velvet demanded impatiently.

"Get a train tonight."

"Why not?"

"You have to get hold of a safe conduct passage . . . ma'am," he said, his words slowing at Velvet's sudden stormy look.

"*Damn!*" Velvet ejaculated. "How long does that take?"

"A week—maybe two . . . under normal circumstances," the young man answered haltingly. He had been the bearer of so much in the way of bad tidings this night, he hesitated to bring more. Yet, as he watched the petite and fiery Velvet, so intent on her rash adventure, he could not bear to remain silent. "I'd be awful surprised if you got one at all, ma'am," he pressed. "With things like they are, they can't just let people go waltzing onto battlefields. Face it, ma'am, the only trains they're going to allow out of New York right now are troop trains." His pale eyes widened at the sudden blue-green glitter in Velvet's. The room seethed to a terrible silence.

"You wouldn't dare," Morgana breathed. Velvet tilted her a challenging look.

"Wouldn't I?"

"Now *that* would be folly." Morgana abruptly sat on a nearby chair, nearly sending herself and it reeling. "I cannot have you thinking what I know you're thinking," she declared, her eyes shifting wildly between Erastus and Velvet. "Tell her, Erastus."

"What should I tell her, miss?" he pleaded fervently. There was danger here, he perceived, but could not imagine its source.

"You tell her," demanded Morgana, "that she is not to even

think of taking a troop train south."

Erastus allowed seconds to pass as his mouth fell open, and his breath failed him. "Oh, miss," he said at last. "She's not thinking about that." He looked, with awe-filled disbelief at Morgana and then Velvet. "You're not thinking *that*, are you, ma'am?"

"That's exactly what I'm thinking," Velvet retorted. "And stop calling me 'ma'am'."

"But, ma'am . . ."

"Now, the two of you, help me finish my packing."

Morgana, twisting a handkerchief desperately, stood. "I'm sworn, this is the most insane . . . the most idiotic . . . They'll take you to the lunatic asylum in Sweetwater sure if you go through with this. Please don't do it, Velvet honey. You ought to remember your condition, if nothing else." Erastus Winthrop heard the words, felt he himself might faint, and took the opportunity to sit right down on the bed.

"Oh, ma'am," he breathed. "Oh, ma'am. You're in a . . . condition? Oh, Ma'am."

"I told you," Velvet stated, as she continued to pack, "don't call me 'ma'am.' "

Chapter Twenty-one

The morning air steamed to restless life. Velvet picked her way across the railroad yard, across broken shards of stones and glass, to the boxcar where perhaps a hundred men stood waiting to board. She tilted her begrimed face down, beneath the wide-brimmed hat, raising her shoulders, and waited with her pack like the others. They seemed a desultory army — some in rumpled uniforms, some in worn, stained, and grimy clothing more suited to their work on upstate farms. They lounged, unsoldierlike, about the barren expanse of the yard. Shouts, forced laughter, obscenities sailed about Velvet. If Erastus was correct, they would make connections with other troops south of New York. Velvet would soon come to know this disordered, irregular army as traveling companions. Naturally, they must not know her. She would keep unfailingly to herself, avoiding conversation, contact. She pulled herself tighter into the soft folds of Cutter's clothes. The smell and feel of them reminded Velvet of him. She knew that, at this moment, she was as lonely for him as she would ever be.

Unprotected, like the treeless, unsheltered railroad yard, from the vagaries of weather and fortune, Velvet snuggled herself into the shadow of the car, the only relief from the mist-dissipating July sun. She chanced a perusal of the long needle of track that cut the empty distance to the horizon, and immediately averted her gaze. She must not think about the journey.

At once, a tall officer dressed in a blue uniform stepped forward. An amorphous path was cleared among the men. He stood with hands on hips, grim-faced, and began to speak. Velvet heard the words only dimly. "Virginia," he had said. As Erastus had directed her, she'd reached the right train. That was really her only concern. Whatever else the man had to say did not pertain to her; she would be leaving the ranks as soon as — or shortly after — they reached the Potomac River. The officer's further words, the men, this place might have been a dream, some incomprehensible unreality.

Velvet was barely astonished as she saw the officer lurch and fall to the ground, the side of his head seemingly shattered. The spurt of blood, the shrill cry of a distant crowd, the scattering of the men around her seemed no more real to her than the past few hours. Not until she was grabbed and flung to the ground did she realize she was in danger.

"What is it?" she asked breathlessly of the man who had apparently saved her life. He glanced over at her as he drew a weapon.

"Draft riot," he answered tersely. "Better try to get to the car, sonny." Shots pierced the air. Rocks hurtled through it. Velvet scrambled, on her belly, in the direction of the train. The hiss of the engine towered over all other sounds, a cloud of steam blinded her. Velvet wadded herself into a tight clot, protecting herself against the missles in the air above her. A sudden, inexplicable weight heaved down onto her. Her breath was jolted from her as, flattened, she struggled to extricate herself. She shoved, and at last rolled free, only to have the weight follow her. It was a man. Limply, heavily, his arms swatted the ground next to her. She turned to look at him, and her vision was filled with blood. Velvet screamed, and struggled to her feet, tried to run; but her legs would not support her. She fell, with her pack, onto the oily shale of the yard floor. It might have been the floor of hell.

"Train's leavin'," a man shouted as he pounded by. Again, unmindful of the cutting stone beneath her, Velvet lifted herself, dragging her body and her pack toward the open door of the car. The dark hole lurched and moved across her vision. She followed it with her eyes, horrified, knowing it would leave her. A hand shot out of the darkness. Velvet grabbed it. It connected with her wrist, dragging her as the train gained speed. Running raggedly, she jumped as the hand jerked her upward. Her strength nearly failing, she gave one mighty heave, and her pack followed her into the moving dark.

"Sheee-it!" a man shouted as Velvet plumped down onto the hard, bumping floor of the car. "We made it!" There was a triumphant whoop, laughing, and general congratulations. Velvet blinked, attempted to acclimate her vision to the dark inside of the train. Except for the brief words "draft riot," she had no idea of what had happened. She peered at the men around her, assessing their expressions. Some were exultant, still others were solemn.

"We lost Benny," one man said grimly. "If I get out of this alive, I'm going to kill every one of those Copperhead bastards."

Velvet settled herself against the relative softness of her pack, in a corner, and continued to watch and listen. It was not until several hours into the jolting, steaming journey that she chanced an inquiry. The man next to her had just awakened from a nap. He rubbed at his grizzly chin, and drew a bottle from the pocket of his jacket. After taking a long draught, he offered it to Velvet. She shook her head and smiled weakly, trying to soften her refusal.

"Better have some, son," the man warned. "Might be the last whiskey you see for a while." He smiled. "Bet you're just a tad sorry you took my hand when I offered it back there." He pushed the bottle toward her. " 'Course, at the time, it seemed the best alternative."

Velvet knew that, short of being rude, she would have to avoid this friendly man's company. She averted her face and tugged at the chin strap that held her wide-brimmed hat in place. Clearing her throat, and attempting to disguise her Southern accent and feminine tones, she said, "Thank you . . . for both your hand and your bottle, but I'm really not very thirsty." The man squinted into the darkness at her.

"What's thirst got to do with anything?" he asked. He paused, looking at her, and Velvet drew herself deeper into her clothes. "How old are you, lad?" the man asked finally.

"N-not very old, sir," she said, drawing away from him.

"I can tell," he said shortly. He took another swig from his bottle. "That's what they're so fired up about."

"What is the problem?" Velvet asked, chancing the question against her better judgement.

The man glanced once again, not quite trusting his eyes, at his callow traveling companion. "Problem is," he stated, "the new draft act lets the rich ones take advantage of lads like yourself." He swiped at his mouth. "Damn shame about it, too. Up until March this was a volunteer army. But them fellas in Congress decided they needed more men to fight the Rebs. Wouldn't've been so bad if they'd just passed a draft law. It ain't that anyone likes getting drafted, mind you, but it'd be a lot easier to swallow if the law was

207

fair." He leaned confidentially toward Velvet. "I wouldn't want this to get around, but those fellows who attacked us today got a point, I got to say it, lad. It ain't fair that anybody rich enough to buy himself a substitute can get out of serving his time; that's all I'm saying. I got to agree with those boys on that. Don't spread it around, though. I'm like to get my ass kicked from here to Richmond, just for saying it."

"Your secret is safe with me," Velvet said, allowing a smile to curve her lips. The man cocked his head, his gaze narrowing.

"It appears, I ain't the only one got a secret on this train," he said. Velvet stiffened. "You're from the South, ain't you," the man continued.

"Yes," Velvet whispered, mightily relieved that he had discovered only a minute portion of her secret. "Yes, I am. But you mustn't tell." The man smiled slyly.

"I won't," he said very softly. He leaned back onto his own pack. "I won't say a word . . . lady." Velvet's eyes widened. She grabbed at the man, pulled him toward her with a force surprising to both of them. Both Velvet and her companion realized suddenly that they had garnered the attention of the other men in the darkened car. Velvet, thinking quickly, let go her hold, and pushed the man away, grabbing, as she did so at his bottle. The man immediately caught the direction of her ruse. "All you had to do was ask," he said gruffly. He turned to the curious onlookers and shrugged as Velvet downed a gulp of the liquid. Her resultant fit of choking made the men even more curious. "The boy's thirst overcame his reason, I'll wager," Velvet's companion said with a smile. The men grunted, some laughed in understanding, and then went back to their own business. "That wasn't smart," said the man from the corner of his mouth. Containing herself at last, Velvet thrust the bottle back toward the man. She gave him a withering glare. He laughed quietly. "Your secret's safe with me," he said, and lay back down.

"How did you know?" Velvet asked much later.

"It ain't hard," the man answered, "to know such things." Velvet eyed him askance.

"What gave me away?"

The man sat up slowly, and faced Velvet. "It's them eyes, lady. Don't think you're going to fool anybody. With them beautiful, beautiful eyes, you're a dead giveaway. But now you got me curious; what're you doing here?"

Velvet felt she owed the man an explanation. "I'm going home," she answered softly. The man shook his head. Velvet faced him squarely. Her hushed tone in no way diminished the intensity of her words. "I have to. Don't you see? War or no war; my family is there, and it's where I belong."

The man lay back down, and said quietly, "You belong in a flower garden, or in a grand ballroom. You don't belong here. None of us belongs here." His eyes closed, and he seemed to sleep.

The train pounded idly, resolutely, on. For two days, the habitual thump of the wheels lulled Velvet into a kind of euphoria. She even managed occasional sleep. She woke fitfully, at a certain point, battling a sudden silence. She bolted to a sitting position. The man next to her touched her shoulder, steadying her.

"Just take it real easy," he said softly. He offered her, as he had before during the trip, a broken piece of greasy sausage. Velvet refused the food, as she had before, her stomach rumbling languidly at the sight of it. She assumed they'd taken another comfort stop, but this time there was an urgency about the delay. The doors of the car scraped open, and blinding sunlight poured into the darkness.

"We'll be walking from here, men," said a voice from the sunlight. Muttered questions, grumblings, and a general stretching and moving of bodies answered the order.

"What's it about?" whispered Velvet. "Is this usual?"

The man shrugged. "Your guess is as good as mine." He stuffed the sausage into his pocket, and stood. Resisting the urge to aid Velvet, he watched as she, too, stood, struggling with her pack. "Oh, lady . . ." he sighed. Velvet looked up sharply. "Sorry," he muttered, and moved ahead of her to the doorway.

As, unaided, she climbed awkwardly from the train, Velvet realized the toll taken by the long ride. Her limbs ached appallingly. She stumbled, but another warning glance reined in her traveling companion's gallantry. A rueful smile crossed his lips as he turned, and began, with the other soldiers, a desultory march.

A soldier, walking the line of marchers, handed out weapons to those who had none. He identified, for Velvet and her friend, the odd shape of the tracks that had stalled the train. "They're calling them 'Sherman's neckties,' " he said. Velvet had looked, horrified,

209

on the twisted metal. Gnarled, charred, desolate, the writhing contours, once a busy railroad track, seemed shapeless symbols of some terrible, vicious sentence. Velvet could not imagine the hatred that had molded such destruction.

"Who did it?" she asked her friend.

"Your Southern boys, I imagine," he answered.

"But why?"

"It's a good bet they don't want us coming down here," the man said with a small laugh. "Can't blame them for that." Velvet looked up at him as they continued to trudge the long, foliated stretch along the track.

"Are they so desperate," she asked softly, "that they would do such a thing?" The man eyed her in bemusement.

"This is war, lady. Didn't you know that?"

"I guess," she said solemnly, "I didn't know what war was."

"You still don't," the man responded. His eyes, keenly focused on the path ahead, offered no explanation.

Velvet had lost track of time. She knew they had stopped for the night, she knew a new day had begun; but how many times had they stopped, how many new days had begun? The land was looking more and more familiar to her. Her weariness forgotten one humid afternoon, she nudged her friend.

"I think we're in Virginia," she whispered excitedly. The man merely nodded. "I knew it!" she exulted. She quickly checked her enthusiasm, however, and lowered her head. "I knew it," she repeated in a whisper. Unable to discipline herself, she allowed her eyes to wander throughout the afternoon, along the familiar, loved landscape. Suddenly, her attention became riveted. The man jostled her when she stopped.

"Come on, lady," he urged. "You can't give up now."

"I'm not giving up," she breathed. "That's L'Étoile de Vie." The man squinted into the distance. Upon a rise, in the heat-misted air, he saw what Velvet saw. He pushed down her pointing finger. "But it's—"

"It's just a ruined plantation," he said sharply. "Just that, and nothing more." Velvet, about to protest, saw a man ahead of her turn to glance over his shoulder at her pause, and then she saw

210

another do the same.

"Yes," she said, swallowing hard, continuing her walk, "that's just what it is." She watched, through the sunset, the tall columns disappear behind them. No one noticed that the little soldier taking up the rear of the battalion, probably the youngest recruit the Northern army had ever had, kept swiping at his eyes.

Once they had bedded down for the night, Velvet made her silent way to where her friend slept. She shook him furtively. He mumbled broken phrases, and then pitched to consciousness. Velvet calmed him hastily. "It's me," she whispered.

"What's wrong?" he asked.

"I'm going home," she answered. The man sat up.

"I figured," he said softly. "You knew that plantation back there."

Velvet nodded. "It was L'Étoile de Vie. It belongs . . . belonged to friends of mine; the Carletons. Sweet Briar Hill isn't far from here." She smiled up at the man. "You've never told me your name," she said. "I'd like to know it."

"Name's McCulloch," he said quietly. "James McCulloch."

"I'm very glad to have met you, James McCulloch," Velvet said. "My name's Velvet . . . McBride. If you ever get to Brandy Station, you look me up."

"You take good care of yourself, lady. This here's Reb territory."

Velvet quirked her brow. "But I'm a Reb," she said wryly.

"That may be," James McCulloch answered, "but your boys ain't going to make too many distinctions when they start shooting at intruders, so you mind yourself."

"I will," Velvet said. "Thank you for keeping my secret."

"And thanks for keeping mine."

"Which secret is that?"

He smiled. "You must've guessed it. It's the one about me not wanting to be here . . . and all that implies," he answered quietly.

"Anytime," she said, patting his arm. "Anytime." In the quiet moonlit dark, Velvet slipped away. James McCulloch watched her leave. He watched until the darkness obscured the lithe figure. "Those eyes'll give her away, sure," he said softly to himself, as he lay down and tried to sleep.

211

Chapter Twenty-two

Velvet had retraced her steps through the soft night forest. As the moon spread its last silver spume upon the shore of the world, she came upon the proud, spent splendor of L' Étoile de Vie. Through the columns, bright shadows traced a haunted path as the moon moved on. Dimly lighted verandas, all too achingly familiar, greeted Velvet as she treaded the once gracefully foliaged, now overgrown, drive leading up to the house. She blinked uncomprehendingly. Some whimsical trick of her memory's famished eye, or the moonshine, or the lustrous dark led her to believe she could see the inside of the house as well as the outside. She blinked again. Still the phantom interiors — hallways, staircases and high-ceilinged rooms — like ravaged specters, loomed in the shadowed grandeur before her as she approached. She saw, at last, what she'd not seen that afternoon. L' Étoile de Vie, that glorious endorsement of the nobility of her homeland, had been savaged. One side of its ornate main front had been torn away. "Oh, God," she breathed aloud. Velvet began to run, dragging herself raggedly toward a thing she could not bear to accept.

A shot pierced the night silence. Velvet gasped and halted her progress, nearly tumbling to the ground. Her eyes widened. She searched the moonlit dark wildly. Another shot rang out. Velvet dove to the ground. She rolled to the relative shelter of a low, arching shrub. Kneeling in its shadow, she peered into the night toward the house. She was sure the shot had come from there. At once, she saw movement on the porch. Men in pale uniforms shouted to one another, their boots making hollow thunder beneath them. She must explain to them that she was not an enemy. She stood. A third shot exploded, serrating the grass near her feet. Velvet scrambled behind the bush, and huddled there. How can I explain if I can't get near them? she wondered, her heart lurching wildly. Trembling, more afraid than she had ever recalled being, she hunkered, pushing herself into the enshrouding foliage. It whispered, rustled against her quivering form, threatening to reveal her concealment. Velvet held herself very still, waiting for another shot. It did not come. Instead, the air around her seethed with a certain gorged silence. Velvet risked a peek around the cover of the bush. She saw no shapes on the porch. The men must have camouflaged themselves—or maybe they'd left. Long moments passed in which her thudding heart slowly eased to a more governed cadence. Perhaps, she thought, with less than certain optimism, they had seen her head for the trees, and realized she was no danger to them—only afraid. She was about to chance another attempt to get to the house, when a low voice behind her riveted her attention.

"Drop the weapon, lad," the voice commanded. Velvet looked down incredulously at her shoulder, strapped and supporting a gun. She had not even remembered that she carried it. With the weight of her pack, it had been merely another encumbrance for her to bear. She hastily slid the weapon off her shoulder, and it fell with a dull thud to the grassy earth. "Now stand up nice and slow, and turn around." Velvet did exactly as she was told. She could not avoid, even in her terror, the sudden, relieved realization that the tones commanding her were distinctly Southern. At last, she could make contact with one of her own kind. She watched the shadowed darkness as a darker form emerged. A man stood up, and moved to her. Before she could make out his features, she saw the charred barrel of his gun glinting dully in the moonlight. It was directed on her. As the figure came near, Velvet cringed away from it. She swallowed hard, forcing herself to speak.

"Please don't shoot me," she entreated breathlessly. "I'm not a soldier."

"Anyone else with you?" the man asked.

"No," Velvet responded hastily. "I'm alone."

"You on the run, son?" the man inquired lazily.

"I'm . . . I'm not . . . what you said. Not that, or . . . anything. I'm going home." Velvet gazed up at him, her eyes softened in the moonlight by fear. The man allowed himself a long pause. Velvet heard him draw in his breath.

"You're a . . . a girl," he observed in awe.

"Yes," Velvet said joyfully, dropping her hands in premature anticipation of a reprieve. A click resonated in the dark silence, the man backed away, steadying his aim.

"Hold it," he ordered, his voice surly. Velvet checked her enthusiasm, and splayed a hand against the man's aggression.

"I understand," she said softly, evenly, allowing no emotion to color her response. She raised her hands warily. She was on dangerous ground, she realized. She'd assumed correctly that this fellow was a Southerner, but he was a soldier as well, and no doubt drilled in practiced caution. She took a long, calming breath. "I am a woman," she began again, "and no soldier. You see I wear no uniform. I am, like you, a Southerner."

"Turn around," the fellow said curtly. Velvet did so. A chill ribbon of fear raced up her spine, but she resisted the urge to shudder. "March," the man ordered. Again, Velvet followed the command precisely. He was not, apparently, about to shoot her in the back. With hard, urgent pokes, he prodded her up the drive toward the house. Uttering a husky summons, loud enough to be heard by his comrades but not loud enough to reach the ears of a possibly concealed enemy, the man brought attention to their approach. Several soldiers hurried out onto the veranda, and several others came from the grounds surrounding the house to join them.

"Is he alone?" asked one of the uniformed men.

"He's no 'he,' " Velvet's escort responded in a hoarse voice. The others gathered quickly, curiously, silently, to assist in the capture of this most arresting prisoner.

Velvet was ushered into what had been the Carletons' graceful library. That room was on the side of the house that had not been destroyed. Still, the wreckage there appalled her. Lofting bookcases, once adorned by polished, leather-bound volumes bore the scars of flaming destruction. Like the outside of the house, the inside walls were charred, starkly barren, and sagged piteously; the draperies hung in tattered scraps against the broken glass of the French windows. Tears popped into Velvet's widened eyes as she viewed the wretched shade of a once-grand salon. Forgetting her own perilous circumstance, Velvet turned slowly as she stood amid the terrible waste. Her hands fell to her sides. On a certain level, Velvet could understand—if she could not accept—the destruction of the railroad tracks she had seen just a few days ago. But how could anyone, any civilized human being, destroy a noble

214

house? And what of the Carletons; where were they?

Velvet glanced around quickly. Behind her, men stood, watching her with guarded interest. Before her, she saw in the dimness of the moonlight, a man sitting with his foot stretched up and resting on Mr. Carleton's French teak desk. Velvet moved to him slowly.

"Who are you?" she asked.

"I might ask the same of you?" the man responded easily. He was obviously in charge, and deeply comfortable in his command.

"My name is Velvet . . . McBride. I live at Sweet Briar Hill. My father is Steven McBride." As she spoke, Velvet felt her confidence rise. She, after all, belonged here. "This is my friend Morgana's house."

"Was," the man at the desk rejoined.

"I beg your pardon?"

"Was," said the man, easing himself up out of the chair. "It *was* your friend Morgana's house. Now it's mine." The man moved toward Velvet slowly.

"Did you destroy it?" Velvet asked, stiffening.

The man stood over her for a long moment. He seemed to be examining her. "No," he answered at last.

Velvet lowered her gaze. The moonstruck darkness had caught the glimmer of mistrust in the man's eyes. She must not allow herself the indulgence of fear, or tears. "I have told your friend that, like you, I am from the South," she began, repressing the rage she felt over the destruction of the house.

"Private Jackson," the man put in. Velvet glanced up quizzically. "You told Private Jackson you were from the South," the man explained tersely. "That's the man who brought you up here." Velvet nodded.

"Yes," she said quietly. "Private Jackson. I told him I am a Southerner . . . a private citizen. And I told him I'm heading home."

"That's all?"

"What more would you like me to say?" Velvet asked, frustration beginning to build. "I've told the truth. I don't see—"

From behind her, a sudden movement caught her attention. "Federal issue," Private Jackson said as he tossed her gun to the man in charge. That soldier caught it with one snaking gesture and held it before Velvet just at her eye level. In the waning light of the moon, the long weapon glinted alarmingly.

"It's not mine," Velvet said carefully, her gaze taking in the full length of the rifle.

"Whose then?" her interrogator demanded.

"They gave it to me, and I . . . I . . . just started carrying it."

"Who gave it to you?"

"Some gentleman from the train. . ." Her voice trailed off. She could not say much more without endangering those soldiers with whom she had traveled South.

"The train?" the man asked easily. His smile glistened horribly in the dark. Velvet swallowed hard. "You wouldn't happen to have been with that little group that went by today, would you?"

"Wh-what group?" Velvet asked, determined to plead absolute innocence.

" 'Cause if you were," the man said, "I ought to know about it." Never had Velvet heard one Southerner speak so malevolently to another. His tones held a cunning cruelty that stunned her. Her gaze lifted, and she saw in his coldness, suspicion of guilt, even . . . hatred. Her mouth dry, she ran her tongue over her lips. Silence resonated around her in the dark.

"I don't know what you're talking about," she said, her voice barely above a whisper.

"I think you do." He paused. "But even if you don't, it won't change things any; that little bunch is walking right into an ambush." His smile deepened as he watched Velvet stiffen. "You've got a friend or two among that sorry little collection, have you?" He turned away. "My, my," he said softly. He sat against the desk and folded his arms across his wide chest. "I'll just bet you'd like to go out right now and warn those Northern boys that the whole Reb army is about to descend on them. 'Cause that's what's going to happen, sure enough. At least, that's what it'll seem like. They'll wake up at dawn with that horrible Rebel yell screaming in their ears. They'll think the world has died, and is shrieking out its last terrible agonies. But," he added, "it'll be them that's dying. Now," the man said, "you want to tell me about that gun?"

In the time it had taken for the soldier to spew his litany of hate against the Northern soldiers, Velvet had gathered what little composure she could manage. She had been a fool to be intimidated by this pompous oaf who was overgorged with his own importance. She had forgotten for a moment who she was, what lessons she had learned at her mother's knee. Perhaps she'd been North too long, she thought wryly. Her gaze fell, allowing the fans of her lashes to sweep the pale curve of her cheeks.

"May I . . . may I take off my hat?" she murmured. She looked up to see the soldier before her hesitate, then nod curtly. Velvet carefully undid the lacing at her chin, and very slowly removed the wide-brimmed hat. At the same time, she raised the perfect oval of her face and let the flaxen-streaked curls of her dark hair swirl down about her shoulders. She looked straight at the arrogant questioner. In the lusterless new light of the milky dawn, she was deeply satisfied to see his gaze narrow and glint. "I know what you must be thinking," she said softly, "and I can't blame you for it. I'd be thinking the same thing were I in your position." She shook her head lightly, helplessly. The gesture, subtle and feminine, caused her curls to form sweet ringlets about her face. "All I can tell you is the truth. Naturally," she added, allowing her eyes to widen and her mouth to form a small pout, "I can only depend upon your belief in that truth. I am, you might say, at your mercy." She lowered her lashes again, splaying her hands at her sides in a gesture of defenselessness. Velvet raised her chin bravely, and cast a sweeping glance over her shoulder. Her eyes took in the other soldiers behind her who seemed all too ready to listen to her explanation — if only she could come up with one.

"You see . . ." she began, searching her mind rabidly for details that would catch the sympathy of these particular men. "My dear, sweet mammy is waiting for me — I just know it. When my family sent me north two years ago, I promised her I'd be back. I told her that somehow, some way, I'd make it back to her . . . even if I died trying." Velvet lifted a dark brow, and chanced another look over her shoulder. Surely, among this collection of roughened, rude soldiers, there was at least one who recalled the sweet mammy of his childhood. "She's going to be so worried," Velvet offered. "I can see the tears just streaming down her tired old face." Velvet clasped her hands to her breast, and chanced a piteous stare into some far middle distance. In truth, her mind conjured that picture of Mammy Jane for her, allowing soft tears to form dewy crystals on her thick lashes. "It was for her that I decided upon this rash course of action. I took the Fredricksburg and Potomac toward Richmond," she continued breathlessly. "It was terrible; a finely bred

daughter of the South traveling alone; vulnerable to all sorts of
. . . danger. But I knew I must go. A kind gentleman, a true
Southern son of chivalry gave me that gun when he realized I was
determined to leave the train and travel by foot to Sweet Briar Hill.
He said, " 'Our gallant lads aren't going to make too many distinctions when they start shooting at intruders.' " James McCulloch
had said those words — sort of — and Velvet knew that the best lies
always had a seed of truth. She smiled as though in pleasant memory. "That dear man had retrieved the gun from a dead Northerner, he told me, and he said he was proud it was being put to such
good use." Velvet angled her chin even higher. "Even if I die tonight," she said, calling up all the drama of the finest tragediennes
she'd seen, "I know that proud warrior would be joyous to learn I'd
come this far. And my dear mammy," she finished, altering her
tone to a sentimental hush, "must know, with her world-weary
wisdom, that I tried to reach her." She bowed her head. "The spirit
of the South is in my heart, and that will never die." Velvet smiled
with inward satisfaction as she listened to the muffled sniffles in the
group behind her. Unfortunately, her inquisitor was not so easily
moved. he merely watched her.

Finally, he said resentfully, "I never had a mammy." Velvet realized that she might have made a slight error in judgement. She did
not succumb, however, to the sudden chill that trickled into her
heart. Keeping her eyes on the floor, she waited for the man's next
pronouncement. It came after a long moment. "Private Jackson,
take this woman to the stable. We'll keep her for a while and see if
her story changes."

Velvet glanced up. "Am I to be your prisoner?" she asked in a
small voice. The man nodded, and a grim smile curved his lips.

"Your sweet . . . mammy will just have to wait a little longer."
He turned abruptly as Private Jackson escorted Velvet outside and
to the stable.

As they walked, their feet crunching on the pebbled path, Velvet
chanced several glances at her guard. In the quickening dawn
gray, she found in his countenance what she had hoped to find —
Private Jackson was one of the snifflers.

Chapter Twenty-three

Silently, Private Jackson lit a lamp, shooed an impatient animal from its stall, and piled hay within. As he worked, he eyed Velvet sheepishly. For her part, Velvet merely waited for the young soldier to finish. He did finally, and with a deferential nod, he ushered her into the stall. She picked her way into the tiny enclosure, frowning at the odor and the rudeness of her prison.

"I'm deeply sorry, ma'am," apologized Private Jackson softly. "I just don't know what to tell you, except try to make yourself as comfortable as possible." He paused. "He'll change his mind; you wait and see." Velvet looked up. Private Jackson's discomfort was apparent. He glanced away. "Honestly, ma'am, if I'd thought it was going to end like this, I'd have let you get away."

"You were just doing your duty," Velvet murmured. She set down her pack gingerly. "Do you know what will happen to me?" she asked. Her eyes were liquid turquoise in the lamplight. Private Jackson shifted uncomfortably.

"I wish I knew, ma'am," he said, his voice harsher than he'd intended it to be. He managed a small, helpless smile. "I mean . . ." He laughed nervously. "The captain's a hard man. I think he resents most folks—rich ones, anyhow. He's always making comments about us 'advantaged' boys—that's what he calls us—and giving us the most tedious, disgusting, dangerous assignments. I knew, as soon as you started telling your story, that he was going to get himself into a growling snit over it. He won't be fit to live with." The young soldier shook his head sadly. "I feel sorry for them Yankees when he gets ahold of them."

"Is he going to attack that . . . group of soldiers he mentioned?"

"He is, ma'am. They're assembling now. Those Northern boys are going to get hit from four sides. They walked by here so

219

innocent this afternoon, but we sent out a rider as soon as we spotted them. There's three other battalions waiting to come down on them at dawn. Captain McCulloch is probably drooling by now." Velvet looked up sharply.

"Captain McCulloch?" she asked. The soldier nodded. "His name is McCulloch?"

"Yes, ma'am," Private Jackson said in puzzlement.

"There's a James McCulloch among those Northern soldiers."

The private shrugged. "I've heard him mention a brother, but I don't see—"

Velvet grabbed a desperate handful of the man's jacket. "Take me to the captain," she implored.

"I can't do that, ma'am," Private Jackson said with a desperation equal to Velvet's own. He attempted to pry her hands away, and to calm her. "Just because the names match up doesn't mean—"

"Please, private—"

"Oh, ma'am, it won't do any good, don't you know that? Don't you know that all over the South brothers are killing brothers? And you'll just make things worse for yourself." He paused. "Listen."

Velvet's attention was suddenly caught by the sound of men's voices. Her eyes widened.

"Are they coming down to gather the horses?" she asked.

"Yes," the soldier said softly. Velvet stared up into his eyes. In that moment of sad communication, the two young people understood fully the hopelessness of Velvet's situation. "If you tell him what you know," the private said, "he'll know you were with those soldiers today." Velvet turned away, struck dumb. At last she looked back at Private Jackson.

"I don't care," she said quietly. "I've got to see Captain McCulloch. I've got to tell him—"

"Tell him what?" He moved to her and grabbed her shoulders. "Don't you understand, it won't make one bit of difference? Even if he would speak to you—and I know he would not—even if you told him what you know, it wouldn't make a difference." His words were emphatic, his tone crushing.

She and Private Jackson listened as the stable came alive with the activity of horses being blanketed and saddled, the clinks and rattles of bridles being slipped on. The young man eyed Velvet one last time, and then stepped from the enclosure, shutting the stall gate behind him. Velvet looked up at the tall barrier. She listened for long moments to terse commands made to Private Jackson about his prisoner. Then the sounds died, as the men and their horses headed outside. Finally, when the stable was once again silent, she called out to her guard.

"I've got to do something," she said. Only silence answered her. "Private Jackson?" she called. Again silence filled the dimly lit recesses of her tiny cell.

"I'm here," he said at last. With his voice, the silence suddenly became filled with the thunder of hooves in the distance.

"You've got to let me out," Velvet said with quiet intensity.

"I can't do that, ma'am," he answered.

"Yes you can, Private." Velvet moved to the thick wooden gate, and leaned against it, caressing it as though it were a lover. "You have no choice. You've done your martial duty, Private, now you must do your moral duty." Velvet went on relentlessly. "Just suppose the two McCullochs *are* brothers. Just suppose that's true, Private; just suppose."

"I don't see how it could be—"

"But suppose it is? Do you want to be responsible for such a horrible possibility—brother fighting against brother?"

"I told you, ma'am—"

"I know," Velvet burst out. "You told me that all over the South brothers are fighting brothers. Does that make it right?"

"It only makes it true, ma'am," the voice said harshly. Velvet pushed herself away from the door. Frustration and defeat warring for supremacy against desperation and resolve.

I am going to get out of here, Velvet thought with determination. She eyed the small prison. High above her there was an aperture. She stepped to it, and reached up. Her fingertips would not reach the sill. She attempted silently to imagine herself piling hay and reaching the opening. Even if she did reach it, however, she realized, as she studied the small slit, that she would never be able to crawl through it. Instead, she concentrated her next scrutiny on the earthen floor. She pushed against the hay, and felt the boards of the stable where they met the ground—only they did not meet the ground. She felt wildly along the bottom of the building, realizing that there was a cleft between it and the earth on which it was built. She quickly looked back at the door. It stood impassively between her and Private Jackson. Velvet called again to him.

"Are you going to stay out there all day?" she asked.

"For as long as I'm told to, ma'am," he answered.

"Would you talk to me, at least?" she said, her tone melancholy and inviting.

"I think I could do that," Private Jackson said. Velvet detected a distinct sympathy in the young soldier.

"I wouldn't want you to compromise your sense of duty," she called out softly.

"It's okay, ma'am," he answered, a smile in his voice, "we're only talking."

"Yes," Velvet said with satisfaction. "What happened to the Carletons?" she asked. She went to her pack, and quietly rummaged through it.

"I couldn't say," Private Jackson answered. "The house was deserted when we got here. Could be they're in Richmond. Lot's of folks have gone there to pay their last respects to old 'Stonewall' Jackson."

Velvet looked up from her search. "Last respects?" she asked.

"Yes, ma'am," said the young soldier. "He passed on. Lost his arm at Chancellorsville. It was a real tragedy. His own regiment accidentally fired on him. How's that for horrible irony?" he asked. Velvet nodded wordlessly. "The irony of the two McCullochs is nothing compared to that," he added.

"I think both situations are appalling," Velvet responded, and quickly altered the adversarial nature of her tone, "don't you, Private?"

"Yes, ma'am, I do. But that's how it goes in a war. . . ." Private Jackson went on, and Velvet tried to listen, though her concentration was riveted, at the moment, on finding something with which to dig. Her hand rested on a kid slipper. She pulled it out of the bag. What in the world, she wondered, had made her bring that? Then she recalled the manner of her packing; she'd not bothered to index her possessions — or even to care what she was bringing with her. She'd grabbed things from the armoire, and simply flung them into her pack. The shoe had a small, high heel. It might serve. She crawled with it to the outer wall of the stable, and began to dig. The earth was hard, but slowly, with her relentless excavation, it began to give way—chunk by chunk. Silence abruptly resonated in her ears, and she realized that Private Jackson had been quiet for some time.

"So you think the Carletons might have gone to Richmond?" she asked, praying that her question would not seem so obscure that the soldier would realize she'd not been listening to him.

"Or to Mexico, or Europe," he said. "Lots of Southerners have left the country—the rich ones, anyway. I don't blame them, either. It's been so bad here, ma'am. Things have changed. One night I wrapped myself in a carpet from a house we went into last winter. It had a pattern of roses, and it made me think about my house in Kentucky. It made me think about the roses climbing over the end of the porch—pink ones, and yellow ones. It's probably starting to get real pretty in the valley now." His voice caught. "I just wonder if the roses are still there."

Velvet found that as she'd been listening to the young soldier, she'd been thinking about her own home, wondering if it had changed. She shook off her reflective mood, and continued her work. She dipped water from the small trough into her hat, and carefully poured it over the ground, making it softer, easier to dig into.

"I wonder about my home, too," she said.

"Are you really heading home like you said?" the private asked.

"Yes, I am."

"How come you were with those Northerners?"

"It's the only way I could get South," she answered. "I had to take a troop train, but we were delayed because of some broken tracks. We had to walk." She heard the soft chuckle. "Did your boys do it?" she asked.

"You mean the tracks?" Private Jackson asked. "We sure did," he responded, not waiting for her reply.

"It seems so . . . frightening . . . so destructive," Velvet said softly.

"Yes, ma'am," the young soldier answered. "It sure is frightening."

Velvet was finding that her efforts were being more than rewarded. The hole she'd made was quite large. Through it, she could see a lightening dawn. She glanced furtively at the door. It remained stolidly closed. "Not as frightening, though," she said to the door, "as the destruction of the Carleton's house."

"That was too bad, ma'am," said Private Jackson, "but, like the captain told you, we didn't do that. We're just occupying the house."

"Who destroyed it?" Velvet asked, and then burrowed down to continue her digging.

"The Northerners, I guess. They been coming down here burning, stealing. You wouldn't believe it, ma'am, what they've done. But I suppose they're looking for food all the time, just like we are. They're as underfed as us, I hear. What I can't understand is, why they think they've got to demolish the houses. It doesn't seem entirely fair to me. It's almost like they're waging a war against the land itself. It's like . . . to them it doesn't matter who wins, as long as our way of life is destroyed in the process." His voice trailed off. "It doesn't seem fair." Again, his silence prompted Velvet to speak. She lifted her head abruptly, bumping it soundly on the wall. She winced and held the wound for a second.

Taking a deep calming breath, she said, "No, it doesn't seem fair, Private." Appalled, Velvet felt the warm stickiness of blood, and hastily examined her hand. She was bleeding profusely, but she knew that any exclamation would betray her. "I . . . I suppose," she said, suppressing a deep shudder, "in order to be completely fair, the war ought to be fought up North, as well as down here."

"That's the truth, ma'am. But you just try to convince one of those hotheaded Northerners of such a thing. We're trying, though."

"And I know you'll keep trying," Velvet ground out, as her own efforts continued. She dug rabidly, entirely abandoning the aid of her little shoe. Fear and pain guided her now.

"You know . . . Velvet," Private Jackson said, his tone becoming intimate, "you never did tell me the true story about why you're here — and with a gun, no less." He chuckled softly. "I'll bet you really do have a sweet mammy waiting for you, though."

Velvet, sliding backward into the stall, answered breathlessly,

"Mammy Jane."

"I knew it. Mine's Abby. She is the sweetest mammy in the whole world. But you know," he continued reminiscently, "she can be awful mean; she's like a hound of hell when somebody crosses her. She was never mean to me, though. She's probably so worried about me — wondering if I'm getting my grits every day, wondering if I'm clean, dry. Yours, too, I'll bet. That's how they are." His voice trailed off into sweet remembrance. "I think I miss her more than my own mother — well, maybe not more. I don't know." He paused, listening. "Don't be too downhearted, Velvet. I know how you must feel. I'll see what I can do with Captain McCulloch." He heard the quiet, muffled urgency of her breathing. "Please don't cry, honey," he said soothingly. "This is no time to give up." He heard the softening of her breath. Perhaps, he mused, she was falling asleep. Poor lamb must be exhausted. Gently bred girls were not cut out for this kind of perturbation. He laughed softly. Once this was over, he would make it a point to get to know her better. She was some unusual little piece of work. In a while, he would talk with her again, find out the truth of her story. Private Jackson felt himself tranquilized by the silence behind the door. No reason why, if she had succumbed to sleep, he should not. He smiled comfortably, and closed his eyes as he slid to a sitting position on the floor of the stable. "Rest easy, sugar," he said gently. "We'll have you out of there in no time."

The sky turned from charcoal to a deep, soft slate as Velvet made her way through the wood surrounding the Carleton plantation. She had decided she would backtrack before heading on to Sweet Briar Hill, and see if she could find a way to warn the Northern soldiers — her former traveling companions — of the impending attack. In her heart, she knew what she would find. If only she'd been allowed to talk to Captain McCulloch. Private Jackson had told her it would do no good, but somehow Velvet believed she could have stopped the captain — at the very least, she could have tried. She swiped at tears as she walked, unburdened now, toward the place where she'd left James McCulloch. She had left her pack behind; it would not fit through the slim burrow she'd made beneath the stable. It was a miracle that she had fit. She looked down at her hands as she stopped the rest against the bole of a tree. Muddied, scratched, devoid of any womanly appearance, they might have been those of a field hand. Velvet ran the roughened fingertips over her forehead, and realized she'd not stopped bleeding. Warm weals of blood trickled onto her hands and down her arms. She leaned her head onto her arms, and allowed herself the luxury of extravagant, body-wrenching sobs.

Velvet was hungry, deeply hungry. She'd not eaten since she'd picked at the meager army meal she'd been offered before she'd left her companions from the train. She was thirsty, hot — the morning was already promising a warm day — bloodied, tired. She leaned back against the tree. Soft breezes caught the thick matting of her hair. She must go to James McCulloch. She must not allow herself to indulge in self-pity. She raised herself slowly, and continued her march. At last she reached the top of a rise overlooking a valley. She sidled her way down the steep hillside, catching onto the branches of low-growing shrubbery to control her descent. At last, she came to the clearing she'd left only the night before. It looked very different in the brightening light of day. She saw amid the foliage what she had feared so much to see. Bodies littered the ground. What had seemed only a dim horror became for Velvet a stark and terrible reality. She moved, her senses alive, to where she imagined she'd left James. She shoved at the limp weight of the form lying on the ground. It was not him. She ran to another prone body, and then to another and another. Each time, she pushed at the man's weight, and each time, as the body rolled over, she looked for the face of James McCulloch. With mounting hope, unmindful of the death surrounding her, Velvet ran from man to man. Perhaps James had escaped the terrible destiny of the others. Perhaps Captain McCulloch had discovered at the last moment that his brother was among these men. Perhaps they'd embraced each other, and . . . At last, horror struck, she heaved against the weight of yet another young soldier, and she saw him. Velvet, for the first time in her young life, viewed the face of death — true death — the death of someone she had known.

The world turned dark, and upside down. Velvet felt herself

falling, whirled mercilessly in a miasma of destruction. She heard a scream, and she knew it was her own. And then she heard nothing.

The sun was fully up when Velvet finally awakened. She lay across the body of James McCulloch. Her heart was drowned in tears as she pulled herself away from his stiffened form. Yet, she found herself unable to cry. Velvet lifted herself. As she stood up, she said a silent prayer, and then did what she knew she must. She reached into the pocket of his dark, blood-stiffened jacket, and drew out the bottle she had known would be there. She lifted it and drank deeply. She felt for money, and took whatever she imagined might be of some use to her. Then she went searching among the other bodies. She found some beef jerky, and ate it greedily. She found hard biscuits in another pocket, and stuffed them into her own. She glanced around one last time before she left. Her eyes settled on James, and her throat closed. She realized she hardly knew him.

At last, Velvet turned away, walking heavily, toward home.

Chapter Twenty-four

Had it been minutes, hours, days? Velvet realized, before the world swirled around her, that the food she'd taken from the dead had been too little to sustain her. She had made it to the top of the rise, and then collapsed. She lay beneath the pinkened sky, feeling the hardness of pain from her abdomen engulf her. She might have swung in and out of consciousness; she could not tell. For long moments, she would be in the dark — a ravaged dark, not a peaceful one — haunted by lingering specters, rising ghostly pale above her. And then, suddenly, blindingly, it would be light. But the light was not the sunlight of a springtime afternoon; it was a hellish light. Crystalline heat stung her, and she writhed against the snaking agony. At last, at long last, she felt a gush of quiet calm envelop her.

Sounds, men's voices, the crunching of boots on dried leaves and foliage, surrounded her. Bird songs lifted her, in the dark, on waves of melody.

The bright was dark; the light diffused in lyrical shadows overhead. Velvet lay quietly for long moments, and waited. What was this place? She wondered idly if she was at home, at Sweet Briar Hill. Perhaps she had been found and taken there. But who was it that might have found her? Who was it that might have carried her home? She heard a sweet sound, a woman sound. Someone was singing far away. Maybe I'm in heaven, Velvet thought wryly. But, of course, I couldn't be in heaven, she reflected; angels are all men — at least that's what the Bible says.

She lifted her head weakly, and out of the shadowed light she saw, coming toward her . . . Arabella. Velvet was home! She bolted to a sitting position, and reeled forward. The figure before her caught her and laid her back.

"Arabella," she whispered, and the smooth, brown young face above her vanished.

Bright water splashed coolly at her feet. It was the gurgling stream that ran through the sweetly green meadows at Sweet Briar Hill. Velvet laughed as she ran to the water's edge. The day was warm, and she lingered at the little stream, dipping her fingertips roguishly into the burbling depths. It was the day of the Carleton barbecue, and Mammy Jane had told her to keep herself tidy until the carriage came around. Arabella was behind her, pleading that she not get herself into trouble.

"Mammy'll tan you for sure, Miss Velvet. She'll tan you, but she'll stripe me bloody," the girl was saying.

"Shoot, honey child," Velvet laughed, "stupid, old, fat Mammy Jane doesn't scare me one little bit! She'll have to catch me before she can tan me." At Arabella's wide-gazed horror, Velvet merely giggled and swiped off her straw bonnet. Tossing it across the lawn, she followed it with her eyes, and gleefully watched its descent onto a nodding wisteria bush. Arabella hastily retrieved the hat, and brushed and smoothed at the ribbons.

"You mess up your pretty things, and Mammy Jane'll skin us both," the girl scolded. "You think old Mammy can't run so fast, but I once saw her outrace a horse." Arabella's little chin lifted haughtily at Velvet's astonishment. "You think I'm funning you? Well, I'm not," the girl insisted. "It was midnight, one night down in the quarters, and . . ." Arabella placed the bonnet firmly on Velvet's head, tied the ribbons beneath her chin, and led her back to the main house, as she continued her story. ". . . there was all this yelling. The men couldn't stop that old pony; it just leapt the fence, and started running as fast as you can ever imagine a horse could run. Well, Mammy Jane hitched up her night dress, and followed it out into the night." Arabella's voice took on a low, mysterious tone. "After a while, she came leading that poor animal out of the dark. It didn't have a chance."

"That doesn't mean she actually outraced it," Velvet scoffed uncertainly, as the little girls made their way across the lawn.

"It doesn't mean she didn't." Arabella insisted soothingly. "Nobody really knows what happened out there in the dark between that horse and Mammy Jane; now, do they?" Velvet shook her head, puzzled at the image of the big woman chasing down a horse. "It's like everybody says," Arabella continued, "you better mind your p's and q's around Mammy Jane. You just never know about what an old, fat lady can do, if she sets her mind to it."

A new respect was born in Velvet for Mammy Jane, and it stayed with her long after she'd ceased to believe the horse story.

Velvet's eyelids fluttered up. Had it been a memory, or a dream, she wondered? Had she been awake or asleep these past moments? The images had been so real — bright, sunny images. Impressions of warmth, of tenderness enfolded her, even as blankets were nested around her shoulders. Arabella . . . *home*. Velvet tried to lift herself.

"Now, you just calm yourself, Miss Velvet," the voice said, as though it had been saying it, like that, for years.

"Arabella?"

"It's me." The face swam above her. Velvet smiled, and closed her eyes.

"Are we home?" There was a silence. "Are we at Sweet Briar Hill?" she asked, opening her eyes. Arabella was clearly above her.

"No, Miss Velvet," the young woman said gently. She sat near, on the edge of the bed. "We're in a hospital, not far from home." Velvet tried to sit up once again, but Arabella restrained her. "You just calm yourself." The girl smiled, and placed a cool cloth over Velvet's forehead. "Arabella's going to take care of you, just like always."

Lights burned incessantly, shimmering over the dark star of Arabella's face each time Velvet opened her eyes. Then, at last, there was sunlight. Velvet was lifted and propped on pillows, and a tray of food was brought. Arabella was there, lifting small portions of broth to Velvet's lips.

"How long have I been here?" Velvet asked.

"Almost two weeks," the girl said softly. Velvet's eyes widened. "Two weeks?" she breathed.

Arabella nodded, and said, "You were real sick, Miss Velvet, half-starved, bruised, cut . . . and . . ."

"And?" Velvet asked, suddenly gripping Arabella's wrist as she lifted it to spoon more broth between Velvet's lips.

Arabella lowered her eyes. "The baby's gone, Miss Velvet," she said quietly. Velvet felt hot tears wet her widened gaze.

"I knew it, I think," she said at last. She lowered her head. "I did

230

it." Arabella grasped her shoulders, and pulled Velvet to her.

"Don't you go feeling guilty, Miss Velvet," she said urgently. "I can't imagine what you were doing out there in that field, but I just know—"

"No!" Velvet sobbed. "I did it, and I know I did." The two women rocked together for long moments. At last, softly, Velvet began to tell her story. She told of the Adirondacks, and her marriage to Cutter, and Jason's pictures, and her need to come home. Velvet related the details of Albany and New York City and her journey south. Arabella listened raptly.

Finally, when Velvet was finished, she said, with gentle certainty, "You did what you had to do, Miss Velvet. Nobody can ever fault you on it." She took Velvet's hands in hers. "You didn't know how all this was going to turn out. You didn't plan it. You," she said kindly, "didn't make this war."

Velvet looked directly into the shimmering dark eyes. "In a way, Arabella, I did," she said in wonder, as though she was realizing her own culpability for the first time. "They told me up north that all I had ever believed—everything I had ever counted on, or supposed to be true—was a lie. I met people there, Arabella, a woman just like you, who told me about herself, about her feelings. I was stunned; I couldn't believe her. But, now," she said softly, averting her gaze, "I do." Velvet was startled by Arabella's sudden, quiet laughter. She looked up.

"Was she really . . . 'just like' me?" the young woman asked. Velvet smiled guiltily.

"She told me something of her life," she said. "Her name was Mary Ann, and she said she was born a slave."

"Well, now," Arabella said brightly, "I guess she was 'just like' me." She stood and wiped at the spilled soup that had stained the sheet. Velvet drew her knees up to her chest.

"I'm sorry," she said solemnly. She looked uncertainly toward Arabella. "I guess I haven't yet learned my lesson."

The young woman sat down once again. "Let me tell you something, Miss Velvet," she said after a pause. "We're all guilty of ignorance. It's no sin to be ignorant. The sin happens when our ignorance is pointed out, and we won't do anything about it." She took Velvet's hands, once again, in her own. "At this moment, I feel sorrier for you than I've ever felt for anyone in my life—including myself. You're feeling guilty about everything that's happened; and guilt's the worst feeling you can have. It can rip your insides apart. But, just remember; guilt is not going to bring back that baby, and guilt is not going to bring back that James McCulloch fellow, and guilt is not going to bring back your husband, and your guilt," she said pointedly, "is not going to end this war. You've got to concentrate on things you *can* do. The past is past, Miss Velvet. You've got to get yourself healthy, like you always were." She paused significantly. "And you've got to get yourself home." Arabella's last words were said quietly, intensely, and Velvet realized the portent in them.

"Are things bad there?" she asked. Arabella merely looked into her eyes.

"Get yourself well. You need to see for yourself," she said softly.

Over the next few days, Velvet's strength returned. With the reintroduction of solid food into her system, and Arabella's careful nursing, Velvet felt she was able to leave the hospital. She chafed daily against the insistence of a young doctor that she remain.

Velvet learned through quiet talks with Arabella that several of the young women from the surrounding plantations had been recruited as nurses, and that many men had been drafted. There was an all-Negro battalion which had been set to digging ditches and to cleaning up the bodies of the dead and wounded. Arabella further informed her that Sweet Briar Hill was indeed still standing, but would go no further in her discussions of the plantation, except to say that all were alive there—as far as she knew.

On a day in midsummer, Velvet fought her usual battle with depression, frustration, and the hospital's young doctor. He had insisted that she remain in his care for another week, but Velvet had decided that her defiance had been in abeyance too long. Arabella found her up and waiting impatiently when she entered to bring Velvet her lunch.

"Get me some clothes," Velvet said sharply, as the young woman entered.

"Now, Miss Velvet . . ." Arabella said hesitantly, setting down the tray and readying herself for a skirmish.

"Don't you 'Now, Miss Velvet' me, Arabella. I'm going home—and I'm going today," Velvet answered sharply.

"But the doctor says—"

"The *doctor,*" Velvet railed with heavy irony, "has no way of knowing how I feel." Arabella recalled, as she had so often these past days, Velvet's well-documented determination. "Therefore," Velvet continued, "he has no way of prescribing what I need. I am not sick," she finished resolutely. "And, if I am, it's this hospital I'm sick of."

Arabella sighed defeatedly. "You'll go whether I get you some clothes or not, won't you," she said quietly. Velvet nodded, offering that sweet, fixed smile of resolution that Arabella remembered with such mixed emotions. That smile had always settled any matter. Whether the smile related to the chasing down of an unsuspecting male, or the acquisition of a new bauble, it had prophesied, as it did today, a thing accomplished. Whether Arabella approved of the decision, or not, had mattered little throughout her young life with Velvet McBride, and her approval mattered little today. She turned wordlessly, and left the room. Velvet wondered briefly if Arabella was going to get the young doctor. Shrugging lightly, she decided it didn't matter. If she had to leave this place in her hospital gown, she would go. She eyed the lunch that had been placed on a small table near her bed. Velvet's appetite was now intact, and she moved to the tray. Sitting with it on her bed, she ate the meal ravenously.

Chapter Twenty-five

She was there. Velvet saw her in the distance, in all her mythic bulk. Mammy Jane was digging for something outside the house, in the front garden. And the house — *it was still standing!* — was still beautiful, like Mammy. Velvet jumped from the little dog cart, and thanked the driver with whom she'd hitched a ride. She began to run, almost before the driver had halted the weary horse.

"Mammy," she called wildly, as she ran the length of the drive, "Oh, Mammy, Mammy Jane!" The old woman straightened stiffly, and glanced around. At last, she spotted the little figure in dowdy muslin running toward her.

"Who is it?" she demanded, scowling in the late afternoon sun.

"It's me," Velvet nearly sang. "It's me. Oh, Mammy, it's me!"

"Who's me?" Before the big woman could adjust her failing eyesight to determine the identity of the intruder, the intruder was upon her. Wrestling joyously to draw herself into the familiar embrace, Velvet bubbled with laughter, trembled with jubilant tears, jumped and bounced and, in general, unnerved the formidable old woman. Mammy Jane held the girl away from her, and gazed keenly at her. A sudden, disbelieving smile of recognition lit her dark, rheumy eyes. "My God," she breathed. "Oh, my God." With that exultation, she drew Velvet into the longed-for embrace. She held her against her heavy, heaving bosom, and rocked her with tender incessant jerks of her big body. "I can't believe it, child," she crooned. "I just can't believe my little Velvet-pie is here with me. Thank you, Lord," she intoned again and again. At last, reluctantly, Velvet extricated herself.

"Oh, Mammy," she whispered tearfully, "I can't believe it either." Velvet took the moment to search the grounds, to assess the beloved sweep of the lawns. Patched brown and barren in spots, they still rolled gracefully down on three sides to the low fences, not meant to keep anyone out, meant only to delineate the Sweet Briar

234

Hill property from the rest of the world. Ornamental tea roses wound their delicate paths through the rails. She thought instantly of Private Jackson's roses in Kentucky, and wondered, for his sake, if they had been left unscathed. Abruptly, she shook off the recollection. She turned her attention to the house itself. It stood in all its elegant splendor in the center of the lawns. High white pillars lofted to a stately second floor where French windows gleamed, unbroken, in the sun. Balconies and balustrades set out in rows along the third floor were untouched.

Breathless with relief, Velvet broke from Mammy Jane's insistent grasp, and ran toward the porch. "It's all here," she cried. "They didn't burn it!" Velvet fell, in exultant laughter, onto the wide steps, and held herself in an orgy of wild joy. At last, as her self-indulgent relief dissipated, she looked toward Mammy, and her face sobered. "I saw the Carletons, Mammy," she said softly. "You wouldn't believe what happened there." The big woman swiped at her forehead with a heavy forearm.

"We heard about it, child," she acknowledged. "We got some things to be thankful for."

Velvet eyed her uncertainly. "We have *everything* to be thankful for, Mammy. We have our house." The old woman nodded sadly. She bent tiredly, and began to capture in her grimy apron the potatoes she'd been digging. A terrible dread began to invade Velvet's soul. She stood slowly. "I think I'll go inside now and see Mother," she said carefully, waiting expectantly for any change in Mammy Jane's demeanor. Seeing none, she added, "Is Pa inside, too?" The old woman nodded.

"Your Ma's upstairs . . . in her room," she said.

Velvet's brow quirked in puzzlement, but her questions went unasked. "I'll just go up then," she said quietly. She turned stiffly, and moved up the steps toward the wide, curve-crowned front doors. She glanced back at Mammy Jane who watched her. "I'll go upstairs and see my mother," Velvet said, not stopping.

Inside, the house, like the Carletons, was bereft of furniture. Carpets had been lifted off of wide-planked floors, leaving beneath wood that was ashen and dully discolored. Dust glistened in the air, disturbed by the opening of the door. Velvet's eyes lingered on the darkened front hallway as she moved to the stairs. She wondered where things had gone. Awed by the emptiness in the great room, she studied places where great statues had graced corners, polished étagères and secretaries had stood in stately grandeur, gilt chairs and finely carved tables had waited to receive guests and their calling cards. She took the uncarpeted steps up the curving staircase one by one, stopping to survey, with each attained height, a new void. Light and shadow played slyly with her vision. Nothing seemed real.

Transfixed, Velvet turned on the landing, and gazed out over the mezzanine. Was the picture of her grandfather truly missing from the wall; was that the darkened wallpaper left by its removal? Or was the picture there, glaring out at her from a dusky neglect? Velvet could not be sure; she did not want to know. She came to her mother's door suddenly and burst into the room.

There on the bed, covered by a light, rose-colored quilt, lay her mother—perfectly alive, perfectly whole.

"Mother?" Velvet asked softly, unwilling to believe her uncertain vision.

Alicia McBride, her hair haloed elegantly atop her head, lifted her eyes from a book. "For glory's sake," she said breathlessly. "It's Velvet."

"Yes, Mother," Velvet cried, lunging for the bed. "It's me!" Alicia sat up to welcome her daughter into her arms. The all too dear and familiar scent of Jasmine encloaked Velvet, sent the warm tingle of remembrance into her heart. "I'm here, Mother," she said into the soft folds of her mother's gown.

"So you are, my darling. How wonderful to see you!" She held her daughter away from her. "But why aren't you up north with Yvonne and Andrew?"

"I had to come home, Mother," Velvet said softly. "I couldn't bear the thought of you all being down here with what's been going on, and me—"

"You won't like it here," Alicia said vaguely. She lay back against the several pillows which propped up her slender shoulders, and idly fingered the lace trim at the bodice of her gown.

Velvet lifted herself more securely onto her mother's bed, and eyed the woman in puzzlement. It occurred to her that her mother seemed to have taken very well to the war. "I know there's been a great deal of fighting in this part of the country—"

Alicia splayed a hand toward her, and arched a brow in annoyance. "I won't hear anymore," she said sharply. "You mustn't bother me about it."

"Velvet watched her mother carefully. "But, surely, Mother, you can't —"

"I *said*," Alicia McBride shot back, "I don't want to hear about it." Her voice was ragged and harsh, and Velvet repressed an immediate desire to question her about such a response.

"Is Pa around?" she asked instead.

Alicia frowned thoughtfully. "Won't you light a lamp for me, my darling? It gets so dark this time of day." She lifted her book, and drew it toward her. Unbelievably, she began to read.

Confused, Velvet raised herself and lit a lamp. She watched her mother. "Did you say Pa was around?" she asked at last, evenly.

"He's most likely down in his study," Alicia murmured. She lowered her book and smiled briefly. "Tell Mammy Jane to fix you a nice little pot pie, darling. You must be starved, after your outing."

"I am hungry," Velvet managed. Her mother's smile deepened.

"Well, you just get yourself down to that kitchen, then. But don't you dare spoil your appetite for dinner," she warned. She waved Velvet away lightly, and then went back to her book. Alicia's air might have been more suited to any pretty, idle summer afternoon many years ago . . . long before the war. Mesmerized Velvet made her way from the room, down the staircase, and along the hallway on the first floor that led to her father's study.

The room was low and deep and, at this time of day, shaded by a side porch. Velvet could barely see into its vacant depths as she pushed the door open. Far shadows, lit by a rill of fading sunlight, seemed to move at her entrance.

"Is that you, Mammy?" a familiar, if quietly haunted voice, intoned.

"It's not Mammy," Velvet managed as she stepped cautiously inside. "Is that you, Pa?" Silence answered. "Pa?" she repeated. "Is it you?" Again, no answering voice responded. Velvet moved to the corner of the room from which the words had come. "It's me, Pa. It's Velvet," she said softly. She stood before a huddled form that looked up at her from empty eyes — eyes in all other respects so like her own.

"My, my," said Steven McBride. "It's my little Velvet."

The wave of dread and unfocused horror that had gripped her, came singing now, like the thrum of hellish demons, into Velvet's consciousness. She backed away, smelling for the first time, the unholy odor of decay that overwhelmed the room, that ungodly smell, that brooding, vaguely skeletal figure of what was once her father overbalancing rational thought, Velvet flung herself wildly through the doorway. Appalled and frightened beyond reason, she staggered down the hallway. Caught up abruptly by the big, brown figure of Mammy Jane, Velvet allowed herself the indulgence of screams. She let herself be drawn into the comfort of thick, soft, welcoming arms, allowed herself to sob out her disbelief, her fear, her confusion.

"I know, child. I know," Mammy Jane crooned, as she rocked the girl, leading her, after long moments, into the big kitchen. "It ain't getting no better for you, is it, my little Velvet-pie?" The big woman sat Velvet down in a chair. "It's a sad, sad day for your homecoming," she murmured. Velvet lifted tear-glistened eyes.

"What's going on here, Mammy?" she cried. "In the name of all that's holy, what has happened?" Mammy Jane did not answer immediately. Instead, she offered Velvet a ragged cloth that passed for a handkerchief, and moved heavily to the stove. She watched as the girl swiped at her nose and eyes. She watched as Velvet slowly but determinedly composed herself. Mammy Jane hid a smile, hastily repressed the desire to run back to the girl and take her into her arms once again. The Velvet she remembered was back.

"Let me make us a cup of tea," the older woman said quietly.

The two women sat late into the evening, over their tea. "And it's been like that since the fighting early in June, child. I don't know what else to tell you," Mammy Jane was saying.

"You mean Mother has taken to her bed, and Pa has . . . has . . ." Velvet could not finish her own analysis of the situation. She turned sharply away. "I just can't believe this," she said. "Pa was always such a meticulous gentleman — in his dress, in his habits. Why, I never remember him taking spirits until after six o'clock in the evening. I remember once Mr. Carleton was exhorting him to have a drink in celebration of some business triumph or other, and Pa flatly refused, and Mr. Carleton . . ." Again, her voice trailed off. She glanced back at Mammy. "And Mother," Velvet nearly whispered, tears threatening once again. "She was the belle of

Brandy Station, Mammy. How can such a spirited woman just lie there and let this happen?"

Mammy shook her graying head miserably. "I wonder that myself, Velvet-pie," she said softly. "But," she added, raising her sad eyes, "maybe it's because I can't really understand what happened here. Maybe nobody can understand. That dear woman up there, just lying in her bed, just living somewhere in a world where there's no war, no loss, won't talk to me. And, until she does, I —"

"Is dinner never to be served, Mammy?" said the gently reproving voice from the doorway. Both Velvet and Mammy Jane looked up sharply, and then back to each other. Alicia McBride glided into the kitchen. "Might I have some of that tea?" she asked. "I swear, Mammy" — she laughed lightly — "since that Emancipation Proclamation of Mr. Lincoln's, you've become lazy as bones. One would never guess we were paying you a salary."

"That tea's cold, honey," said Mammy Jane gently. "Let me make up a fresh pot."

Alicia sat in the chair vacated by Mammy, and looked knowingly at Velvet. "Mammy understands my little chiding remarks," she said. "She knows I love her for staying. She's the only one who did, can you imagine?" She looked up and caught Mammy in an affectionate glance. "No matter what that cold-hearted rail-splitter says, she'll always be our mammy." She leaned toward Velvet, and placed a soft hand over hers. "She's a treasure, and we must appreciate her," she whispered as though Mammy were not in the room. "She's all we have left."

"Would you like your supper down here tonight, Miss Alicia?" Mammy Jane asked.

"I think not," Alicia said, yawning. "I think I'll have it upstairs, as usual. I seem to have the spring fever more powerfully than ever this year. I just want to sleep all the time."

"It's summer, Mother," Velvet said evenly.

"Well, that's exactly what I'm saying, Velvet darling," her mother answered earnestly. "This affliction just doesn't want to go away; it just hangs on and on. I am sworn, I just can't credit how tired I am. Next thing you know, I'll be sleeping round the clock." She laughed roguishly. "Now wouldn't I just be the scandal?"

"You'll feel better, honey," Mammy Jane said softly, "soon's the weather changes."

"Oh, I know that, Mammy," said Alicia. "And I am counting on feeling better soon. But I'm so concerned because I just know I'm not going to feel up to giving my end-of-summer ball. And you know how everyone just dotes on that particular event. Why, they depend on it." She swept a look over both her listeners. "It isn't generally known, but I've invited Mr. Damien Archambault down to design my gown," she said confidentially. "Now, don't either of you breathe a word about that. But I'm afraid," she finished, her tone altered, "it won't matter much if I don't recover from this malaise of mine."

Velvet sat back, closing her eyes. The picture of the elegantly plump and manicured Monsieur Archambault drifted across her internal vision. What would that gentleman think of all this, she wondered. She glanced around the barren kitchen. There were no evidences of the gracious life that had been directed from this space, no copper pots hanging from the curving wrought-iron pot hold above the stove, no smells of exotic spices wafting from the ovens, no kitchen girls, no meat tenders, no . . . nothing—just the barest minimum of necessities. As in the other rooms, all indications of gracious living had vanished. Again, Velvet reminded herself to ask Mammy Jane what had become of everything.

"I've met him," she said, at last, to her mother.

"Who, darling?" asked Alicia.

"Damien Archambault," Velvet answered. "He's very nice."

"How did you happen to meet him?"

Velvet smiled at the memory. How long ago had it been? "I was in New York City with Morgana," she said. "He's an acquaintance of hers, and we had dinner. I'm afraid," Velvet laughed ruefully, "I did not make the best of impressions."

"Oh, how awful," said Alicia, startled. "How could such a thing happen?"

"I'll explain it sometime," Velvet said gently. "In any case, Mother, Monsieur Archambault will not be coming down here this year, I'm afraid. You see—"

Alicia stood abruptly. "Bring my supper up, Mammy, as soon as it's prepared," she said, and swept from the room.

Velvet exchanged looks with Mammy Jane. "Are you really being paid a salary?" she asked wearily.

Mammy Jane smiled. "Do you think I'd take money from this

family, Velvet-pie," she asked, "even if there was money to take?"

"No, Mammy," Velvet said softly. She rested her head on her arms. "I wouldn't mind some supper myself," she said wistfully. "What have we got? Mother suggested a pot pie."

"Oh, child, there ain't been no pot pie in this house in months," said Mammy Jane. "We got potatoes, turnips, and a skinny chicken out back that's still breathing because he's got no feathers and less meat on him." She shook her head sadly. "I'll fix you something, child, but it won't be no pot pie." She paused significantly. "Tomorrow come, though," she said gently, "and maybe Mr. Whitney — I should say, Major Whitney — will come by with some supplies."

Velvet looked up sharply. "Brett?" she asked. Mammy Jane nodded solemnly.

"He comes by every few weeks, and brings us what he can. But the need's so great, honey, that he ain't always able to—"

"Brett Whitney," Velvet breathed, her eyes suddenly alight.

"Now don't you go getting your hopes up, Velvet-pie," said Mammy Jane sternly, as she peeled potatoes over the iron sink. "I said 'maybe.' "

"When was he last here?" asked Velvet, standing.

Mammy Jane thought for a moment. "Been about three weeks," she recalled. "Just about that, I think."

"And how often did you say he comes by?" Velvet urged.

"Oh, child," Mammy Jane scolded, "you're thinking Northern time. Nothing happens down here that regular — not anymore." She turned and leaned tiredly against the sink. "We wait, child. We wait for everything. We wait for supplies that may, or may not, come; we wait for shooting that may, or may not, come; we wait for the end of war that may, or may not, come. Why, we've given up counting on anything. We live from day to day. That's the only thing that counts now — getting through this day."

Velvet sighed, and sat down heavily. "I'm not used to waiting," she said petulantly. Mammy Jane merely smiled, and resumed her work. Her Velvet-pie was indeed back.

Chapter Twenty-six

Sunlight thickened in the room. Velvet lifted sandy eyelids, and looked out over the bare expanse of grimy wallpaper and wooden floor. She raised herself onto one elbow, swiped wearily at her sleep-clouded eyes, and then lay back. Her bed had been spared, but the mattress was gone, and she lay on a rude and lumpy piling of rags. Another day had begun, she thought wearily. Mammy Jane had said all that counted was getting through each one—each day—and here was yet another to be gotten through. She sighed, and pulled her knees up, lifting them over the side of the bed. She'd been at Sweet Briar Hill one month. In that time her curiosity had been sated in long talks with Mammy Jane. Velvet had discovered that most of what the family owned had been taken by the Yankees. Each delicate family treasure had been pocketed, each room plundered, each corner of the great house pillaged, until there was nothing left. She gazed around at the emptiness that closed in on her each time she bothered to think about it. She lowered her chin into her hands. Velvet could not escape the images that bore into her heart. The little, antique, porcelain lantern clock that ticked so loyally, so long, on her mantelpiece had been a gift from her father on her fourteenth birthday. She raised her gaze to where it had stood. Why would the Yankees have taken it? she pondered; surely it was not worth a great deal of money. But Mammy Jane had said that "anything worth anything" had been confiscated. Velvet's eyes swept to where an armoire had stood between two tall windows. Yes, she thought reasonably, that was a piece worth stealing—worth selling. Red oak, in the fire pattern, that piece had been valued at hundreds of dollars. It could be sold. The money gotten from its sale could feed a great many soldiers. Velvet could even understand—if she could not accept—the seizing of mattresses, pots, carpets, silverware, paintings. These items could be used by the soldiers, or sold to buy boots . . . or guns. But

242

why was her mantel clock taken? Why had her little mother-of-pearl toilette set been stolen from her? Why had hundreds of gowns, shoes, hats been torn from upstairs rooms . . . why had a conch shell, lovingly cherished from a vacation on a South Carolina beach, been snatched away? Why?

The battle of Brandy Station, it was called; the biggest cavalry battle of the war, they said. The Union had crossed the Rappahannock in force twenty-five miles above Fredericksburg to find out what Lee was up to. James E. B. "Jeb" Stuart had effectively impeded the blue troopers, and the Confederacy had won yet another victory that June. The Confederacy had won that battle. . . . Velvet moved to the window and stood staring out at the parched lawns. "We won," she said softly. She glanced back at her bedroom, stripped, dismantled, ravished. "We won," she repeated in an awed whisper. Tears formed, unchallenged, on her lashes. "If we won," she asked in wonder, "why was everything lost?"

The day had worn heavily on, from morning into the early afternoon. Velvet's time was taken with brief periods of reading to her mother, fetching pots of rose-hip tea for her father—which he refused—and helping Mammy to dig in the gardens for potatoes and turnips and whatever else they could find. It was past noon when both women looked up to see a lone rider on the drive up to the house.

"It's him," Mammy breathed, as she wiped at her perspiration-smeared face with her apron.

"Who?" Velvet asked.

"It's Major Whitney."

Velvet's eyes widened. Her hands went immediately to her tangled hair. Pins aside, thick tresses had slid in tousled profusion from the top of her head. She attempted to smooth into some sort of order the thick masses, but the task seemed futile. She hastily dabbed at her face with the hem of her grime-stiffened gown. Oh, this was too much, she railed inwardly. That Brett Whitney should see her this way . . .

He was upon them—his tall, wide-shouldered, golden self above them in the sunlight. Velvet managed her most eloquent smile. His big brown steed skidded to a halt.

"Why, Brett Whitney," she breathed out, as though his presence had not been anticipated for days. "Whatever in the blessed world brings you to Sweet Briar Hill?" It might have been a lazy Sunday afternoon four years ago.

Brett Whitney bounded from his horse, and ran toward Velvet. Taking her into his arms, he swung her up from the dusty ground. "Oh, God," Velvet honey," he exulted. "You're back!" Holding to each other, the couple laughed wildly, embraced, and lingeringly, longingly gazed at each other. "I can't believe it, sugar," Brett said at last.

"Neither can I, Brett." Velvet laughed breathlessly.

"But why, honey?" he said after a pause. "Why did you leave the North? Didn't they tell you how bad things were down here?"

"That's why I left," Velvet said softly. She drew away from him; after the initial joy of their reunion, his manner seemed somewhat forward to Velvet. She understood, of course, that times were different now, but she could not allow that to change things between her and her idealized Brett Whitney. Theirs had always been a special relationship. Velvet had lost so much; she would not lose that. She looked up at him, and forced a teasing smile. Folding her hands before her, she tilted her tousled head. "I couldn't let you all have all the excitement, now could I?" she asked.

Brett laughed, and swept off his gray hat. Offering a low bow, he said, formally, "You haven't changed one bit, Miss Velvet." He straightened, and added solemnly, "Thank the Lord." He drew a small package from his saddlebag and handed it to Mammy Jane. "You'll find some flour in there, Mammy," he said, "and a few other things that might enhance your table tonight."

Velvet laughed and placed her hand delicately into the crook of his arm. "In any event . . . *Major* Whitney," she said as they walked toward the house, "I had to come down and see for myself what a success you've made of yourself."

"You heard of my being made major?" he asked.

"Well, just since I've been back. We've had no mail up north for over a year, and Mammy tells me you've received none from me." She tilted a glance toward Brett. For the moment, she determined, though she could not tell why, it was best that Brett not know of her marriage to Cutter. "But I had a feeling," she chattered on, "that you would do something wonderful for our blessed cause. What

244

better way to serve us, Brett," she said gravely, "than to lead men in our defense?"

Brett Whitney smiled. "And that, sugar, is exactly what it's been up to now — a defense."

"Now don't you be modest, Major Whitney," said Velvet, playfully, leading him up onto the porch. "Mammy told me how brave you all were a few weeks ago here at Brandy Station. She told me how courageously you fought."

Brett nodded. "We were brave," he said quietly.

"And you won," Velvet added perkily. Again Brett nodded.

"We won," he acknowledged. Velvet ushered him to a pair of tottering porch chairs, on which they sat.

"Do you think we could have something to drink?" she asked Mammy Jane who had followed them up to the house.

The older woman smiled sadly. "I'll see what I can find, child," she said. She glanced briefly at Brett Whitney, and moved into the house. Velvet turned her most dazzling, her most persuasive smile on her company.

"Now you must stay and share our newly acquired bounty, Major Whitney." She giggled girlishly. "I just can't get used to calling you that, Brett." He crossed one neatly creased leg over another, and sat watching her. Velvet took full advantage of his attention, attempting to ignore her own dishabille. She must dazzle him with personality alone, she decided. "You must tell me how it happened. These days, I hear, men are often promoted right on the field of battle. For enormous bravery, I daresay," Velvet exulted. "Is that how you became a major, Brett?"

"In a way," he answered. His gaze narrowed. "Do you really want to hear this, honey?"

"Whyever wouldn't I want to hear it, Brett?" she asked breathlessly. Let him go on and on, she concluded smugly. It might take his attention from her temporary lack of grooming. She nestled into her chair, and offered him a rapt and solemn regard. "Do go on . . . Major."

He hesitated, then began softly. "As Mammy told you, we did manage to push the Yankees back, here at Brandy Station," he said. "But that isn't how I earned my particular addition." He leaned forward, resting his arms on his knees. "You see, I rarely engage in battle anymore." He glanced up at Velvet. "At least, not the sort of battle that occurred here. I am a member — the leader, in fact — of a rather elite battalion of men."

"Are you?" Velvet asked, interested.

"Yes. It isn't generally known, but we have been commissioned to hunt down and capture criminals of war. It's a dirty business, sugar, but one that must be done." He glanced once again at Velvet from whom he had turned. In her regard he found only sincere absorption in what he was relating. He sat back, relieved. He had risked the truth of his lowly — but well-paying — station, and the risk had paid off. Uninitiated as she was, Velvet could not realize the significance of what he had told her. With any luck at all, Brett Whitney might obscure that significance for some time to come. He crossed one knee over the other and smiled, folding his hands comfortably across his broad chest. "As for dinner today," he said easily, "I am afraid I must decline." He watched the pretty disappointment that clouded Velvet's face. "But I shall promise, on my honor as a gentleman," he said, leaning forward once again, "that I shall come by tomorrow — if the invitation still stands." He smiled. "Does it, sugar?"

"Why naturally, Major," Velvet said, brightening. "You have what we shall refer to as a *standing* invitation." They both laughed. Brett stood.

"It would give me no end of pleasure," he said with a formalized courtliness, "to stay on today, Miss Velvet, but I am afraid I must go. Duty calls." He laughed.

"Are you on the trail of a dangerous criminal?" she asked, sweetly tremulous as she rose.

Brett placed his hat onto his head. "I am," he said seriously, his mouth forming a grim line. "One of the *most* dangerous." Velvet walked him to his horse, and allowed the barest brush of his lips on her hand. She waved as he rode off, and then, when he was out of sight, frenziedly hurled herself back toward the house.

She exploded into the kitchen where Mammy Jane was boiling rain water for lemonade.

"The major brought us two lemons," the older woman said brightly.

"Save them for tomorrow night," Velvet commanded breathlessly, with the air of an agitated field marshal. She paced across the kitchen like a general, scrutinizing a new command. "We must have linens, silver, stemware—" She rounded on Mammy Jane. "Is there any of that left?"

"I told you, child—"

"I don't care what you told me," Velvet exhorted, "there must be something left—somewhere! Major Whitney is coming to dinner tomorrow, and we have to be ready for him. Now we are going to scour this big house, and we are going to come up with everything we need."

"But, honey—"

"And, we are going to sober up Pa, and get Mother out of bed, we are going to prepare a lavish dinner—"

"Velvet-pie," said Mammy Jane sharply. The two women, both surprised at the elder's harshness, abruptly stopped and stared at each other. "Child," Mammy Jane said finally, soothingly, "I know you want what you want, but that don't make it possible. There's nothing 'lavish' about turnips and potatoes, and that's all we got."

"We've got a skinny chicken," Velvet shot back levelly.

"We got that," Mammy Jane conceded.

"And we've got some flour," Velvet went on relentlessly. "And we've got lemons for lemonade, and we've got roses for the table, and we've got a host and a hostess, and we've got a guest. We've got everything we need for a party, and, by the Lord who made my bones, *we're going to have a party.*" Silenced by Velvet's vehemence, Mammy Jane merely stared at the girl.

Finally, she said softly, "We ain't got a table."

Velvet's gaze darkened. "Then we'll, by heaven, make us one," she ground out. She spun crisply, and slammed out of the kitchen. Mammy Jane smiled ruefully. If she knew anything at all about Velvet McBride, she knew that tomorrow night, at Sweet Briar Hill, that girl would be presiding over a party.

Chapter Twenty-seven

Velvet had, as she'd promised, scoured the house. She'd come up with little, but what she did find, she made full use of. An old curtain served as a cloth for a table rigged from a set of saw horses from the barn and topped with some rough boards she'd also found there. She had scrubbed at the curtain until it was pristine white, and then dried it in the sunlit air. She would cut roses tomorrow, and lay them, without benefit of vase or bowl, at the center of the table, she decided. The resulting arrangement would be appealing, rustic and homey, would speak of a delicately untamed wood world; she might even use the motif at some future time — when her fortunes had been returned. There were few lamps in the house — one by her mother's bed — and they would serve for a low, dramatic lighting of the table. Napkins were made from several rags of various colors and patterns, carefully washed and artfully folded. The few plates and pieces of flatware would serve — stains, nicks, and scratches obscured by the lack of light. Her table would be fanciful, if improvised. There would be no dinner music — Velvet's favorite being the second movement of Mozart's Piano Concerto in D Minor, played by a small chamber orchestra — but Velvet would throw open the windows, and early evening birdsong would accompany their dinner conversation.

She and Mammy Jane had decided upon the menu. There would be a chicken stew, flavored with wild onions and wild thyme, a turnip pie, and berries, gathered from the hillside, for dessert. It was a simple, lyrical evening Velvet had planned; the focus being not on the food and the accoutrements, but the company. The McBrides might be temporarily without funds, or possessions, but they had something that could never be taken away; the McBrides had breeding. Breeding would tell.

Velvet sighed tiredly as she lay down on her rag bed, diminished now by four remnants which had become napkins for tomorrow's dinner table, and thought out how she might approach her father. Alicia had been thrilled at the prospect of entertaining the elegant Mr. Whitney — Velvet had thought it best not to mention that he was now a major in the Confederate army — and had even managed several long moments of concentrated thought on how the evening should proceed. She offered to read, after dinner, from her favorite poet, George Gordon, Lord Byron, and wondered absently, after a time, what particular poem she should read. Velvet had pronounced the idea inspired. She had left her mother mulling over her choices, and happily anticipating the following evening. Steven McBride was a different problem. Velvet had approached him, had entered the dreaded lair where her father sat huddled and silent, and had apprised him of her plans. She had pleaded with him, reasoned, and finally demanded that he participate. In the end, Velvet could not tell whether he had even heard her.

Neither she nor Mammy Jane knew where his private stock was hidden — Mammy Jane confessed she'd never seen him leave the house, and Velvet had made a cursory search of the study, finding nothing — and so it was impossible to control his intake of whiskey, or whatever it was he was drinking. If necessary, Velvet resolved, she would drag her father bodily from that room, and force him to sit at table. She was not going to allow dinner to proceed without at least a ceremonial host. If silence and drunkenness were her father's defenses against the terrible reality of the war — as denial was her mother's protection — then let him be silent, or drunk, or whatever he wished to be. He would be it, by heaven, at her table.

Velvet fell into a kind of charged sleep. Her dreams that night were of the morrow.

The morning broke, as summer mornings will, with glittering, fine rain. By ten o'clock the sun had blossomed, and a rainbow appeared — the covenant, Mammy Jane exulted, that the Lord had made with Noah, promising the world would never again be destroyed by water. Velvet, who had studiously gathered rainwater in buckets, mentioned, while Mammy Jane rejoiced, that she would not be opposed to whatever water the Lord chose to send. Velvet needed a bath.

By noon, every window in the house had been thrown open, the table had been set, the skinny chicken had been sacrificed, Alicia was deciding what stanzas she would choose to read from *Don Juan*, and Velvet's only dress was being aired. She stood before it now, in her muslin chemise — borrowed, along with the dress, at the hospital from Arabella — and wondered how she might freshen its appearance. It flapped breezily on the back line, and Velvet only vaguely perceived Mammy Jane's scolding, from the kitchen, that she must get her shameless self inside.

"Imagine," Mammy Jane humphed, "standing outside the house in your shimmies." She watched Velvet reproachfully as the girl came thoughtfully into the kitchen.

"Have we got any ribbon, Mammy?" Velvet asked absently.

"We got no ribbon, we got no lace, we got no silk flowers," Mammy Jane said resentfully. "If I told you once — "

"Have we got — "

"Nothing," stated Mammy Jane impatiently. Velvet slid onto a stool.

"There must be something. . . ," she reflected, undeterred by her mammy's sullenness. Velvet smiled at last. "I'll put fresh daisies in my hair, and I'll adorn my dress with jonquils," she decided. Mammy Jane merely eyed the girl wryly. The child never gave up. "I'm going to take my bath now. Can you help me?"

By the late afternoon, the world was cleansed and dried and freshened, as was Velvet. Warm breezes rippled her freshly washed flaxen-streaked hair as she wandered out to the twining rose bushes to choose just the right blossoms for her table. She had chosen to let her curls drift freely about her shoulders, lifting one side only and catching it with a spray of wild daisies. She had pinned jonquils at the hem of her dress, and they swung and swirled at her feet as she walked. The effect spoke of early summer zephyrs and dew, of lightness and youth.

Velvet had been momentarily daunted by the image of herself in the darkly veined fragment of a mirror she'd found in her search of the house. She saw what she'd never thought to see staring back. Her face was pale, ravaged by adversities. It had never occurred to her that one's experiences could affect one's looks. She had become philosophical finally, and reflected that, up to the point of her decision to come home, she'd had few "experiences" on which to base such an assumption. Her life in the South, and then in the North, had been relatively unscathed by hardship. Even in her worst moments, those she'd spent fighting her physical attraction to Cutter, and when she'd been faced with the naked fallacies of her upbringing, Velvet had known certain comforts. She had always enjoyed certain accommodations, if not advantages. She had known, even then in those darkest days of her mental torment, that she was protected by her own innocence. Yet, as she thought back on it now, despite Cutter the wild, Cutter the impossible, Cutter the untamed, she was still the woman she had always known herself to be. Despite her ravaged emotions back then, she was, to say nothing of being clothed and fed, treated with a certain deference by everyone around her—comforted by that deference. Now everything had been torn away. Velvet had been stripped of the accommodation of innocence. She could never again claim that she "didn't know," she could never claim specialness, she could never claim inexperience—or that she was the exception to the rule. Velvet had grown up in the last months; she had become, through her experiences, a woman—fully responsible for herself. The knowledge frightened her; it vitalized her; it riveted her to one purpose. Velvet knew she must explore every avenue of survival. At the moment, she did not know exactly what that meant. She was weighted by the damage done her parents by the war. Could that damage be healed? In the weeks since her arrival at Sweet Briar Hill, she did not—could not—venture into that morass of wounded emotions. But, she reflected, why had she come? What, after all, had been her purpose if not to help them? She had seen Jason's pictures. She had known she must be with her family in their ordeal. But her own mental pictures had never conjured up the waste, the human misery she had found.

It was time, she resolved, to put aside her own timidity, and begin to do what she'd come to do.

Velvet cut roses with a new resolve. In the late afternoon sun, each blossom seemed to shimmer with its own purpose. She picked only the fully matured flowers, those which had lived the fullest life, those that offered the most glowing picture of purpose fulfilled. She carried them back to the house, her head high, her step light with anticipation. Tonight was the beginning. If Brett Whitney had been helpful to her family before, he would, after tonight, remember the McBrides most generously from now on. There would be flour in their bin, chickens in their yard, provender on their table. That's where survival begins, determined Velvet. She would show Brett simple, yet earnest, hospitality; and should he happen to steal a kiss, Velvet would be properly, and zealously, astonished—and she would invite, with her maidenly blushes, more visits, and, if necessary, more kisses.

She laughed as she saw Mammy's look of bewilderment.

"You plan to put all those flowers on the table?" the older woman asked.

"I do," Velvet said, skipping into the dining room with her arms full of roses. Recklessly, she tossed the blossoms onto the jerry-rigged table, saving a few for the centerpiece. Then she stepped back to survey her work. With a few adjustments, she deemed the table perfect, and ran upstairs to see if her mother was ready.

"I had this on when they came." The low, whispered words greeted Velvet, as she stepped into her mother's room.

"What is it, Mother?" Velvet asked. She moved to Alicia, conscious only of the vacant stare, the wild emptiness in her mother's eyes. The emptiness clouded; tears came and were as suddenly choked back.

"I've nothing to wear," Alicia said archly. "I simply, quite simply, have nothing to wear. You must tell our guest that I am indisposed—and do make my sincerest apologies." She turned and lay down on the bed, drawing the coverlet up to her chin. Velvet stepped to her slowly. She'd not thought of what her mother might wear for tonight; it had not entered her mind.

"I think you look particularly lovely tonight, Mother," Velvet ventured. "Your gown is—"

"My *gown*," Alicia shot back, "is particularly inappropriate for a dinner party." She turned onto her side. "I'm not hungry anyway," she muttered.

Velvet felt herself stiffen. Swift anger rose. "Couldn't you just try, Mother?" she heard herself say. "Couldn't you just try for tonight? For heaven's sake, nobody cares how we look anymore." The words died in Velvet's throat as she watched her mother turn slowly, challengingly toward her.

"I care," Alicia proclaimed softly. Velvet's heart tilted in her breast.

"I know that, Mother," she said gently. It was precisely because Alicia McBride still cared that she had tucked herself away in this bedchamber, because she cared that she could not accept the horrors that had overwhelmed her. Alicia cared about loveliness, she cared about gentility; and the world was not lovely — or genteel — anymore. Velvet stepped to the side of the bed and sat with care. "I gathered roses, Mother," she said kindly. "Would you like me to pin some to the neckline of your gown?" Alicia's brows quirked with interest. "I'll go down and get the loveliest of the blossoms," Velvet went on softly. "I'll choose only the perkiest, prettiest ones. We'll pin them along here," she said, pointing to the places in the lace of her mother's dressing gown where the flowers might best serve. "We'll all be so disappointed if we don't hear you read *Don Juan* tonight."

Alicia smiled wickedly. "Do you really think my choice is appropriate?" she asked. "After all, it is rather a depraved little piece."

Velvet laughed. "I think the choice an excellent one. We should all be exposed to a bit of depravity now and then."

"And it *is* romantic," Alicia responded exultantly.

Velvet nodded and patted her mother's hand. "Wickedly romantic," she said. She straightened and went downstairs to get the roses.

Steven McBride proved to be a tougher case than his wife. Velvet was forced to drag him nearly bodily out onto the porch. She made sure that her mother and father were both seated on the wobbly porch chairs by the time Brett Whitney arrived. When he did, Velvet was pleased by the picture of untainted domesticity she and her parents presented. Never mind that her father swayed slightly in his chair, and made little eye contact with anyone; never mind that her mother wore a nightgown with roses hanging flaccidly from the neckline; never mind that Velvet stood, having no more chairs to offer, they were, all three of them, together — the image of gracious hospitality.

Mammy Jane had been instructed to serve the lemonade as soon as Brett arrived, and she did so. Velvet stood, drinking hers stiffly, as Brett leaned against the porch rail and told her parents how well they looked. When they went in to enjoy their dinner, the porch chairs had to be brought along. Velvet attempted to make light of the inconvenience, saying airily, "We're just pioneers in the

253

field of entertaining."

"More like poor whites," her mother responded archly.

" 'Crackers'," Steven McBride said. Everyone glanced at him. It was the first word he'd spoken, and his blue-green eyes sparkled zestfully. Velvet knew the first moment of dread. It had never occurred to her that her father might talk. If he did talk, what might he say, she wondered. She set her little chin rigidly.

"Will you head the table, Pa?" she said sharply. Steven obediently sat on one of the porch chairs indicated by his daughter. He was smiling vacantly now, and Velvet decided that dinner must be served immediately. She looked quickly at Mammy Jane who nodded in understanding, and began to serve.

"What a pretty table, darling," said Alicia, and Brett nodded and smiled his agreement. "How clever of you to eschew all ornamentation," Alicia continued.

"I've always said" — Velvet laughed bravely — "that we put too much value on *things*. We must take more account of the beauty of nature — and fine company." She tilted a glance at Brett. "After all, things will disappear. And when they do, what have we got but each other?" Velvet realized that she was rambling, but she felt a break in the conversation might spur another unfortunate comment from her father. As it was, he only sat before his food, staring it down. She glanced at her mother appreciatively. At least Alicia was trying — commenting on the fine food, on how handsome Brett looked. In both respects, she was correct. Velvet resolved that she must compliment Mammy Jane on her excellent dinner, and she must mention, at some point in the evening, how handsome Brett looked tonight, polished, pressed, and a thorough treat to the eye. Velvet watched him gratefully. It was so pleasant to see someone at Sweet Briar Hill who'd not been ravaged by the war.

The foursome sat a long time over their berries and tea. Alicia read successfully from Lord Byron's "wickedly romantic" poem, and, at last, as evening darkened the room, Brett explained that he must be leaving. He took advantage of the moment, however, to inquire of Steven McBride if he might call upon his daughter, and Velvet smiled longingly. Brett, at least, had not forgotten his elegant manners. She watched her father's reaction to the request, hoping he might merely nod his approval, and allow the matter to end.

Instead, the older man stood shakily, shoved his face into Brett's, and asked, "How's the bounty-hunting business these days, Whitney?" Brett recoiled from the whiskey fumes of Steven's breath, and Velvet, wide-eyed, disbelieving, stepped between them. "That's what he is," Steven proclaimed, undaunted. "He's a bounty hunter! He hunts down men — for a price." He shoved Velvet aside, and advanced on the dubiously retreating Brett Whitney. "Now isn't that a disgusting business for a man to take up?" Steven went on. "He's called 'the meanest man in the South,' and that's how he got the job. No *civilized* fellow would take it!" Abruptly, Alicia burst into tears. Velvet managed to work her way between the two men, risking injury from the wild flailing of her father's arms. She shrieked for Mammy, who immediately led Alicia from the room, and pushed at her father, who fell sprawling to the floor.

"How could you, Pa?" she demanded. In response, Steven McBride lay down at her feet, and immediately began to snore.

Horrified, Velvet took several long moments to compose herself. She glanced sheepishly at their guest. "I'm so sorry, Brett," she murmured. Brett swept his hat from a nearby table.

"I'd better go," he said grimly.

"Let me walk you outside," Velvet responded, taking his arm and leading him hurriedly from the room. This was surely the worst night of her life. Wordlessly, the couple made their way to the porch. As they stepped down onto the lawn, Velvet felt charged with the necessity of somehow softening her father's unforgivable behavior. "I just can't tell you how ashamed I feel," she said at last. "I had such a lovely evening planned. I never dreamed—"

"My only regret," Brett said turning to her, "is that you had to learn the true nature of my work." Velvet looked up at him, her brows quirked in puzzlement.

"What do you mean, Brett?" she asked.

"What your father said is true, Velvet," he answered. "I am little more than a bounty hunter. I hunt down men considered war criminals by the South. When I find them — and I always find them," he continued ruthlessly, "there is little chance of their survival. A name given to me by the government is a death sentence for that man. If I don't shoot him in the course of my duty, he is given a military trial. You may imagine for yourself the outcome

255

of such a trial."

"And are you called . . . 'the meanest man in the South'?" Velvet asked, awed.

"Yes," Brett said crisply, "I am." Velvet blinked, and turned briefly away. Then, as quickly, she turned back. The turquoise of her gaze glittered in the moonlight.

"To be perfectly frank," she said softly, "it matters little to me what you do. We've all compromised our values, Brett. We've had no choice." The quiet night breezes played in the halo of his hair, and Velvet watched as his lips lowered to hers. She did not turn her face away, but accepted his kiss. In the deepest recesses of her conscious thought, she knew she must remain objective toward Brett Whitney. He was, after all, doing nothing more immoral than those soldiers who raised their guns to murder strangers—men they'd never met. She would have bet that James McCulloch had not known his killer. And if he had? Was it less immoral for a brother to slay a brother? Velvet allowed Brett's lips to search hers. She allowed his arms to encircle her. Faint stirrings, remembrances, called to her. She lifted her own arms and entwined them around muscled shoulders. Her fingertips tunneled into coarse curls at the base of the strong column of a neck. She felt herself drawn to the hardness of a broad chest. Her breasts tingled at the recollected abrasion of manly fur against yielding flesh. Her lips parted, allowing the invasion of a searching tongue.

Strong hands demanded access. Velvet felt the bodice of her gown give way to searching hunger. Hot, moist kisses breathed their way down along the arch of her throat. Her hair, sweetly wrenched, quivered against the naked flesh of her shoulders. Primal need rose from her belly and, with heated fingers, seized her soul. Velvet moaned, more alive than she'd been in weeks. Her longing flesh ached for relentless rapture. Her heart sang: *Cutter. Oh, Cutter.*

Brett Whitney lifted her in strong arms.

"Wh-where are you taking me?" Velvet asked breathlessly, sudden awareness gripping her.

"We'll go around back, sugar," Brett said, his voice a rasping whisper.

"Wait! Brett, you can't—"

His steely grip tightened. "Can't what?" he demanded, still

walking with her toward the back of the house.

"You can't do this, Brett—" Velvet struggled wildly in his arms. At last he stopped and looked down at her. His green eyes, in the moonlight, were flecked with pinpoints of gold. "You can't," Velvet said weakly. "We . . . can't."

Brett Whitney arched a moon-silvered brow. Above her, he seemed a righteous, analyzing god. "You said yourself we've all had to compromise, sugar," he growled.

"I know that, but—"

"What are you afraid of, Velvet?" he asked roughly. "Are you afraid the neighbors will condemn you? Are you afraid society will think you tainted? There is no 'society,' as you remember it, sugar; and your neighbors have no objection to doing exactly what you're doing to get what they want."

"I . . . I don't understand, Brett," Velvet responded earnestly. He paused, and then slowly, reluctantly, set her down on her feet.

He raked long fingers through the golden tousle of his curls. "What did you think this was all about?" he demanded at last.

Velvet tugged at the edges of her bodice, struggling to cover herself. "I don't know what you're saying, Brett," she stated impatiently. "You ask me what I think 'this' is all about. What do you mean by 'this'? I asked you here tonight to share a pleasant evening. I let you kiss me because—"

"Because you wanted to be kissed," he said roughly. Velvet lowered her gaze. She had wanted to be kissed, it was true.

"I did want to be kissed," she murmured softly. Abruptly, she felt her shoulders jerked in a hard grasp. She looked up sharply.

"Don't you know that the old rules do not apply?" Brett ground out. "Don't you know you have only yourself to answer to?"

"My rules still apply to me," she rejoined. "I do not intend to give myself to just any old body who happens along, Major Whitney."

"Oh, come now, Miss Belle of Brandy Station, Virginia," he said harshly, "what is the point of pretense now? Don't you realize what's happened here? The 'Old South' and all its delicate little courtesies are gone. You're not a *belle* anymore, you're a woman—and a hungry woman, I might add. If the war has taught me nothing else, it has taught me to take the things I want when they become available to me."

"Then you had better get used to the fact," Velvet snapped,

struggling away from him, "that I am not one of those *things* available to you, Major." She lunged away from Brett Whitney, and was startled that, very suddenly, he let her go. She stumbled, and was startled again when he did not leap to her aid. She looked up at him in wonder. He only smiled. Velvet's gaze darkened. "Rudeness, I see, has survived the war," she said quietly.

He laughed. "Velvet honey," he said, almost heartily, "little courtesies will need to be earned from now on."

"I'm sure I don't know what you mean, Major," Velvet said archly. "It seems to me that . . . I daresay . . ." She was looking into his keen gaze. She knew exactly what he meant.

"There is a little encampment not far from here," he said evenly, his smile fading. "There are twenty or so women in that little encampment, all displaced from their gracious Southern mansions—all members of your pleasant circle of former belles." He paused. "Do you happen to remember a shy little mouse by the name of Lisa Mae Bloomer? Lisa Mae understands—as you do not—what the war has done to all of us. Lisa Mae is the proud possessor of a fat cow, a weekly supply of honey, and a generous allotment of just about anything else I can get my hands on." He eyed Velvet significantly. She could not repress her astonishment.

"You mean . . ." she breathed.

"That's exactly what I mean, sugar."

She stiffened, and said in wonder, "You *are* the meanest man in the South."

Chapter Twenty-eight

For as long as she could remember, Velvet had felt a friendly, patronizing disdain for Lisa Mae Bloomer — now she pitied her. It was odd, thought Velvet, how she seemed to be learning some new feeling every day. She had believed that, as of yesterday, she was deeply initiated, thoroughly versed in every phase of human nature. She had planned so carefully how she would handle the Brett Whitney of her youth and young womanhood. Her plans had not included his transformation from gentleman to cad. Cad! she said to herself, and nearly laughed at the appellation. Cad was a word she might have used years ago with no concept of its true meaning. Someone was a "cad" if he waited until the last moment to invite you to one party or another. He was a "cad" if he attempted to steal a kiss, if he bandied your name about, if he remarked impolitely regarding your new bonnet — or didn't mention it at all. How many times had she called this young man, or that, a "cad"? She had thought it of Cutter, but he was no cad. He was bold, it was true. He was impatient, thoughtless, arrogant. . . .

"Oh, Cutter," she said aloud. Tears came, unannounced. Velvet's heart clenched. "Where are you?" she breathed into the quiet, dogwood-laced air. Why am I missing him so just now? she wondered. She leaned back against the bole of the tree, and felt the soft grasses beneath her. Very near this spot, last night, she had considered succumbing to the will of Brett Whitney. She was still considering. Her traditional values aside, Velvet knew the arrangement Brett had proposed was at the very least . . . practical. But she could not repress her outrage — and the thought that if Cutter had accompanied her south, she would not be facing such a choice. But Cutter had gone his own stubborn way.

The fact was, she'd not been sorry to see him go. If she'd felt abandoned in New York City, her response had been temporary — momentary. Cutter had been horrible to her. Their marriage had come completely apart. There had been no reason in the world for them to continue their relationship. She glanced down and touched her belly. Her tears flowed freely as she thought of their child that might have been. Perhaps, for the first time, Velvet had a glimmer of what she had lost. There had been a certain . . . love between her and Cutter, but, given their strong personalities—her own willfulness, she conceded—it had not had a chance to mature. Once their trip south had begun, circumstances had played havoc with whatever chance they'd had to form a lasting relationship. And now Cutter was gone.

Velvet swiped at her tears. He was probably, she determined, up there in the Adirondacks with her cousin Nicole, nursing his bruised ego and blaming Velvet for the breakdown of their marriage. It would be just like him to—But that wouldn't be like him, she thought suddenly. Cutter would not run to another woman's arms, no matter how willing the woman. Velvet did not know how she could know such a thing, but she did. In her heart, she knew Cutter loved her. The abrupt knowledge overwhelmed her.

Velvet straightened, and then stood, unable to contain an apocryphal joy.

"He loves me," she said breathlessly, awed by the revelation. Why had he left her, after all? He had left because he hadn't wanted to hurt her! That was love!

Velvet began to run. She must tell someone. She made for the house, praying that Mammy Jane was in the kitchen. Doggedly, her desperation mounting, she charged up the long path, over the lawns, and burst into the house. She called to Mammy through the hallway, and finally reached the kitchen. She must get the words out very quickly, before the beautiful, wonderful, remarkable truth disappeared.

"We're married!" Velvet erupted breathlessly. "Cutter loves me, and we're married!" Mammy Jane eyed the girl disbelievingly.

"What's that, child?" she said.

Velvet swallowed and gulped in air. "I met a man, Mammy, a strong, handsome . . . terrible, mean . . ." Velvet began to laugh. "J. Eliot Cutter is his name, and I thought him the most roguish of creatures, and—"

"Now, Velvet-pie, you just calm yourself. You're overheated, honey." Mammy Jane moved to Velvet, and led her to the stool.

260

"I'm just fine, Mammy," Velvet insisted, still laughing. "I have to tell you about Cutter!"

"All right, girl, tell me," said Mammy Jane beginning to feel some of Velvet's excitement. "But you just calm yourself right down to a walk first. I won't have you getting the vapors." She waited for Velvet to catch her breath. "Now you tell Mammy Jane everything about this terrible, wonderful boy."

Velvet began her story slowly, as Mammy lowered herself comfortably into a nearby tottery chair. Starting with her first lonely weeks in the Duffy household, and ending with her marriage to Cutter and their trip south, she spared no detail. She told Mammy about the child she had lost—and was sorry she had done so, for the old woman's eyes became moist with tears.

"Now that's a real shame, Velvet-pie," Mammy Jane said softly. "Old Mammy would love to have had a little chick to cuddle again." She gazed sadly at Velvet. "That must be the worst part of all you've been through," she murmured.

Velvet nodded. "I don't think," she said quietly, "I've ever felt . . . guilt before, Mammy."

"Well, now, I won't have *that*," Mammy said sternly. "We don't know why that baby was lost. I know the Lord," she added righteously, "and he don't explain such things—even to me. Now, you know my Dahlia?" she asked. Velvet nodded, for she remembered well Mammy Jane's sturdy daughter. "That child never should have been born. I was not fifteen when I conceived that child," the older woman continued. "And I wasn't healthy like you, girl. Talk about hungry . . . That was when I lived at the McPherson plantation, and they didn't feed us hardly. When they *did* feed us, they didn't give us nearly enough, and it was always wormy. Some of us, the brave ones"—she chuckled—"ate the worms, just to stay alive. But not me! Well now, I remember it was so hot that summer, and Dahlia was little more than a twinkle in my eye, and . . . well . . . I took it into my head to get myself off of that plantation. I was a disobedient little thing in those days," she said, shifting comfortably in her chair. "I'd heard about a place north of New York City where runaways could find a safe home. I'd heard about it all right, and a fellow name of John Brown, and I decided I was going to go there. Now let me see," Mammy recollected softly, "that was in August of forty-one that I went slogging through them

261

swamps — we were in Georgia at the time — and Dahlia was born that next March. I got myself caught, in the meantime, and that old McPherson whupped me; hung me up by my wrists, and whupped me good." The room deadened to silence as Mammy finished her story. "If anyone asks you what this war is about, Velvet-pie," she said softly, "you tell them that. But that's not why I told you that story," she continued after a pause. "I don't want you — or anybody — feeling sorry for me. I told you that story because I wanted you to hear what I went through while I was carrying Dahlia. *And she got born.*" Mammy Jane stood and touched Velvet's cheek. "Don't you go blaming yourself, child, for that baby's loss; I won't have my little girl feeling guilt over something she couldn't help." The older woman smiled shrewdly. "We're going to have a little one here soon anyway, you know. Dahlia went off, got herself married, and she and her husband . . . and their little one are planning to come back to Sweet Briar Hill one day; Dahlia told me that when she left. She said, 'Mama, I'm leaving, but I'm coming back.' Her man, George, is going to make them some money. We'll get this plantation back to where you'll be proud of it. There'll be fine food on the table . . . maybe Dahlia will even buy us a table." She chuckled.

Velvet managed a smile. "Thank you for sharing your story, Mammy," she said quietly. "Thank you for helping me with my feelings of guilt. And, mostly . . . mostly, thank you for just being you." She took Mammy Jane into an embrace. The two women enjoyed the warmth of their mutual love for long moments. Finally, Velvet said gently, "Until Dahlia does come back to save us, we must think of something to get us through the next days."

"Shoot, child," Mammy said, moving to the sink to wash the potatoes she'd dug early in the day, "we'll get through. The Lord will —"

"The Lord," Velvet said sourly, "has his hands full. I'm afraid we're going to have to look after ourselves." Mammy Jane's rich laughter filled the room. Velvet looked at her in surprise.

"Honey," the older woman said, "have you got any idea how many hands the Lord's got?"

"I guess I don't, Mammy," Velvet said with a small laugh of her own. Mammy Jane's faith was remarkable, but at the moment food and money, not faith, were needed. Velvet stood, and moved absently to the sink. Lifting a potato — she'd come to hate them — she rolled it over her fingertips. The coarse, muddied feel of it irritated her. She tossed it ungently back onto the wooden counter. "Last night," Velvet began slowly, "Major Whitney offered me a proposal."

Mammy Jane looked at her in startled and delighted surprise. Her expression quickly changed to one of puzzlement. "You're already married, child," she said.

"It wasn't . . . marriage he proposed," Velvet said carefully. Mammy's expressive face immediately registered disapproval. "I felt the same way at first," Velvet went on quickly, "but now, after considering our desperate situation, I've . . . reviewed the idea." Velvet looked pointedly away from Mammy. "Mother and Pa can't go on much longer this way. Somebody in this house has got to do something." At Mammy Jane's silence, Velvet glanced at her. She was startled to find deep sadness in her eyes.

"Didn't my story tell you anything?" the woman asked. At Velvet's questioning look, she added, "That Whitney boy — major or no — is offering you nothing but slavery. He told me once, 'Mammy, I've been going to free my slaves for years.' And I said to him — this was *after* the Proclamation, but I was polite anyway — I said, 'Well now, maybe you ought to've followed your good instincts, sir.' I said, 'Maybe this war never needed to happen, with such good men as you around.' And you know what he said to me, child? He said, 'Mammy, somebody will always be enslaved, 'cause there's always going to be rich, and there's always going to be poor.' Well, I say" — Mammy sniffed — " he's right, but not for the *reason* he says. Somebody is always going to be enslaved, *I* say, because there's always going to be people around who'll take advantage of human weakness. You're hungry right now. Well, I'm hungry too. Miss Alicia's hungry, and Mr. Steven's hungry — if he only knew it — but that don't mean any one of us is going to be taken advantage of. You put your faith in the Lord, Velvet-pie," Mammy finished, " 'cause the Lord won't ask nothing for *His* generosity."

Velvet sighed deeply. She had been wrong to confide in Mammy Jane. The woman was wise, it was true, but frustratingly unrealistic. It was fine for her to spout platitudes about putting one's faith in the Lord, but that didn't seem to be putting anything but turnips and those mealy potatoes in their stomachs. Hindered by Mammy's words, but not entirely stalled, Velvet's "review" of Brett Whitney's proposal went on.

She decided she must be the mistress of rationalization; she could, on a moral level, dismiss his offer, but on a more pragmatic level it made perfect sense. Why should Brett simply give away his bounty? He had a perfect right to expect something in return . . . didn't he? After all, nothing in this world was gotten for nothing . . . was it? People paid for what they wanted. Unfortunately, she had no resources. There was only the one thing she could offer Brett Whitney in return for his generosity—and that one thing was herself.

Velvet made yet another tour of the house. The remnants of last night's dinner awaited her in the dining room. Though the dishes had been cleared away, the roses remained—wilted now. She lifted a fragile blossom. Somehow, in the throes of its own death, the rose smelled more sweet than it had during the halcyon days of its life. Its pungent aroma stayed with Velvet as she made her way, first to her mother's room to check on a sleeping Alicia, and then to Steven's study.

"What shall I do, Pa?" she sighed to the inert figure who huddled in a chair—the only furniture in the room. As she had expected, her father responded with silence. Velvet moved slowly, heavily, back through the house. She surveyed the wedding cake moldings of the ceilings, the high arched French windows, the parqueted flooring—architectural symbols of Sweet Briar Hill's former grandeur. But what had become of that grandeur? It had fallen to uselessness. What good were symbols now? When everything within that noble framework came to nothing, of what use were exterior accommodations? Of what use was Velvet's maidenly persona now? Too much had happened to her—as too much had happened in this house—for her to go on with the pretense that she was anything other than a vessel for her own instincts for survival. She had been reduced to little more than an animal. Why should her corporeal impulses end with Brett Whitney? The only real sin here, Velvet decided, would be the sin of dereliction of duty. Once committed to the task of survival for herself and her family, she must follow that pledge to wherever it led. If Brett Whitney—and his spurious offer—was the path of survival, then Velvet would take that path.

She entered the kitchen once again to find Mammy Jane — and Arabella.

"Hello, Miss Velvet," the woman said brightly.

"Why, Arabella," Velvet said, running to her and embracing the woman. "What brings you all the way out here?"

"Didn't I tell you?" Mammy said smugly. "The Lord — and Arabella — have provided."

The younger woman merely smiled. "I brought a little bit of sugar, and a little bit of corn meal," she said, chuckling. "I don't think *that* puts me in the same breath with the Lord."

"You'd be surprised," Velvet said wryly, inspecting the small sack of provisions that Arabella had brought. "Where did you get it?"

"Sad to say, Miss Velvet, we got wounded prisoners over to the hospital. Whatever they got on them when they're captured, we take and divvy up. The doctors take most for the hospital, but they give some to the workers over there to take home to their families. Well," she said warmly, "the McBrides have been 'family' to me for most of my life. Your Ma and Pa have been kind to me, Miss Velvet. They bought Mammy and me off the McPherson plantation about the same time, though I was just a baby, and Mammy was all grown up." Velvet nodded guiltily, for she recalled with a shudder Mammy's story. "And that purchase was providential," Arabella went on. "Mammy and me began to get treated like human beings here — no more whippings, no more starvation. Well, now we're free, God be praised; but I don't think either of us will forget your family's kindness, not after what we'd been through."

"Amen," said Mammy Jane softly.

"I will never know how you can all be so forgiving," Velvet said, in awe.

"We're not *all* forgiving, Miss Velvet," Arabella said gently. "We're just like your folks. Some of us is, and some of us isn't."

Velvet's heart twisted in her chest. Again, she had put these two very individual women into a neat categorical slot. She must not let that happen again. She smiled, repressing her guilt for the moment. "I feel very fortunate to know you both," she said softly. "I hope — once this war is over — we can be just friends."

"We'll see." Arabella laughed.

265

She sat her stool confidently, and Velvet realized how much the war had changed her. Velvet recalled the small, submissive child Arabella had been, and how she'd grown at Sweet Briar Hill into a cheerful, robust young woman. She'd always been completely deferential, though, and never expressed an opinion or questioned authority. Now Arabella had an authority of her own. The change was subtle, but obvious. All changes, Velvet supposed, began with small manifestations and grew more obvious with time. Lisa Mae Bloomer had obviously changed. Nothing in the world could have convinced Lisa Mae, years ago, to have the relationship she now had with Brett Whitney.

Velvet shook off that unpleasant reflection. She wanted to enjoy Arabella's visit. She said, "How are things going for you, at the hospital?"

"I like my work," Arabella answered seriously.

"It's noble work," Mammy Jane offered sagely.

"Yes, it is," said Arabella. She laughed. "Only thing," she added, her tone altered, her voice trailing, "I feel so bad for those boys. They're hurt and scared. And those Northern boys—the prisoners—are so far from home. It just doesn't seem right. Most of them are decent boys. I go around and make friends, when I get time. There's this one fellow," she continued, leaning toward her listeners, "who's got the devil in him, I am sworn." All three women laughed. "He got himself shot up something awful, but you'd never know it. Every day he nudges me, and asks me if I maybe got a gun hid under my petticoat. I say to him, 'Mr. Cutter, sir, it's none of your damned business *what* I got under my petticoat.'"

Arabella laughed riotously, and it was several moments before she realized she was laughing alone.

"Did you say, 'Mr. Cutter'?" Velvet asked, her face drained of color.

"Yes, honey," Arabella said worriedly. "You know that boy?"

Mammy stepped to Velvet's side, and embraced her. "That 'boy,'" she said worriedly, "is her husband."

Chapter Twenty-nine

"This is the craziest thing I've ever done in my life, Velvet McBride." Arabella's whisper was high and hoarse. Velvet grasped her shoulders, and pulled her down into the shadows of a small outbuilding that leaned lazily in the sun.

"Dammit, Bella, keep your voice down!" she commanded, her own voice lifting to an urgent, and inadvisable, stridency. Quickly altering her tone, Velvet whispered, "Do you want us discovered before we even have a chance to—" Her words were cut off abruptly as a gray-coated soldier paced by, about twenty feet from them, in all his martial menace. "See?" Velvet admonished once he had passed. "They're everywhere."

"Well, we knew that," Arabella rejoined, keeping her indignation hushed. "I told you we should have waited till night."

"All right, then," Velvet intoned, her regard darkening, "we'll wait till night. That just leaves Cutter in their hands for, at least, another three hours; is that what you want?"

Arabella cast her a disgruntled frown. "I'm just being sensible," she insisted. She watched uncertainty and frustration cloud Velvet's face. "I know how you must feel, but this is insanity," she went on with quiet gravity. "Will you, for once in your life, listen to someone else?" Velvet's recklessness had been much the source of humor among the servants at Sweet Briar Hill. Her willful ways, throughout her growing-up years, were often satirized in the quarters—not unkindly, and with some affection—but Arabella could not now allow that rashness to be the undoing of both of them. "*We* could end up being taken prisoner, and then where would your husband be?" she reasoned.

Velvet folded her arms petulantly across her breast. Forbearance is not this girl's strong point, Arabella reflected with wry tenderness; and she capitulated with difficulty. "It'll be dark soon," she went on more gently. "If we can just be patient, we can get up to the stable without them spotting us."

"And then what?" Velvet muttered. "I think my plan was far more sensible."

"As I remember," Arabella sighed, "your 'plan' was hardly a plan."

"I still think it will work," Velvet challenged.

"Keep your voice down," Arabella admonished. They both huddled, in necessary silence, at the side of the building as the soldier returned. When he had once again passed, Velvet continued.

"I will find Private Jackson; I flatter myself that he held me in some esteem. He will help us."

"How can you be sure?" Arabella insisted.

"I just am," Velvet rejoined petulantly.

"You just *hope*," said Arabella.

Velvet regarded her dubiously. "All right then, I *hope* Private Jackson will help us. What else have we got to hope for?" She turned away in vexation. "If only they'd not transferred Cutter from the hospital . . ."

"It's his own fault," Arabella said, attempting to interject some humor into the bleak situation, "for being so all-fired ornery — and getting well so soon."

"Is he well, Bella?" Velvet asked, turning with sudden earnestness to her companion. The woman nodded with certainty.

"They wouldn't have transferred him to L Étoile de Vie if he hadn't recovered," she said soothingly. "They send all the prisoners here once they're well." She sighed. "Unfortunately, this is just one step away from a military trial. And, from what you've told me about Cutter and his activities up north, we both know how that's going to turn out."

"Yes," Velvet reflected aloud. "We were told," she said sadly, "that his reception here in the South would not be a generous one." She quirked her brow in puzzlement. "I wonder what brought him down here in the first place?"

"He never shared that," Arabella said softly. "For all he was a cooperative patient — and a charmer — there was something about him . . . a sadness or . . . something that you understood was, well, private." Velvet bit at her lower lip, and wondered why on earth Cutter had placed himself in the present danger. He was nothing short of impossible, she determined silently. She determined, too, that Arabella was correct in insisting on their using the cover of darkness.

"We'll know soon enough," Velvet said after a moment. "And, I think," she added, looking directly at Arabella, "we ought to wait until darkness falls before pursuing our plan."

Arabella merely smiled. Old habits die hard, she thought ruefully. Velvet McBride was not one to relinquish control of a situation easily.

"You're probably right," Arabella said softly.

"It's the only sensible thing to do," Velvet assured her, as though she herself had just then thought up the idea. "Now all we have to do," she added, "is come up with the 'plan'." At that moment, the soldier repaced his apparently appointed route. Velvet watched him, as she and Arabella huddled in the gathering afternoon shadows. "He's obviously guarding some strategic position," she observed. "And he's only one," she added significantly. The young women looked at each other.

"Do you think we could?" asked Arabella. They were both silent as he passed them heading back to his apparent starting point.

Velvet pulled her down at last, and they hunched together very close. "We might overpower him," Velvet said. "We might somehow, the two of us, get his uniform and his gun. Then I could impersonate him, and just waltz right up to the stable."

"Why should you be the one to impersonate him," Arabella said quickly. "I'm bigger than you; I'll do it." Velvet lifted an elegantly winged brow. Arabella received the implied flaw in that plan, and laughed. Velvet silenced her immediately, and Arabella hastily repressed her mirth. "All right, you do it," she whispered. "but then what will I do?" Velvet frowned, thinking.

"Perhaps," she said slowly, "you could fashion some sort of diversion. You could run up to the house, and pretend you're being chased, and tell them—"

"This is all on the assumption that I don't get shot the minute they spot me," said Arabella wryly.

"They won't shoot you," Velvet said impatiently. "They *are* gentlemen, after all."

"They didn't act very 'gentlemanly' toward you," rejoined Arabella.

"Well then, maybe you ought to walk," Velvet said with finality. "That way, you won't seem so threatening . . . but, of course, how can you say you're being chased if you're walking—"

"Maybe we should do just what we did when we went to the hospital," interjected Arabella. "I'll just go up there—*walk* up there," she added, "and say I'm inquiring about the health of their latest prisoner. I could say the doctor sent me from the hospital."

"Is that done?" inquired Velvet.

"Never been done before," said Arabella, shaking her head. "But who's to say it might not be done? This war hasn't erased *all* traces of humanity, has it? I mean *some* doctor might still be interested in the welfare of his patient, wouldn't you think?"

Velvet sighed. "I'm not sure, Arabella," she said softly. "I never cease to be amazed at what this war has done to seemingly civilized people." She glanced up at her companion. "We in the South were the most civilized people in the world once." At Arabella's silence, she quirked her brow.

"How 'civilized' are people who keep other people as slaves, Velvet?" Arabella asked after a pause.

"I know," Velvet answered quietly, lowering her gaze. "I know exactly what you mean. But on another level . . . I mean . . ." She lifted her eyes. "At one time, no gentleman in the world was ever more gentlemanly, more chivalrous, than a Southern gentleman. And, now . . ."

"But that was all just—"

"Playacting," Velvet finished for her. "I know," she added resignedly. "But I miss it."

Twilight had darkened the surrounding lawns to a deep, rusty purple. Lengthening shadows cast a shivering dusk over the world. It was in these tense shadows that Velvet and Arabella came up with their plan. Its foremost manifestation was to be carried out now. Velvet stepped into the path of the pacing guard. He stopped abruptly, cocking his head into the darkness, not sure of what he was seeing.

"It's me, Velvet McBride," said the shimmering form before him. "I was a prisoner of your Captain McCulloch a little over a month ago, and I left rather . . . unceremoniously."

The soldier's recognition was immediate, and apparent. He raised his gun and cocked it. "Put your hands up," he commanded. Velvet did so, but slowly.

"I am no danger to you," she said carefully. "As you see, I'm unarmed." The soldier moved closer to her. "I only came back," she added, her tone hesitating and helpless, "in order that I might clear my name. Captain McCulloch believed me to be a spy . . . or some such thing . . . and I just couldn't bear the thought that he might still carry that presumption." The soldier moved still closer, and Velvet managed a small, ingratiating smile. "You understand, don't you, sir?" she said. "A lady's good name is so important to her. It would never do for me to endure the onus that your most dynamic captain has placed upon me. And now that I'm back at Sweet Briar Hill, my family has urged that I come here to —"

"Why didn't your daddy come to speak for you?" the soldier demanded. Velvet lowered her eyes sadly, and the man, regretting his unfortunate question, hesitated, and at last shifted his aggressive posture. "I apologize most profoundly, ma'am," he said with concern. Lowering his gun, he added, "Have you no brother, or an uncle who could plead your situation with the captain?" Timely tears glazed Velvet's eyes. Again the young soldier damned the war for the impossible situation over which he now presided.

"It's not your fault, sir," Velvet murmured. "May I lower my hands?" she inquired sweetly.

"Oh, of course, ma'am," the man said with awed apology. "I'm so deeply sorry." He bowed, nearly scraping the ground between them, and then stepped to Velvet. "We'll get you right up to the captain, Miss . . . ."

"McBride," Velvet said gently. "But, do you think my speaking to him will do any good? Isn't it just possible he might toss me right back into that godawful stable?" she asked.

"I can't imagine even Captain McCulloch doing such a thing, Miss —"

"McBride," Velvet interjected.

"I remember," the man smiled. "I'll never forget that name, ma'am." He took her elbow, and began to lead her up to the

271

house. "After all, Miss McBride," he continued, "the captain's a reasonable man and you're giving yourself up. He couldn't still believe—" Velvet stopped him with a fluttery hesitation.

"I can't help but be frightened," she said, suddenly breathless. "Oh, my, I do think . . ." Abruptly, she teetered and swooned, falling to the ground at the astonished soldier's feet.

"Oh, ma'am," he gaped worriedly, bending over her and setting down his gun. At that, Arabella lunged from behind the small outbuilding, and, with a shriek, she ran through the shimmering darkness toward where the young soldier was kneeling in the grass. He twisted, amazed at the hellish vision, then grabbed for his gun, but Velvet sat up suddenly, and shoved him off balance. Arabella had reached them, and kicked the gun from his reach. Scrambling for it, Velvet crawled away from him while Arabella jumped onto the man's chest, pinning him down.

"Hold it," Velvet commanded, leveling the gun at the struggling couple. Arabella lurched away quickly, so that the man might not hold her hostage, and ran to Velvet's side. Slowly, the soldier recognized his own peril, and stood facing the two women.

"Well, well," he intoned, with a small smile. "I have been what you might call gin-rummied."

"You might say that," Velvet rejoined curtly. "Now move." She indicated with the barrel of the gun the back of the outbuilding. She knew, if she were to be successful with her plan, that she must not indicate the distressing fact that, even if necessary, she could not imagine how to use the gun—except perhaps to hit him with it. She maintained as stern a demeanor as possible. "Hurry up, soldier," she commanded. The trio moved to the blackness of the shadows. As planned, Arabella drew Velvet's gown down around her feet, and Velvet stepped from it. Arabella tore it into strips, while Velvet held the man prisoner at the point of the gun.

"You ought to be ashamed of yourself, Mammy," said the man softly, as Arabella commanded that he remove his own clothes, and then tied him. Arabella looked down at him finally, and stuffed the last of the scraps of Velvet's gown into his mouth with, perhaps, more force than was completely necessary.

"I ain't your Mammy," she said emphatically.

Velvet laughed, relieved, and lowered the gun. "You were

272

right about one thing, Private," she said. "You won't soon forget the name Velvet McBride."

Hastily, she slipped the soldier's uniform on over her chemise, and she and Arabella began their walk up to the house — Arabella leading, at the point of Velvet's gun.

"You know something?" Arabella observed in a whisper, over her shoulder, as they walked. "I've always noticed that, when there's a man around, your Southern accent gets thick as winter honey."

Velvet stifled a small laugh. "Thick enough," she whispered back, "to ooze over a young soldier and trap his heart." Both women suppressed giggles.

They moved slowly but steadily up the drive to the house, finding themselves at last at the bottom of the steps. Several soldiers saluted Velvet, and attempted to make some inquiry as to the circumstances under which she'd captured the young Negro woman, but Velvet proceeded with Arabella into the house, and went directly to where she recalled Captain McCulloch kept his office. Greeting him smartly, she stepped back, allowing Arabella to tell her own story. Captain McCulloch stood, a little surprised at the intrusion, the silence of the apparently very young soldier, and the arch-browed confidence of his captive.

"I am Arabella Barret from the hospital," the woman said. "I've come to inquire —"

"Let the soldier explain your presence," said the captain, eying Velvet. "What's her story, Private?"

Velvet cleared her throat, indicating with a cough, that she'd lost her voice. "Cold, sir," she said in a hoarse whisper.

"I see," said McCulloch irritably. He looked back to Arabella. "Explain yourself then," he said.

"The doctor over at the hospital asked me to come to see you, and find out about the status of one of your prisoners," Arabella said, with no indication of the nervousness that assaulted her in the presence of this most menacing captain. "He wants to know —"

"Which prisoner?" asked McCulloch curtly.

"Cutter," Arabella responded quickly. "J. Eliot Cutter." McCulloch's eyes narrowed. "The doctor felt he might be . . . might be . . ."

273

"Might be what, girl?"

"In pain," Arabella said, thinking quickly. She'd not believed that she and Velvet would get this far. She had certainly not anticipated an interrogation. "The doctor says he was shot up bad, and he wanted me to . . . to check on him."

"Check on him?" McCulloch said slowly. "The man is a prisoner of war." He stepped around the French teak desk and faced the two women in all his polished, soldierly splendor. Velvet's eyes lifted; she was awed by the military authority he represented. He flashed her a scrutinizing regard, and her gaze quickly lowered. The captain looked back to Arabella. "Are we now indulging our prisoners, girl? Are we inviting Northerners down here to enjoy a bit of pampering? Even our own lads get less than private medical attention." He paused, then crossed the room, circling slowly around the two intruders. Arabella and Velvet remained absolutely still. "Answer me, girl," said McCulloch, his tone quiet, menacing.

Arabella cleared her throat. "It's only that . . . the doctor told me," she said, thinking quickly, "Cutter was such an important prisoner. Major Whitney said when he came to get Cutter to transfer him to here . . . Major Whitney told the doctor you all wanted Cutter alive."

"That we do," conceded McCulloch, allowing a small smile to etch his firm lips. "That we do, girl. We want that particular prisoner, now that he's well, to go to trial . . . so we can hang him." He watched Arabella stiffen almost imperceptibly. He noted, too, the small shift of the young soldier's feet. "Problem, soldier?" he asked. Velvet hastily shook her head, and pulled the brim of her hat down further over her eyes. " 'Cause, if there is," he said softly, "we can have this lady here look at you." His eyes drifted back to Arabella. "Or is it only this Cutter fellow you enjoy nursing?"

"I . . . I don't understand," Arabella said, attempting nonchalance.

"Oh, I just got the feeling that maybe you were inquiring not for the doctor but for yourself, girl. Might that be the case?"

Arabella drew back her shoulders. "It is not," she stated.

"I think it is," McCulloch said levelly. "I think it is. Isn't that what you think, soldier?" he asked. He stood now very close to

274

Velvet. She stepped back a small pace, but the captain merely advanced on her. "Too bad about that sore throat, Private," he said. "I hate to see any of my boys in pain." He glanced at Arabella. "I've got some nursing instincts myself, girl. Did you notice that?" Arabella nodded mutely. "I'm glad you noticed, 'cause I wouldn't want either of you to think me a monster." He laughed, but the sound was not a merry one. There was deep cruelty in the sound, even danger. Velvet shuddered in the warm, twilit dusk of the room. She chanced a look up at Captain McCulloch. He was regarding her calmly, and she turned away, perceiving that cruelty now. Icy dread washed over her.

"I guess we'd better go," Arabella said hastily. "I'll tell the doctor—"

"Turn up the lamp, Private," McCulloch ordered. A bright light flared, dispelling shadows. The captain grabbed Velvet's arm, twisting it painfully behind her back. With his other hand, he tore that hat from her head, and entrapped her free arm. Her gun clattered to the ground, and Arabella grabbed for it. Another soldier took her. The scuffle suddenly over, silence gripped the room. "Well, well," Captain McCulloch said at last, quietly, "my little spy has returned."

Velvet, trapped against his hard chest, looked up at him defiantly. "I'm no spy, and you know it, Captain," she spat out.

McCulloch nodded, raising a sand-colored brow, and smiled. "Yes," he said, "I do know it."

"Then, dammit to flaming hell, let me go," Velvet grated, her eyes flashing blue-green fire. She struggled against McCulloch's steely grip. For her efforts, she was merely held tighter, his muscular arms like unyielding leather straps around her.

"Do not fight me, lady," he drawled softly, and with a hint of amusement. "If you do, you'll find yourself in a losing battle."

Velvet's rage flashed. "I'll find myself at odds with *you*, Captain McCulloch, whether you let me go or not." She wriggled mindlessly, flaxen-streaked curls flying out. McCulloch seemed to hold her effortlessly, and this increased her frustration. "Let me go, damn you, sir!" she shrieked. The captain, containing his apparent mirth, glanced over his broad shoulder.

"Clear this room," he said to the several soldiers who stood, looking with awed curiosity at the amazing one-sided battle. De-

275

spite Arabella's loud protests, they all left. Abruptly, Velvet stopped struggling.

Looking up, her eyes wide and tear-struck, she said, "You won't hurt Arabella, will you?" McCulloch's silence served only to darken her regard. "She's done nothing, Captain," Velvet said solemnly.

"Except," McCulloch rejoined, "aiding and abetting the attempted escape of a known criminal."

"Cutter hasn't even been tried yet, and you call him a criminal," said Velvet. She watched the humor fade from McCulloch's face.

The captain paused. "One might ask how such a man inspires such loyalty in a beautiful Southern woman like yourself," he said, not really expecting an answer.

"He's my husband," Velvet shot back.

Again, McCulloch paused. His brow lifted. "I see," he said. By degrees he let go his hold on her.

"Besides that," Velvet added, massaging her wrists, "how could you possibly know that Arabella was attempting to aid his escape? How do you know she wasn't telling the truth?" McCulloch's regard hooded.

"I don't," he answered evenly. "I also don't know why you're here, and in that ridiculous getup. Would you care to explain yourself?" Velvet hesitated. In her fury, she had not even begun to think of an explanation to offer him. The captain watched her. "I've got all night, Miss McBride . . . or should I say, Mrs. Cutter?" When again, Velvet failed to respond, McCulloch sat on the corner of Mr. Carleton's desk, and folded his arms across his chest. "Let me be honest with you, madam," he said, "you would be in a great deal of trouble, if it were not for the information I received from Major Brett Whitney."

"Brett?" Velvet gaped.

McCulloch smiled narrowly. "Brett," he repeated. "Major Whitney and I spoke at some length about you. After your . . . unfortunate escape from our little prison, I made some inquiries. The escape itself rather astonished me, to speak the truth. I might add that Private Jackson was appropriately chastised for his rather lax handling of your imprisonment."

"You didn't hurt him, did you?" Velvet interjected with concern. "It wasn't his fault, you know."

"My, my," McCulloch drawled. "Such a passionate little heart. Does your concern for others know no bounds, madam?"

Velvet's lips tightened. "My concern, Captain," she gritted out, "is for those unjustly dealt with."

"Yes," McCulloch sighed, lowering his gaze. "Unfortunately, those who might benefit by your compassion seem to suffer terrible trials just from meeting up with you."

Velvet paused. She had no rejoiner. The truth was, if the choice had been made between her own survival and that of Private Jackson; she'd make the same choice again. Arabella was another matter, however. Velvet had to get both of them out of there, and she had to get Cutter away from this place as well. "I want to see my husband," she said finally, lifting her little chin.

"Oh, I have no doubt of that," Captain McCulloch said.

"May I see him?" Velvet asked firmly.

"How do I know you won't try to help him escape?"

"I won't," Velvet answered, lying unabashedly. "That was never my intention—or Arabella's either. She was only helping me."

"Major Whitney assured me you were no spy," said McCulloch slowly. "He assured me you were a true daughter of the South, but then, he was not aware of your marriage to a Northerner."

"I am still a daughter of the South, Captain McCulloch," Velvet said tartly. "Anyone who doubts that ought to come to Sweet Briar Hill. We are a most traditional family."

"Word is," said McCulloch, lowering his gaze in mock despair, "that your daddy has taken to the drink, and that your mother's—"

"Don't you dare speak of my mother, sir," Velvet grated. "Have you no shame? Is there nothing left of civility?"

McCulloch looked up sharply. "Civility"—he sneered—"is, and always was, for the rich. As a boy, madam, I was called a 'cracker' by apparently 'civilized' people like yourself. I was taunted and ridiculed by little girls dressed in laces, as you were most likely dressed." He stood and moved toward her. He stopped directly over her, and glared down into her eyes. "Why should I show you any courtesy, madam? Answer me that."

"B-because . . ."

"Because what, madam? Because you demand it? Because, by virtue of your birth into an aristocratic family, you are entitled to it?" Velvet pushed herself away from him, but he followed, circling the room. "You might have come to me humbly. You might have sweetly requested—"

"And how far would that have gotten me," Velvet shot back.

McCulloch's arm snaked out and caught Velvet's. He snapped her to him. "I don't know that it would have gotten you any farther than this," he ground out, "but you might at least have tried. Instead, you come to me this way—using the uniform of your own cause to deceive me. Did you think me so stupid that I wouldn't recognize your foolish little ruse?"

"I . . . I didn't . . . think," Velvet answered.

"No," he pushed her away, "you didn't." McCulloch presented his wide-shouldered back to her. "Your kind never does, madam," he said softly. "Do you know what I would have given," he said after a long silence, "to have lived in a place like this when I was a boy, to have had your advantages?" He faced her. Velvet looked away. "My brother was the intelligent one in our family," he continued. "He left Virginia when he was still a boy. He knew—"

"Your brother?" Velvet asked, lifting her gaze.

"My brother, James," said McCulloch. "He went north a long, long time ago, to New York City. He's probably a rich man by now, working in some Northern industry. People have a chance up north. Down here, once a 'cracker' always a cracker." Velvet shut her eyes against the tears that formed abruptly. James McCulloch was this pompous captain's brother, after all. And yet, the captain knew nothing of his brother's soldierhood—and death. Velvet would not be the one to tell him. Let him imagine James sitting somewhere in a leather-appointed office, a captain himself—of industry. Velvet sat heavily in a nearby chair, her head lowered. She felt truly humbled now. This war—this terrible, terrible war—had done so much to so many, had caused more suffering than one life could contain. She looked up at the man she'd thought spiteful and dangerous only moments ago. She saw him now—the truth of him—as a man who'd ordered, unknowingly, the death of his own brother in deference to . . .

278

what? To a cause. Tears came freely now. Velvet did not attempt to stop them.

"I'm so sorry," she whispered.

Captain McCulloch stiffened. "Sorry for what, madam," he said brusquely.

"I suppose," Velvet murmured, swallowing, "that I'm sorry I was dressed in laces, while you . . ." Her voice broke. McCulloch moved toward her, watching the glitter of her tears against the sooty thickness of her lashes.

"Your husband's a lucky man," he said huskily. "He will die, it is true, but he has much for which to be thankful. His physical wounds are fully healed, and he will spend the last hours of his life knowing that he has inspired the love of a remarkable woman. This is not the case for many of the men who fight this war." Looking for long moments into the aquatic pools of her eyes, he said finally, "I'll send for him."

Chapter Thirty

For the first time in over a year, Velvet understood her original, and painful, attraction to Cutter. He stood before her now, chest bared, in all his manly magnificence. He was so tall, so wide-shouldered, the young soldiers who escorted him into the room paled in contrast to his onyx-haired, gray-eyed perfection. Wrists tied behind his back with thick ropes, his curls falling in jet tousles over his forehead, his gaze silver in the lamplit dimness of the room, he might have been a mythic god; even in his bound condition, humbling every other being on earth. Velvet gasped and ran to him. He could not return her embrace, but he lowered his lips wordlessly to her upturned ones.

"Oh, Cutter," she breathed, and touched his shoulders. She laughed breathlessly as she ran her fingertips over his coarsely stubbled jaw, caressed tenderly the thick tangle of his curls. "Oh, love." She entwined her arms around the strong column of his neck, and smiled into his eyes. "I never imagined how much we meant to each other till you were gone."

"Nor I, princess," he intoned. He looked up, his flint-eyed gaze resting on McCulloch. "Might I be unbound while I greet my wife," he said; it was not a question. The captain studied him for a brief moment. The two men were of a height. Finally, McCulloch gave a curt nod, and Cutter was hastily untied.

"Don't try anything, Cutter," McCulloch ordered, and with his men, after a softer, arch-browed glance at Velvet, he left the room.

Immediately, Velvet was swept into Cutter's strong embrace. His lips consumed her. Each moist breath, each powerful caress, each longing word, penetrated the hard hurt that she'd endured, and healed it. She felt warm, life-giving passion energize her every pore. She was alive, each sense tingling. He held her to him at last, his heart thrumming, generating life in her breast. He cradled the back of her head in one big hand, pressing her to his chest as though he would never release her.

"Oh, Velvet," he groaned over and over. "I was a fool to leave you." She pushed against the hard-muscled expanse of his embrace, and looked up into his eyes.

"No, love," she murmured. "I was the fool. I shall always regret—"

"Do not regret anything," he said gently. A corner of his firm lips twitched, threatening a smile, and his gaze glinted. "We did our best to fight this thing between us—the thing we've both known was there since the day we met—but it was stronger than us. It has won, princess."

"Yes," Velvet affirmed. "Love has won." They held onto each other, declaring with their hearts what their minds now knew. "Oh, Cutter," she sighed at last, "I cannot bear to see you this way."

"Bear it well, princess," he said softly, "because I am more alive at this moment than I have been in a very long time." He held her away from him, and his smile was full and deep, his even white teeth glinting in the lamplight. "I have been little more than a walking corpse since I left you in New York City. Prison is now a minor annoyance, sweet."

Velvet's eyes became wide and solemn. "Prison is not our concern, love," she said. "They want to hang you." To her amazement, Cutter laughed deeply.

"There is a little battle going on right now up in Gettysburg, Pennsylvania that will ensure my freedom very soon. These bloody Rebs won't have time to hang me." Velvet turned from him abruptly, and Cutter's exuberance was immediately checked. "I'm sorry, princess," he said gently. "I didn't mean to disparage your beloved South, but—"

"Oh, Cutter," she replied with irritation—his arrogance still had the power to move her to that. "Do you think I care who wins this war? Don't you know," she added, gazing up into the pewter depths of his eyes, "all I care about is you?" Velvet's irritation grew as she spoke. "They've already got you hanged, don't you know that? Your activities with the Underground Railroad are unforgivable, as far as these 'bloody Rebs' are concerned." She lowered her gaze abruptly. "You're considered a war criminal, love," she went on. "Your fate is all but decided." Cutter did not

281

speak for a moment, and she lifted her regard. "I've come here to help you escape," she said grimly, "and that is what I intend to do."

His smile threatened, but Cutter merely arched a dark brow, and asked, "And how did you intend to manage that?"

"I haven't decided," said Velvet, her confidence leaving her, and her own arrogance taking hold. "But I will. Arabella and I got this far. . . ." Her expression suddenly altered. "Arabella," she gasped. "I need to find out what they've done with her." She lurched past Cutter toward the door, but his hand shot out, and he grabbed her.

"If you're speaking of the pretty young woman from the hospital, she's fine, princess. I saw her as they brought me in, in the other room." He drew Velvet to him. "Is she in on this little plan of yours?" he asked, his amusement still perilously close to the surface. Velvet nodded. "I wondered what she was doing here," he said. Velvet's eyes were wide and solemn as she looked up into his.

"We're not leaving without you," she stated. Cutter slowly released her. He was marginally convinced that this little wife of his was serious.

"Velvet," he said kindly, "I know you want to help me, but —"

"And I will, Cutter," she answered him. "Don't try to discourage me. I might tell you," she added archly, "that I escaped from this prison myself not long ago." Cutter's brows furrowed in sudden astounded puzzlement.

"What are you talking about?" he thundered. "They wouldn't have dared —" Velvet raced to him, and pressed her hand against his lips.

"Please, Cutter," she entreated. "Do you want to bring them all in here?" She held onto him, attempting to soothe the tension she felt in his body. "I came down here on a troop train," she said quickly, "and I was captured. It's all right, love," she murmured. "I'm all right, I promise." Cutter pulled away from her hold.

"Oh, God," he said quietly. "I was even glad for a while you didn't stay in New York City." He turned, and impaled her with his silver regard. "I had attempted to join the twenty-third New York Cavalry, but my presence in the army, they said, might prove a liability. It was the first inkling I had that the Confederacy considered me a criminal. They told me to head north; they

282

told me my mere presence would endanger every soldier in any battalion to which I might be assigned." He lowered his gaze. The memory obviously caused him great pain. "They pleaded with me to go home, and wait out the war—a war in which I believed," he said softly, "a war I was forced to let other men fight for me." He turned away from her.

"Cutter," Velvet said quietly, "you have done more in the pursuit of your beliefs than most men. Instead of killing, you have saved people, given them new lives. You've nothing to be ashamed of."

He faced her again, repressing his deep hurt. "I was halfway back to Northville," he explained stiffly, "before it occurred to me that you probably would not stay with Morgana. I retraced my path, and reached New York just as the draft riots were ravaging that city." Velvet nodded.

"A riot broke out just as I boarded the train," she said, shuddering as she recalled that bloody day. Cutter moved to her and held her.

"You must have been only hours ahead of me," he said quietly. "I found Morgana, and she told me what you'd done. I started south immediately." He laughed softly, and looked down into the perfect oval of her face. "I suppose I might have expected it," he said, brushing an errant curl from her soft cheek, "but I admit to being murderously angry at the time."

"It's a good thing, then," Velvet murmured, "that you didn't catch up with me till now." This impudence in her piquant, green- blue gaze, the reckless tousle of her star-frosted curls, the small smile that curved the perfect bow of her lips, all did elfin combat with Cutter's resentment.

"Oh, yes," he groaned, drawing her, roughly, deeper into his hard embrace. "What in the name of God am I to do with you?" he breathed hoarsely into her thick curls.

"For one thing," Velvet said softly, "you are going to let me get you out of this place." His laugh now was husky, and resigned.

"Little princess," he said with tender reverence.

At that moment, the door burst open. Captain McCulloch stepped into the room. "It's time, Cutter," he said sharply. Two men accompanied him, and they took Cutter's arms roughly, binding his wrists once again.

283

"Is that necessary?" Velvet looked imploringly into McCulloch's eyes, and they both caught the sudden dangerous narrowing of Cutter's.

"I'm sorry, madam," said McCulloch stiffly. "Get him out of here," he ordered his men. Cutter was unceremoniously shoved through the door. The captain looked quickly at Velvet, and then, as quickly, away. "Your husband is, after all, a prisoner," he said rigidly.

"I'm aware of that," Velvet answered evenly. She was not unaware of McCulloch's discomfort. This, she reasoned, might somehow work for her. She moderated her tone. "I am aware there's a war going on, Captain," she said mildly, "and that you have certain . . . duties to perform." She watched as McCulloch turned slowly back to face her, and her eyes took on a melting softness, her voice was warm. "I wouldn't want to interfere with those duties, but surely you can understand my distress." McCulloch nodded, reluctantly conceding the point.

"I understand," he said tersely. He moved to her, and stood before her, his hands placed, with military austerity, behind his back. "But you must understand a few things, too." Velvet regarded him intently, and McCulloch took a long breath. "J. Eliot Cutter is a prisoner of war. He has been accused of high crimes against the government, not the least of which is treason. No matter how I may feel about his wife," he finished, hesitating only barely perceptibly, "I am bound by law to—" McCulloch abruptly swung away. "You'd better go, Mrs. Cutter," he said harshly. "There is nothing I can, or intend, to do for your husband. There is no plea for him outside a military court."

"I see," Velvet murmured. "In that case, Captain McCulloch, I shall go."

"Yes," McCulloch answered. "And do us both a favor, madam," he said turning back to face her, having regained his composure. "Don't come back here dressed as a soldier again. It won't do you one damned bit of good." There was only the hint of amusement on his face as he continued. "Your eyes, you know," he said softly, "will give you away every time."

Velvet repressed her own smile. "Will Arabella be leaving with me?" she asked. McCulloch nodded.

"I've told my men to release her."

"Thank you." She paused. "Goodbye, Captain."

"Goodbye . . . Mrs. Cutter."

Flames purled ominously as night breezes sent their light shuddering into the soft air. It was moments before the stillness of L'Étoile de Vie was shattered by harsh shouts, pounding footfalls, scrambling bodies. Velvet and Arabella watched, from the back of the stables, the once-great house endure a second fire—this one its sure ruin. They raced to the front entry of the stable as they saw soldiers running away from it to the house. The locked door provided only a momentary barrier as they shouted for Cutter. Several men heaved their bodies through it, thereby realizing their own liberation and nearly trampling the two young women in their bid for freedom. Cutter was among them. He grabbed Arabella and Velvet in his flight, and dragged them both along a narrow path and away from the plantation. He raged blindly through low-growing foliage at a pounding run, keeping both women firmly in tow. The fire, the shouts, the destruction of L'Étoile de Vie was far behind before he dared pause. When, at last, he did, Velvet and Arabella collapsed at his feet. The three of them breathed raggedly, gratefully accepting oxygen into their exhausted lungs. Cutter threw himself to the ground near Velvet.

"Now what's this all about?" he rasped, as he rolled toward her.

"You didn't ask for an explanation a few minutes ago," Velvet gasped. Cutter managed a wry laugh.

"Come on," he said to both women, and, grasping their wrists, he resumed their ragged flight.

They reached Sweet Briar Hill on a fading shaft of moonlight, as the horizon appeared in a pale ribbon of dawn. Velvet led them all to the attic rooms, and they huddled there at last, laughing, gasping, and attempting not to awaken the rest of the house.

Velvet and Arabella told him how they'd been escorted home, after he'd been brought back to his cell. They explained tolerantly that they had gone back and set the fire; yes, they had temporarily abandoned their womanly kindheartedness and had done that terrible thing to Morgana Carleton's home; and yes, they had risked the lives of the Confederate soldiers encamped at

L'Étoile de Vie.

"Is what we did so awful, love?" Velvet finally asked. "We saved your life."

Cutter shook his head in disbelief. He glanced at Arabella. "You never did have a rifle beneath your petticoats," he said incredulously, "but you had something far more formidable."

"What's that, Mr. Cutter?" she asked playfully.

"You had a container of kerosene." The three young people dissolved into wild, effusive laughter. At least part of their hilarity, at that moment, was surely the result of unrestrained relief. It was not long before they realized the danger they'd put themselves in, and attempted to collect themselves.

"Now, remember," Velvet warned softly, as she and Arabella headed for the ladder that would take them down into the main house, "be as quiet as possible, love. I'll get back up to you as soon as I can." Cutter nodded in the moon-silvered dark of the tiny, low-ceilinged room.

"It seems," he intoned, not altogether in jest, "I've exchanged one prison for another."

Velvet and Arabella made their way down staircases and through quiet hallways, to the kitchen. Silently, they entered the room, only to find Mammy Jane positioned judgementally before them.

"What in the Lord's name you two been up to," she demanded. Hands on hips, feet planted firmly apart, her voice and presence projecting the arrival of moral order to guilty consciences. Dipping their heads, neither young woman ready — or able — to explain herself fully, both Velvet and Arabella merely mumbled indefinable utterances, until at last Mammy Jane having had enough of their mutterings, demanded, "Now what's going on?"

"I ought to get myself back to the hospital," Arabella said weakly.

"You should," Velvet agreed piously. "They might be needing you there just now." Both women noticed that Mammy Jane was not to be put off. Her bottom lip determinedly set, she folded heavy arms over her heavy breasts and waited. Finally, with painful dispirit, Velvet told their tale.

"What else were we to do, Mammy?" Velvet entreated at last when Mammy Jane responded to their story with only silence.

"We couldn't just leave Cutter there to be hanged."

Soft clucking sounds of disapproval rumbled up from the older woman's throat. "The two of you ought to be ashamed of yourselves, burning down that poor house," she said softly. "Your consciences are going to bother you for a long, long time. Still," she added, attempting to reason out the events of the night for herself, "there wasn't too much else you could do."

Seizing this softening of her mammy's strict moral code, Velvet said, "What else *could* we have done, Mammy? It was the only weapon we had." Her hopeful demeanor was quickly crushed.

"Now that he's up there," Mammy reproved, "what are you going to do with him? They'll come looking for him, I am sworn. And what are you going to say?"

"None of us know anything about any of it, Mammy," Arabella said soberly. "We have to say we know nothing of the fire, and nothing of the escape."

"And that," rejoined Mammy Jane darkly, "puts the black mark of a lie on our souls."

"Oh, Mammy," Velvet groaned. "Do you really think God will punish us for saving a man's life?"

Mammy Jane hesitated and frowned. It was obvious she was in a deep state of moral confusion. Making her decision, she touched Velvet's cheek at last. "Velvet-pie," she said softly, "the only thing God's going to punish me for right now is if I don't get some good home cooking into that boy's stomach." She looked at Arabella briefly. "Thanks for the corn meal, honey," she said. "You stay for breakfast now; I'll make some muffins." Then turning away, she went to the stove. Both girls glanced at each other guiltily as Mammy was heard to grumble prayerfully, "Thought I brought the two of them up better than that, Lord. What more can a Mammy do?"

Chapter Thirty-one

Velvet had brought a small lamp to the tiny attic room. She came quietly, stepping over broken things and scraps left by the Union soldiers. She knelt carefully as she set the lamp near the place where Cutter lay, his breathing even and deep. She looked down on him. Tenderness overwhelmed her. He had come to find her, had abandoned the sweet freedom of his beloved Adirondack Mountains for . . . perhaps . . . a greater love — a love for her. Cutter might have avoided the makeshift Confederate prison, he might have avoided the humiliation of capture, the further humiliation of hiding here in the musty attic at Sweet Briar Hill. But he had avoided none of that, had, in fact, risked his very life for her; he had surely known the danger that traveling south would hold for him. Velvet leaned down, brushing Cutter's coarsely stubbled jaw with her lips. "Oh, love," she breathed softly. In the half-light, shadows played on the muscular hills and hollows of his bared chest, dark fur against pale bronze. Velvet could barely restrain herself from running aching fingertips over his loved flesh. She eased herself away. There would be time for them, a time when tenderness, when ready passion, when sweet need might be served. Velvet must leave now to face the inevitable intrusion of questioning. The soldiers would come very soon. They would want to know if Cutter was here. They might even search for him. She shuddered against that invasive possibility, and jumped when a big hand grasped her wrist.

"Don't leave me, princess."

The hoarse whisper startled her. "Go back to sleep, love," she said gently. "Mammy Jane is making food. I'll bring it up later."

"I am hungry, sweet," he answered softly, "but not for food." Slowly, he drew her down to him. "Stay with me awhile."

"Oh, Cutter," she protested irresolutely. "Not now, love." But her protest died, the urgency of time retreated, as he relentlessly took her deeper into his embrace. Velvet had little choice, as he drew her to his lean, warm length, but to submit to the swell of hungry necessity that budded suddenly in the depths of her yearning soul. She had not felt like this in so long. As Cutter stroked the tender, needing flesh of her arms and breasts and belly, she abandoned resistance, gave herself as she once had so long ago to rapture. His hot kisses feathered along the arching column of her throat and then to the budding peaks of breasts. He devoured her. She might have been a drop of dew consumed by the sun, lifted to the hot, illusive heights of liquid ecstasy. She might have been a silvered wave melting on a moonstruck shore.

Cutter drew himself over her. In the dark his power radiated like sun-touched night. Her body arced to his generative force. Sun and shadow, light and darkness, swept through her soul. He lingered over her, his lips, his tongue, his hot breath, his virile strength delaying time. Day or night, sun or shadow, had no authority — only Cutter. He took long, sweet leisure with her, treading time.

"Velvet . . . love," he whispered huskily over and over. "I have waited so long to hold you in my arms." Long, captured moments of relived rapture, present pleasure, encloaked them. Velvet lifted her heart to him, opened her soul.

"I am yours, love," she breathed into the consuming drift of time. "Forever." He took her then. Swelling starshine, moon-silvered dawn were torn away in the heat of sunstruck day. By main force, the hardened steel of desire pierced the softer, yielding flesh of dawning hunger. Velvet cried out, the tearing power of blazing light ripping into her soul, masculine resplendence overbearing her gentler hunger. She opened herself more fully, flowering to the harder necessity, allowing the supremacy of sun over shadow, of glistening light over shimmering warmth.

She gasped raggedly at the sudden, stunning burst of golden rapture that magnified all her senses. She knew the pungent sweetness of rarified zephyrs, the exalted harmonies of the spheres. In that heaven-washed moment of rarest ecstasy, Velvet touched the sun.

Shuddering against her, Cutter tightened his embrace as Velvet lingered in the shimmering mists of repletion. They drifted together on cool shadows, tenderly holding each other in pillowed bliss.

Velvet nestled into the deep resting place of Cutter's muscled arms. She had not felt this way — loved, cherished, restored — in a very long time. She sighed against his manly hardness as he drew her closer, deeper into his embrace. He stroked the warm hollows of her flesh. She had needed him for so long. Long, wordless, heaven-scented moments passed before they both heard the muffled clop of horse's hooves outside on the ground below.

Cutter glanced quickly down at Velvet, and she sat up rigidly. "It's them," she whispered. "They've come for you." Fearfully, she reached for her clothes, such as they were. She slipped her muslin dress over her head, and brushed a kiss against Cutter's cheek. He grasped her arm.

"Don't be afraid, love," he whispered. "I'll be watching."

"You stay up here, Cutter," she admonished him. "I will signal somehow if they decide to search." Reluctantly, she left him, the heat of their mutual desire ebbing slowly. Cold fear replaced the warmth as she descended the attic ladder, then hastened along the upstairs hallway to the main staircase. Looking down into the sunlit hall, she saw, to her amazement, the golden presence of Brett Whitney. But why would it not be Brett? she reasoned; Cutter was, after all, his prisoner. In the shadows of the landing, she gathered her resources. At her last meeting with Brett, there had been the question of her submission to his repugnant proposal. That was what she must remember, address herself to. She must seem to know of no other reason for Brett's "visit." She must appear tranquil, hospitable, cheerily resigned to his proposal. She must know nothing of the fire and the escape. With her right foot, in the manner of grand Southern ladies, she began her descent.

"Why, Major Whitney," she said lightly, as she made her way down the stairs. "I suppose you've come for my answer. I must tell you that I struggled long and hard with your . . . rather bold suggestion, but I've come to the conclusion that, no matter the cost to me, I must—"

"Where is he, Velvet?" Brett said sharply as she reached the ground floor.

"Who?" Velvet asked, her voice projecting honeyed innocence. "What are you talking about, Major Whitney?" In the sunlit shadows of the main hall, Velvet smiled up at him. His menacing frown did not daunt her. "For heaven's sake, Brett, what is troubling you? One would think—"

"I know all about your little escapade last night," he said, grabbing her shoulders. "Don't play the simpering belle with me." He snapped her to him, and would have shaken her mercilessly had not Mammy Jane appeared at the dark, shadowed end of the hallway.

"Don't anybody knock at doors anymore?" she demanded. "Well, if it isn't Major Whitney," she amended. "I am sworn, if it isn't a real pleasure to see you again so soon, sir." She moved heavily along the hall, smiling broadly. "My, my," she mused brightly. "You just never know who's going to stop by these days. Won't you join us for some breakfast—"

"Both you women stop this nonsense," Brett ejaculated. "I want Cutter."

"Cutter?" Velvet repeated in a small voice, her confidence deserting her. Brett eyed her narrowly.

"You did not apprise me of the fact that you were married, *Miss* McBride," he said with a jaundiced smile. "I had to hear it from a rather unexpected source. Captain McCulloch also told me that you paid a visit to him last evening—an unusual visit to be sure. He found one of his men tied and gagged not far from the house. Captain McCulloch and I can come to only one conclusion concerning Cutter's escape." Velvet looked quickly at Mammy Jane, and cursed that woman's lack of guile. Her eyes were wide and fearful.

"Escape?" Velvet breathed. She fluttered to the bottom step, and sat there breathlessly for a moment, hoping to divert Brett's attention from Mammy Jane's obvious show of guilt. "Brett," Velvet said, apparently recovering herself, her voice too full of conciliation she was sure, "whatever do you mean? Now, I fully admit to visiting L'Étoile de Vie last evening, I even admit to . . . well . . . the use of unladylike means of gaining entry to the house. But . . . how can you accuse poor me of abetting an escape? How could I possibly engineer such a thing?"

"The Carleton house was destroyed last night," Brett said curtly. "By fire." He regarded Velvet obliquely. "Am I to believe you had nothing to do with that?"

"How can you imagine I would destroy Morgana's home," she said with found indignity. "How can you think such a thing?" she covered her face with her hands. "Oh, Brett, what have we come to that you could believe such a thing?" she asked helplessly. She lifted tear-glazed eyes to his, and slowly stood. "I only visited him, Brett, because I believed it to be my wifely duty. Do you really believe I loved that Northern savage? Do you really believe I would help him escape?"

Brett suddenly grasped her arm and pulled her roughly down the hallway to the front door. He stepped outside. Velvet saw what she had feared. Several men sat their horses impatiently.

"These men," said Brett Whitney, "will attest to the fact that you risked your life to gain entry to the house, to visit that 'Northern savage.'" Velvet recoiled from the accusation in their regard. "Now tell me again that you don't love him enough to help him escape." Squinting against the glare of morning light, Velvet looked up at Brett. She mustered years of aristocratic breeding.

"How dare you, Major Whitney!" she gasped. "I suppose you have bandied my name about in the company of these young ruffians. For shame, sir," she finished, and would have turned back into the house, but Brett grabbed her roughly.

What happened next astounded Velvet due to the simplicity of its execution. She saw Brett's hand go up, its hard knuckled surface above her. As if in slow motion, it descended. The resounding crack, the white hot flash of hot pain appalled her. She fell, as if thrown, down the steps of the porch and tumbled onto the ground below. She lay — the world above her, whirling blue — in the grass, and tasted blood.

Alicia cried out softly. Steven was above her, blotting out the blue world. Hooves danced, dust was raised.

"How dare you, sir!" Velvet's father was saying. He was lifting his daughter in his arms. Velvet's lids fluttered. Brett was there, struggling with Steven. Velvet held tightly to him.

"Pa," she breathed, and placed her head on his long-loved shoulder. "Oh, Pa." Nothing else was real. The warm weal of blood that trickled from her lips, the struggle between men, her mother's sobs, all evaporated in the loving bond between Velvet and her father. He was there for her. Transported into the cool shadows of the house, into the safe haven of rooms she'd loved,

Velvet felt warm, protected. Mammy was placing moist cloths on her face. "Oh, Pa," Velvet said finally. She looked up into eyes so like her own. "You're all right." It took many moments, warm moments of tender forgiveness, for reality to intrude.

"If he's here," Brett Whitney was saying roughly, "you'd better tell me." Velvet glanced foggily toward the voice. Brett stood above her, faintly golden. She looked around the room. Mammy Jane was there, and Alicia. Steven knelt at Velvet's side. Even Arabella was present.

"He went north," Arabella was saying.

"Then you admit to helping him escape," Brett charged. Arabella nodded.

"But he headed north. You don't think he'd stay here, do you?"

"I don't know what to think," Brett snarled. Several uniformed men stood with them, and he glanced sheepishly in their direction. "Wait outside," he ordered curtly. He looked back to the little band of McBrides as the soldiers left the room. "I need to sort this thing out," he said.

"You may take my word as a gentleman, sir —" Steven began.

"Or shall I take your word as a drunkard, sir?" Brett rejoined. He cast a withering glance over the now-silent group. "I want Cutter," he said quietly. "I could arrest all of you. I could take this house apart in search of him, but I am aware that, if you're hiding him, you are probably hiding him all too well." His eyes drifted to Arabella and then to Velvet. "I doubt either of you would be stupid enough to hide him here. My time will be better spent heading north with my men; Cutter couldn't have gotten far. But I warn you all," he said, his gaze sweeping the gathering, "I will be back." He saw the flicker of relief in Velvet's eyes, and amended his decision. "In the meantime, I will be ordering Captain McCulloch to send several men here to search the house and grounds," he said evenly. "If Cutter is here, you'd better see to it he is *well* hidden." He turned stiffly and left the room.

"Lord, what has happened to that boy," said Mammy Jane in the silence that followed Brett Whitney's departure.

"War has happened, Mammy," Steven McBride answered softly. "War. War has happened to all of us." He stood heavily. Velvet watched him, realizing that he'd carried her to his study.

"Pa," she murmured. He looked down at her. "What made you

leave this room? What brought you out to the porch?" She looked quickly to her mother. "And you, Mother, what brought you from your bed?" Her parents looked into her eyes, and then at each other. "We're still a family, aren't we?" Velvet went on. "War or no war, we're a family." Her gaze drifted to Arabella and to Mammy Jane. Nothing would ever be the same for the people in this room, and yet, somehow, between them nothing had really changed. For Velvet, it was as though years had melted away. The love and support she'd felt in this house all her life was here. That was what had brought her back home in the first place. She had needed to experience that again. After the terrible truths she'd found up North, she needed to reaffirm her belief in, and love for, the people she had grown up with. Her life had not been a lie then, she thought with relief; and her heart sang as, slowly, she surrendered herself to sleep.

Chapter Thirty-two

Velvet's awareness came in eddying waves of consciousness. First the resonating sound of a man's anger leapt at her from the darkness. A woman's lighter voice, pleading, touched familiar chords. Pounding feet, a door bursting open, Cutter's face above her brought her to full awareness.

"What has he done!" Cutter thundered. "What has the unholy bastard done to you." Velvet made an attempt to sit up, but the pounding in her head stalled her efforts.

"I'm not really hurt, Cutter," she soothed.

"She'll be fine, Mr. Cutter," insisted the woman's voice. Velvet looked beyond Cutter's shoulder to find Arabella in the doorway. "I've looked her over, and she's fine." Cutter took Velvet's shoulders in his strong arms, and sat, cradling her, on her bed.

"I'll get the bastard, princess," he said softly. "I'll get him for you." Velvet closed her eyes in resignation.

"No, Cutter . . . please," she murmured.

"Why wasn't I called?" he demanded, shooting a glare at Arabella.

"You weren't called, Mr. Cutter," she replied acidly, "because that might've gotten us *all* hanged. As it is, Major Whitney—"

"Major Whitney," Cutter snarled.

"Major Whitney," repeated Arabella firmly, "left us alone because he was in such a hurry to chase you. He damn near threatened to arrest all of us."

"I'll kill the son of a bitch," Cutter intoned as he brushed tenderly at a wisp of flaxen curl that clung to Velvet's cheek.

"That may be," Arabella rejoined, "but for now, you're going to get yourself back up into that attic till we think of a better place to hide you." Velvet's eyes fluttered open.

"Please, Cutter," she whispered. "He's sending men." She struggled to a sitting position, her eyes suddenly wide. "I remem-

295

ber that, Bella," she cried hoarsely. "Brett said—"

At the mention of the major's proper name, Arabella saw the sudden glint in Cutter's eyes, and interjected. "Major Whitney threatened," she said hastily, "to send a search party over here."

"Brett?" Cutter asked stonily.

Velvet looked at him. "That's his name," she answered. "And he . . . he . . ." Her voice trailed off, as she realized the sudden menace in Cutter's silver gaze. "I've known him for years, love," she soothed. "We grew up together."

"Then this sickening transgression of his is trebled in my eyes," Cutter grated. He gently laid Velvet down, and paced the room like a panther. Looking sharply at Arabella, he demanded, "Where did he say he was headed?"

"I don't know," she answered, suddenly frightened.

"Cutter," Velvet said, struggling up once more, "you cannot do this." His gaze hooded as he glanced at her.

"Do you protect the bastard?" he asked.

"No, goddammit!" she cried, astonished at her own outburst. She lay back down, the sudden pain in her jaw reminding her that she'd just suffered a serious injury. Cutter moved quickly to her side. "No," she repeated softly, "I do not defend him." She gazed up into Cutter's eyes, and placed a small hand on his chest. "How could you think such a thing, love?" Was their bond so fragile, she wondered, that Cutter could doubt her so easily? Tears of frustration leapt to wet the sooty tangle of her lashes. "Oh, Cutter," she sighed, and turned her head. She felt rough fingertips take her chin and draw her face back. Velvet saw Cutter's tear-softened gaze, and, for the first time since she'd known him, she realized that in him was a nearly unbearable anguish. She lifted her arms to entwine them about his strong neck. This powerful, vulnerable creature she loved needed comforting as much as she did. She drew his lips down to hers.

It was at this moment that Arabella wisely chose to leave the room.

"Forgive me, princess," Cutter said gently, his lips against hers. He held her away from him, cradling the back of her tousled head in one large hand. "You have so much to think about, and now," he said smiling roguishly, "you must consider the passions of an inflamed husband."

"It's all right, love," she declared. "I don't blame you for wanting revenge, nor do I blame you for . . . for . . ." she glanced away — "for questioning my relationship with Brett Whitney." He started to speak, but she placed her fingertips over his firm lips. "I've made so much in the past of our Southern sensibilities. I've held our gentlemen up to you as a standard by which you would always be judged, but I promise you, love, that standard no longer applies. I have learned so much, Cutter." Suddenly, without preamble, her arms were around him. The force of her embrace was enough to throw him off balance, and he responded with a kind of dubious acceptance of it.

"What is this?" he questioned softly.

"Oh, Cutter," she sobbed, her voice muffled in his wide shoulder, "I have been such a bad wife to you. I've been so lacking in . . . in consideration for you, for what you might be feeling. I suppose," she said, sitting back and sniffing loudly, "I believed I was protecting myself, in a way." She looked up at him and her eyes were wide and solemn, her tones deeply sincere. "I was so afraid of you, Cutter," she said softly. "I was afraid of your ability to be open and honest with me because I knew that meant I might have to be open and honest with you, and if I did that, Cutter, if I was open and honest with you, as I wanted to be so often, I might have to admit that . . . that . . ." Velvet swiped at her nose in vexation.

"That you loved me?" Cutter asked, his mouth twitching, threatening a smile. Velvet nodded forlornly.

"And I think I always have," she said wretchedly.

"Is that so terrible, princess?" he said gently. Velvet looked up at him in disbelief.

"How can you even ask such a thing, love?" she gasped. "You were always so rough and . . . and rude and demanding, and I was taught that men ought to be . . . courtly."

"And I was taught that women were supposed to be defenseless and adoring," he said, his smile no longer repressed. "It would seem," he added, lifting her chin with one roughened fingertip, "that we have both learned something, sweet."

"Yes," she said softly, her smile matching his. "The most important thing I've learned, Cutter, is that I love you."

"And I love you, princess."

Heart-stopping moments were being passed in the kitchen of Sweet Briar Hill as the family waited for the outcome of Cutter's anger. They half expected to see him rage down the hallway, cursing and making violent threats against the vile treatment of Velvet by Major Whitney. It was with relief that they watched him enter with an unsteady, but recovered, Velvet on his arm. They relaxed somewhat when he greeted them with a wide, unthreatening smile.

"You've met Arabella, of course," said Velvet, taking over the amenities, "and this is Mammy." Cutter swept the old lady a courtly bow, which impressed her deeply.

"He don't look so mean to me," Mammy Jane said, looking with uncertain disapproval at the unshirted Cutter. Velvet hastily drew Cutter away from her guileless scrutiny, and introduced him to her mother and father.

"These are my parents, Steven and Alicia McBride," Velvet said proudly. "Mother and Pa, my husband — J. Eliot Cutter." The two older people nodded greetings, and Velvet felt that her heart would burst with gratitude. It was not long, however, before she realized that there was much work to be done in that arena. Steven excused himself wordlessly and returned to his study. Alicia merely smiled, apologized for her lack of proper dress, and retired to her room, breathlessly requesting that Mammy Jane bring her some tea. That woman shook her head sadly and directed the rest of them to seat themselves around the jerry-built dining table.

"I got corn muffins and potato pancakes," she said sternly, "and nobody in this house has had any food today." Once seated, the three younger people immediately began to talk of their next move.

"Be sensible, Velvet," Arabella was saying, "you can't hide him here. Whitney is sending the whole damned Confederate army—"

"He's not sending the 'whole' army," Velvet replied, stuffing a large piece of muffin into her mouth. "He's sending a few men."

"Excuse me, ladies," Cutter broke in, "I am not used to putting my fate in the hands of women. It seems to me—"

"It seems to *me*, Mr. Cutter," Arabella rejoined, "that you have little choice in the matter."

"Really, love," Velvet agreed, "why don't you just let us figure this out?" Cutter deferred the impulse to point out that their last venture had been less than organized, though he admitted reluctantly that they'd gotten him out of the prison. He listened in restive silence to their plans.

"What about taking him to the women's encampment south of here, near Crystal Hill?" offered Arabella.

Velvet winced inwardly. She knew that to be the encampment where Lisa Mae Bloomer must be, her plantation being the very Crystal Hill named by Arabella. "I don't think so," she said reflectively. "Brett—I mean Major Whitney—mentioned that he takes food to those poor ladies." She looked quickly at Cutter, and noted with some frustration that he was watching her reaction to the suggestion. She could never tell him what Brett Whitney had proposed to her, nor could she mention what he was getting in repayment for his generosity to the women at Crystal Hill. Already, Velvet sensed that violence could erupt between the two men, if they ever met, and she wanted to avoid that possibility at all costs. Cutter was even now enraged by Brett's brutality toward her; he would be further angered if he knew the sort of man Brett had become. Velvet must guard her reactions very carefully from now on. A confrontation between the two men would surely mean the death of one of them, and she would not allow it to be Cutter. Better to avoid that confrontation in the first place, she determined.

"Well, he can't head north," Arabella sighed. "Whitney's headed that way."

Their speculations were suddenly cut short by the thunder of hooves at the front of the house.

"It must be the soldiers from L'Étoile de Vie," Velvet gasped, and nearly shoved Cutter toward the staircase. "You've got to get up to the attic," she said breathlessly.

"We'll stall them," Arabella said. "And pull up the ladder after you're up there."

Cutter attempted to protest, but the women were too insistent, too urgent in their insistence, too headstrong. Cutter obeyed finally, taking the stairs a few at a time, and hiding himself, in a self-determined compromise, at the top of them. He would not again leave Velvet vulnerable to attack. He listened keenly as the two young women moved to the door.

They were rushed by several gray-coated men who burst into the hall. "We're here on orders from Major Whitney," one of them said, saluting Velvet briefly.

"I'll take the upstairs, sir," said one of the young men.

As that soldier started for the stairs, Velvet managed to insert herself into his path.

"Why, hello, Private Jackson," she said on a startled breath. The young man stopped abruptly.

"Miss McBride." He gaped.

Velvet barely noted that several men had pushed past them on their way to the kitchen and the other rooms, and she scarcely heard the order shouted to the others to search the grounds.

"Let me accompany you," Velvet said hastily, as she quickly stepped up the stairs ahead of Private Jackson.

"Oh, ma'am, I don't think—"

"I heard you got into terrible trouble over me," she babbled as they climbed the stairs. "Now isn't that just like the army; they hardly ever give you credit for anything, but they'll sure enough punish you for doing something wrong. I hope you hold no animosity in your heart, *dear* Private Jackson, for what happened between us. I'd just feel terrible—" She stopped suddenly, horrified, as peripherally she saw Cutter back into the shadows against a near wall. "I hope you all won't disturb my mother," Velvet said, deliberately turning the young private so that his back was to Cutter. "She's in here." Velvet opened the door hastily, and allowed Jackson a brief look inside. Alicia, sleeping, did not acknowledge their entrance, and Velvet shut the door. "Now that's Mother's room, and this," she said reverentially, "is mine." Private Jackson seemed awed to silence as she led him inside. "I'm a little ashamed to show you where I sleep," Velvet added in a deliberately small voice. "Nothing much was left to us after the battle here in June." Velvet allowed a tear to fall unchallenged down her cheek as she raised her small chin. "You understand, Private, great families have great pride."

"I do, ma'am," said Private Jackson as he sadly surveyed the bare room. His eyes fell with embarrassment on the bed of rags. "You . . . sleep there?" he asked quietly.

"Yes," Velvet said simply. She lowered her lashes, allowing

them to sweep the curve of her pale cheeks.

"Jackson," called a harsh voice from downstairs. "Have you finished up there?" The young man immediately stepped out onto the mezzanine.

"Yes, sir!" he called back. He turned back to Velvet. She managed a small, brave smile.

"I'll show you the rest of the rooms, Private Jackson," she said softly.

"Oh, ma'am," the boy said solemnly. "I will not put you to further humiliation; you've been offended enough as it is." He took her hand respectfully. "Forgive a poor soldier for doing his duty, ma'am," he added, and brushed her hand with a devout kiss. With that, he turned and left the room. "Nothing up there, sir," he called as he raced down the stairs. Velvet stayed in her room as the soldiers departed noisily. She did not realize that she'd been holding her breath for some seconds until Cutter entered.

"Well done, princess." He smiled as he took her into his arms. Velvet exhaled with relief, and fell into Cutter's embrace.

That night, for the first time, Velvet and Cutter shared a truly harmonious marital bed.

Chapter Thirty-three

On the gentle slope of Cemetery Ridge near a small Pennsylvania town, Confederate General Robert E. Lee's Napoleonic vision of the destruction of the Federal Army was itself destroyed. The 'little battle" of which Cutter had spoken, the Battle of Gettysburg, had turned the tide of the War Between the States. Union soldiers had marched into Vicksburg, the city having been surrendered to General U. S. Grant. Emaciated, nearly naked, the proud young soldiers of the Confederacy were forced, in some cases, to accept the largess of their deadly foes.

The summer of 1863 was passing at Sweet Briar Hill with some predictability. Cutter's presence lightened the load somewhat for Mammy Jane and Velvet. He set traps of his own devising daily, while Velvet foraged for wild onions and sassafras buds. Arabella had warned them that their main business must be to ward off diseases such as scurvy. Food was a constant source of concern.

Arabella had reported that McCulloch's soldiers were abandoning the encampment and prison at L' Étoile de Vie, and Cutter and Velvet responded almost in unison, with some irony, that it hadn't been much of a prison as far as they were concerned.

Supplies filtered in from the hospital where Arabella still worked, but, she reported, even the horses were dying now from lack of grass. Virginia had become a wilderness of scrub oak and thorny undergrowth.

The hot days of early autumn became hot humid nights, and Cutter and Velvet sat on the front porch, overlooking the once-opulent lawns of Sweet Briar Hill devising plans that might save their little family from starvation. Money became Velvet's principle preoccupation. She believed it would cure all their woes.

"Velvet," Cutter said reasonably one night, "money, for it's own sake, won't do this shattered world of yours much good." Velvet looked up sharply, her eyes like chips of turquoise in the moonlight.

"What are you talking about, Cutter?" she demanded. "Money is the only important thing in the world. If we had money, we could be just as we were before. We could have food on the table, I could fix the house, and mother would get out of bed, and Pa would—"

Cutter shook his head ruefully, kindling Velvet's resentment. "All over the South, princess," he said quietly, " 'speculators' hold back food for higher prices. Men disgrace themselves by their greed. Money, in and of itself, has little intrinsic value. Oh, it might buy us food at bloated prices, but it will not cure the real problem." His moonlit gaze swept the land. "There is really only one thing that will save your beloved South."

Velvet quirked a winged brow and leaned toward him. "What is it, love?" she asked.

He glanced at her. "In the weeks I've been here at Sweet Briar Hill," he said slowly, "I have concluded that, if it is to survive, the South must do what it does best; it must return to the richness of its origins. These great plantations need to be planted again. The war will end, princess, and the North will win; and Northern industry will take over this land. In order for your family and others like yours to survive, in order for them to continue the gentle patterns of the life they knew here, they must somehow avoid that tide of Northern domination."

"I don't understand, Cutter," Velvet said softly.

Cutter looked away from her. The grim truth that life, as Velvet had known it, was over was more than he could bear to tell her. Gentle families like the McBrides would be swept away in the cruel flood of the war's end. In Cutter's eyes, they were ill prepared for the hard realities of the greater battle that waited them. He stood abruptly. Velvet watched him in startled amazement as he strode toward the great front door. "I'm going in to talk to your father," he said grimly.

"But Pa doesn't talk to anybody," Velvet said.

"He's going to talk to me," Cutter stated.

303

Steven McBride's study was silently dark, and the lamp Cutter brought with him as he entered made golden shadows on the floors and walls. They brushed the room with fluttering strokes, illuminating the isolated emptiness. Cutter saw Steven, huddled in a corner in his big chair.

"Sir," Cutter said softly, raising the lamp. In the dim light, Steven McBride lifted red-rimmed eyes toward the intruder.

"Get out, son," he murmured thickly.

"No, sir," Cutter stated emphatically. "I will not get out."

Steven mumbled unintelligibly, and weaved as he turned away. "Suit yourself," he finally intoned.

"I think not, sir," said Cutter. "If I were to suit myself," he added softly, "I would be headed, with my wife, up to the Adirondack Mountains. I would be, if I were to 'suit myself,' exploring the thin soil of those mountains, discovering the beauty of a rare and treasured geological history. That's what I would be doing, sir, if I were to 'suit myself'. Instead"—he paused briefly—"I am here, with you. And I intend to stay here, sir." Cutter lowered the lamp, and rested on one knee before Steven McBride. That man finally turned slowly to face him.

"What do you want?" Steven finally said hoarsely. "Why don't you just leave me alone?" Cutter lowered his eyes against the ruin in his father-in-law's haggard gaze.

"Leave you alone," he repeated gently. "To die?" he asked, lifting his glinting regard suddenly.

"Yes," Steven said.

"That," Cutter answered him, "I cannot do. I might add, sir," he went on mildly, "that, knowing your daughter, I am more than a little surprised that you would choose the coward's path."

"You say that to me"—Steven sneered—"knowing nothing of what has happened here."

"Why don't you tell me what has happened here?" Cutter said, resting his arms over one knee. Steven glared at him for a long moment, and then turned unsteadily away. Huddling deeper into his chair, he remained for some moments relentlessly silent. Then, Cutter watching him steadily, he began to talk.

"I had a life here once, Mr. Cutter," he said quietly. "My

father and his father before him, and his father and his, created a life of privilege and power." He looked quickly at Cutter, and then away. "They called my great-great-grandfather a 'cavalier.'" Steven laughed sharply. "The legendary cavalier Southern planter, Mr. Cutter, is exactly that—a legend. There was never any such thing—not really—not in the McBride ancestry, at any rate. We were hard workers, the McBride men; we never sat on our grand porches, sipping our juleps, instigating duels and gossip. All that," he said, his voice faltering, his hand sweeping out feebly, "all that . . . foolishness . . . is a myth. I will grant you," he conceded with a tired smile, "it is a fine myth. However," he added bitterly, after a pause, "it is one that I find personally offensive. All my life, Mr. Cutter, I have considered myself a man of the land. I have loved the land, nurtured it, and received from it great bounty. With that great bounty I fed my family, clothed them, kept them safe." He looked steadily at Cutter. "You might say I kept them very well, Mr. Cutter. You might, in fact, accuse me of usurpation in their behalf—or more reprehensibly in my own behalf. You might accuse me of many sins. You might, with your righteous Northern sensibilities, accuse me of seizing what was not rightfully mine, of exploiting not only the land but other human beings as well. Do not bother to accuse me of such things," Steven drawled quietly, "I have already accused myself. This war has brought into the world the terrible bright light of truth, and that light shines most acutely on my sins. And yet," he went on sadly, "I never meant for it to be so. I never meant to sin.

"I am a proud man, Mr. Cutter. I pride myself on many things. I am well read, cultured, a fair and honest gentleman." He managed a small laugh, and stood slowly, pacing the room. "A gentleman," he repeated regretfully. "Do you know something, Mr. Cutter?" he asked. "I have never had a mistress." He paused. "Now, why would I find it necessary to apprise you of that fact?" he questioned rhetorically. "I suppose," he said, "I find it necessary because the myth of the cavalier planter embodies the myth of the cruel white Southern master, lording it over his household, terrifying his slaves, taking women of any color at his will to satisfy his sybaritic instincts." Again Steven McBride laughed softly. "Maybe that is true of some men, Mr.

Cutter, but I suppose I wanted you to know it isn't true of me."

"I do know it, sir," Cutter answered.

"I suppose my little Velvet has told you how . . . pleasant life was here at Sweet Briar Hill before the war."

"She did."

"And I suppose you have chosen to dismiss her fine memories, trivialize them, to give her notice that her belief in the sweet circumstances of her youth were built on the vile notion of slavery." When Cutter did not answer, Steven leaned down and touched his shoulder. "Of course you did, Mr. Cutter. What else could you do? That's what you believe. Well" — he sighed — "now I believe it, too. But I didn't then, lad," he said gently. "Oh, no, not then. I believed in my life, Mr. Cutter, and the life I had created here at Sweet Briar Hill." Steven sat again in his big chair. "When I said before that I received great bounty from the land, and used that bounty on behalf of my family, I meant my whole family. Everyone that ever lived at Sweet Briar Hill is my family, Mr. Cutter." He looked for a long time at his son-in-law. "Can you understand any of what I've said?" Cutter nodded, and stood. "Have a drink, Mr. Cutter," Steven said as he produced a bottle of whiskey from the floor next to his chair. Cutter took the bottle and held it to his lips, enjoying a long draught.

"Have one yourself, sir," he said finally, "and let it be the last for a while."

"I think I will have one," said Steven, "but I do not think it will be my last."

Cutter drew back his shoulders. "I've heard your story, sir," he said. "Now hear mine." Steven nodded amiably, and drank from the bottle. "My story," said Cutter, "is shorter than your own, but it tells of a truly decent man, a man who does not deserve the suffering he is inflicting upon himself and his family." Steven lifted an amused brow.

"Anyone I know, Mr. Cutter?"

"I wonder," Cutter answered. "If you knew this man, sir, you would want to help him, because, like yourself, he is a virtuous gentleman. He has never deliberately hurt anyone in his life, this man, though he accuses himself of that. He lived a life he believed in, a life his forebears made for him. Something happened to that man, Mr. McBride. Some great and powerful event happened in his life, and that event taught him a very great lesson. He suffered a great deal with the pain of that enlightenment. But that pain was nothing to the pain he has inflicted on one who loves him very much." Cutter paused significantly. "The other day, sir, you were there to protect your beloved daughter from the cruelty of a man who is supposed to be a gentleman. You stopped him from manhandling her because I was not there to stop him, and she was so grateful. Couldn't you help her again, Mr. McBride? Another cruelty threatens her in the form of another man. Protect her, sir, from that cruel man. Stand up to him as you stood up to Major Whitney. Tell him it is his indulgence, his surrender to his own pain that is causing pain in others. Tell him that his wife is suffering. Tell him that those he loves, those who have depended upon his strength and his humanity — the sweet and noble Mammy Jane and Arabella — are now suffering from the lack of it. Tell him that, sir," Cutter finished. "Maybe that will help him." Steven was silent for a long moment. At last, he looked up.

"You're a wise man, Cutter," he said softly. "But changes such as the one you suggest, don't happen simply because we want them to. Guilt does not fall off like petals from a dying flower."

"No," Cutter agreed, "guilt does not go away so easily. Perhaps the secret is to live with guilt, and, perhaps, to make what we are guilty about better."

"But what if we cannot make it better? What if we are destroyed by it?"

Cutter lifted a brow. "Are you destroyed, sir?" he asked. "Or are you merely in the process of self-destruction?"

Steven McBride shook his head in disbelief. "Where did my daughter find such a man?" he said softly.

"If you ask her," said Cutter laughing, "she will tell you she found me in the 'godforsaken wilderness' of northeastern New York State. She will tell you, too, that she didn't very much like what she found."

"Didn't she?" Steven said with a rueful smile. "I suppose she thought she would have been happier with one of our fine

Southern gentlemen . . . like Brett Whitney." He looked seriously at Cutter. That man's reaction—a slight stiffening of his shoulders, a slight narrowing of his gaze—was barely discernible. "And, once," Steven continued, "that may have been true. You see, Cutter, Brett Whitney wasn't always as he is now either. He was a good lad once. I knew his father, and respected him. The Whitneys were one of the finest families in Virginia. Had this war not happened—"

"But it did happen, sir," Cutter interjected.

"Yes," Steven responded. A less impaired gentleman might have noted the change in Cutter's attitude, but Steven McBride only smiled. "Where do we go from here?" he asked simply. Cutter's stance softened.

"Where, sir?" he asked.

"How do I begin?"

Cutter paused. At last, he stepped to his father-in-law, and held out his hand. "You begin," he said gently, "by shaking hands with your new son-in-law."

"That I'll do," Steven said, standing and taking Cutter's hand. "That I'll do."

"And then," added Cutter, "you go out and tell your daughter that you love her."

"Was that ever in doubt?" Steven McBride's rust-colored brow lifted.

"How could she not doubt it, sir?" Cutter asked.

Steven paused. "I shall go to her on one condition," he said finally. "That condition is that you call me Steven." Cutter smiled broadly, repeating the name, and, his arm firmly around the older man's shoulders, he went out onto the porch with Steven.

Velvet's eyes in the summer moonlight were wide and startled as her father appeared with Cutter. "Pa," she breathed.

Steven took her into his embrace. "Oh, daughter," he said, "your pa's not been much of a 'Pa' these last days."

Velvet drew away from him. "You helped me when it counted," she said kindly.

They walked arm in arm down off the front steps and out onto the moon-laced lawn. Cutter accompanied them, keeping a respectful distance. He listened as Steven explained the hard battle he'd fought with himself. He listened as Steven told Velvet that, ragged and beaten down as they were, cowed by the vagaries of fortune, they would be once again a family.

"We can do it, daughter," he said quietly. "I know that now.'"

Beneath the shadowy veil of a locust tree, Velvet stopped. She took her father's hands in hers. "Pa," she said solemnly, "you must tell me about Mother. You must tell me how she came to be the way she is." Steven shook his head slowly.

"I wish I knew," he said on a deep, sad breath. "Alicia was the strong one. Our whole life together, she was the one who bolstered me. She gave me her strength—the strength to be what I needed to be for all of you." A sparkle of amusement drifted into his gaze. "You always pictured me as the patriarch, the leader of this family," he said. "But your mother was the one who allowed that image to prevail. It was," he added quietly, "an image." All three people sat down in the lush grasses beneath the tree. "Alicia Deschênes," Steven said, almost reverently. "How I doted on her. Little did I realize," he said smiling, "when I first brought her here, how little doting she required. Oh, she played the part of the pampered Southern belle very nicely. Liquid of eye, fair of face, she was as delightful a mistress, as precious a jewel as adorned any plantation hereabouts. What I hadn't realized," he said with a small smile, "was that she was playing a part—for me. I realized, somewhere along the line, that what I had on my hands was a willful little French-Canadian sprite." He paused. "Do you know something?" he said fondly. "I think if I'd brought her to a swampland, she'd have fit in there, too." He turned away and swiped at his eyes. "I am being every bit as sentimental as your mother always told me I was," he said with a rueful laugh. " 'Always the poet,' she said to me. Always the poet." His tones became solemn. "I think I've had too much of the drink to make any sense."

"You make perfect sense to me, Pa," Velvet said.

"And to me, sir," Cutter added quietly. He offered Velvet an arch-browed smile. "I now begin to understand the complexities of a certain sprite of my own acquaintance." He munched contentedly on a piece of willow grass. "You know, Steven," he said seriously, "what has happened to your wife, it seems to me, is that she is denying the truth of what she has experienced in this war. It happens to strong people. They are strong for so long, and then . . ."

"Cutter," Steven said darkly, "you cannot imagine what happened here."

"No," replied Cutter. "I cannot imagine what the two of you have experienced." He raised his eyes and their pewter depths caught the moonlight. "It is hard for any of us to know the minds and hearts of others. That is why," he said, looking from his wife to his father-in-law, "we have been given the gift of speech. We are able to communicate our thoughts and our feelings. Sometimes that's difficult — especially when we do not fully understand them ourselves. It is those times — when we do not really know ourselves — that we most need each other." He paused, and reclined onto the grass. "It is those times that test the true extent of our separation from the animals. What civilizes us?" he asked rhetorically. "What makes us different from beasts? It is nothing more — or less — than our ability to communicate with each other." Cutter pillowed his hands beneath his head.

"In theory, love," said Velvet softly, "that is a very pretty and profound philosophy. But we cannot *force* Mother to speak of what troubles her."

"Why not?" said Cutter quietly.

"It would be cruel," Velvet murmured.

"Sometimes, princess," he answered, "we must be cruel in order to be kind."

Chapter Thirty-four

Hot summer thundered into fall. News came through Arabella from the nearby hospital that the U.S.S. *New Ironsides* had been heavily damaged by Confederate torpedo boat *David,* but a Union victory at Lookout Mountain and Missionary Ridge in Chattanooga, during the time of a total eclipse of the moon, had left the Confederacy with a stunning defeat.

At Sweet Briar Hill, Cutter and Steven McBride worked together, turning the ground for the next spring's planting. They had spent long days planning which fields to sow. They did not trouble themselves wondering where the money would come from for the seed, or where the hands would be found to undertake the monumental task. It was Velvet who worried, and pragmatically so, how they would manage the rejuvenation of the land, to say nothing of how they would feed themselves in the winter to come. She and Mammy Jane had gathered the fruits of summer, preserving them. They had dried a portion of the meat from the animals Cutter had trapped, and had pickled several different kinds of vegetables grown throughout the summer. Still, even with Arabella's offerings from the hospital, Velvet realized that they had barely enough food to get them through the next few weeks.

It was early in December, a tepid, sun-filled day, when Dahlia, Mammy Jane's beloved daughter, arrived at the plantation with her two babies. Velvet, overjoyed to see the young woman so dearly remembered from her youth, was thrilled by the prospect of children at Sweet Briar Hill, but she despaired at the plantation's growing list of dependents.

Dahlia's husband had become a member of the Colored Volunteers stationed at Duvall's Bluff, Arkansas. She had stayed in Little Rock until his troop had been transferred, then, experiencing an aloneness she had never in her life known, she had

311

decided to come back to Sweet Briar Hill—and her mother. Mammy Jane might have been handed a star from out of the farthest, most spangled regions of the sky. Her two grandchildren, both boys—John Brown, the eldest, and Abraham Lincoln Tull—were little more than babes, and Mammy Jane relinquished them to their mother only on the occasions when they needed to be nursed.

John Brown Tull, just two years old, had already begun to walk. The family shared the chore of keeping track of the vitally curious little rakehell. It was many weeks before an often-exhausted Arabella admitted that her voluminous list of chores at the hospital kept her less busy than John Brown.

Nearly weaned from his mother, the husky toddler provided yet another concern for Velvet. It was one thing for adults to go to bed hungry in these terrible days, but it was entirely another that a child should go unnourished.

Brett Whitney had mentioned a fat cow and a weekly supply of honey, she reflected tiredly on one particularly sodden afternoon in January. The women's encampment at Crystal Hill had never been very far from Velvet's mind these past months. She wondered often not if but when Brett Whitney would come back to Sweet Briar Hill. She wondered, too, if she would be tempted by another proposal from him. More than that, Velvet feared a confrontation between him and Cutter.

The family had managed so far to anticipate—even if only by seconds—the arrival of soldiers at the plantation. The sound of hoofbeats on the road would be enough to send one or another of them flying out to the fields or into the house to hide Cutter. The initial search of the dwelling, having turned up nothing, had alleviated any fear of further search, but now they worried that Major Whitney or some other soldier might recognize Cutter if he were to be visible. The members of the household had managed to hide any food stores in Steven's secret place for hiding whiskey. The loose flooring beneath his big chair in the study no longer hid bottles, it now hid jellies, dried meat, and pickled vegetables. Troops of soldiers would make a quick sweep of the kitchen—Mammy Jane having left one or two jars of something or other out for them to find—and would apologize for the necessity of having to confiscate the family's food, then leave. Still, everyone in the house knew, from the occasional inquiry concerning Cutter, that he was being sought. And Velvet sensed it was only a matter of time until Brett Whitney sought him out at Sweet Briar Hill.

Now, on this heavy, exhausting winter day, she thought of Brett Whitney not only as a threat but as a source of nourishment for the ever-growing John Brown Tull. If there was, in fact, a fat cow at Crystal Hill, Velvet must have it.

She made her decision rapidly, almost without thinking. Arabella had arrived home from the hospital in her little pony cart not moments ago, so Velvet snatched a heavy shawl from the newel post in the hallway, and made her way from the house. The little pony whickered piteously, but Velvet eased, with a lump of the family's precious sugar, his reluctance to be once again harnessed. Spurring him gently, she began the ride to Crystal Hill.

The sky was dark and sullen with low moonlit clouds by the time Velvet reached the encampment. Several women and a few mammies came out of their tents at the sound of her approach. The occasional rains that day had left muddy puddles dotting the ground, and campfires made tiny golden spots of flickering light among them. Velvet could barely believe what she was seeing. Women who had been reared in luxury were now reduced to the protection of a few yards of canvas stretched over wooden frames among the trees. She alit gingerly from the cart, and stepped over the damp grasses to one of the ladies. She recognized her as a one-time contender for the position of belle of the county. Sadly, shabbily clothed, emotionally frayed, the two young women greeted each other.

"Is it you, Velvet McBride?" the other asked tentatively.

"It is," Velvet said gently. "Only now I am Velvet Cutter." The two women embraced, held to each other for a long moment, perhaps to recapture their once benign and oh-so-joyous rivalry, and then spent sorrowful minutes detailing briefly the last few months of their lives.

"The name Cutter sounds familiar to me," said the young woman after a time.

"I am not surprised," Velvet answered.

"Is he a local boy?"

"Not really," Velvet demurred. She asked finally where she might find Lisa Mae Bloomer.

"Her tent is that last one at the end of the row," the young woman told her. At that, several children burst ebulliently from a nearby tent, and danced around her skirts. The mammy who stood by shooed them back inside.

The young woman shrugged a nonchalant shoulder and smiled. Velvet's eyes widened. "They're not all yours," she breathed. "Three of them are," she said. "They really ought to be in bed. It's so hard to maintain any discipline here. Thank God for Mammy."

Velvet's heart twisted. One day that young woman's husband would come home, and she would greet him with his dear family. Velvet had greeted Cutter with nothing but poverty and hardship. One day, she thought, she would give him a child. That day, it seemed now, might be long in coming. For the moment Velvet must attempt to provide for the children they already had to care for. She said a warm goodbye to the young woman, and made her way carefully down the row of tents to Lisa Mae's.

Velvet could find nowhere to knock and so she called out. The answering voice did not sound at all like that of her girlhood acquaintance. Cautiously, Velvet drew back the flap of the door.

"Lisa Mae?" she asked softly.

In the dim light of a hanging lamp, the figure of a woman sat rigidly on a cot. "What do you want?" she demanded.

"It's Velvet."

"Who?" the woman said stonily.

"Velvet . . . McBride."

The young woman stood slowly and said, "What do you want?"

Velvet hesitated. She had not envisioned warmth from Lisa Mae, but she'd envisioned . . . something. She had certainly not anticipated hostility. Lisa Mae, in all their years together, in all their little rivalrous matches, with all that Velvet had done to tweak her prim and proper vanities, had never shown the slightest belligerence. No matter the provocation, Lisa Mae had remained studiously and prudishly aloof. Velvet flinched inwardly from this present aggressiveness, but did not allow her

314

reticence to show.

"I've come to ask a favor of you," Velvet said quietly.

The young woman began to smile, and her smile became a harsh laugh. "Indeed," she said finally, cruelly. "And what favor is it you think I will grant *you* of all people."

"I want your cow," Velvet said, without hesitation, "or at least some of its milk." Lisa Mae placed her hands firmly on her hips and stepped to Velvet. In the low lamplight, she had been viewed only dimly. Now the hard lines of bitterness, resentment, and even malevolence became apparent to Velvet.

"War does humble one, does it not?" said Lisa Mae. "It seems to be the great equalizer. That used to be death or taxes, but now it's war. Have you a little bastard to care for, Velvet? Did some marauding Northern soldier come into Sweet Briar Hill and ravish you, dear? Did he leave you with a little—"

Lisa Mae's cruel taunt was abruptly cut off by Velvet's stinging slap. Unexpected, deeply enraging, the assault threw Lisa Mae off balance, and she reacted immediately. Lunging for Velvet, she bared her teeth and meant to grab at the tousle of Velvet's once-admired curls.

"Don't you dare," Velvet snarled as she grasped Lisa Mae's wrists. With all her strength Velvet threw the girl to the ground.

"You bitch," Lisa Mae shrieked. She jumped up and swung out, catching Velvet's cheek with a close-fisted blow. Velvet retrieved her balance, and threw her body into the maddened Lisa Mae. They both careened to the floor of the tent, wrestling wildly. Their screams caught the attention of the other women in the camp, and some came to stand in the doorway, wringing their hands and watching helplessly as the two frenzied women battled. Writhing furiously, Lisa Mae attempted to twist away from Velvet, but, with the power of her own desperate need, Velvet managed to get herself on top her opponent and to catch her wrists, pinning them to the ground. Straddling Lisa Mae's chest, Velvet held her furiously, knowing she would lash out at the slightest lapse in strength.

"You call me a bitch, Lisa Mae Bloomer," Velvet grated breathlessly, "and yet you would keep that from me which my family needs most."

"That cow is mine," Lisa Mae snarled. "I live on the favors it can buy me!" The watching women turned away in embarrassment. They had all sold something of value to Lisa Mae in return for a pint of milk. Daily they came to her with offerings in order that they might feed their children. They were embarrassed about her, about the desperation that forced them all to stoop to such bargaining. And they were embarrassed for her, for her deep greed.

"Oh, Lisa Mae," Velvet gasped hoarsely, as she continued to hold the writhing woman. "You cannot expect me to believe that you would—"

"Believe it," Lisa Mae snapped back. She paused in her frenzy to impale Velvet with a stinging glare. "Every woman here had access to Brett Whitney's terms. I was the one who accepted them. Should I sell myself so cheaply that my debasement amounts to nothing?" She made one last attempt to free herself from Velvet's clutches, and then, at last, lay back, breathing harshly. "Get off me," she grated.

"Not till you compose yourself," Velvet rejoined.

"Composure is a luxury," Lisa Mae returned hotly. "I haven't time for composure." Still, Velvet judged that Lisa Mae was ready to concede at least the physical battle. By degrees, Velvet released her hold, and stood, ready to resume, if necessary, the struggle. She would not leave without a concession of another sort.

"I need that milk, Lisa Mae," she said quietly.

"What have you got for sale," Lisa Mae shot back as she lifted herself from the ground. At Velvet's silence, the other woman merely smiled. "It is a simple matter, Velvet McBride. You want something—I have something. A bargain is struck."

Velvet sat heavily on the cat and watched as Lisa Mae eyed the gathered women defiantly.

"Isn't that a fact, ladies?" Lisa Mae asked, lifting her chin. "We do business here at Crystal Hill, just like men."

"But we're not men," Velvet said into the silence that followed. Lisa Mae rounded on her, and Velvet stiffened in anticipation of another struggle.

"No," said Lisa Mae, "we're not men. But we are the product of their war, dammit. We starving, homeless women and children are what they've made of us. And, by God, I at least—" she snapped a derisive glance at the women at the door—"intend not to submit to that circumstance without a fight. I am not garbage to be trampled on by the booted feet of honor-bound soldiers. Where is honor now? Where is honor to be found in all of this? There is none." She sneered. "The men live by their own rules—they make war, and profit from it. Well, I live by their rules, too."

"We all wanted this war, Lisa Mae," one courageous woman said softly. "We all believed it was right."

"And now?" asked Velvet lifting her gaze and taking in all the women. "In a way," she said quietly, "Lisa Mae is more right than the rest of us. The problem is," she said sighing heavily, "that *right* is not always *good*." She targeted Lisa Mae with a pleading stare. "We are supposed to be the makers of manners," she said gently. "We are supposed to be the civilized ones." She stood slowly, and bent to retrieve her heavy shawl from the ground. She lifted it in both her hands, and held it out to Lisa Mae. "It is all I have," she said softly. Abruptly, Lisa Mae's eyes became glazed with tears. She turned away suddenly.

"Do you know how hungry I've been?" she asked in a tired, tormented voice. She turned back and lifted her chin defensively. "They came at night," she said harshly. "They came with their guns and with their sacks, and they took everything. They shot my father. They . . . they took my mother and me for their marauding pleasure . . . and they . . . used us again and again . . . until their *duty* called them to other places. Then they burned our home . . . and left." Her lips quivered, but Lisa Mae staunchly went on, through a veil of deep emotion. "I promised myself, after I watched Ma die, that I wouldn't let those smarmy Northerners—or any man—win another victory over me. I would *live!* I promised myself. And I am living." She swiped at the tears which came freely now. "I am alive, by God, and I'll do anything I must to stay alive."

A small, shabbily dressed woman separated herself from the others and stepped farther into the tent. She looked up into Lisa Mae's eyes, and said, "We understand. We . . . know." Lisa Mae fell into her gentle embrace, and the other women gathered around the two suddenly, forgiving, holding on. Velvet waited quietly. There was a healing going on here, and she was not part of it. For a moment she prayed that these women, together, might find ease in their tortured reunion.

Slowly, Lisa Mae drew herself from the group and faced Velvet. "Do you know how hard it was for me to sell myself to a man who used to beg for your favors?" she asked. Velvet lowered her gaze.

"Brett came to me, too," she murmured. She lifted her eyes. "I've been seriously considering his offer."

Tears came anew to Lisa Mae's gaze. "Oh, Velvet," she whispered, "don't." She took Velvet's hands in hers. "I've sacrificed myself, but you mustn't." Lisa Mae looked back at the others, desperation in her eyes. "I've learned something tonight," she said. "I've learned . . . how alone one can be."

"But you're not alone, Lisa Mae," Velvet said sharply.

"I know that now," she answered. She sat on her cot. "I've been thinking for a long, long time that it was me against everyone else in the world."

"I know the feeling," Velvet said with a small laugh. Lisa Mae raised her eyes. "I won't go into detail," Velvet said gently, "but, believe me, when the pattern of my life was destroyed, I knew that feeling. Mother and Pa sent me North. . . ." Velvet detailed, though she had said she would not, the story of her past three years—the matter of the Duffys and Cutter. "And now," she said finally, "I am here, and trying to reconstruct something—a life—that may have had no validity in the first place." Her gaze swept the assembled women. "I am so confused," she finished quietly.

"Yes," agreed Lisa Mae. Velvet stood slowly.

"I have a thought," she said. "Why don't you all come to Sweet Briar Hill. There are still a few outbuildings left, and we have rooms in the house. Perhaps, together," she added uncertainly, "we can—somehow—create something new." The women glanced at each other, debating with their eyes the prudence of such a move. Outside, the threatening winter storm rumbled, hastening their decision.

"We'll come," said Lisa Mae abruptly. "I don't know how we'll move everything." She laughed.

"And I don't know how we'll feed you all once you get there," added Velvet, "but we'll be together at least." She hesitated for only a moment before continuing. "We need each other," she said with certainty.

It was very late before Velvet, in the company of Lisa Mae Bloomer, some of her belongings, and the cow, made her way back to Sweet Briar Hill.

They rode up to the house to find it as ablaze with light, in the darkness, as it could be, considering the shortage of candles and lamps. Velvet swallowed hard, knowing that she should have apprised the family of her flight, but knowing as well that if she had, they would have discouraged her. Beyond that, Velvet had given little forethought to her venture. She prayed that the appearance of Lisa Mae and her cow might abate any scolding the family had planned. As Velvet alit from the dogcart, Cutter charged from the house. Lisa Mae flinched, and Velvet held tight to her.

"Cutter," Velvet cried with forced enthusiasm, "look who I've brought home!" Wordlessly, Cutter grasped her arm and dragged her up the steps, into the house, and to their bedroom. This next scene, Velvet acquiesced silently, must be enacted between married people — alone.

Cutter fairly threw her down onto their bed. "What in the name of bloody hell do you think you're doing?" he thundered. "Where have you been?"

She attempted to calm him with a soothing drop of her shoulders and a tilt of her head. "For heaven's sake, Cutter, why are you so—"

He grasped her shoulders, and snapped her to him, his dark brow ploughed in anger. "Goddammit, woman, don't you know how dangerous it is for you to go out on your own? What in God's name got into you?" Anger rose and was abruptly dissipated as Velvet was enfolded in a rough embrace. "God*dammit*, woman," Cutter groaned. "What in hell am I going to do with you?" His voice muffled in her curls, he went on. "For the love of *Christ*, don't you know how much I adore you? Don't you know—"

"Cutter," Velvet said insistently. "I'm all right." Still he clung to her, needing to be assured, it seemed, that she was really there. She drew away from him at last, and looked into the silver depths of his gaze. "I know how much you love me," she said

319

softly. "I know how worried you must have been. I never should have gone off like that."

"Why did you?" he asked darkly.

"I didn't think, love," she said. At his sudden rigidity, she placed her small hands on each side of his face. "I forget, Cutter. I keep forgetting about the war; and yet I'm thinking of it every minute of my life." Her voice broke, and Cutter reluctantly resigned himself to the knowledge that he could not simply muscle an explanation from her. Velvet rested her head upon his wide chest. "I knew we needed milk. I knew the women at Crystal Hill had a cow. I knew I had to go there. That's all I knew, Cutter," she sobbed. She sagged in Cutter's embrace, and he helped her to the bed, to lie down. Nestled in his arms, she continued softly. "I know that, now more than ever, we must think before we act, but I . . . forget."

Velvet was exhausted. Her mind and her body had been wearied by months of deprivation. She had been frustrated by weeks of her inability to speak with her mother about Alicia's withdrawal. Cutter stroked and caressed Velvet's rigid flesh. He, too, needed respite—certainly from the terrible images he'd conjured up of what might be happening to his wife, but also from the longer-term frustration he felt at not being able to provide properly for her, or to protect her as a man wants to protect someone he loves. Though Velvet had never told him of her ordeal after she'd left New York City, he'd heard snatches of the story from Mammy Jane and from Arabella. He knew the horror of what she'd been through at the hands of the vicious Brett Whitney. Even now, his anger, though often repressed, seethed at the thought of that barbarous attack. They were both exhausted—due to their own separate horrors.

Wordlessly they clung to each other as the minutes passed, as sleep finally came to them.

Chapter Thirty-five

Mornings came gently to Sweet Briar Hill. By the end of April, the damp, raw, winter chill had passed, but there was enough coolness in the air to entice Velvet and Cutter to remain snuggled together on their newly acquired mattress, beneath their newly acquired blankets. Cutter usually awakened first and rolled languidly to his side to watch Velvet, still asleep, in the half-light of dawn. She had not yet gotten used to the luxury of sleeping on a real mattress, tattered and saggy though it was, beneath real blankets, holey and patched though they were, and lingered in near-sleep, smiling, for long, hedonistic moments. It was at these times that Cutter felt closest to her. He imagined her in her former life, sweetly bathed and perfumed before she went to bed, awakening to hot breakfasts and nothing more difficult to decide than what frock to put on that day.

"Cutter?" she breathed. And the word was a question. He lifted a lock of her gold-streaked hair, nearly translucent in the arriving sunlight. "Love," she murmured.

"It's me, princess."

Velvet turned toward him and snuggled herself into the hills and hollows of his warm embrace. Her heavily lashed eyes fluttered open. "So it is," she said softly. Her smile deepened. "Let's not get up today," she purred into his chest. She felt the tenderness of warm morning kisses feather down along her cheek and neck. Her head fell back, allowing access for Cutter's bolder passions. His tongue and lips explored the regions of her naked flesh, newly awakened to morning pleasures. She allowed herself to fully open to his hunger. Her ripened senses tingled with the caressing moistness of his mouth, as he feasted greedily on buds of sweet fulfillment. Like wood nymphs, naked, freely exploring fresh grasslands in the dewy morning light, they threw off the confinement of their blankets, and writhed in their tousled field. Lushly, verdantly Cutter's hunger engulfed Velvet, and kindled ticking tongues of hot need in her.

No longer a romp, their lovemaking became a muscular satyr's pursuit of a yielding undine. Cutter took her buttocks in his big hand and lifted her to him. Startled, Velvet's eyes flew open. The throbbing penetration filled her, and her arms lifted to encircle his neck. She drew him down to her, and together they were swept into a frenzied world of pulsing rapture. Elevated and sublime, that world shuddered and pulsated with urgent demands. Hungry rills of need shattered to expose the sated couple to a sudden, sun-shivered world of perfect repletion.

"Oh, Cutter," Velvet moaned in her rapture. "Oh, love." He held her close to him, and she, needing to keep that rapture for a moment longer, held to him, holding him inside her, in her soul.

They lay together, listening to the perfect, sweet music of their mutual bliss. It was long moments before they realized that the young and ever-curious John Brown Tull was knocking and calling at their door.

"Shush, John Brown," an irritated Dahlia admonished her son. "You hush now, and come down and drink your milk." Footfalls padded to silence down the hall, but the interrupted demands of the little boy reminded the couple that they must leave their sleepy world of love and passion, and join the family for the day's work.

Cutter lifted a brow and looked down at Velvet, nested in his embrace. "I thank you, princess," he said with heavy irony, "For your delicate suggestion that we put a lock on that door." Velvet smiled lazily.

"I thought you might appreciate it, love," she murmured. They took a few more moments to move luxuriously and tenderly against each other, to vitalize themselves for facing the hard days and exhausted nights ahead, and reluctantly got out of bed.

The house and grounds of Sweet Briar Hill had become filled with people, and it became the main focus of Steven and

322

Cutter's days that the planting should be done as soon as possible. Now, at least, they had the hands to accomplish their goal. Each day they went out to the fields, organizing their little band of workers—most of the women and children who now lived on the plantation, and depended upon its support for their very lives. Ground was turned, divided into plots. They had decided to plant ten acres for the first year. Eight of those acres would be relegated to tobacco, which Steven believed they could sell for an enormous profit. Cutter reluctantly agreed. The other two acres would be reserved for food. Anyone who could work did so. The rest, the very small children and the infirm, stayed at the house to begin the cleaning and restoring Velvet had resolved must be done.

She had set herself the chore of washing down the wood molding in the formal parlor. The lovely wedding cake carvings were heavy with dust and soot, and Velvet dug into the delicate patterns with her soapy rags, determined to make them sparkle in the dappled sunlight as they once had. She could hear, in the quiet afternoon, the sounds coming from the fields. She heard, much to her delight, soft laughter coming from upstairs where her mother sewed and read with several of the older women. What ribald tales are they reading on this pleasant afternoon? she wondered. Perhaps they were reading Master Shakespeare's bawdy dialogue between Mistress Quickly, hostess of the Boar's Head Tavern in Eastcheap, and Sir John Falstaff, degenerate and lovable friend to Prince Hal. Perhaps . . . Her ear picked up another sound. It was the pound of hoofbeats on the road in front of the house. In itself the sound was not unusual these days when battles raged all around them in the wilderness areas of Virginia. She wondered, as she always did, if she should run to tell Cutter. Abruptly, she realized that the sound was indeed a warning. The horses were turning into the drive. Velvet threw down her cleaning paraphernalia, and leapt from her perch. She ran blindly to the kitchen to apprise Mammy Jane of the impending intrusion—and possible search. Mammy Jane bundled her thick body through the narrow kitchen door and rang the cowbell that signaled the approach of soldiers. Its dull clang echoed over the land as Velvet ran back through the house to meet the troop head-on. She skidded to a halt before the front door, and composed herself before stepping to the thick portal to open it and to welcome her "guests."

Adopting her best sugar-coated smile, and the most deferential, questioning tilt of her head, Velvet went outside to stand on the porch. The horses approached, and it was not until they were nearly to the front walk that Velvet recognized, with the deepest horror she'd known in months, the figure of Brett Whitney astride the foremost mount. Before the horse had even stopped, he dismounted and strode to the porch.

"Velvet, honey," he called out, removing his plumed gray hat and sweeping her a bow. He made his way, two steps at a time, up to her side, where he stood smiling. "How are you, sugar?" he asked as he approached.

Velvet's heart lurched in her breast. She did not abandon her smile, however, and held her hand out rigidly. "Why, Major Whitney," she said, with forced brightness, "if this isn't the surprise of the world." She had an image of the hectic activity going on at the back of the house, and, with that in mind, determined to keep the major and his soldiers cooling their heels for as long as possible at the front. Brett brushed her hand gallantly with his lips. "You're looking very well, sir," Velvet murmured, her tone, she hoped, sounding intimately welcoming. Her gaze swept the assembled soldiers. "You haven't come to take our food, now, have you?"

"Why no such thing, Velvet honey," said Brett Whitney expansively. "My men live very well," he added with confidential roguishness.

"I'm so glad to hear that," Velvet returned, attempting with all her resources to unclench her teeth. "Someone has to these days."

"You're so right, sugar," Brett said with a hearty laugh. "You're so right. If I've learned nothing else through this most terrible war, I've learned that we need to keep track of our priorities." He eyed her expectantly, and Velvet tried to keep her lips curved in a sweet and uncomprehending smile. Brett continued lazily. "I suppose you've learned a thing or two as well," he said, his last words rising questioningly.

"Oh, I have, Brett," she said softly, solemnly, as though her recent hard life had taught her nothing if it hadn't taught her that. In truth, Velvet reflected as she looked up into his hard green gaze, she had begun to realize that priorities—not necessarily Brett Whitney's priorities—must be faced. She altered her expression hastily, as though a sudden thought had assailed her. "Won't you sit down out here for a moment. I'd like," she said, lowering her eyes modestly, "if you won't take offense, to discuss something with you."

"Why of course, sugar," Brett said solicitously. "I shall send my men out back to water their horses."

"Oh," Velvet nearly squeaked, "we have a trough right there, right at the side of the house, Brett." She pointed to the nearby watering trough. "With all you gentlemen coming by, we thought it best to move it so you wouldn't have to go so far."

"How thoughtful of you, sugar," he said. "You are ever the gracious hostess." Naturally, he could not know that Velvet and Mammy Jane and Cutter had moved the trough when Cutter had first arrived to avoid having soldiers going to the back of the house— so there would be less chance of them spotting Cutter.

Velvet led Brett Whitney to the rickety porch chairs. They sat, he comfortably—one long leg casually resting upon the other—she at the edge of the seat. "I suppose you've been to Crystal Hill?" she asked. Brett nodded.

"It's been abandoned."

"Yes," Velvet said, hesitating. "All the women are here, Brett."

"I rather suspected that. The trail of their leave-taking was not hard to follow."

"It took us weeks to move them," Velvet said, forcing a certain childlike lightness. "I just couldn't bear to see them all idling there in the wilderness." She looked up suddenly, her mouth forming a small, delicate moue. "The war's right here, Brett," she said with wonder. "We can actually hear the guns some days." Again, Brett nodded.

"Grant's begun his push across the Rapidan toward Richmond. He has one hundred eighteen thousand men to Lee's sixty five thousand. It's a sad time, sugar," Brett said, his gaze

325

lowering in what Velvet knew to be false woe. This man, this opportunist who made his money off the hardship of others, could only see the end of the war as another path to easy wealth. Velvet's resolve stiffened. If Brett Whitney wanted profit from this war's end—if that was his objective—perhaps she could provide the path. For weeks her father and Cutter had speculated on how they might acquire the materials to plant the acreage at Sweet Briar Hill. Velvet would not give herself to Brett, and she would not allow Lisa Mae to sacrifice herself, but perhaps, even without that incentive, Velvet could provide an even greater motive to force the greedy Major Whitney to help. Brett glanced up at her through a hooded gaze. "Is Lisa Mae among the women you've so generously taken in?" he asked.

Velvet smiled brightly and said, "Of course, Major. Lisa Mae is the very reason I went to Crystal Hill. You mentioned, our last night together, that you had provided her with a 'fat cow.' " Velvet laughed, as though the memory were simply a pleasant episode to recall on bright days, on sunny porches. "Mammy Jane's daughter, Dahlia, came home with her two children, and we needed milk for them."

"Dahlia," reflected Brett Whitney aloud. "Oh, yes," he said, "she was that uppity girl who left with her husband. As I recall, he was recruited into Colonel Page's band of sable warriors."

"That's right, Brett," agreed Velvet. "Well, now she's back. So I went to Lisa Mae to see if she'd share some of the bounty she'd enjoyed through your kind generosity." Brett merely watched Velvet, a smile threatening at the corners of his mouth. This little minx was nothing if not brazen.

"I see," he intoned.

"Well, anyway," Velvet went on pertly, "Lisa Mae and the others were just so pathetic out there in their little tents, and I thought . . . I thought . . ." Her voice broke, and Brett watched as Velvet placed trembling fingertips to her lips. "I just couldn't stand to see them like that, Brett."

"Of course you couldn't, my dear," Brett offered.

"So I invited them here. You know, Brett," she went on, altering her tone, and casting him a sweeping sidewise glance.

"I still haven't forgiven you your rough handling of me that last day. But, when I saw those unfortunate women, and realized how much you'd helped them, I could not but admire you." She managed a troubled smile. "And you asked so little in return for your generosity."

Brett Whitney eyed her uncertainly. Was the vixen telling the truth? Had the war made her a liar? He could not be sure where this attitude of hers was leading. He resolved to listen, to judge when the time came.

Velvet went on. "I've realized in the months since you left that what you asked of me was not so terrible. Everyone should profit somehow, Brett." She looked into his eyes with unfailing earnestness. "If someone has something to offer, he should not give it away for free. That's just stupid." Her eyes in her pale face were serious, and liquid with unvarnished honesty. "If you have something — and others want it — you have a right to ask a fair price for it."

"That's true," said Brett, still deciding. At last, he asked quietly, hopefully, "Do you have something you wish to sell, sugar?"

Velvet laughed lightly, the music of the sound dancing delicately on the major's senses. "Indeed I do, Major," she returned. "Indeed I do." Slowly, her expression changed. There was in it an unfocused hardness, a businesslike callousness that made Brett Whitney recoil. The war had definitely changed this sweet Daughter of the South, and he was not sure he was going to like that change.

"The last time we met," Velvet said, her tones precise, crisp, uncharacteristically unplayful, "you offered me a proposal, Major Whitney, now I offer one to you. I now have the resources — in the women I brought from Crystal Hill — to plant about ten acres of my land. I'd like to put at least eight of those acres into tobacco. The problem is, I've no money." She looked straight at him. "You have money," she said, "and I want some of it." Brett leaned back in his chair, almost in relief. He smiled fully.

"And what are you offering as collateral, sugar," he asked.

Without hesitation, Velvet said, "Sweet Briar Hill." Brett's look of genuine astonishment gave her the deepest sense of satisfaction she'd ever known. He could not have perceived the unwieldy thump of her heart within her chest. "If I fail to meet my debt to you, Major Whitney," Velvet added, "I shall turn over my home. It is as simple as that." She paused delicately. "If, as you say, the war is nearly over, and I do not pretend to know about such things" — Velvet resolved that she must keep up at least a pretense of haplessness — "then tobacco and other products of the South ought to skyrocket in value." She lowered her gaze. "It makes perfect business sense, does it not, Major Whitney." Brett could only nod blankly. No matter the outcome of the war, no matter the outcome of this bargain, he could not lose.

"Sugar," he said raptly, "you've made yourself a deal."

Chapter Thirty-six

Velvet had not thought it out. She had not planned. Once again, her rash and reckless instincts had ruled the possible effects of cold reasoning. The papers had been drawn up and signed before Steven McBride could make protest. Brett Whitney had made the point, expansively, that it seemed silly to plant merely eight acres when Steven could plant thousands. They decided, finally, that fifty acres would be put in that year. Brett would arrange details of the planting, and Velvet was not to worry her pretty head about any of it. Women, he told her, needed to concern themselves with trifles — household affairs and raising children. Velvet did not remind him, as they strolled back out onto the porch, that it was, in fact, women who would be making his fortune for him.

He swept her a chivalrous bow when he left, assuring her he would be back to keep an eye on his interests. Velvet's heart thumped wildly when Brett assured her that his "interest" included not merely the crass details of money and profit.

"Perhaps, when this war is over," he said slyly, "when we are all back to normal, I might call upon you, sugar." Velvet managed a modest smile.

"That would be lovely, Major," she murmured, "though I must tell you, you have a great deal of apologizing to do."

"I know it," he said solemnly, holding his plumed hat reverently to his broad chest. "And I couldn't be more sorry that the exigencies of this terrible, terrible war have forced me into such ungentlemanly behavior. It's only that my very livelihood — not to speak of my considerable reputation — depends on finding these dangerous war criminals. The government pays me very well for my efforts," he added with a caustic smile. His expression altered as he said, "I shall spend the rest of my life making it up to you." Velvet's startled eyes lifted to his. "I've risked my life trying to find that rogue of a husband of yours," he added.

"Have you?" Velvet said, feigning concern for him. "My, my, Brett, how awful for you."

"Yes," he said, watching her keenly. "I have a feeling he is somewhere hereabouts. I'll find him," he said. "And when I do, I shall see to it that he hangs. Then," he added pointedly, "you will be free to accept my suit." Velvet swallowed. She did not answer for fear that the hollowness in her tone would betray Cutter. She managed a smile of agreement, and waved tranquilly as Brett and his men rode off.

Velvet stepped into the front hall, and was immediately assailed by first Cutter and then the rest of the family. She gasped at Cutter's stinging grasp, as he cut off her progress down the hall.

"You realize, of course, I'll have to kill the bastard," he said bitingly.

"How could you have done this, daughter?" her father bawled at her.

"Lord, child," huffed Mammy Jane in uncharacteristic admonishment, "we'll lose our happy home, sure."

Velvet faced first one, then another reproof without getting the opportunity to defend herself. Her father shook his fist.

"Dammit, girl," he thundered. "Suppose the crops fail? What are you going to do then; give the whole damned place to Whitney?"

"I don't know what's got into that child," Mammy Jane agreed.

"I did the only thing I could think to do!" Velvet shot back at them finally. She faced each one in turn. "You won't have to kill him, Cutter," she said firmly, "because I will not allow a confrontation between the two of you." She turned to father. "You've been complaining for weeks, Pa, that there is no money to plant this land. Well, I got you money." Velvet turned at last to Mammy Jane, blue-green fire in her glare. "What's gotten into me, Mammy, is this bloody war! I do *not*," she finished, addressing them all, "intend to sacrifice my husband to a ruthless bounty hunter. I do *not* intend to give our home away. The crops will *not* fail, and, *dammit*, Brett Whit-

ney's money *will* save our lives. That's all I care about." At her final words, Velvet turned sharply and made her way up the great staircase.

In her room, no one having dared to follow her, Velvet sat alone, each accusation replaying itself in her mind. What had she really accomplished, she wondered, by bargaining with the devil? With Brett Whitney constantly around, overseeing his investment, how could she, in fact, prevent a confrontation between him and Cutter? How could she predict that the weather would favor their little crop? How could she even say that she had done the "right" thing? She had tried to protect the interests of those who depended on Sweet Briar Hill—her father's interests and her mother's interests, Lisa Mae's interests, Cutter's interests, little John Brown's interests, and his brother's, and—dammit—everyone's interests. She had tried, kept trying. What more could she do; what more did they want of her? Angry tears blurred her vision. She strode to the window that overlooked the lawns, and pounded with clenched fists on the sill. *Damn them all! Damn them for reproaching her!*

A soft click at the door both startled and angered her. She turned, ready to do battle.

"I heard the yelling downstairs," her mother said quietly. Her questing eyes took in Velvet's mood, but that did not send her away. Instead, Alicia stepped farther into the room, closing the door behind her. "I understand that you are not in a humor to talk, but I am going to talk anyway." She moved to the bed, and sat at the edge of the mattress, her hands folded primly before her. Velvet leaned heavily against the sill. Her mother often adopted these talkative streaks. There was little choice but to listen, for she would not be put off. Velvet folded her arms, suppressed her frustration, and let her mother go on. "In my day," said Alicia with a soft smile, "where *I* came from, it wasn't enough to be possessed of a pretty face; a girl needed what we used to call 'sand' if she was to survive. Your Aunt Vonnie and I weren't slighted in either respect."

"I know that, Mother," Velvet murmured, attempting to cut short this annoying habit of Alicia's, replaying the past.

Her mother splayed a hand and said gently, "I know you do,

331

darling, and so I shall make this brief. Of late, I have looked a great deal into my past, because sometimes, whether we know it or not, that helps to define the present. Hasn't it seemed odd to you that your mother should recall so precisely things that happened to her so many, many years ago, yet seems to know nothing of her present circumstance?" Velvet looked with interest now at Alicia's sudden, seeming lucidity. "I know it must have disconcerted you all, and yet . . ." She lifted her chin in Velvet's own gesture of defiance. "It just has seemed so much easier to ignore it all. And I have, quite successfully, I think." She lowered her gaze. "But, I'm not the demure flower your father thinks me to be," she said, smiling. "I'm a tough little nut, just like"—here she raised her eyes—"my daughter." Alicia paused. "It took this moment, this very moment for me to realize it. I don't know what any of this is about—I don't know what the war is about—but I heard that verbal battle downstairs; I heard you standing up to the most important people in your life—the most loved people—and, suddenly, it dawned on me that the terrible things that happen to us can either destroy us or they can make us strong. I think I've decided that I'm *not* going to be destroyed."

"Of . . . of course you're not, Mother," Velvet said, gaping at the woman she'd tried so hard to reach all these months. She moved to her mother, and took her hands. "You do know, then, that there is a war going on."

Alicia nodded slowly. "I remember how it all started. They came to me," she said, "each in turn. They told me—Dahlia and her husband, and Quamina, and Arabella, and the others—that they were leaving; and, one by one, they did leave." Alicia was staring straight ahead, remembering. "They left that day, and the next, and the next; only Mammy Jane stayed." She looked up at Velvet, who realized that her mother was recalling the effects of the Emancipation Proclamation. "Finally, there was just your Pa and me and Mammy Jane. It was so lonely here. And then, one day, those others came." Her eyes suddenly filled with tears, but her expression did not change. "Those boys were so young, Velvet darling. You would not believe how young they were." She smiled into Velvet's eyes. "I couldn't give your father a son," she explained, "and some of those boys might have been the son he never had. They came," she continued, "and we gave freely of everything we had; it didn't matter to us whether they wore blue uniforms or gray ones. Mammy Jane would grumble so." Alicia laughed softly. Then her expression changed suddenly to one of wide-gazed terror. "Others came, too—with guns and . . . cruel words. They were so . . . young . . . so very, very young; they were just little boys." The tears flowed down her pale cheeks. "Your father and I tried to hide things, but those youngsters ranged the house . . . from top to bottom. They took your seashells," she said at last, looking up, startled suddenly by the thought. "I always wondered why. Then the fighting began between those little boys. Little boys . . . fighting . . . dying . . . right on our front lawn, Velvet darling. Can you imagine? Your father and Mammy Jane and I hid. For three days, we hid, waiting for the guns to stop. And then they did stop, and I made your father move those dead boys off the front lawn because I said I didn't want to look at them anymore. I made him bury them . . . somewhere. And Mammy Jane and I read our Bibles, and Mammy Jane sang to me." Alicia paused on a breath. "And then I went to sleep." She rested her head against Velvet's breast, and Velvet began to rock her mother slowly, rhythmically, very gently. "I said I would be brief, Velvet darling, and I haven't been."

"It's all right, Mother. It's all right," Velvet whispered.

"They were so young," Alicia said, tenderness in her voice. "And your father always wanted a son . . . ." Her voice trailed off. "But he's always cherished his little girl more deeply than his own life; and I know how much you love him." She looked up at Velvet. "And when I heard you standing up to him and to your beloved mammy and to that nice boy you're married to, I knew that something important had happened. And I said to myself, 'Alicia,' I said, 'that girl has something very important to stand up for. Otherwise she wouldn't be shouting.' I said to myself, 'People don't shout over just trifles.' I knew I'd raised a tough little nut, but I didn't know how tough you were until today. And, suddenly, I remembered how tough I used to be. I remember the day I told my mother and my daddy I was going to marry Steven. I remember the day I left Deschênes. Oh, I didn't care what else happened in the whole world, as long as I could be with your pa. That was the only time I ever shouted at my father." She smiled. "He forgave me, though, and your pa will forgive you — no matter what you've done."

"I hope so, Mother," Velvet said softly.

"He will, and so will the others."

Bright summer melted into early fall. The vivid scents of ripe life wafted over the plantation. News came from the hospital that Atlanta had been destroyed. The ominous rumble of artillery — sometimes to the north and sometimes to the south — told everyone at Sweet Briar Hill that the war was not very far away. Reenlistment, it was said, was popular among Union soldiers who had mustered out and then, scenting victory, wanted to be part of the war's final days. General Grant had taken yet another try at Richmond. But Richmond, Steven McBride assured them all at nightly suppers, would never fall. That was impossible.

Brett Whitney visited the plantation often. He was ever deferential, even to Lisa Mae, who made it her business to face him and to let him know that she knew he was not the gentleman his well-trained demeanor announced him to be. Brett took her taunts in stride, and even, very publicly, forgave her. Privately, he told Velvet that it was she who had suggested the arrangement they'd had.

"How unfortunate," he said one refulgent, late autumn day, as he and Velvet strolled out onto the porch, "that such a lovely girl chooses to debase herself so uncharacteristically with lies."

"Perhaps," demurred Velvet, "Lisa Mae simply has a random memory."

"We really should forgive these things," Brett conceded, "but I think it best simply to forget. We ought to build our lives from here, don't you agree?" Velvet found it difficult to agree with anything that Brett Whitney proposed, but she realized that she could not reveal her true feelings. The plantation had become too dependent on Brett Whitney — or, more accurately, on Brett Whitney's money. The plantation was, remarkably, showing a profit. For the most part, the fighting of late was focused south of Virginia, in North Carolina and Tennessee. Velvet was managing slowly to restore the grandeur of the main house at Sweet Briar Hill. She had procured, with Brett's relentless aid, some paint, bolts of material for clothes and curtains, and even precious linens. Mammy had made overalls for John Brown Tull and his brother Abraham Lincoln, and the seedy, uncared-for appearance of people, house, and grounds was at last giving way to a certain bright newness. The lawns had been reseeded, the trees pruned, the shrubs manicured. There was, for everyone at Sweet Briar Hill, a sense of pride in the restoration. They took on a dignity, even as they worked in the fields, that they'd not had in a very long time.

The winter came and went, as winters will, with almost will-o'-the-wisp quickness. Columbia, South Carolina had been burned by the marching Sherman, Charleston had been evacuated, and Abraham Lincoln—the original Mr. Lincoln—had been inaugurated for his second term as President of the Union. Abraham Lincoln Tull of Sweet Briar Hill passed the event with little knowledge of its significance. It was in March that his father, George Tull, Dahlia's husband, came home to apprise the family that he had been mustered out at Little Rock, Arkansas. He did not speak much of his experiences with the Colored Volunteers, rather he spent a great deal of time helping Cutter and Steven build furniture. Velvet watched the men with a jaundiced eye, and complained to any other female who would listen that, once again, the men had shut them out.

"Nothing ever really changes," she said resentfully. "It's just like we didn't even exist. It's like it was before the war; never mind that we've planted and hauled and starved just like they have." She huffed and accused and lamented sourly about the house and grounds, and finally resolved that she would simply ignore this brotherhood of males. Her resolve, however, did not extend to her nights with Cutter.

Languidly, purposefully, they made splendorous love, and Velvet announced, to the deep joy of everyone at Sweet Briar Hill, that soon there would be another little Cutter to enjoy the bounty of family love that encloaked the plantation.

"Oh, daughter," her father rejoiced, "it'll be grand to have a little one about the house." Velvet laughed.

"Pa," she said, "you have more little ones about this house than you can count."

"I know," Steven conceded, "but now we'll have a real little McBride to inherit Sweet Briar Hill." Velvet and Cutter glanced wordlessly at each other. "You will," said her father, "see what you can do about having yourself a boy."

"The only thing I regret," said Alicia wistfully, "is that I never saw you married, Velvet darling. I would love to have been there. But, of course, that would have been impossible." She smiled softly. "Still, it's a mother's dream to see her only daughter married."

"The marriage," Cutter returned dryly, "was the social event of the Adirondack season."

"I'm sure it was," Alicia said seriously.

"It was . . . just an ordinary wedding," said Velvet hastily, shooting Cutter a narrowed glance. "It was lovely, but . . . ordinary." Velvet turned back to her mother.

"You know," said Alicia brightening suddenly, "it just occurred to me. Why couldn't we have a wedding here?"

"I think that would be a grand idea," Steven offered enthusiastically. He turned a tender regard on his wife. "And you call me a poet, my love." Alicia happily lowered her gaze. It had been so long since she and her husband had shared an intimate moment; now that intimacy had begun for them again, she felt, in his strong presence, like an adolescent girl. She glanced back at him, and smiled modestly.

"My romantic tendencies were learned at the feet of a master, Steven darling," she murmured. He laughed heartily, and then Velvet's parents looked back expectantly to Cutter and her. That couple merely gaped. "Won't you have a wedding just for us?" pleaded Alicia.

"I . . . I suppose . . . it would be all right," stammered Velvet.

"Like your father," Cutter said huskily, "I think it would be a grand idea." He looked down into his wife's bewildered gaze. Remembering the day of their first wedding nearly three years

336

ago, they shared for a quick moment those lusty, innocent days when two people, two temperaments, two cultures, two different worlds clashed, blended, rose, and fell. Velvet and Cutter had been so different, so irrepressibly prideful of their own individual powers. And now they'd come together somehow. It seemed a miracle. Perhaps, reflected Velvet, a miracle was an occasion for celebration. She glanced first at her mother, then her father, and finally at Cutter.

"You're right," she said softly, "a wedding here at Sweet Briar Hill is a grand idea."

Chapter Thirty-seven

Velvet and Cutter sat serenely in a pew at St. Paul's Church in Richmond. They'd undertaken the dangerous, yet necessary, and exciting journey because Velvet had insisted that she wanted to be married by the same minister who'd married her mother and father. She intended to ask the minister to come back with them to Sweet Briar Hill. Beyond that, Velvet had not seen Richmond in many years, and decided that only there might she find a gown worthy of the occasion of her second marriage to Cutter. Resigned to the trip, resigned to a Sunday sermon—resigned, he supposed, forever to his wife's whimsy—Cutter enjoyed the balmy breezes that wafted in through the open doors of the pleasant church. He felt Velvet's urgent nudge, and glanced at her.

"It's the president," she whispered with rapt impatience. Cutter's eyes scanned the room, but could find no one who even vaguely resembled the pictures he'd seen of Abraham Lincoln. He shrugged and shook his head. "There," insisted Velvet, pointing as discreetly as possible to a man a few rows ahead on the other side of the center aisle. It was then Cutter realized that the deep-eyed gentleman to whom Velvet was pointing was Jefferson Davis, president of the Confederacy. "I saw him once, when he was inaugurated here in Richmond, years ago." Velvet's proud smile reminded Cutter that the war between their states was not over; though, when Fort Fisher in Wilmington, North Carolina, fell that past January, with the defeat of that last Confederate port, it was resolved that the war was ended. The gentleman who now sat alone this quiet Sunday had not been willing to admit defeat. Cutter wrapped his big arm around Velvet's shoulders, and smiled down at her.

"He's a great and proud man," Cutter whispered to his wife. Velvet nodded worshipfully. They watched him for some moments, and saw, to their bewilderment, a man in a gray uniform tiptoe down the aisle and hand the president a telegram. Turning pale, Mr. Davis stood and wordlessly left the church. Velvet and Cutter were not the only parishioners who'd read the historic message on the face of the man who had tried so desperately to bring the war to a peaceful but noble end for his tottering South. At once murmurings began, and people began to evacuate the church. Cutter and Velvet were carried on the tide of escape.

Outside, the streets were thronged with civilians and soldiers. Conveyances of every description were being commandeered and fights were breaking out at street corners. The sounds of gunfire reached their ears, and Cutter dragged Velvet into a nearby storefront. From there they watched, horror-struck, the frenzied evacuation of the once-proud city. Velvet's eyes became riveted on a spot not far from where they stood. She pointed suddenly, and the people stilled for a quick second while flames exploded into the sky.

"The tobacco warehouses!" someone shouted. With a sickening roar, flames erupted and fire engulfed those buildings and spread hungrily out to the rest of the city. People scattered. A tempest of shattered glass burst next to Cutter and Velvet, and they recoiled as mobs of men, women, and children rushed the building. Someone, a small woman in a patched bonnet and apron, exhorted others to help her smash bottles of spirit for which the looters made desperate grabs. As Cutter and Velvet ran through the mobbed streets, the reek of whiskey that flowed through the gutters assailed them. Catching fire, the liquid trails burned in bright blue, red, and yellow waves. The hungry inferno roared up at unexpected places among the frightened crowd. The rapid series of explosions that followed indicated the blowing up of the ironclads — armored vessels which had arrived only recently, and which had given the people of Richmond such hope. Hoses were unfurled, but futilely as it was discovered that they had been cut. Thus the hungry cauldron that was Richmond, Virginia, blazed relentlessly until the city was consumed.

Cutter and Velvet had made it to Capitol Square. They huddled there, Cutter, with his own body, protecting Velvet from the flying tatters of fiery refuse that seethed in the smoke-blackened air. Time and place lost all reality as isolated volleys of gunfire were replaced by the rampaging roar of cannon. The sights and sounds and smells of destruction and death surrounded them.

Very late, the guns stopped and there was simply silence. The occasional sound of running feet, the crash of shattering glass, or the shriek of human pain were the only sounds — the last groans of a dying city — in the moonlit air.

Slowly, Velvet and Cutter raised themselves and assessed their damages. They held to each other fiercely at last, thanking God that they had escaped with their lives, the horror of the fall of Richmond. Above them, like a Greek monument in the midst of the ruins of Athens, the old Capitol building stood alone in the silvered night.

Cutter and Velvet had made it back to Sweet Briar Hill. For both of them, though they had experienced much poverty and pain there, the plantation was a haven of peace and tranquility. The planting had begun, and the women worked in the fields on these gentle spring days. The children romped and worked by their sides. It was said that General Lee had visited General Grant at Appomattox, at the courthouse there, and then at the McLean House, where he'd signed the articles of surrender and parole. Joseph E. Johnston surrendered to Sherman in North Carolina, and General Kirby Smith surrendered at Galveston. The settlement of the war had cost the country an estimated total of 600,000 dead on both sides.

Velvet and Cutter did not fully explain the horror of the fall of Richmond, but instead assured the family that the impossible had happened. The war's end was emphatically celebrated. The people at Sweet Briar Hill were happy only that the fighting was over, and that each of them could begin to rebuild their lives.

The news came in mid-April: President Lincoln had been assassinated by an obsessed actor, and a Mr. Johnson, who had been vice president, would be organizing what was being called the reconstruction of the South.

340

Velvet and her mother began to plan, in earnest, the wedding that was to be held in June. Though they could not secure the services of the minister at St. Paul's, who had married Alicia and Steven, Mammy Jane assured them that she would take charge of finding a man of the cloth to preside. The gown Velvet would wear was a problem not easily solved. The white velvet that had been gotten and made into portieres for the main parlor would simply not serve for a June wedding, Alicia insisted. She insisted, too, that somehow they must secure silk for this very special gown of all gowns — watered silk would be best, of course. Velvet thought immediately of Brett Whitney, and wondered if the war's end had increased his fortunes. He had not visited the plantation in some time, and that suited Velvet very well. As long as he paid them well — probably not nearly as well as he was paid — for their tobacco, she was satisfied. She wondered, though, at his lack of interest in their operation after months and months of diligent, though unwelcomed, attention. Now would be a perfect time for him to make an appearance — now when silk was needed so desperately.

It was a soft morning at the beginning of May that brought the few inhabitants scattered inside the house to the front porch. A carriage was pulling up — a carriage so laden with packages and luggage that it sagged and teetered, in its progress, beneath the weight. Velvet stood, watching its arrival curiously, with Mammy Jane and Alicia and several of the older women. Some wealthy acquaintance, it occurred to all of them, must be visiting. But none of them knew anyone who was wealthy — except Brett Whitney. Velvet wondered breathlessly if she should apprise the people out back that Brett was here. She paused just long enough to realize that the figure she saw in the isinglass window of the carriage was female, and with her was a middle-aged man.

At last, her red hair emblazoned against the wide brim of her rose-colored bonnet, Morgana Carleton stepped down from the carriage. Smiling, even laughing in gleeful triumph at the stir she'd caused, Morgana stepped, hoops and plumes bobbing, up the walk to the porch.

"Hello, you all," she called out. She reached the bottom of

the steps and looked up, shielding her eyes with a gloved hand. "Velvet," she said. "Thank heaven. Hello, Mrs. McBride, sugar," she called genially. "And there's dear old Mammy Jane. I see you've got a couple of little pickaninnies flapping at your skirts." She turned and waved to her traveling companion. "Come ahead, honey," she called to him. "They're all here." She bobbed up onto the porch and kissed the air in the general direction of Velvet's cheek. "I didn't know what we'd find," she said lightly. Then she turned her attention on her companion, and Velvet recognized, as he walked toward them, the pudgy and perfectly manicured figure of Damien Archambault.

"Bonjour, ladies," he said, bowing with courtly deference. Alicia McBride was properly impressed when she was introduced, and held out her hand in the manner of a modest belle.

"Monsieur," she breathed, "I have admired your lovely work for years."

"I am sure you have," said Damien, with what little humility his high status in the world of fashion would allow. "And I," he said, his eyes sweeping the elegant house, "admire your lovely Sweet Briar Hill."

"Wait till you see L'Étoile de Vie," Morgana said cheerfully. "It has twice the size and twice the grace of this old house." She laughed at her own good-natured barb, and suddenly Velvet's heart lurched. She'd meant, so often these last days, to write to Morgana in New York and apprise her of the fact that the Carleton plantation had been destroyed, but she'd avoided the dreaded task until, now, it was too late.

"I thought you might have stopped there first," she offered weakly.

"Oh, I just couldn't, sugar," said Morgana. "Mummy and Pa are arriving from Europe next month, and nothing will have been opened up there. I thought Damien and I would just impose ourselves on you all till they got here and got everything settled. You don't mind, do you? I hope you've got room for us."

She had addressed her last words to Alicia, who merely nodded blankly. "Of course," she murmured, not having the faintest notion what else to say. Actually, not a bedroom at Sweet

342

Briar Hill was unoccupied. Something would have to be done to accommodate Morgana and her exalted guest.

"You can bed down with one of the other women," said Mammy Jane with the nonchalance of one who cares not a fig about the impression she is making.

"I beg your pardon, Mammy dear?" asked Morgana sweetly. "Did you say something?"

"Things will certainly be arranged for your visit," said Velvet hastily, as she led the visitors into the house. Morgana swept into the parlor, confident that her luggage would be properly and efficiently trundled into the house.

"Come, Damien," she burbled, "and see this gracious parlor." Together, the two newcomers swept an appreciative look around the room. "And we thought you all were living in poverty and want down here," Morgana said lightly.

"Aren't you going to bring in your bags?" called out Mammy Jane. Alicia nudged her, and she and the other women, along with the driver of the carriage began to unload the luggage. Mammy Jane offered a grudging thrust of her bottom lip when Alicia indicated silently that she, too, should assist. "Those two are younger and stronger than me," Mammy Jane muttered, as they all helped with the bags. In the parlor, Velvet played hostess.

"This has all been recently done over," she said, indicating proudly the gold and white motif. Velvet did not mention that she, herself, had done most of it. She'd made the walls the soft yellow of the evening sun; she had sewn the floor-to-ceiling draperies and valances in pillowy white velvet to match the clouds that sailed over Sweet Briar Hill on bright summer days. She'd seen old, patched chairs reupholstered in the bright, patterned golds of ash-tree leaves in autumn, and had hooked together thick fillets of pale, creamy wool to make the tidy rugs that lay in carefully arranged disarray over the polished oak floor. Damien Archambault nodded approvingly.

"Most satisfyingly tasteful," he said in his disarming French accent. Morgana regarded him icily for only the breath of a second, and then began to pull off her gloves, finger by deliberate finger.

"It is restful," conceded Morgana, "if a tad seedy." She

glanced about expectantly. "After our long trip, I am sworn," she sighed, "I could do with a pot of tea."

"Oh, certainly," Velvet said hastily. "I'll get some."

"Let the darkies do it, sugar," said Morgana lightly, with a certain questioning challenge in her voice. "I have been just so impatient to hear about everything that's been going on." She sat down primly, and adjusted her wide skirts. Looking up at Velvet and seeming to enjoy her indecision, Morgana went on. "We'd heard the workers had all left, but I see Mammy Jane's still here." Her last words lifted questioningly.

"Well, that's true, Morgana; the workers left after the proclamation, and . . . and Mammy Jane's still here. . . . Dahlia's here, too, and her husband George and their two children. And"—here she laughed with forced brightness—"Arabella never went very far away in the first place—only to the field hospital a few miles up the road. . . ." Her voice trailed off. "But," she finally continued, "they're all so very busy what with one thing and another, so . . . I'll just get the tea." At that moment, Alicia swept into the room, for all the world the grand and elegant hostess—no one would guess she'd just finished lugging Morgana's things into the house. Velvet stepped to her gratefully. "Won't you entertain our guests, Mother?" she said, and moved hastily from the room.

"That woman is trouble, Velvet-pie," said Mammy Jane narrowly as she helped Velvet prepare refreshments in the kitchen.

"Oh, Mammy," said Velvet with a lightness she did not feel, "she just got here. Why are you assuming the worst?" Velvet busied herself placing tiny muffins on a plate, and attempted to ignore Mammy Jane's silence. At last she turned, and faced the older woman. "Morgana is used to . . . certain amenities, a certain deference being paid to her. We can't just . . . Oh, Mammy," she said softly. "She has no idea what's happened here. Can't we all be just a little bit patient with her?"

Mammy Jane looked sternly into Velvet's pleading gaze. Slowly, with a disapproving grunt and an emphatic drawing in of her lower lip, Mammy Jane capitulated. She handed Velvet a dish of sliced carrot bread, and some rolled napkins for the tea tray.

"I ain't saying I approve of this," she mumbled.

"Arabella and Dahlia will approve even less," Velvet muttered woefully as she arranged the tray, dreading the next few hours. She offered Mammy Jane a weak smile of gratitude, and left the room.

In the parlor, Alicia and the guests were involved in an animated conversation about French fashions, and they barely noted Velvet's entrance. She poured tea, and attempted to listen to the talk of rolled hems and deepening necklines. She looked up, startled by Damien Archambault's question.

"So you want the most *glorious* of wedding gown?" he said with avuncular approval.

"Gowns," said Morgana flatly. At Archambault's questioning look, she smiled sweetly, hastily amending her attitude. "You must use the plural there, sugar. 'The most glorious of *gowns.*'"

"Of course," said Damien with an apologetic smile. "My English is not yet . . . *parfait.* But my hands are those of *un maître.*" He added proudly, "I have designed and sewed for your Mrs. Lincoln."

"Oh, that dowdy old thing," derided Morgana. "I cannot tell you how glad I am that she's out of Washington. They say she's gone loony, you know. Of course"—she laughed—"I *always* thought she was a little 'off.' But then who wouldn't be, being married to that crude rail-splitter? They say he started this whole war because he was part darky himself." She sipped delicately at her tea. "Not," Morgana added with a shy smile, "that I know anything about the war."

"You're very fortunate," said Alicia seriously.

"Oh, I know that, Mrs. McBride, sugar," returned Morgana with deliberate solemnity. "Mummy and Pa were so right to send me north back in sixty-two. And I was . . . so right to have stayed where I was put." She offered Velvet an arch-browed and apparently friendly reproof, and then smiled at Alicia. "Mummy and Pa toddled off to Europe, of course."

"Yes, we'd heard," answered Alicia with a quick, hesitant look toward her daughter. "They were wise to have left."

"They were spared a . . . great hardship." Velvet's sorrowful glance prompted Morgana to rise and delicately set her cup down.

"I think Damien and I ought to be shown to our rooms," she said peremptorily. She brushed out her skirts, and smiled to those in the room. Velvet hesitated briefly.

"I'm . . . I'm sure we can arrange something. You see, Morgana, we've rather . . . opened our home to. . . ." Velvet's voice trailed off. She rallied somewhat finally and said, "Unfortunately, the war has made certain . . . adjustments necessary."

"Is that so?" asked Morgana innocently.

"Many women and their children were forced . . . because of the war to band together, and take up residence in . . . well, encampments — to protect themselves." Velvet was not anxious to open the wounds, so recently salved, of the women of Crystal Hill. She was startled by a voice from behind her.

"You'll be sharing my room, Morgana," said Lisa Mae Bloomer. She stood in the doorway of the parlor, her arms folded across her breast. "Won't that be fun?" she added with a smiling challenge.

"Why, Lisa Mae," said Morgana tightly. "Whatever are you doing here?"

"I was raped," rejoined Lisa Mae, "my parents were killed and my home was plundered by soldiers." She tilted her head. "Velvet and her family very kindly took me in."

"Did they?" murmured Morgana uncertainly. "How . . . sweet."

"Oh, it wasn't really sweetness that determined their generosity. We've helped each other, you see, through this very" — her gaze swept derisively over Morgana's rose-patterned gown — "unglamorous period of our lives. It's been hell here . . . sugar." The last word was emphasized significantly.

Morgana looked with puzzlement at Velvet. "Then you have other guests," she said.

"About thirty," said Velvet regretfully. "But I am sure we can arrange something for you," she added, glancing hopefully toward Lisa Mae.

That woman nodded. "Morgana will stay with me, and Monsieur Archambault will take the attic room."

"But what about Mammy Eliza and Sue Calhoun and her

daughters?" blurted Alicia. She looked sheepishly at Morgana and then at Damien Archambault.

"They're all settled in with—" began Lisa Mae. She was interrupted sharply.

"Well, we certainly didn't mean to cause—" Morgana said.

"No, no," Velvet interjected, rising quickly, "You haven't *caused* anything, Morgana." She shot a thankful look toward Lisa Mae. "We have everything arranged." She waited a few seconds for the embarrassment of the moment to pass, and then said, the lightness of her tone, belying the gravity of her determination, "Let's get the two of you settled, and then we can talk about . . . everything." Velvet said the last word hesitantly. She knew all too well that soon she would have to tell Morgana there was no one to wait on her; she would have to tell her that the myth of the cavalier and the belle was not only passé but now completely unrealistic; she would have to tell Morgana of the burning of L'Étoile de Vie—and who was responsible for that final destruction.

For the moment, however, Velvet determined that she must attempt to make Morgana's passage into this new life in the South as painless as possible. Remembering her own cruel introduction to the war, Velvet hoped to spare Morgana; indeed, she would try to spare anyone the harshness of that experience. She would delay, for the moment at least, the ordeal Morgana would face soon enough as she was forced to reconstruct her life.

Chapter Thirty-eight

Velvet stepped, with Morgana, into the room that her guest and Lisa Mae would occupy. "It is small," Velvet said apologetically, "but I'm sure it will serve . . . for the time being."

"Of course it will," said Morgana with an obviously forced cheerfulness. She glanced around at the piled boxes. "I wonder where I shall put my things, though," she mused aloud in some irritation.

"We've all learned to make do, Morgana," said Velvet gently. "It hasn't been easy, you see."

Morgana quickly looked at Velvet. "Oh, I know that, sugar, it's just . . . well," she said with a small, helpless laugh, "I'm used to accommodations that are a bit more . . . accommodating."

"I understand," Velvet said. "But you must understand, too, that things have changed a bit here in the South."

"Well, I can certainly see they've changed here at Sweet Briar Hill," Morgana responded. "I haven't seen one painting, for all the walls are freshly washed, nor have I seen a piece of crystal or silver. I thought I'd die when you served tea in that old ceramic teapot. And you, sugar," Morgana went on in disbelief, "you look more indigent than you ever looked in Albany. I didn't want to say anything in front of your dear mother, but you all look like the wrath of God." Morgana began pulling gowns from boxes, and fluffing them crisply. "Mammy Jane has never let herself go so shamefully. That dress of hers has been patched so many times, I'm surprised it even stays on her big fat body. She's a disgrace to this fine house, is what she is."

"Mammy Jane's no disgrace to this house," Velvet put in with more vehemence than she'd intended. Morgana looked over her shoulder sharply. Velvet amended her attitude, and said tiredly, "We're all doing our best, Morgana."

"Well, sometimes 'best' is none too good when it comes to those lazy darkies," she shot back.

"Please don't say things like that," Velvet said quickly. "I mean, we . . . we don't talk like that here."

"Oh, yes," said Morgana with a certain superiority, "we're now all equal; isn't that what 'His Majesty Abraham the First' said? Well, *I* think it's disgusting," she said, turning away. She looked back slyly. "Naturally, since your husband's here, I suppose we must defer to his rather crude sensibilities." She paused. "Where is that handsome old thing, anyway? Last time I heard, he was going to join the army."

"He tried," said Velvet tentatively. She was not sure how much Morgana knew of Cutter's reputation. Now that the war was officially over, however, and all power taken from the Confederacy, she could feel safe in disclosing his whereabouts; her mother had already spoken of the planned wedding. Still Velvet hesitated. She knew that a confrontation between Cutter and Brett Whitney must be avoided. "Cutter came looking for me," she said finally. "He is here at Sweet Briar Hill. But, promise me," she added quickly, "that should Brett Whitney come by, you will not mention that fact."

"Brett?" asked Morgana with a lift of a cinnamon-colored brow. "Have you seen Brett?"

"Yes," Velvet admitted. "He is responsible for much of what we now have. You see, Morgana," she continued, lowering her eyes, "the war robbed us of everything. Hungry soldiers stole from us even the clothing in our closets." She looked up to see, with a certain reluctant satisfaction, Morgana's look of astonishment. "We had nothing until Brett Whitney agreed to finance the planting of our fields last year. With the profits he advanced us, we were able to make the house and grounds at least livable. It will be a very long time before we are able to afford the luxury of paintings or silver teapots." She managed a small laugh. "But we are happy here. Compared to some, we have been very fortunate."

"Compared to whom?" Morgana said wryly.

"Compared to me, for instance," said Lisa Mae, who stood now just inside the door. "You'll have to move your stuff, sugar. I don't have much," she said sharply, "but what I've got, I'm keeping tidy." She swept past the two women, and began to clear away Morgana's things from what she considered her part of the room. "You'll have to live out of a trunk for a while, Morgana." Velvet noted a hardness in Lisa Mae that she'd not seen since that young woman had arrived at Crystal Hill that first night. And there was something else in Lisa Mae's regard as she eyed Morgana. There was a certain envy. It was this that frightened Velvet more than anything. If, after all they'd been through, Lisa Mae could feel jealous of the ostentation and falsehood that Morgana represented, then there was little hope in Velvet that Lisa Mae had learned anything at all.

Morgana glanced tartly at Lisa Mae. "Maybe you can be content living out of a trunk, my girl," she said, "but I can't."

"Who said I was 'content,' Morgana?" Lisa Mae rejoined. Her gaze drifted to the window, and she distractedly surveyed the scene outside. "I'm far from content," she grated. She looked back at her two old acquaintances. "I'll never be satisfied until I've stopped living out of a trunk, until I've got enough money so I can live like a queen. I'll do anything to get it, too," she added harshly. "I'll take any opportunity that shows itself. You wait and see—both of you. I'm going to leave here soon, but I'm coming back. And I'm coming back a rich woman."

Morgana smiled wickedly. "This opportunity you describe can't come soon enough for me, Lisa Mae honey. I need room for my things."

"You'll have your room very soon, Morgana." Lisa Mae smiled back at her. "And no matter the sacrifice, no matter the personal compromise, I'll have my opportunity."

"You have changed, Lisa Mae," said Morgana with a sly smile, "and not for the better, I must say. Any woman who—"

"Any woman who has lived through the hell of this war," interjected Lisa Mae, "is entitled to live out the rest of her life on her own terms. That's what I intend to do."

"That's what I've always done," said Morgana with tranquil superiority. "And look what I have to show for it. Look at me, Lisa Mae Bloomer. Can you really hope to match what you see? You're a little late . . sugar."

"I may be late, Morgana," the other woman stated. "But I am no less determined." Her gaze flicked over Velvet, and she continued. "I am leaving within the week," she gritted out. "And the next time you see me, I won't, as God is my witness, be dressed in rags."

"We need to talk, Lisa Mae," Velvet said wearily. Then she realized with a sudden terrible sadness that there would be no talk with Lisa Mae. A relentless determination had overtaken the woman. At the sight and scent of the lavishly turned out Morgana, reason had fled her. Velvet knew suddenly, with an interior shudder, that Lisa Mae was doomed to a horrible certainty of her own making—of the war's making. How differently individuals responded to similar influences, she thought in wonder. Where would Lisa Mae's response to the horrors of the war carry her? It had carried her once to terrible compromise in the lustful clutches of Brett Whitney. Would it do so again? Velvet made a silent prayer against such an inevitability. She cast a rueful look at both women, and left the room. She knew that she was powerless against Lisa Mae's resolve. She must accept what the circumstances of the war had wrought, but she was deeply pained by, deeply sorry for, the woman's lost gentility. Velvet's own resolve, however, began to assert itself. In her own heart, somehow, she would find peace. Despite all that had happened, Velvet would know serenity—and she would not burrow back into the falseness of her former life to find it. She would find it within herself. Still, she mused, with a sorrowful smile, the thought flowing through her like a whispered wish, she would love just once again to look as lovely as Morgana Carleton.

Downstairs, Velvet attempted to lose herself in preparations for dinner. As she and Mammy Jane and Arabella, just home from the hospital, sliced vegetables and cold meats, Velvet wondered distractedly how she might keep peace,

351

until Lisa Mae decided to leave, in a household that had been a haven. It was just before dinner was served that a refreshed Morgana appeared in the kitchen. Smiling enthusiastically, she asked if there was anything she could do to help. Velvet recalled, with a tender twist of her heart, her own less than successful attempts to become a part of the family life at her Uncle Duff's. She smiled encouragingly, and told Morgana that she might roll the napkins. This must be exactly how her dear Aunt Vonnie had felt, trying to find jobs for Velvet in her sweeping gowns.

"We wouldn't want you to get your pretty dress spotted," she said kindly.

"Oh, this old thing." Morgana laughed lightly. Still, she rolled the napkins, and kept up a steady stream of gay conversation. Velvet barely heard the tales of Morgana's glittery life in New York. She could only look covetously on the "old thing" that Morgana was wearing. It was a pale green creation in the most diaphanous organza that Velvet had ever seen. She did not really envy Morgana . . . not really. But her own tired cotton frock seemed so much more shabby in the face of Morgana's opulence. In fact, all of Sweet Briar Hill seemed less satisfying than it had that morning.

The men came trooping into the kitchen, having washed outside, and exclamations of welcome—and admiration—followed before Mammy Jane announced dinner with more force, everyone thought, than was completely necessary.

The table in the dining room was, as always, filled with good food and joyous conversation. Velvet realized a moment of uneasiness as Arabella, Mammy Jane, and Dahlia and her husband George along with their children sat down for dinner. Velvet noted, if no one else did, that Morgana eyed them all with some puzzlement and more than a little disapproval.

"Is your table always this . . . full, sugar?" her guest asked coolly. Velvet nodded wordlessly, and wondered whether Cutter had caught Morgana's censorious posture. She needn't have worried, she reflected sourly, since Morgana was already fully engrossed in laying the full measure of her considerable charm on the gentleman in question. "I think it's just wonderful what you all are doing," she called down the laden table to Steven and Cutter. "You're just so brave, is what you are. My piddly life seems like nothing compared to what you all have been through." She ate heartily, complimented just as heartily, and, by the time dinner was over, enjoyed the status — as she always had — of "belle of the ball." The days of knights and their ladies might be over, but, for that brief time at Sweet Briar Hill, as the family enjoyed their dinner, Morgana Carleton had managed to sweep everyone back to those fairy-tale days. Only Damien Archambault, and of course, Lisa Mae, seemed untouched by Morgana's twinkly, much longed for gaiety. Life, Velvet had to admit, had been rather drab hereabouts for a very long time. Morgana brought a certain sparkle to the table. Velvet could not blame her husband and the other members of their family for being fascinated with Morgana's charm and wit. Still, she eyed Cutter dubiously. He was obviously enchanted. It was, then, with some gratification, that she noted Damien's regard drifting to her — and particularly to Arabella.

Dinner was cleared by everyone, and, as Velvet and Arabella cleaned the dishes and flatware, Damien Archambault strolled out to where they worked in the yard. The soft, scented night made him smile, and Velvet could not help but smile back in greeting. She swiped at a stray curl that had fallen against her cheek.

"Why aren't you with the others in the parlor, *monsieur?*" she asked.

"Why should I be in there?" he asked in his broken English. "I would much rather enjoy this magic night with two lovely ladies, here in this magic garden."

Arabella laughed softly. "There is no magic here, *monsieur*," she said as she swished a plate in the rinse water before wiping it.

"Isn't there, *mademoiselle?*" Damien Archambault stepped over the stubby grass, his hands magisterially placed behind his back, and said, "In my country, we believe there is magic everywhere. Would the two of you like to hear a pretty story? It may help to pass for you this time of drudgery." Both

353

women nodded, and listened raptly as they continued their work. "There was once a beautiful princess," he said softly, his voice broken music in the night, "and she had a beautiful friend—an exotic friend who was also a princess, but from a faraway land." Velvet and Arabella smiled at each other. "These two princesses were forced to live in poverty in a beautiful, but rather seedy, castle. It was so sad. They had to do terrible and demeaning work for a wicked woman of great riches. They were very kind to this woman, though she was not kind to them." He shrugged in eloquent Gallic fashion, and continued. "What can I tell you, except that these two *mademoiselles* were merely . . . kind? But," he said with warning, "what the wicked lady did not know was that they were grander ladies than she. It would have frightened her—terribly—had she known that. And so, the princesses did not tell her. They waited and remained kind. One day a sorcerer came. He had no riches, but he had great magic in his hands. He turned the princesses, one day—one very special day, a wedding day—into the grandest ladies anyone had ever seen." He smiled an elfin grin. For all his elegance, for all his continental polish, he was nothing if not a mischiefmaker. "And so will I do that for you." He cocked a graying brow, and regarded the two young women impishly. "But we will tell no one, eh?"

"Our lips are sealed," Velvet giggled. Damien stepped toward Arabella, and he became serious.

"Did you know," he asked, "that in Paris our most elegant models of women's couture are African women of great beauty and great stature? It is a fact," he said admiringly. "And none have I seen more . . . *magnifique* than you, *mademoiselle*." He bowed low, and lifted Arabella's hand, brushing it with his lips. "You will see for yourself one day—that wedding day I mentioned." He bowed to Velvet, and once again to Arabella, and left the yard.

"He's going to make you a dress," Arabella said raptly, as she watched him go, "the most . . . *magnifique* dress in the whole world, for your wedding."

Velvet eyed her obliquely. "I don't think my dress is going

354

to be nearly as . . . *magnifique* as the one he intends to make for you . . . sugar."

Arabella regarded her friend shyly. "Do you think he really meant it?" she asked.

"I do," Velvet answered in mock solemnity. "It will be a wonderful dress." She lifted a shoulder flirtatiously. "It will be just perfect for scrubbing these dishes," she added sweetly, "Which we will never get done if you don't give me some help." Both girls found themselves laughing over the steamy water as they finished their now not so tedious work.

Warm spring breezes danced over the land. Bright new growth was everywhere. Virgin plants lifted their newly awakened verdancy to the sunlit sky, and hope nestled in the hearts of everyone at Sweet Briar Hill. Most of the women and their children had left to join their husbands; slowly, the plantation family was diminishing. Velvet had seen to it that each woman and her brood received several dollars from the carefully hoarded advance given the McBrides by Brett Whitney in anticipation of enormous profits from their tobacco crops. This year promised to be even more rewarding, and she told each woman as she left, that more money could be expected. Steven and Cutter had managed to hire a great many mustered-out soldiers to do the work formerly done by the women. Sue Calhoun had commented wryly that she rather resented being displaced; she had, she admitted, rather enjoyed the wages she'd earned as a sharecropper. "What can we do, though?" She sighed. "The men are back from the war—they have to have some means to support their families." It did not go unnoted by all the women, however, that they'd not done a bad job in that particular male sphere, when it counted.

It was mid-May, after General Taylor had surrendered all remaining Confederate troops east of the Mississippi at Alabama, that Velvet, arranging a bouquet of day lilies on a newly constructed front-porch, saw the gray-uniformed rider coming at a pounding gallop up the road before the house.

She recognized the plumed hat, the proud set of the shoulders, and knew it to be Brett Whitney. She took a quick, composing breath, glanced toward the back of the house, and moved hastily off the porch in order to meet him on the drive. His horse skidded to a halt, raising clouds of dust before her.

"Why, what brings you here, Major?" Velvet asked with forced brightness as she squinted up into the sun. From the height of his saddle, he looked down on her.

"I've got rather bad news," he said grimly.

"Oh, it couldn't be that bad, Brett," she rejoined girlishly, but her heart pounded beneath her breast. Brett Whitney swung down from his saddle.

"I'm afraid it is," he said tersely. "It's taken me this long to assess the damage, but I can tell you this; the profits I expected from your tobacco will not be forthcoming. Therefore, the money I advanced to you is money owed."

The world swirled inside Velvet's head. She felt she might swoon, but she held herself rigidly against such weakness. "Wh-whatever do you mean, Brett?" she asked, determined to maintain that "helpless female" posture he seemed to enjoy but to get to the reason for this disastrous turn of events.

"Where is your father?" he asked.

"Oh, please, let's not bother Pa with this; he's out in the fields." She placed a small hand on his wide chest, and looked straight up into his green gaze. "I shall be strong, Brett, I promise."

Brett Whitney hesitated, then stepped toward Velvet, taking her elbow gallantly and leading her to the porch. They sat down, and Brett told his unpleasant and world-turning story. Most of it, Velvet had guessed. She remembered all too vividly the burning of Richmond. She recalled that someone had shouted the tobacco warehouses were burning. She did not know, however, that it was her own tobacco that was destroyed. She looked up, startled by Brett Whitney's final statement.

"The terms of our agreement, then, state that I become the owner of Sweet Briar Hill," he was saying. "Naturally, I would be less exacting about my demands for repayment if I had some guarantee that again this year I might benefit by your even larger crop," he said with icy determination. Velvet watched him evenly, showing little emotion. She felt at once relieved and horrified. So he was not about to take the plantation; this had been her nightmare. But, it was also a fact that once again she must submit her family to a repugnant alliance with a man they detested.

"Naturally," she said finally. But her stomach lurched. The hatred she felt for Brett Whitney could hardly abide another year of putting up with his repulsive presence in her life. And yet, what could she do? Short of turning over the plantation to him, she had little choice in the matter but to partner herself once again with this detestable money grubber.

"You will apprise your father of my terms," he said silkily, knowing that he had triumphed. He wondered, watching Velvet nod obediently, why he'd ever been concerned. "I shall draw up papers, and bring them tomorrow," he said rising. "You know," he added, lifting her reluctant hand to his lips, "now that the war is over, and that scoundrel of a husband of yours is gone—maybe dead—I should very much like to press my suit. I cannot tell you how generous I would be, had I a . . . cooperative business partner."

The blow came like lightning—explosive, deadly—and sent Brett Whitney hurtling down the steps, into the dust at the bottom of the porch. *"Son of a bitch!"* he railed, looking for the source of the murderous jolt. Before he could speak another word, Cutter was upon him. Brett rolled from under his lunging assault, and attempted to counterattack, but Cutter hammered punch after battering punch into his face and abdomen. Brett's powerful forearms were no obstacle to Cutter's killing rage. A fist rammed like a ball of shot into the Southerner's middle, and Brett doubled over, gasping and choking, and at last falling to the ground.

"No, Cutter," screamed Velvet. She threw herself down off the porch, and ran to her husband. His jaw locked rigidly.

"Get back," he grated, his even white teeth clenched in animal fury.

357

"Don't, love," she pleaded, sobbing, grabbing at his powerfully muscled arms that were rigid with waiting for his writhing prey to recover so that he might finish him off.

"The bastard needs killing," he ground out, pushing her away once more.

"But not by you, lad," shouted a voice from the front doorway. Both Velvet and Cutter turned to see Steven McBride. Alicia came and stood with him, and then Mammy Jane.

"Your business has been *saving* lives, John," called out Alicia.

"You get your tail in here, boy," Mammy Jane said sternly, adding her voice to the general frenzy, "before you do something you're sorry for."

"Oh, Cutter," Velvet urged, "don't you see that killing him won't do any good? They'll hang you for it—then what will I do, and what will your son do?" At this last, Cutter paused. He regarded Velvet in disbelief. She veiled her gaze and placed her hands delicately over her abdomen.

"Son?" Cutter asked, bewildered. Brett Whitney, choking in air, pushed himself from the ground.

"You goddamned . . . you . . . stinking . . ." His voice was barely audible, and he spit blood. He looked up murderously, as he straightened himself, his green gaze taking in the whole family. He swiped at a weal of blood pouring from his ruined nose. "We meet at last," he grated in a hoarse whisper. "I've got one thing to tell you, Cutter—*boy;* you've just killed it for all of them." Cutter stepped to him, and grabbed his lapels.

"Have I?" he gritted out. "Then maybe I'd just better kill you. Huh—*boy?*"

Velvet's fingertips flew to her mouth. "Please, Cutter," she moaned, for she knew that her husband's words were not an idle threat. "If you love me," she pleaded, "if you love our child, please don't do this." Cutter glanced over at her, his dark brow ploughing in frustration. A storm of indecision raged in the iron gray of his eyes. At last, in a cyclonic tempest of determination, he threw the battered Brett Whitney away from him. That man tottered and stumbled across the lawn, and at last, caught his balance. Clutching himself protectively, he made a staggering retreat to his horse. Mounting it with ragged haste, he wheeled the animal. Before starting off, and with the protection of his mounted position, he paced the animal toward the house. Keeping a safe distance, his green gaze swept the people gathered there.

"This ignorant Northerner has cost you all something very dear to you," he shouted out hoarsely. "You'll be served eviction papers tomorrow." With that, Brett Whitney spurred his horse and rode at a gallop from the plantation that he now owned.

"A child," Cutter said on a breath. Velvet nodded. He reached out and touched her cheek. She looked into the liquid silver of his gaze and delicately placed her hand over his.

"Your child, Cutter," she said quietly, "and mine." He smiled and tears welled in his eyes.

"Out of this horror has come the most precious of life's treasures," he reflected.

"The most precious," Velvet agreed, smiling warmly. As twilight enveloped them, they sat on the bottom step of the porch. The rest of the family had made their way inside, carrying Brett Whitney's words with them. Now those words echoed on the warm evening breezes, and Cutter frowned.

"Whitney intends to take your child's legacy, Velvet," he said solemnly. "But I will not allow that."

"Nor will I, Cutter," she replied. "Nor will I."

Chapter Thirty-nine

The news of Sweet Briar Hill's endangerment swept the inhabitants of the plantation. They descended upon Velvet with their savings. Arabella, Mammy Jane, the remaining women all wished to contribute to the plantation's preservation. Velvet felt an especial twinge of sorrow when Morgana came to her with all the money she had in the world.

"And when Mummy and Pa return, they're sure to help," she assured her. Velvet knew she must soon inform Morgana of what had happened at L' Étoile de Vie. In the meantime, she smiled kindly at the donations, but forlornly refused them, reluctantly giving notice that for all their generosity, the people living on the plantation could not save it. Collectively, they had not enough money to buy an acre, much less the hundreds of acres of land that made up Sweet Briar Hill. It occurred to them as they sat around the supper table, late that night, that they might be able to save at least the house and a few of the fields.

"I don't think Mr. Whitney is much in the mood for bargaining," said Steven McBride softly.

"For that," said Cutter sharply, "you may all thank this 'ignorant Northerner.' " He stood and stepped away from the table. Raking long fingers through the tangles of his jet curls, he paced the dining room.

"Now, John Eliot, sugar," Morgana piped, "you mustn't blame yourself. After all—as I understand it—it was Velvet who made the devilish bargain in the first place." She looked hastily at Velvet, and lifted delicate fingertips to her lips. "Oh, honey, I'm so sorry. It's only that—"

"I know, Morgana," Velvet said tiredly. "It's only that you're absolutely right."

"Now, darling," said Alicia. "You mustn't blame yourself."

"She's right," Arabella said, moving along the table to Velvet's side. "You did what you had to do under the circumstances." She did not note the sudden narrowing of Morgana's gaze.

"Arabella, honey," Morgana said more than sweetly, "why don't you clear away these dishes. It just doesn't seem right, our all sitting around amid the rubble of dinner discussing our poverty." She laughed lightly.

Arabella hesitated only a moment before lifting the first few plates from the table.

"Let me help," said Velvet attempting to avert tension between the two women.

"I'll do it," Arabella said quietly. She looked straight at Morgana who simply smiled. "I don't mind a bit," said Arabella, and she continued to clear.

Damien Archambault listened attentively to the various financial possibilities that were tossed about for a few moments more. "I wish that I was in a position to help you," he said softly, "but, unfortunately, I have not the resources here in America." He looked woefully toward Alicia. "And you such a dear . . . *admiratrice* — how do you say — enthusiast of me. I wish I could do something for you, madame. In fact," he added with a bright elfin smile, "I may be able to do something for you. If nothing else, I can help you with your supper dishes." Abruptly, he stood, and began to clear the rest of the table. With his neatly sleeved arms filled with dishes, he made his way to the kitchen.

Even in the face of their great despair, everyone managed laughter. Cutter's mirth ebbed before that of the rest, and as sober deliberation returned, he quietly left the room. It was not many moments before Morgana excused herself.

The star-silvered night left dappled shadows on the lawns. Morgana treaded softly over the long grasses, and spotted her prey at last. "John Eliot," she called out quietly. Cutter turned at her approach.

"Hello, Morgana," he said. His silver gaze impaled her, and she flinched inwardly. This would not be easy. She had wanted Cutter since the day she'd met him, had yearned for those strong heroic arms to hold her, enfold her in their masculine necessity. She looked up, allowing, thanks to her deeply cut neckline, her throat and rounded breasts their fullest display.

"I feel so sorry for Velvet," she murmured, knowing that she must approach this man differently than she might approach others of her acquaintance. She could not depend upon his willing compliance with her brand of seduction. She could not turn him against Velvet, and so she must seem to be — as he obviously was — in complete sympathy with her. And, perhaps, with any luck at all, John Eliot Cutter had a weakness or two that Morgana might play upon. "That poor little wife of yours is trying so hard to help everybody." She lifted a pale arm and brushed languidly at her bright curls. "Dear me, she is the most valiant of women."

"Yes," Cutter said huskily.

"I just don't know what I'd do in her position," Morgana sighed. She began to walk, strolling randomly across the lawn. As she had hoped, Cutter followed. "As a matter of fact," she continued with a small, moonstruck smile, "I do know what I'd do in her position." She paused, glancing up at Cutter. "Do you know what that is, John Eliot?"

"I have no idea, Morgana," he answered.

"I think I'd take my . . . extravagantly handsome husband, and leave this place."

"Where would you and your . . . extravagantly handsome husband go?"

"We'd go up to New York City, or, even better, to Albany." Morgana laughed lightly. "You're still quite a celebrity there, you know. You could probably get yourself elected mayor, or something."

"Really," Cutter said, lifting a brow and smiling back at her.

Morgana nodded. "My friend, Eben Conway, has political ambitions, and he told me he was glad you'd left Albany. He said" — here, encouraged by Cutter's seeming interest, Morgana stopped and turned, looking directly into his eyes — "he said, you'd give him a run for his money if you decided to run for any office — and he's got a lot of money, John Eliot. Why you and Velvet could live like royalty in that city. Naturally," she added, "Velvet would never leave Sweet Briar Hill." Morgana frowned disconsolately. "It's such a shame she's so devoted to her home. If you were my husband, I'd be devoted only to you." Cutter's smile deepened.

"I doubt, lovely Morgana," he said quietly, "that you could be 'devoted' *only* to anyone."

"Well, I could," she answered back, more forcefully than she'd intended. "I mean," she said, altering her tone, "I could be devoted if I were properly . . . motivated. And, if it wasn't . . . devotion — strictly speaking — that a man was looking for; well, I could provide that, too." Her eyes, nearly translucent in the starlight, beckoned as she lifted her head and ran silken fingertips over Cutter's rough jaw. He caught her wrist, and the touch sent fire through Morgana's veins. Slowly, he stepped to her.

"You are sweetly satanic temptation, Morgana," he said roughly. Her scent perfumed the air between them. "And I am sorely tempted." Morgana's heart thumped beneath the ripe white swell of her breasts. "But I love my wife," he said, "and —"

"And, what?" she breathed. "Does that preclude —"

"Yes," he answered, and a smile etched his firm lips. "It does."

Morgana twisted away from him, and said, "I don't see why." She was all perfume and petulance, and Cutter laughed, the sound coming from deep in his wide chest.

"You, Morgana Carleton," he said gently, "are a rare jewel; there aren't many like you left."

"Like me?" she huffed sourly. "For heaven's sake, John Eliot Cutter, *you're* the rare one."

"Maybe so, Morgana," he conceded amiably. "Maybe so."

It was very late before Cutter made his way to bed, and Velvet was softly asleep. Her breathing, even and deep, filled the room with a kind of night fragrance that always enchanted him. She murmured incoherently, her voice a whisper on the night wind from the open window, as he snuggled beneath the light coverlet, taking her to him.

"Where have you been, love?" she asked sleepily, and she nestled cozily into his embrace, her moon-tossed curls against his chest.

"I've been walking, princess," he answered, "wrestling with my guilt."

"You mustn't feel guilty," she whispered. She raised her lips, taking his in a tender caress. He looked down at her, warm, sleep-softened in his arms and smiled. He placed a big hand on her cheek, and her eyes unclosed. "Promise me," she said softly.

"I shall promise you anything in the world, princess," he answered huskily. Velvet lifted her arms and entwined them around his neck, her fingertips brushing the thick curls that lay there. He drew her to him. The warmth of his tenderness embraced her. Feathery sensations lingered achingly beneath her flesh, as he stroked her lovingly, awakening, with practiced touches, familiar hungers.

Moaning softly, pressing herself temptingly close to him, writhing invitingly in his embrace, Velvet felt the tender application of hand and heart that only loving lovers give. His rough hands, so strong, delicately stroked her breasts and hips, buttocks and thighs. Hands, so capable of violence, savored unhurriedly each yielding place, each hungry, swelling bud of her desire. Blood quickened, pulses throbbed. Her lips parted, achingly eager for the invasion of his great power. He raised himself over her and arched her to him. In the starlit darkness, she could see only the muscular form of him, lingering above her, intensifying her need for him with teasing torment. His mouth, his lips, his tongue savored her. Arcing tongues of rapture spread from her belly to heat those places of cungingest need. She spread herself like a canvas on which he created burning patterns of rapture — and necessity.

She drew him close, craving the masculine hardness of him against her softer senses. Yearning for the rapacity of his hunger, she yielded to the manly roughness that took her, savagely exposing that place of tenderest resistance. She gasped, cried out at the throbbing hunger, the pounding pungency of his will. Inhaling sharply, holding to that supremest moment of rapture, she clung to him, raking his strong back with her nails. Breath came in moaning exhalation as she felt that sudden, soaring epiphany of release.

"Oh, Cutter," she gasped. Her female senses were alive with womanly repletion, and the star-shot world flared, then slowly dimmed. "Oh, love," she breathed, and writhed against him, the abrasion of his manly fur pleasingly provoking on her tender flesh.

Cutter lay for a long, long time with her held to him. Unlike him, she drifted soon into sleep. He knew, at that moment, that no matter the will of this little creature nestled so trustingly in his arms, he would abide that will. He could not be without Velvet. He must help her find a way to save her home, and then, if Sweet Briar Hill was where she wanted to stay, he would stay there, too.

The sun burst cheerily over the horizon the next morning. Velvet roused herself slowly, unwillingly, from her slumber, and woke smiling. She reached out for Cutter, but he was not there. Lifting herself to a sleepy, sitting position, she assumed she'd slept late and that he was already out in the fields. She swiped at the tangle of her curls. Looking out, across the sky, she realized that it was only a little past dawn. Perhaps, he was downstairs having breakfast. She pushed herself reluctantly from the tousled bed, and shrugged into her tired, cotton frock. She made her weary way down to the kitchen to find only Mammy Jane and Arabella there.

"What are you doing up so early, Velvet-pie?" said Mammy in that whispered way reserved for morning talk.

"I wouldn't be up myself, except for John Brown Tull," said Arabella wearily. "That boy got me up before dawn—"

"Where's Cutter and Pa?" asked Velvet.

"Well," Mammy Jane said, "your pa's just stirring now. I was about to fix corn cakes; the men are coming up the road to start their field work."

"And Cutter rode out ages ago," Arabella said.

Velvet looked up sharply. "Where did he go?" she demanded. Arabella raised an unconcerned shoulder. "Well, didn't you ask him?" Velvet said.

"I saw him from my window," Arabella responded, suddenly concerned. "Is anything wrong?"

"I'm not sure," Velvet said softly. "It's only that he was feeling so guilty last evening. I thought . . . Well, I just hope he's not about to do something rash."

"Like go and kill Brett Whitney?" Arabella said, dread in her tone. Velvet nodded, and took the coffee offered her by Mammy Jane.

"That boy's not going to kill anybody," said the older woman with certainty. "Oh, he's got it in him, all right, but he's also got too much goodness in him. Like Miss Alicia pointed out, he's a life-giver, not a taker of lives. God made him that way; He ain't' going to take away that goodness all of a sudden." Arabella and Velvet exchanged a dubious glance.

"I just wish he'd left a note," Velvet said quietly at last.

The morning passed with deadening slowness. Velvet waited for the eviction notice to come as Brett Whitney had promised it would that day. At long last, she and Mammy Jane spotted the agent of their destruction. He was a lone figure, thin and prim, riding in a small wagon.

"It must be him," Velvet whispered.

"A 'Daniel come to judgement,' " Mammy Jane whispered back. They waited expectantly on the porch, as the little man descended from the wagon.

"I believe you ladies are expecting this," he said, his final words lifting in question. Velvet forced herself to take the paper extended toward her.

"Is there nothing we can do?" she asked in a small voice.

"Yes," the gentleman said officiously. "You can come up with two thousand dollars — or its equivalent — before the end of the week."

"Its . . . equivalent?" asked Velvet.

"Something of equal value," the man stated primly. His eyes swept the two shabbily dressed women and then took in the painted, clean, but poorly accoutered house. "If you should suddenly find yourself with that sort of . . . wealth, I can be contacted in Richmond." He touched the brim of his black hat, and made his precise way back to his wagon. Without further word, he was on his way, leaving Velvet and Mammy Jane watching his departure forlornly.

"The end of the week," Velvet murmured blankly.

"As your pa said, Velvet-pie," Mammy Jane offered, "Mr. Brett Whitney is in no mood to bargain."

Chapter Forty

"I insist we ride out today," Morgana said as she ate heartily of her late lunch.

"But Morgana," Velvet said, with more desperation than she'd intended, "it's so late."

"I don't care," Morgana returned petulantly. "I want to see L' Étoile de Vie. If we're going to have a wedding here, I want to get my jewels out of Pa's safe. Can you imagine; that old poop wouldn't even let me take my pearls to Albany—much less my sapphires? And I do miss them so." She pouted.

Velvet and Mammy Jane glanced at each other, hiding—or attempting to hide—their anxiety. "Now, child," Mammy Jane began.

"I'm *not* your child, Mammy, and"—Morgana arched a brow in Velvet's direction—"I *do* insist." Velvet felt a sudden emptiness in her stomach. She lowered her eyes. The time had come, she resolved. She'd kept the truth from Morgana far too long. The dreaded thing must be spoken.

She lifted her gaze. "Morgana," she said evenly, "there is no more L'Étoile de Vie." The other woman merely watched Velvet; she showed no emotion. "It's gone," Velvet said earnestly, spurred by Morgana's dispassion.

"Gone?" Morgana asked.

Velvet nodded.

"I'm afraid I haven't the faintest idea what you're talking about, sugar."

Velvet sat down near Morgana, and began her terrible story. Morgana's expression was like an opal in the shifting of its disposition. She seemed perplexed at first, then irate, then, finally, quietly wrathful. She stood. "You're telling me," she seethed, her voice an uncharacteristic grate, "that . . . *you* burned up my home?"

"I had no choice, Morgana," Velvet cried. "You've heard the whole story; you can't possibly blame me."

"You *bitch!*" Morgana forced out the last word. Her face was a mask of hatred as she swung out her hand. Velvet shut her eyes tightly against the expected blow — but it did not come. Her eyes popped open to find that Mammy Jane had caught Morgana's wrist in a vicious grip. "Let me go, you dirty old darkie!" the younger woman shrieked.

"You take your trashy violence out of this kitchen, girl," Mammy Jane growled. "We've had enough of hurting." Slowly, warily, as she felt tension ebb, she let go her hold on Morgana's wrist.

That woman wrenched away. Bitter tears welled in her eyes. "I'll get you for this, Velvet McBride," she shot out. "Just don't you, for one minute of your life, think I won't." She turned sharply and fled from the room.

"Thank you," Velvet said softly to Mammy Jane.

That woman delicately smoothed the brightly colored kerchief that covered her head. "Ain't a reason in the world to thank me, honey," she answered piously. "It was the Lord give me the strength to stop that girl. But I'll tell you one thing, Velvet-pie," she added gravely, "you watch out for her. She's a bad one — always was. I'd do some mean praying, if I was you."

Velvet nodded sorrowfully. Perhaps, one day, Morgana would forgive her. In the meantime, there seemed so many other things about which to pray.

The day had begun, and ended, badly for Velvet. She sat on the porch of Sweet Briar Hill's main house as the twilight faded into night. Her husband apparently had deserted her — at least that was what she felt. All day she'd expected him. All day she'd wondered and worried about what had drawn him away, what had kept him from the house. She'd gone to the fields and not found him. She'd explored every nook and cranny of the vast estate, and all the while, she'd lingered in a liminal world, hating him for leaving her at such a time, loving him, torturing herself concerning the possibilities of his going. Had he determined to find Brett Whitney? Had he decided that, with brute force, he would change the man's mind concerning the plantation? Had his just desire for revenge forced him to kill their detested enemy?

Or, had he simply decided that Velvet, their child yet to be born, and the financial woes surrounding the plantation were more than he cared to deal with. These notions tormented Velvet. They whirled like serrate-backed monsters through her thoughts, lashing out with great force to terrify her. She hugged her knees protectively to her chest as she watched the darkness thicken. Once again she was with child, and, once again, without a husband.

Morgana stepped from the house. Velvet looked up at her sudden appearance, not certain what to expect. Tension between the two women was suddenly dispelled.

"I realize," Morgana offered softly, "how . . . unfair I've been." She swept onto the porch in a rustle of satin and heavy perfume.

Velvet tilted her a puzzled regard. "You . . . realize . . ." It was so unlike Morgana to "realize" anything. She was a completely narcissistic creature, driven only by her own egocentricity.

Morgana sat near her, and offered a weak smile. "I'm so ashamed," she said.

Velvet's eyes widened.

"Are you sincere, Morgana?" She gaped.

Morgana nodded wordlessly, and Velvet detected a sincerity in the woman's response that could only be born of true remorse.

"I'm so relieved," she said on a breath. "You can't imagine how I've dreaded telling you the truth."

"It must have been awful for you," Morgana replied sadly. "But you had no choice. I know that now." She looked directly at Velvet. "I'd have done exactly the same thing." Her tone altered abruptly. "Why, you've been crying!" the young woman observed with a small gasp. "Now, you must tell me what's wrong; we've been friends too long to have you keeping anything from me." Velvet took a breath. She was not sure how friendly she and Morgana had really been — she was not sure how friendly they were now. Still, perhaps because of their long acquaintance, perhaps because of what they'd recently shared, the woman deserved an explanation.

"It is many things," Velvet said at last.

"Well, I hope this isn't over L'Étoile de Vie; that's water over the dam," Morgana commented. "Is it about Sweet Briar Hill?" she asked in a rush. "I just know it is, and I could kill Brett Whitney for what he's doing to you. If I had any money or jewels, I'd give them to you. But . . . well, you know all about what happened to my jewels —" Her expression changed, and she said, "What's really bothering you is that nasty husband of yours. I knew," she said, her voice trailing. "I shouldn't have mentioned all those things to him. . . ."

"What things?" Velvet asked, looking up sharply.

"Oh, didn't he tell you?" asked Morgana, her eyes wide with astonishment.

"I don't know what you're talking about, Morgana," said Velvet. "But if this has something to do with Cutter's disappearance, you'd better speak up."

"Well, it's really nothing, sugar. It's just that when your husband and I were together last night —"

"You were . . . together?" Velvet asked on a quick breath.

"Didn't he tell you that, either? Oh, my" — Morgana huffed — "he really is a devil. I shall never understand men. It was all very innocent, after all." She eyed Velvet obliquely. "I suppose he thought you might be jealous; but why would you be? That's so silly."

"Yes," said Velvet uncertainly.

"Well, the point is, I was telling him about what Eben Conway said to me up in Albany. He told me that John Eliot could write his own ticket if he ever decided to go back there. He could live there in celebrated status; he could have anything he wanted . . . money, women —" Morgana quickly stopped herself, and hastily raised a hand to her mouth. "Oh, I'm such a dull-witted old thing," she gasped. "I didn't mean that." Velvet felt a sudden horrible numbness wash over her. She gazed at Morgana wordlessly, her eyes wide. Morgana reached over and patted her hand. "For heaven's sake, Velvet honey, I didn't say that's where he went. Besides," she added solicitously, "why would he want any other woman when he's got you?"

Why, indeed? Velvet's heart thumped dully in her breast. Of course that was what Cutter had done; he had gone to Albany, to the freedom and celebrity he deserved. Tears came slowly to her eyes. And why should he not leave her? Why should he stay to share the anxiety and uncertainty of her future? They had made splendorous love last night; a kind of parting love, perhaps. It

371

was the end for Velvet. She allowed the heart-wrenching torment of her soul to pour out. Morgana stayed consolingly at her side, the warm dark hiding the first real smile of satisfaction Morgana had known since leaving home.

The two young women rode out the next morning. Velvet felt they'd shared much the night before, and she felt their friendship was strong enough to withstand the thing they both had to do. Morgana had seemed frightened, vulnerable, and, at the same time, resolved.

Grimly, they rode up to the house—or, rather, to the parched and blackened place where it had stood. The lawns had grown up, foliage over-arched the charred and ragged stone of the foundation. Wind blew restlessly among the ruins of L'Étoile de Vie.

"It's really . . . gone," Morgana murmured, as she gazed at the emptiness where once her home had stood, so proudly, so long ago. Velvet noted the hardness that suddenly shadowed Morgana's eyes. This was a time for her to be alone, she decided, to wrestle with her conflicts, to hate Velvet if she needed to.

"I'll leave you for a while," she said quietly. Morgana did not seem to notice her going.

Velvet crossed the lawn slowly, heavily. Ahead in the distance, she saw the stable, now deserted, where both she and Cutter had been imprisoned. She moved toward it, remembering.

The door opened, nearly by itself. She stepped into the cell, and smiled softly when she saw the repair that had been made where she'd dug herself out. Rude boards had been sunk into the ground, and nailed tightly to the wall. The straw, sweet-smelling now, where she'd thrown her pack, and forgotten it, invited her. She sat down tiredly. How long should she wait for Morgana to collect herself? she wondered. How long did it take to collect a lifetime, to renew a love of life, to heal a wound of such depth—

Her hand, as she tunneled her fingers through the straw, struck something hard and cold. Velvet looked down, lifting the object. In the dim, dappled sunlight she saw, winking up at her, the shimmer, glitter, glint of her beloved emerald necklace.

Chapter Forty-one

The little "Daniel come to judgement" had been contacted. He had received Brett Whitney's "pound of flesh" — the cold, brilliantine sparkle of Velvet's emeralds had at last found their true value. They had become the vehicle by which Velvet discovered what *she* truly valued. She'd saved Sweet Briar Hill; it now truly belonged to the McBride family. There was no question that the plantation would survive. In a way, however, nothing had really survived the long and destructive War Between the States. And Velvet's triumph was hollow. She had looked into the abyss, had realized the nothingness — the sad empty lie — that had been her life. Somehow, she must go on from there.

She would not spend her days yearning for what she had lost. She determined that she must begin anew. It helped her that Morgana Carleton reinforced each day the fact that Cutter was no true partner in life. "He'd never have left you," Morgana preached, nearly hourly, "if he'd really loved you." And, of course, she was right. In Velvet's moments of deepest sorrow, she clung to that which vitalized her. She clung to that new life that existed inside her. It was that life on which she must now focus. That life would be the beginning of Velvet's existence. She planned how she would raise her child — without prejudice, without artifice, with a true respect for natural patterns. The child — daughter or son — would learn from Velvet no preternatural cunning. It would exist in a world of truth. It would grow tall and honest, be confident in the beauty the world could offer if left to its own devices. Man-made patterns of existence, artificial designs, devious behaviors that tore away at the truth of humanity's basic goodness would not be part of its experience. Velvet would teach her child to love. She would teach her child to give freely, and to depend on no manner-makers to guide its passage through life.

What pattern am I describing? she wondered as she sat beneath the shade of a dogwood. What was it that was so familiar about her plans for her child? Her eyes widened. It was . . . Cutter. It was the way he'd shaped his own life. Up there, among the lofty summits of the Adirondack Mountains, in the mists of jagged peaks, sparkling ponds, tall pines, he had built a life based on perfect truth. There he had lived, believing in the nobility of all men, believing — and trusting — in the supremacy of nature.

He had come to her, in the beginning, with no artifice — spurred only by his love . . . . And his lust, she reflected with a small smile, as well as her own. He'd sensed their mutual attraction from the start, and allowed no courtly games to distract him from what he knew must happen between them. Had she been less guarded, Velvet thought wryly, less time would have been wasted. And yet, each moment she'd spent with Cutter was precious to her now. Each event became a moment to be cherished in the history of their lives together. If only they'd been able to go on . . . together. Tears, unplanned, unchecked, wet her cheeks. "Oh, Cutter," she said aloud. The word, the name, was carried on a breath of wind. The wind wafted back to encloak her consciousness.

"Don't cry, princess," the wind said. Velvet looked up. Over her, he stood. Bronzed, tousle-haired, gray eyes laughing in the sun, Cutter held his arms out to her.

Velvet lifted herself slowly. Not fully believing, not fully trusting in his existence, she moved into his embrace. Muscled arms enfolded her, warm in the warm sunlight. At last she looked up. Touching his face, she said softly, "You're back, love. I'm so glad. I could have lived without you, but I'm glad I don't have to."

There was general rejoicing that evening at Sweet Briar Hill. Over a hearty supper, Cutter explained that he'd gone to Albany, that he'd returned with a sizable loan from Eben Conway, and that he'd secured the services of his friend, the Very Reverend Harmon Taylor, to officiate the wedding. It was with some bewilderment that he learned that, in his absence, those details had been attended to. The debt owed Brett Whitney had been paid off, and Mammy Jane had been promised by her old friend and spiritual advisor, the Very Reverend Alvin Brown, that he would preside at the Cutter nuptials. Steven McBride averted his eyes for only a moment before announcing, with ironic amusement, that he'd managed to find and secure the spiritual services of the man who'd presided at his marriage to Alicia, the Very Reverend Robert Basler.

"I think I always knew, John, that you'd come back," he said with a soft smile.

"Poets are often prescient," Alicia offered with a fond laugh.

"Poets live with hope," her husband returned. "Though for a while," he said regretfully, "I lost mine." He glanced from Cutter to Velvet. "But now hope has returned. I see great hope for the future of Sweet Briar Hill. We shall have an heir." Velvet reached out to touch her father's hand.

"You will have an heir, Pa," she said gently. "We shall all have one. But that heir is not to be born at Sweet Briar Hill."

"I don't understand, daughter," said her father.

"Our child will be born in the unchallenged vastness of an Adirondack mountain forest," she said, smiling up at Cutter.

He raised a dark brow. "Not," he asked, "in a 'godforsaken wilderness'?"

"No, love," Velvet answered softly. "Not a godforsaken wilderness."

"God doesn't 'forsake' anything," stated Mammy Jane righteously.

Steven offered her a resigned smile. "You're right, Mammy," he acknowledged. He looked ruefully at his daughter. "I had such . . . plans for that baby," he said.

"And so have I, Pa," she returned gently. "I hope you understand."

"He will," said Alicia. "He will."

The three "Very Reverends" stood, Bibles poised, before the

fireplace in the great parlor of Sweet Briar Hill. Velvet waited, that balmy June night — her wedding night — on the landing of the staircase. Her gown, created for her by a prideful Damien Archambault, was of an icy blue organdy. Crystal beads spangled the voluminous skirts and bodice. As she descended, the beads glinted, catching the candlelight and throwing sparkles of heavenly, glistening light on every surface in the room. In her hair, Velvet wore a garland of baby's breath woven with more crystal beads. But it was her maid of honor, Arabella, who made the most graceful and elegant display.

Unadorned with any jewel, her tall, dark form was draped in a gown of palest lavender chiffon. Its long opaque sleeves, barely veiling her arms, wafted diaphanously as she followed Velvet down the stairs. Flowing down to a deeper lavender the hemline trailed out delicately as she walked. Ribbons of the deeper lavender and of the pale blue of Velvet's gown adorned the small lavender bonnet that sat proudly on her mane of black curls. From the high lace collar to its swirling hemline, a long row of tiny buttons covered in chiffon marked the center of the dress. The two young women, as they walked across the hallway to the parlor, felt like the princesses Damien had promised them they were.

Velvet had decided that she would not have her father give her away in marriage. She and Cutter would give themselves to each other; they would be partners in life from this day forward.

The ceremony was long, meaningful to each person gathered in the warm parlor, for each holy man offered his own insights — according to his own philosophy — on marriage, on partnership, on love.

When the wedding was over, Velvet tossed her bouquet and it was caught by a startled, sobbing Mammy Jane. There was general hilarity as the guests eyed the Very Reverend Alvin Brown who was, it was well known, a close friend, perhaps an intimate friend, of Mammy Jane's. That woman hid her embarrassment, and her pleasure, in the determined supervision of the laying of the wedding buffet.

The party was cresting to a joyous peak when, abruptly, a

reproving murmur went through the guests. There, at the entrance to the parlor, stood Lisa Mae Bloomer. On her arm, tall and handsome in his evening coat, was Brett Whitney. Velvet made her way toward the couple determinedly. The crowd was now silent. Once before them, Velvet rigidly extended her hand.

"I'm so glad you could come, Lisa Mae," she said quietly. "I hoped, when you left Sweet Briar Hill, that we might see each other again." Lisa Mae took Velvet's hand in greeting.

"Of course you know my husband," she said, her smile challenging.

"I do," Velvet answered, lifting her small chin. "Though I had no idea you two had married. How are you, Brett?"

That man cocked a golden brow. "Very well," he said lazily.

"Very rich," Lisa Mae added with a sly smile.

Velvet averted her eyes. "Won't you two join us in celebration of our marriage?" she murmured.

"We have a gift for you," Lisa Mae said. She held out a small, elaborately wrapped package. Velvet took it. As she unwrapped it, Cutter came to stand at her side. Arabella stood nearby, along with Steven and Alicia. Mammy Jane watched them. Velvet looked up in disbelief after opening the present. "It's your emerald necklace," Lisa Mae said. "I made Brett give it back to you."

Velvet took Lisa Mae in a warm embrace. "Thank you," she said gently, "but . . . I cannot accept your gift."

Lisa Mae's face creased in puzzlement.

"Why not, for heaven's sake?" she asked.

Pausing for a brief moment, Velvet found herself reflecting on her answer. "It . . . it doesn't go with my dress," she said at last, with a sudden bright smile. "It doesn't go with *anything* I have anymore." She laughed infectiously. "But thank you for the thought—both of you." She turned to her guests. "Everyone," she called out, "please welcome the newly married Lisa Mae and Brett Whitney." Cutter offered the couple a stilted bow.

"Do join us," he said, and then, with Velvet, he turned and joined their guests. Lisa Mae and Brett found themselves standing alone at the entrance of the parlor, very much apart from the joyous festivities. It was not long before they left the wedding reception.

Morgana Carleton, too, had found herself, throughout the evening and for the first time in her life, not the center of attention. Cutter's return had made the innuendo she had attempted so hard to advance a complete failure. Velvet, the little fool, had been all too willing to forgive her husband, and to accept his paltry excuse for disappearing. Beyond that, she seemed so irritatingly . . . serene these days. She had settled herself very neatly into a new life that was still a puzzle to Morgana. As soon as her parents returned from Europe, Morgana determined, she would begin to piece together her own life. The Carletons would probably buy a townhouse in Richmond, and she could restore her status as premier belle. She would not settle, as Velvet had, for a quiet, boring existence as wife to a geologist — *of all things* — in the godforsaken wilderness of those Northern mountains. What had she ever seen, she wondered, with a certain fretful uncertainty, in John Eliot Cutter? Brett Whitney, on the other hand, still piqued her interest. She might remember, in the very near future, to pay a congratulatory call on that handsome and elegant, and apparently very rich, son of the old South — and, of course, on his mousy little wife.

"Enjoying the party, Morgana?" asked a female voice from behind her. She turned, an extravagant smile curving her lips, to find Arabella standing there. Her smile faded abruptly.

"You might do well to learn, missy, how to address your betters," Morgana said sharply. Arabella smiled, and Morgana turned away, saying "Your bad manners are exceeded only by your arrogance."

"And your unwillingness to change is exceeded only by your vanity," said Arabella mildly. Stunned, Morgana turned to her. Arabella continued. "*You* might do well to learn how to address your *future*, Morgana."

Morgana lifted an elegant brow. "If you lived at L'Étoile de Vie, you'd learn some manners, girl."

"But I don't live at L'Étoile de Vie," returned Arabella, "and neither do you. We've both had a recent change of address," she continued. "I hope you find yours as satisfying as I find mine." Morgana's eyes narrowed. Arabella did not bother to take up the challenge. Instead she turned. Damien Archambault, hidden by Arabella's height, stood behind her. Taking his arm, she walked off without further word.

Steven and Alicia watched the exchange. A sense of destiny had lain over them for weeks now. "We had all better learn how to address our futures," said Steven.

Alicia nodded. "Tomorrow our house will be all but empty," she said quietly. "With all the women gone and Arabella going off to France . . . and our darling Velvet leaving . . ." Her voice trailed off, and she fought tears. At that moment a sleepy John Brown Tull came whining and rubbing his eyes toward them through the crowd of guests.

"What's the matter, old fellow," Steven said, swooping the little boy high into his arms. John Brown giggled, and nestled against Steven's chest. "Did you say our house would be empty?" Steven asked Alicia with a wink.

"Let's take this little darling upstairs to bed," said Alicia softly. The two of them walked from the parlor and across the hall. Together, with Mammy Jane's loved grandson between them, Steven and Alicia ascended the stairs.

Chapter Forty-two

The little town of Mayfield, New York, glittered as resplendently as any grand city in the world. The gathering of the cream of Adirondack society was occasioned by the visit to the county of the Mozart Society of Northeastern New York State. Mr. and Mrs. Chapman-White were among the guests who had been patrons of the auspicious event, along with the Giffords and their son Cain, the Andrew Duffys, the young and popular Jason Amsterdams and the John Eliot Cutters. The reporter for the *Mayfield Gazette* took down the names rapidly as the couples entered the Grange Hall in the center of town. Giddily, he asked them for quotes, so that he might include their words along with his story.

The Duffys and the elder Amsterdams arrived together and told the reporter that they were thankful the war had ended, and that their families — such fine friends all these years — were united at last. The Chapman-Whites were, naturally, thankful the war was over, and had great hopes for the future of Mr. Chapman-White's lumber business. The Giffords agreed, adding only the revelatory tidbit that their son Cain, back from the war, had decided to pen his experiences in the form of a novel, and to open a general store.

The vibrant — and very *enceinte* — Juliette Amsterdam née Duffy, on the arm of her proud and blushing husband, was grateful for his success as an artist, and informed the reporter that the adored Jason had just signed a contract with *Harper's Magazine*. The couple's leisure time, she mentioned enthusiastically, was spent acting with the local community theater.

The Duffy's older daughter, Nicole, a dark-eyed sophisticate who had recently bobbed her hair, was looking forward to her ensuing move to New York City where she would pursue an academic career — and perhaps, a husband.

But it was the fabulous Mr. and Mrs. J. Eliot Cutter that piqued the reporter's interest most of all. Mrs. Cutter, the luminous Velvet, wore an enchanting frock of palest azure — as only she could — which was as lustrous with crystal beads as the Adirondack night with stars. The gown was, of course, an original by the internationally famous French designer, Damien Archambault. Mr. Cutter, the celebrated hero of the Underground Railroad, was interviewed about his new position as head of the department of geology at the local college.

When asked who was minding the recently arrived littlest Cutter, the couple told the reporter that he was being tended to by that ever-reliable citizen of the world, Hanna Clark. It was agreed by all that the baby boy — named Steven Andrew — would, with such illustrious and high-minded parents, be an asset to the community in which he was born. ⌐

Snuggled beneath the blankets of their bed the next morning, Velvet and Cutter read the newspaper account of their fabulous night. They were duly impressed by some of the revealing tidbits, a little concerned about the public mention of Juliette's pregnancy — though they were sure that Jason and she had taken it in stride, and had probably revelled in the roguish audacity of the reporter — and were amused by the rhapsodic description of Velvet's gown.

"If he only knew it was my wedding gown." She giggled. "And almost a year old."

"I imagine Hanna was happy to have been mentioned," Cutter said laughing. He pointed to the "citizen of the world" reference. "She'll never go back to Ireland now that she's famous here," she added wryly.

"I really don't blame her," Velvet said, contentedly resting her head on her husband's muscular shoulder.

"Don't you?" Cutter asked.

"No," Velvet murmured. "Famous or not, I never want to leave these mountains." Cutter looked down at her. She was as delightful to look upon as she'd been the day they'd met. The soft whisper from the cradle next to their bed caught their attention.

Cutter leaned down and scooped Steven Andrew into his arms. He held his son tenderly before handing him to his mother. She drew the cloth from his sturdy little boy and, unburdened, his arms and legs stretched and beat gently against the air. His little face turned immediately to his mother's breast, and he began to suckle. To Cutter the sight was breathtakingly beautiful.

"I'm glad," he said reverently, "that I came to your rescue that day so long ago — even though you did not require rescuing."

Velvet looked up at him through the veil of her lashes. "Didn't I, love?" she asked softly.

Cutter laughed huskily, and drew both her and their son into his embrace. "Maybe we both needed rescuing," he said. Velvet nodded, and gazed up into his eyes.

"If ever I lose sight of what is truly important in life . . . please do not hesitate to rescue me," she said seriously.

"And, if I," said Cutter, "become arrogant, demanding, uncompromising, or . . . *too* impatient —"

"I shall very quickly," Velvet interrupted, "rescue both our son — and myself." They both laughed.

Beyond them, outside, the mountains, shimmering with white pine, sparkling ponds, and ages-old bedrock, looked on benevolently. In the flower of this springtime season there would be no storms, no sliding shale, no floods, or icy winds. Those things would come, perhaps — the vagaries of Adirondack weather being what they are.

GOTHICS A LA MOOR — FROM ZEBRA

ISLAND OF LOST RUBIES
by Patricia Werner   (2603, $3.95)
Heartbroken by her father's death and the loss of her great love, Eileen
returns to her island home to claim her inheritance. But eerie things begin
happening the minute she steps off the boat, and it isn't long before
Eileen realizes that there's no escape from *THE ISLAND OF LOST RU-
BIES*.

DARK CRIES OF GRAY OAKS
by Lee Karr   (2736, $3.95)
When orphaned Brianna Anderson was offered a job as companion to the
mentally ill seventeen-year-old girl, Cassie, she was grateful for the non-
troublesome employment. Soon she began to wonder why the girl's family
insisted that Cassie be given hydro-electrical therapy and increased doses
of laudanum. What was the shocking secret that Cassie held in her dark
tormented mind? And was she herself in danger?

CRYSTAL SHADOWS
by Michele Y. Thomas   (2819, $3.95)
When Teresa Hawthorne accepted a post as tutor to the wealthy Curtis
family, she didn't believe the scandal surrounding them would be any concern of hers. However, it soon began to seem as if someone was trying to
ruin the Curtises and Theresa was becoming the unwitting target of a
deadly conspiracy . . .

CASTLE OF CRUSHED SHAMROCKS
by Lee Karr   (2843, $3.95)
Penniless and alone, eighteen-year-old Aileen O'Conner traveled to the
coast of Ireland to be recognized as daughter and heir to Lord Edwin
Lynhurst. Upon her arrival, she was horrified to find her long lost father
had been murdered. And slowly, the extent of the danger dawned upon
her: her father's killer was still at large. And her name was next on the
list.

BRIDE OF HATFIELD CASTLE
by Beverly G. Warren   (2517, $3.95)
Left a widow on her wedding night and the sole inheritor of Hatfield's
fortune, Eden Lane was convinced that someone wanted her out of the
castle, preferably dead. Her failing health, the whispering voices of death,
and the phantoms who roamed the keep were driving her mad. And al-
though she came to the castle as a bride, she needed to discover who was
trying to kill her, or leave as a corpse!

Contemporary Fiction From
Robin St. Thomas

Fortune's Sisters
(2616, $3.95)

It was Pia's destiny to be a Hollywood star. She had complete self-confidence, breathtaking beauty, and the help of her domineering mother. But her younger sister Jeanne began to steal the spotlight meant for Pia, diverting attention away from the ruthlessly ambitious star. When her mother Mathilde started to return the advances of dashing director Wes Guest, Pia's jealousy surfaced. Her passion for Guest and desire to be the brightest star in Hollywood pitted Pia against her own family—sister against sister, mother against daughter. Pia was determined to be the only survivor in the arenas of love and fame. But neither Mathilde nor Jeanne would surrender without a fight. . . .

Lover's Masquerade
(2886, $4.50)

New Orleans. A city of secrets, shrouded in mystery and magic. A city where dreams become obsessions and memories once again become reality. A city where even one trip, like a stop on Claudia Gage's book promotion tour, can lead to a perilous fall. For New Orleans is also the home of Armand Dantine, who knows the secrets that Claudia would conceal and the past she cannot remember. And he will stop at nothing to make her love him, and will not let her go again . . .